The Triqan

1

Trilogy

The Key
to
Yamal

Tyler Appleby

The Key to Yamal
Copyright © 2015 by Tyler Appleby

The Key to Yamal is the first of three books in the youth fantasy series, The Triqan Trilogy.

First printing – November 2015

For more information:

Website: thecorzanitecubicle.wordpress.com

Cover picture by Tyler Appleby and Jennifer Appleby
Interior design and typesetting by Tyler Appleby
Edited and Proofread by Steve Appleby, Jennifer Appleby, Linda Boyd, Carole Appleby, Mike Appleby, Mikal Applewhite, Eric Greninger, Hally Phillips, and David Skirko.

For my friends, who motivated me
For my family, who supported me
For Jesus, who inspired me

Contents

1
The Training Begins

Contents

2
The Realm of Y

Contents

3

The Dragons of the North

A Brief History

In ancient times, when civilization was young, the country of Aena was flourishing in the land of Domilia. A fair King sat on the throne in those days, ruling over the land with justice and righteousness. He was respected and adored. At the King's right hand sat Governor Ogrion, the strong and powerful ruler of Yamal, the largest Province in Aena. Ogrion enjoyed a luxurious life as the second-in-command, but he was not satisfied. His thirst for power was insatiable. He wanted nothing less than the throne itself. He persuaded many powerful leaders to turn against the King. With their help, he formed a massive army and declared war on his home country.

Fought on the Plains of Adur, a barren wasteland, it was called, "The War for Power." It was the largest war in the history of Aena, and tens of thousands of men died protecting their country. The War for Power stretched over several months, and, eventually, the King of Aena managed to drive Ogrion back into the towering Ratkon fortress, located in the Southwest corner of Yamal Province. There he stayed, cut off from Aena by the treacherous Wilderlands of Kar.

It has been a thousand years since this fearsome battle, and the King has since passed his reign down to his descendants, and they to theirs. Since then, more cities have been built and technology has improved greatly. Aena has been split into five self-governing Provinces. But now, the time has come. Reports are heard in Aena about a rebellion stirring. Rumors say that the current King Ogrion of Yamal, named for his ancestor, is preparing for war. These rumors have reached King Nunor of Aena's ears, and he plans to stop this disaster before it begins. The question now is: "How?"

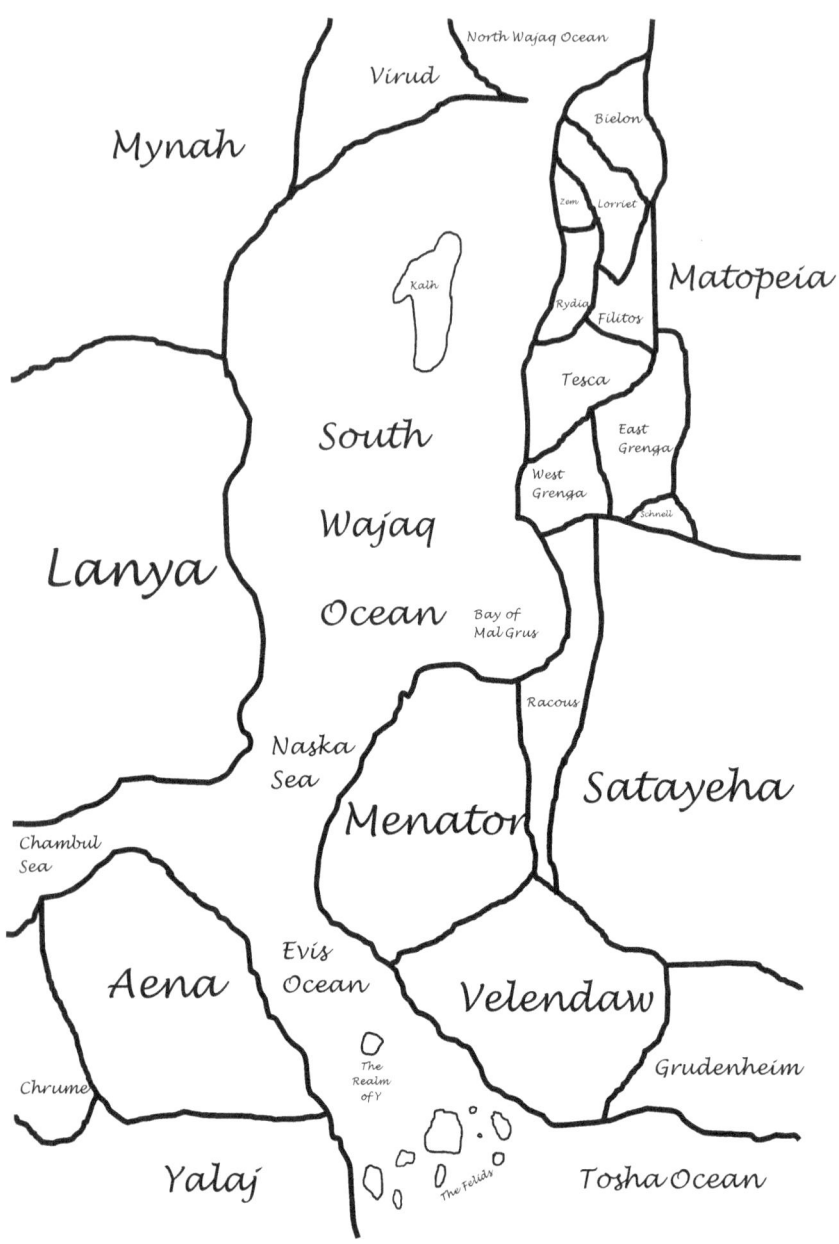

The Northwest Lands of Domilia

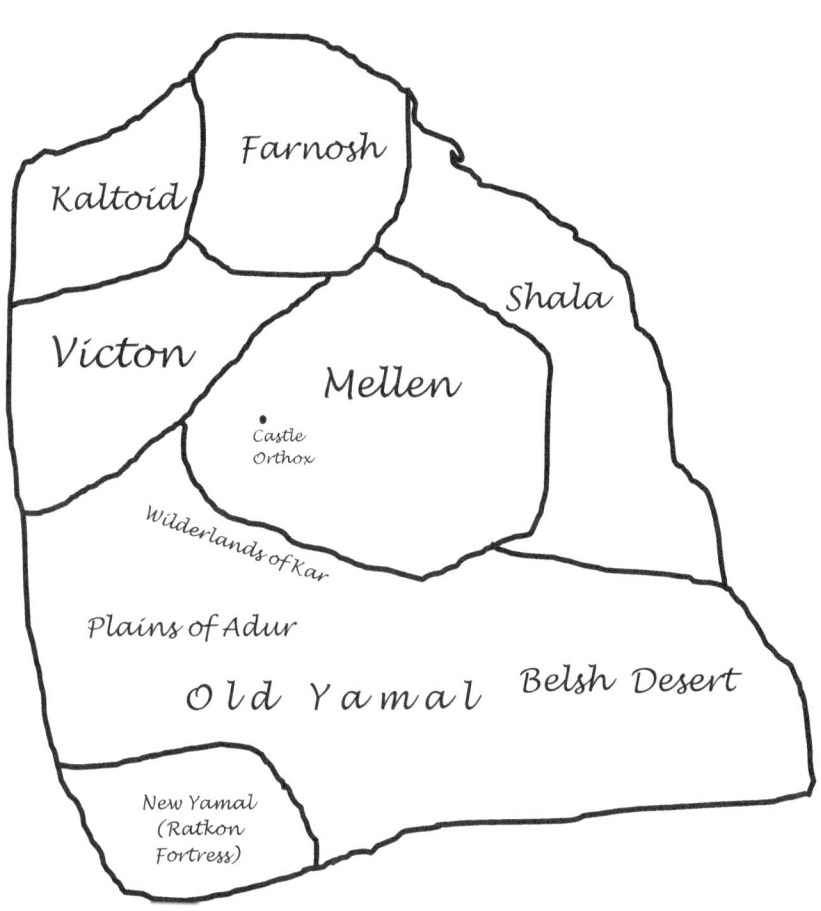

Kaltoid
Farnosh
Victon
Shala
Mellen
• Castle Orthox
Wilderlands of Kar
Plains of Adur
Old Yamal
Belsh Desert
New Yamal (Ratkon Fortress)

The Country of Aena

Part 1

The Training Begins

1

...

Beguilement

"WHY DO YOU PESTER ME WITH SUCH NONSENSE?!"
The huge warlord thundered. "GET OUT OF MY SIGHT NOW!"

The lanky servant jumped back in shock at the outburst, nervously running his hands through his disheveled brown hair. Remembering the proper procedure, he bowed submissively to his incensed master.

"Y-yes, K-king Ogrion!" His fearful face revealed the awe in which he held his ruler. Shuddering, the servant quickly backed out the door, bowing and scraping the whole way.

Ogrion slumped back in his seat as the heavy door to his throne room boomed shut. He rubbed his hands over his deeply set eyes, trying to clear them. His face was crimson from yelling, and sweat seeped profusely from his pores.

Someone might describe the king as old, due to his gnarled features, but his aged looks came from the stress of governing a nation. His face was wrinkled and craggy, although he had scarcely reached his forties. Despite his appearance, Ogrion's body was powerful and strong. He was a master warrior whom no one dared to challenge. At this time, however, he wasn't fit to fight at all. He was exhausted. The interior of his subterranean throne room was so stifling that he longed to go aboveground for just a day.

I need to get some more airflow in this fortress, he mused. *It's sweltering in here!*

Easing his aching body further into the plush seat, Ogrion sighed in pleasure at the comfort. His back was stricken with twinges of pinching pain from standing for so long. All in all, his lengthy conversation with the meek servant had turned out fruitless. His subjects had been trying to convince him to consider a petition about increasing ration sizes for the hungry soldiers of the royal army. As far as Ogrion was concerned, however, it was complete nonsense. His face wrinkled with distaste as he thought about how many hours he'd spent debating this subject with his followers.

As he sat there brooding, Ogrion began wondering what to do about the pitiful King Nunor. He didn't actually know Aena's monarch. Many conflicts had arisen between Yamal and her mother country, originating centuries before Ogrion's time. It had all started with his ancestor, Ogrion the First, who waged a war against Nunor's ancestor, the King of Old, for the freedom of Yamal. That war had been born out of an insatiable lust for power, and in the end, the borders of Yamal had been pushed back to the seat of power where Ogrion sat now, the immense Ratkon Fortress.

Although Ogrion the First had achieved his goal of an independent nation, he had stirred up enough hatred for his family line that his descendants would never again be welcome in Aena.

As Ogrion sat on his elaborate throne sulking about the past, he began speculating ways to gain access to the country of his dreams, Aena. In his mind, which had been twisted by the opinions of others, the only way to be acknowledged in that glorious country was to oust the current ruler.

He had already sent spies to the castle. Infiltration had been easy. His real problem, though, was how to get the other king off the throne. *I could give them true freedom!* He daydreamed. *If only I could be king! My ancestor did all he could to destroy Aena's reputation and usurp power, but he ended up being banished to this miserable fortress! I will be greater and more powerful than Ogrion the First ever dreamed of becoming! I will be a king with a forceful hand!*

Ogrion stared at nothing in particular, his mind wandering into imaginative fantasies of the monarch he was destined to be.

Suddenly, something changed. An odd stillness permeated the atmosphere.

Ogrion's body went rigid in his chair. His hands gripped the armrests of his throne so tight that his knuckles whitened.

What's happening?! He thought desperately, a terrifying feeling of claustrophobia pushing in around him. He tried to shout for help, but his mouth wouldn't work. A surge of terror filled his body as he realized that he was rendered utterly helpless.

As if he wasn't scared enough already, a snaky voice slithered into his mind, sounding like a knife running through sand.

"Ogrion, hear me."

What? He thought, a motionless shiver racking his body. *Who... who's that talking in my head?*

"Just your conscience," it echoed through his mind, giving him the strange, hair-raising sensation of being watched.

As he mentally trembled with fear, Ogrion pondered his frightening situation. Then, his sensible side broke through, and an idea popped into his head.

I-I'll consider listening to you if you l-let me move my body, he bargained, although the prospect of hearing this voice for any longer made him stammer.

Instantly after he said it, he could move again.

"Good," said the voice in a satisfied tone. *"You may speak aloud now, for no one can hear us."*

"What do you want?" Ogrion queried in his normal voice, relief rushing through him when he felt his mouth move.

"I have come to give you counsel, o great and wise ruler."

Confusion washed through his body at this. Was it even possible for so hideous a voice to be so flattering?

"You have a problem with the king of Aena," it continued. *"I seek to help you overcome that problem."*

Although he was unpleasantly surprised by this voice's knowledge of his personal broodings, Ogrion's curiosity got the better of him. "What do you propose?"

"You must declare war against the land of Aena."

"What?!" Ogrion exclaimed. The prospect of challenging one of the most powerful nations in Domilia sent a shot of dread through his nerves.

"You heard what I said!" It shrieked. *"Declare war against Aena, and I will allow you to become its ruler, to oust that incompetent King Nunor."*

A strange dizziness came upon Ogrion as he sat there. His head spun as ideas of power and freedom flashed through his mind. This being's plan was beginning to sound appealing.

"What must I do?" He asked in a dazed voice.

"You must stop Nunor from obtaining an item. A key, in fact. If he gets it, I... you will be done for." So enveloped in his thoughts by this point, Ogrion didn't even notice the slip.

"Yes. I know of what you speak. How must I stop him?"

"I will give you more details later. But for you to complete this task, there is one more step you must take."

"Yes?" Ogrion asked, staring blankly into space. His glazed-over eyes barely registered a luminescent red mist seeping through a crack in the wall. It swayed hypnotically, wafting towards him with the cadence of a slow-moving stream.

The ribbon of light weaved through the air until it was levitating directly in front of his face. A sweet, metallic smell pervaded his nostrils.

"Accept me," the voice hissed mesmerizingly.

In a voice that was not his own, Ogrion whispered, "Yes."

A hideous scream filled the air, and the glowing, red haze lurched towards his face, filling his nostrils, his mouth, his eyes.

With a bloodcurdling shriek, Ogrion lurched forward, his vision red and a metallic film coating his tongue.

Just as he hit the ground, the last vestige of Ogrion's sanity shattered.

"Welcome."

2

...

The Visitor

Samuel opened his eyes and looked at the ceiling of his room. He watched a fly slowly drone through the air. He examined the patterns on the wooden boards above him. Then he heard the obnoxious snoring of his middle-aged father emanating from the next room. Samuel smiled.

He was a farm boy. With a strong build and muscular arms, he stood at five feet, eleven inches tall, large for a fifteen-year-old. His light brown hair was thick and full, sweeping to the side as it met his brow, and his sharp eyebrows contoured his deep blue eyes, making his face seem pronounced. His angular jaw and upper lip showed signs of the light, soft hair that came with adolescence.

Samuel stood up, stretching his arms into the air and shaking his head. He yanked his brown trousers off of a wooden bar that was connected to the wall and pulled them on. The tall youth slid his arms into the sleeves of his warm leather jacket, which was lined with a layer of wool.

Where Samuel lived, it was usually warm in the late spring, but when one awoke so early in the morning, there was always a slight chill to the air. The gray clouds in the sky were daunting, but he could tell that the sun would soon burn them away.

After he finished dressing, Samuel walked out into the main room of his house. Illuminated by the faint gray light of the morning, he could see his family's small kitchen lining the wall, and their only table standing stoically in the center of the room. He shook his arms to get his blood moving and looked towards where his parents slept at the opposite end of their small house. The eerie stillness of the room was broken only by the sound of his father's pronounced snoring.

Shaking himself out of his thoughts, Samuel grabbed the two pails and the basket by the front door and stepped out into the chilly morning. Now that he had left the warmth of his house, he felt the biting chill of the foggy air piercing his body. He folded his arms across his body and shivered, keeping a hold on the three containers.

Samuel looked to the left and saw the long stretches of fertile cornfields and in the foreground, his family's large, brown barn, its tall roof stretching majestically into the sky. He saw the darkly colored doors at the front, their handles projecting out as if beckoning for him to come inside and bask in the heat radiating from so many living bodies.

Giving in to its inviting call, Samuel strode briskly over to the building and cracked open one of its doors. As he closed it behind him, the stench of animals and manure swept over him and permeated his nostrils. Wrinkling his nose, he crept silently past the gates behind which muscular horses rested peacefully, careful not to disturb their deep slumber.

Seeing his favorite animal up ahead, a wry smile broke out on Samuel's face. "Hey, girl," he whispered softly as he swung open the sturdy gate. "How's old Margaret doing this morning?" She swished her tail, hitting him affectionately in the leg. Her fine coat of short, soft hair was colored the rich hue of mahogany. Margaret's familiar smell hovered around her spacious stall: A mixture of fresh grass and dry hay mingling together for a single, pleasant scent.

"I just need to get some milk," Samuel stated in a reassuring voice. "Don't worry, I'll be done in no time." He set down the basket and water pail and put the old, dented milk bucket beneath Margaret's bulbous udder. He knelt down, feeling the sharp prickle of straw beneath his knees and proceeded to fill the pail near to the brim with rich, creamy milk.

"There we go," Samuel said, standing to his feet and hefting the full pail with his thick farmer's arm. "All done! See Margaret? That wasn't so bad." He backed out of the pen and closed the gate, Margaret grunting lovingly. With dexterous hands, Samuel kept the milk bucket level and made his way through the tranquil barn towards the exit.

Pulling his wool jacket tighter around him in the frigid air, he turned and stepped towards the chicken pen. Having left the warmth of the barn, a cloud of steam rose off of the milk, mixing with the fog already in the air. Samuel crouched down and extracted a flexible section of watertight fabric from his pocket, stretching it over the top of the milk pail.

Samuel set the milk and water pails down by the mesh of sticks that made up the fence and peered over the top, holding the egg basket in his other hand. The chickens, always early risers, were up and gossiping noisily.

He stepped slowly into the partitioned area, softly closing the rickety gate behind him and being careful to avoid his family's ornery rooster. It had been known to attack encroaching humans with its sharp beak.

Samuel grimaced at the memory of one such experience.

As he carefully searched for eggs, something triggered some sort of a sixth sense in his mind, causing him to freeze. There had been movement, he was sure of it. Something the color of dry soil had flashed in his peripheral vision for only a moment before it disappeared.

A feeling of dread seeped into Samuel's nerves, adrenaline pulsing through his body. There had been clawed footprints and missing chickens earlier in the season, signs of predators. After these sightings, his father had warned him to be careful as he did his chores, for no one knew when the mysterious creature would strike again.

He gently set down the half-full basket of eggs he had been gathering and reached a slow hand over to his father's favorite shovel, which Marken had fortunately left out that night. Although it was a meager weapon against a predator, it was all he had. Samuel lifted his head and gazed into the thin fog that hovered over the farm, making it look smoky in the gray morning light. His hands gripped the makeshift weapon tightly in white-knuckled apprehension.

Samuel slowly turned his head, scanning his surroundings. He wondered if what he had seen was just his mind playing tricks on him, but then he noticed something else. It was the chickens. They were silent.

He glanced at the hen nearest to him and gulped. The feathered creature was standing stock-still, staring into the deep shadows around the chicken coop at the far end of the pen. Samuel peered into the thick darkness, his eyes wide and the hair on the back of his neck bristling with suspense. He wondered if he should call out to his father, but his throat was tight and the snoring Marken probably wouldn't hear it anyway. His stomach muscles clenched as he realized that he was the only one who could do anything. It was all up to him now.

A loud gurgling squawk sounded from the darkness of the coop and then was quickly silenced. Every muscle in his body was taut with foreboding as he slowly straightened his back, clutching the shovel desperately. He took a quick step forward and stopped, straining his ears for any telltale sounds of a wild animal.

Then he saw it.

Out of the shadows to the right of the chicken coop, a feral creature came slinking out. Its sleek, tawny fur bristled with aggression, and its ears were flattened against its head menacingly. The vicious-looking cat trained its cold, amber eyes on Samuel and hissed, pulling its lips back in a fierce snarl and baring its bloodstained teeth. On the ground next to it lay its most recent prey: A fat hen with dark blood draining out of its still body.

Its tail twitching back and forth, the panther approached Samuel and let out a throaty growl.

Sweat streamed down his face, and his arms shook with fear. He bent his arms and held the shovel before him in a defensive position. Scared out of his wits, Samuel bared his teeth and snarled at the panther, shaking the shovel in front of him with the hope to intimidate it enough to make it leave.

Instead of being frightened, the wild cat growled once again and leapt forward, its claws sharp and gleaming.

Samuel ducked out of the way, barely avoiding the panther's snapping fangs. The creature turned and once again prepared to pounce.

All traces of fear, besides his pounding heart, gone from his body, Samuel adjusted his grip on the shovel. When it leapt a second time, he was ready.

As the bloodthirsty animal flew through the air, Samuel twisted his body and slammed the shovel into the side of its head, knocking it to the ground.

In an instant, the panther was back up again, shaking the dizziness out of its head and readying to attack.

But Samuel wasn't waiting.

With a haphazard lunge, he jumped forward and brought his weapon down onto the creature's head, stunning it. He followed up with a shocking blow from the right, sending the already woozy panther flying through the air. It hit the ground with a sickening crunch, landing on its head and wrenching its neck.

Samuel stared at his defeated foe and let the shovel drop out of his hand. He fell to his knees on the ground, exhausted. His breath came in deep drafts, and his heart was like a thundering drum.

Coming to his senses, Samuel stood up and set the shovel softly against the fence. He walked over and retrieved the three containers he had set down. He left the dead panther behind him and exited the pen in a daze. The chickens were continuing about their normal business, clucking and squawking as if nothing had happened.

As he walked towards the house, some movement near the rough, dirt road caught his eye. Wondering if it was another predator, Samuel looked up and peered into the gray mist that surrounded his family's farm.

In the pale morning light, he saw a lone stranger strolling briskly down the road towards town, his head tilted downward. He was wearing a long, black cloak that undulated as he walked, its cowl pulled far over his head.

That's odd, thought Samuel, still disoriented from his recent battle. *I've never seen someone come past here* this *early in the morning.* He continued watching until the mist congealed around the man's figure, enveloping him in white.

The incident with the cat was still reeling through Samuel's mind as he stepped through the door to his house. This had happened before in the past, but never this dramatically. Samuel decided to tell his parents about the panther later, for at the moment he was too traumatized to talk about it.

The orange sun was just rising, as his mother Lora opened the wooden shutters on the window, allowing the cold house to absorb a modicum of heat. Her golden hair flowed down her shoulders, and her blue eyes twinkled. For being a middle-aged adult, she was pretty; at least her husband thought so. To Samuel, she was just "mom."

As Samuel walked through the door, the delicious aroma of spicy sausage and savory eggs filled his nostrils: one of his mother's favorite breakfasts. He shut the door gently behind him and placed the smooth, brown eggs in a large, metal jar. He nestled the container deeply into a barrel of ice near the front door. As he felt the cold radiating off of the sparkling chunks, a memory crossed his mind of the jovial man who had sold it to them at the market.

His claim, "Here's some fresh, freezing ice from the mountains!" had seemed funny. As if it could be anything other than freezing.

With a delicacy that came only from years of practice, Samuel carefully drained the contents of the milk pail into a couple of jars before snugly placing them into the barrel. His

23

footsteps creaking on the floorboards, Samuel set the sloshing water pail down next to the black potbellied stove that had been purchased only recently. Its bulbous body sat squatly underneath a long, shiny pipe that reached to the ceiling and out into the open air. Through the barred door, he could see flickering flames licking at a dry log, as if tasting it before the meal.

When Samuel's mother had bought it, he had been ignorant as to what its use may be. However, when he had lain down next to it for the first time, feeling the warm glow of the orange coals in the sharp cold of winter, he had realized how important such an improvement was.

"Good morning, Samuel," his mother, Lora, said cheerfully as he carefully set the water down next to the stove. "Breakfast is just about ready, so could you wake up your father before the rafters fall down around us?" Samuel grinned openly, forgetting the terror of his recent encounter with death and finding comfort in the earth-shattering roar that was emanating from his father's lips.

He walked softly into his parents' small bedroom, feeling the sound amplify as he passed through the doorway. He grabbed his father's thick shoulders, shaking him up and down. "Dad!" Samuel called loudly, fracturing the deep sleep that had come over his slumbering parent. "Mom says she would like the house to stay standing, so could you please come out to the table for breakfast?"

His father, Marken, awoke with a start, sitting up sharply in bed and nearly smacking Samuel in the face.

In Samuel's mind, his father was analogous to a troll. He was big, hairy, and loud. Marken's thinning hair was draped over his face, and his wiry chest hairs poked randomly through the thin cotton shirt he wore. His thick beard was bedraggled, and one side of his face was red and textured from sleeping on his side.

Marken stared at Samuel in confusion for a few seconds, his green eyes bleary and brain not completely active. "Did I do it again?" He asked, finally realizing who was the butt of the joke. Samuel nodded, hiding a grin. "Great!" He exclaimed in a sarcastically drawn-out voice. "Every time! I'm tellin' you, it's natural! I can't help it! So stop makin' fun of me!" Marken paused his tirade and sniffed the air, the sweet aroma of breakfast filling his nostrils.

Forgetting his annoyance in an instant, Marken flipped the cover back and stood up, saying, "All right! You win! I'm comin'!" Samuel walked out of the room as his robust father pulled on his well-worn clothes. Marken walked out the door to the wooden table in the center of the room, where Samuel and Lora were already waiting.

"Goood mornin'!" He exclaimed joyously, lifting his hands into the air.

In a sardonic voice, Lora replied, "Your shirt's on backwards."

After eating a delectable breakfast of sausage and eggs, Samuel sat back in his chair, feeling energized and ready to start the day. Both his parents had long since finished eating; he was the one who ate the most in their family. As he sat there waiting to be dismissed, his mother addressed him.

"Samuel," Lora began in a tone that her experienced son knew very well, "I put some copper shards in your bag while you were outside. I need you to go to the market today and get me some cloth. If possible, could you get the dark green cotton your father likes? He needs some new trousers. As you can see, his leg hair is showing."

"I thought it was always showing," the sly youth replied.

"Hey!" Marken said, huffing indignantly.

Ignoring him, Lora continued. "You can go to Valentina's place to get it. Last time we were there, she promised to give us a discount." She stood up and lifted Samuel's leather satchel off the floor. "I made some bread yesterday and put a couple slices in your pack for when you're hungry."

"Thanks, mom." Samuel excused himself from the table and took the satchel from his mother. "I'll be back soon, although I hope not soon enough to help dad with the corn for supper!" What he was *actually* thinking about, though, was not being there when they discovered the panther.

"You won't get out of that one, boy!" Marken said, a smile dancing in his eyes as he stood from the table.

"We'll see about that," Samuel said. He kissed his mom quickly on the cheek and gave his dad a half-hug. "See you later!"

"Be careful, honey!" That was his mom. Always worrying.

"I will. I promise!"

Vale was a small town.

Filled with stocky log houses and shops, it was the only town for miles around. The picturesque nature of Vale appealed to many visitors as well. The brown wood of the houses contrasted with the dark green of the pine trees gave the town a richly colorful appearance.

From dawn to dusk, busy people could be seen scurrying about their daily tasks. While standing atop the hills that surrounded the village, one could observe streams of people below moving through the streets like ants walking in a naturally created pattern.

When the first explorers set foot on the future site of this city, "Vale" was the first idea that came to their minds for a name, due to its location. The quiet town was situated in a valley next to a dense forest that bustled with wildlife. This forest lay at the foot of Nolai Mountain, the home of the Great Elk. These majestic, sleek-coated creatures had the tastiest, juiciest meat of all the animals in the region. Many who tried it thought that it was the best in the world, explaining its costliness.

About two hundred people lived in Vale now, trading with each other in friendship and harmony. Before Samuel's time, there was a disturbance of the peace when a mysterious carnivore slunk into town and began devouring the locals' livestock, much larger than the more common panthers that haunted the area.

When word got out, the biggest, strongest men hunted this creature down and killed it. Great prestige was heaped upon the man who managed to accomplish this feat. Fortunately, the atmosphere of Vale had not been disrupted like this for quite some time.

Samuel headed through the cobblestone streets, searching for the humble stand of his mother's good friend, Valentina. She was a kindly woman, who possessed the gift of gab. The two ladies had met when Lora was looking through the market for cloth to make clothes for her newborn son. Valentina had been eager to help, and had given her a discount because of her situation.

Some time after that, when Samuel was older, Lora had invited Valentina over for dinner, and they had talked until past midnight. His mother always told him that good friends should be able to have long conversations, but nevertheless, the young Samuel was surprised when he woke in the middle of the night and they were still talking.

From that experience, a deep friendship was born.

Samuel spotted the stall he was looking for up ahead and walked up to it, smiling at the woman that perched lightly on a wooden stool inside. It wasn't a large vending stand, but the bright colors of the cloth she was selling made up for that. Long lengths of colorful fabric hung from the wooden bar that stretched across the top of the stand, displaying their marvelous patterns.

Valentina stood up and leaned on the counter of her stall, her bright face beaming. "Hello, Samuel," she greeted him in a friendly voice. "What brings you to the market today?"

She was the same size as Samuel's mother and around the same age as well. Dark brown hair flowed down the back of her head to her shoulders, curling in to frame her soft face. Her cheery, green eyes shone brightly at Samuel, reflecting the morning sun.

"Hi, Valentina," Samuel said. "Mom told me to come and get some of that green cotton my dad likes so much."

"So she's making him new pants?"

"Yep. When my mom says his old pants are done, they're done." They laughed.

"I'll go get you some." Valentina hurried into the back of her stall to get the cloth.

Samuel stood next to her stand and watched the crowd of people milling around in the market. He gazed at the bustling shoppers, seeing people that had obviously come from other Provinces, such as beefy miners from Victon and swarthy sailors from Shala.

As he stood there, something hauntingly familiar caught his gaze. Nearly fifteen yards away, a man in a black cloak stood shadily against the side of a log cabin, his eyes trained on the mobs of people in the street.

Samuel peered closer, his heart leaping into his throat as he realized what he was seeing. It was the stranger that he had seen on the road!

Samuel's hands started shaking as if they were remembering the terrifying incident that morning. *Who is this guy? I've never seen him around here before. I wonder what he's doing.*

As if he was reading Samuel's mind, the man turned his head until he was staring directly into the surprised boy's eyes. His scrutiny caused a shiver of cold to run down Samuel's back, making him twitch uncomfortably.

"Here, honey. I assume you want two lengths?"

Samuel flinched and then looked over at Valentina, who had come back to the front of her stall unnoticed.

"Um, yeah," he said absently, scratching at the back of his neck. Samuel unobtrusively turned his head back to look at the cloaked stranger. He was gone!

"Are you okay, honey?" Valentina's concerned voice pierced through the fog of mystery that surrounded Samuel's mind.

He turned back to her, shaking his head to clear it. "Yeah, yeah... I'm fine." *Who is this guy? It's almost like he was waiting for me to get here just so he could disappear and scare me!*

Valentina's expression was still suspicious, but she accepted his answer anyway. "Well... okay, but if you need help with anything, let me know. Alright?" The expression of concern in her voice was obvious.

Samuel nodded quickly and dug the copper shards out of his satchel, handing them to her.

"Thanks!" He said with the best smile he could muster and waved a hand in farewell. Samuel walked back through the crowd, peeking warily behind himself every once in a while, but there was no one except busy shoppers.

When he reached the dirt path that led to his farm, Samuel began mulling over reasons why this man would suddenly disappear as soon as he saw Samuel. As he thought about it, he realized that he wasn't apprehensive about the man because he had seen him twice in one day. The reason he was so uneasy was the man's clothing choice.

No one Samuel had ever met wore black as an everyday color. To most people, it was considered a color of mourning; black was something that people wore only when a relative or close friend had passed away.

That guy definitely wasn't grieving. But what was *he doing?* As Samuel pondered this, a disturbing thought crept into his mind, making him shiver with apprehension. *What if he was wearing all black so that he wouldn't be seen?*

3

...

Stalkers

Zane's breath was even and steady as he swung the long pickaxe repeatedly into the solid wall of stone in front of him, chips of rock flying every which way. Sweat pouring down his face, the massively built youth pounded ruthlessly on the rock face, never faltering in his incessant pattern of swing, smash, swing, smash.

Finally, the pickaxe struck a weaker point in the rocks, and a huge section of stone crumbled down to the ground.

Zane straightened his muscular body as much as he could in the cramped tunnel and wiped his brow. He let out a deep sigh of contentment as he stared at the chunk of rock he had gouged out of the tunnel.

He turned to the man mining next to him and said, "I'm gonna take a break. See ya guys in a bit!" Zane turned and made his way to the entrance of the tunnel, leaning his dented pickaxe against the wall as he went. He made his way through the maze of passageways, having memorized it long ago.

Zane approached a wooden platform that had crude railings built around its edges. It was placed in a large tube that led from the surface to the mine. Heavy-duty ropes were tied to the corners of this platform in order to pull the miners up and out.

Zane stepped onto the contraption. "Hey, up thar! I'm ready ta come up!" His deep voice thundered up the shaft and entered the ears of the brawny men who worked the elevator.

"A'right!" He heard them yell back down.

With a few creaks and groans, the light, wooden platform was slowly lifted into the air, carrying its lone passenger out of the mine.

Zane stood patiently and with perfect balance, his hands folded comfortably behind his back. He was a tall boy. At fourteen years old, he had surpassed his village's tallest men. Now he was eighteen and stood at six feet, eleven inches. He had never met anyone taller, and he didn't figure he would.

Intense features decorated his face. His short, black hair was cut flat on top to keep it out of the way when he was mining. His eyes were a creamy, dark brown that sparkled when he laughed. His other features all had the same characteristic in common: they were big. He had a broad nose, wide ears, and a firm, angular jaw. All in all, his face could have been that of a bear's.

One wouldn't usually consider him attractive, but what he lacked in beauty, he made up for in strength. If someone insulted his looks in front of his face, they would need to watch their back for weeks to come.

As he reached the top of the pit, Zane squinted in the bright, noonday sun that was pouring through a break in the clouds. He surveyed the grassy rest area, looking for someone. *There he is!* Zane thought, seeing a barrel-chested man leaning against a tall rock, the sun reflecting off of his shiny, bald head.

Zane walked over to his father, Bilt, and greeted him casually. "Hey, pa."

"Hey, son," his aged father replied in a raspy voice, turning to him with a smile that displayed his many broken teeth. "How've ya been doin'?"

"Better'n you, I bet," Zane replied, leaning back against the rock and putting his hands behind his head. The mines were like a furnace; the body heat of all the working men radiated throughout the tunnels, making it uncomfortably warm in the depths of the earth. Zane relished the chance to feel the light breeze blowing through his hair.

"Ya got that right," said Bilt, scratching an aggravated spot on his wrist. They watched a group of loud, well-muscled miners crowd onto the elevator to go into the mine.

"Ya findin' anything down thar?" Zane asked his father after resting in silence for a few moments.

"As a matter o' fact, we 'ave!" Bilt's broken-tooth grin shone again.

"Watcha got?"

"Well, Shmidt over thar hit a big stash o' coal 'bout first thing t'smornin'. I reckon it be 'bout fifty pounds o' it!"

Zane opened his mouth to reply but then shut it. A strange looking man was walking towards him, a deep, black cowl pulled over his head. The cowl was connected to a long cloak that billowed behind the man as he walked. What surprised the large boy however, was the man's height. *He... he's taller than me!* Zane thought incredulously. *He must not be from this village. I was sure that I was taller than everyone here!*

"Hello," the stranger said, pulling back the deep cowl from his head. He definitely wasn't from Victon Province. He may have been tall, but his face didn't have the big bones common to Zane's people. *Who is this guy?*

"Wal, good afternoon ta yew 's well!" Bilt said in reply, grinning and completely oblivious to the man's daunting composure. "Yer obviously not from these here parts. What brings ya here?"

"I'd like a word with this young man," the cloaked stranger said, his deep voice seeming to carry through the ground and resonate in Zane's chest.

"Wal, go right ahead!" Bilt exclaimed, leaning back on the stone pillar once again and looking up expectantly.

The man looked pained. "Actually, I would like to speak with him alone."

"I guess ya can." Bilt spun around and walked away from them, whistling out of tune. He looked back every once in a while to check on Zane, but he figured that his son could take care of this. Zane, on the other hand, felt apprehensive about the tall man, although he didn't know why.

The man waited until Bilt was out of hearing range and then began. "My name is Yakob." He stepped forward and offered to shake Zane's hand.

Zane enthusiastically obliged, hiding his suspicion. "Why, hello, Yakob! I'm Zane. What can I do fer ya?"

Although Yakob was big, Zane was stronger. The tall man winced and pulled his hand away before Zane could dislocate his wrist. "I would like to ask you some questions."

Without giving him time to answer, he continued. "Do you use a weapon?"

Zane swatted at a fly absently. *I guess it wouldn't hurt.* "Not much," he replied. "Except for bashin' an axe against a wall a' stone every day."

Yakob nodded. "Understandable. And are you good at... ahem... bashing?"

"I guess," Zane said, shrugging. "I can break some a' them there rocks pretty derned fast."

"And you are... eighteen years old?"

"Eighteen and one half, yessiree." *Now how did he know that?* Zane hoped that his surprise didn't show on his face.

"Thank you for your time, Zane." The stranger said, concluding the short conversation. Yakob stood up and nodded to the confused boy.

"The least I can do," Zane said, standing up as well. "I wish ya luck on yer journey back to wherever ya live."

But Yakob was too far away to have heard him. The tall man had seen the first opportunity to leave and had taken it.

As Zane watched Yakob walk across the grassy field towards the woods, he couldn't help but wonder why this man was here and what he wanted with him.

Zane flexed his massive bicep, feeling the muscles ripple powerfully underneath his skin. For the other man's sake, he hoped it was good.

<><><><><><><><><><><><><><><><><><><>

Kari crept through the woods, crouching down so her movement wasn't obvious. The sunlight shone through the trees, splashing spots of light on the forest floor. Birds chirped cheerfully in the distance, but Kari paid them no mind. She was tracking.

There you are. Now don't move.

Up ahead, a large buck paused its steady movement and bent its head, chewing the delicate grass that grew beneath its feet.

Trying her best to move slowly, Kari pulled a razor-sharp arrow from the quiver hanging from her hip. She drew the bowstring back to her cheek, knowing that she only had one shot, so she'd better make that shot count. She shifted her leg back a bit to obtain a more propitious stance.

Her foot landed on a small, dry branch, which cracked sharply in the silence of the woods.

The deer jerked its head up and scanned its surroundings with large, intelligent eyes. Kari hoped that she was being still enough to not be detected. Some of her long, black hair dangled in front of her face, giving her a partial camouflage.

Compared to the average size of the seventeen-year-old girls in her town, Kari was tall. She stood at about six feet even and looked down on most of her neighbors. She had flowing, raven black hair that hung to her waist when not tied up in some sort of braid. Her eyes were dark and calculating, colored deep green like her father's. Her thin lips were low on her round face, and her petite nose was centered between her eyes and mouth. Kari's pale skin would have been perfectly smooth had it not been for the cuts and scratches that marked her face from years of hunting in the wilderness. Many of the boys in her town considered her a stunning beauty, but she shunned every one who approached her. After hearing of bad experiences from her many older siblings and thinking of the teasing that would most certainly come from her younger siblings, Kari had vowed to stay away from boys until she found the right one.

Kari kept her entire body riveted in place as she watched the lone buck survey his surroundings, wondering if he would see her.

Eventually, the suspicious deer decided that nothing was wrong and bent down to munch the fresh grass.

Kari exhaled quietly and lifted her bow again, sighting on the deer's chest, where its heart would be. She breathed in deeply and then pushed the air out, waiting for the moment when her body was motionless between breaths. At that point, she released the arrow.

The silent, brown dart flew true through the air, making no sound. The deer felt a sharp, burning sensation in its chest and tried to sprint away, but instead, it fell haphazardly on its side and twitched violently before finally lying motionless.

Kari stood to walk over to her kill, but before she could, an odd sound reached her ears. She turned around, trying to locate its source. Not seeing anything, she decided to investigate.

After skulking forward for about twenty yards, she happened upon an old, dirt road that was sheltered from the bright sun by the trees of the forest. Staying in the brush, Kari watched as a lithe, black-cloaked man made his way down the road.

Before she had time to process his appearance, a vibrant humming sounded from the other direction. She realized that it had to be the sound she heard in the woods.

Kari turned and peered that way, keeping her body low to the ground. For some reason, a worm of uncertainty had started wriggling in her chest. *How often do people actually come down this road?* Nevertheless, she kept watching.

A short, stout man was ambling along the road, humming to the tune of an unknown song. His head was pale and devoid of hair, and his belly showed that he had drunk one too many beers.

Kari recognized him. He was a beggar that had shown up in her town earlier in the year. No one knew where he had come from, and no one knew his name. He spent his time sitting at street corners, asking passersby for money or alcohol.

The man in black stopped in the middle of the road and greeted the other, shaking his hand in camaraderie. They apparently knew each other.

The men began speaking in lowered tones, but Kari was able to make out some of the more important words, such as "castle" and "Nunor."

All of a sudden, Kari's heart skipped a beat. *That man just said my name!* Although spoken in a quiet voice, she had heard the portly man say, "Her name is Kari," clear as day. She watched in apprehension.

The man in black nodded nondescriptly and patted the other on the back. With that, they both turned around and began strolling back the ways they had come from as if nothing had happened.

As soon as they were both out of sight, Kari made her way through the shadowed woods back to the deer carcass. As she walked, she thought about the meeting that was obviously prearranged. *Whatever those two men were talking about, it involved me. And they said the name of the king! I don't remember doing anything wrong!*

Kari looked behind herself in fright, jumping at shadows. She made a mental note of the buck's location and ran in the direction of her town to fetch someone stronger than her, thinking the whole way that some black-cloaked man was following her.

She didn't know what those two men wanted with her, but whatever it was, it couldn't be good.

Ruth pushed open the wooden door to the hospital and walked briskly inside. The low ceiling stretched to the end of the long, central hallway, at the end of which were two sturdy doors. She had just come back from the small store across the road after buying her and her brother's lunches: a loaf of fragrant, brown bread and a chunk of white cheese.

She walked down the long hall lined with matching doors toward her brother, Gordo, who was helping a patient in the large main room. A wooden sign hung above the entryway, which read "Treatment Room."

She was sixteen years old and spent her time running the hospital, which was the only place one could get medical help in her town. Besides being extremely organized and good at medicine, Ruth had a certain aura of leadership surrounding her. The few staff that manned the hospital knew she was in charge and looked up to her, figuratively, anyway.

Physically, she was shorter than most girls her age. Being only five feet, two inches, she had been harassed about her height many times as a young girl, which inspired her interest in the study of medicine. Now, instead of being hurt, she was helping others.

Ruth had learned her many healing skills from an aged woman who served as a healer for the village her entire life. She had known everything, from stitching cuts and mending broken bones to creating tonics and diagnosing diseases. With Ruth's organization and leadership skills, the two of them had teamed together to create a hospital.

Ruth's strawberry blond hair came down a couple inches past her shoulders. Her delicate eyebrows highlighted the gentle contours of her shining blue eyes, which sparkled whenever she was cheerful. However, she was very skillful at making them seem dark and stormy when patients refused to comply.   The young medic's caramel features gave the impression that she had spent some time in the sun. Her brother, Gordo, claimed that she was pretty, but she had always passed it off as him patronizing her. What she didn't realize, though, was how right he was.

Gordo's face was very similar to Ruth's. The only noticeable differences were his darker hair color and his broad nose. Although he was three years younger, some people mistook them for twins because of their marked similarities.

"What's going on, Gordo?" She asked after opening the doors and setting the food down on a clean counter. She pushed her long hair behind her head and donned a white, cotton cap reserved for nurses.

Looking up at her, Gordo replied, "This man cut his arm, but he doesn't want me to bandage it. He wants you to confirm that it won't get infected." He looked at Ruth with exasperation evident in his expression.

Ruth glanced at him knowingly and bent over to look. The short, thin slice along the man's arm was slowly oozing a trickle of blood. Although he was a full-grown adult, his face was contorted in pain as if his entire limb had been severed.

Ruth cleared her throat and straightened her back. "You have a pretty bad cut there, sir," she began, stating the obvious. "I'm sorry to say it, but the only way it won't get infected is if you let us treat it the way we have to."

"Will it hurt very bad?" The man cringed pathetically.

"Not if you let us take care of it quickly," Ruth replied, folding her arms behind her and looking at him sympathetically.

Hesitating at first, the man eventually resigned to the inevitable. "Very well. Carry on." He squeezed his eyes shut and clenched his fists.

Ruth rolled her eyes at her brother and said, "All right, Gordo. Get working on it." She walked back out of the Treatment Room and strolled down the main hallway, nodding to one of her elderly employees.

The hospital was a fairly large building with many rooms for recovering patients. Each had a numbered door that opened to the central hall, and a window that opened to the outside for fresh air. At the end of the hall opposite the entrance was the Treatment Room, where they worked on the patients one at a time.

Several of her workers were going to and from rooms, checking on the patients' welfare. Most of the staff were older folk who enjoyed volunteering to help people, for in Ruth's hospital, there was no charge to get medical treatment. People who worked for her wouldn't be looking for a way to earn money. They would just be looking for a way to help.

Ruth obtained the small amount of money she needed from hunting. She was an expert knife thrower and snare setter, often catching small game to sell to her good friend who owned the general store across the street.

It would be easier for her if her father helped provide. Unfortunately, he had wasted himself away in the town's many taverns ever since Ruth's mother had been kidnapped by a looting band of thieves. He rarely gave her help in the hospital, and if he needed money, he would sit out in the streets and beg.

Ruth shook her head in disgust at the thought of it. It was much more honorable to earn one's money through hard work. As she was thinking about this, there was a light knock on the front door. Ruth strode quickly down the hall and opened it, expecting another patient. When she saw who it was, however, she was quite intrigued.

Before her stood a man clothed completely in black. His deep cowl was pulled back from his head, revealing his weasel-like face. A short sword hung at his side, signifying that he was some sort of warrior. All in all, his presence made Ruth very curious.

"Can I help you?" she asked kindly.

"I hear that you have medical expertise," he inquired, his voice light and airy. He withdrew his left hand, which had been hidden behind his back. "As you can see, I have a problem."

On the palm of his hand was a bloody slit that stretched from the base of his little finger to the base of his thumb. Ruth noticed that the edges of the cut were clean and straight, obviously the work of a blade. It must have been done recently, as well, for it was openly flowing.

"Yes. You look like you could use some help," Ruth replied, not at all shocked by the injury. "Come in." She beckoned for him to follow her.

The strange man walked behind her to the Treatment Room, where Gordo had just finished binding the other man's arm.

"This man's hand is hurt," Ruth informed him as she walked past him to a wooden counter.

Gordo helped his whimpering patient up. "Alright," he replied, pointing out the extra bandage on the table. The pitiful man limped exaggeratedly out behind him, cradling his wrapped arm.

Gesturing for the cloaked man to sit on the low table, Ruth grabbed a section of thick cloth from a shelf and handed it to him. "Press this onto your hand for a few moments while I prepare the bandage." The man took the fabric and did as he was told.

While she was mending his hand, Ruth asked what had been on her mind since the stranger came in. She was always curious about her patients' wounds. "So how did this happen?"

"I was attacked… by a knife."

"Ouch." *And how did it get on the palm of his hand?* They stared at each other for a second, each assessing the other person.

After he was bandaged, the black-cloaked man stood up and said, "Well, I'd best be going now." He nodded abruptly and made his way down the hallway to the door, lifting his wrapped hand behind him in farewell.

As soon as the door swung shut, Ruth leaned against the table, staring at nothing in particular. *A mysterious man in a black cloak… with a cut on the* palm *of his hand from what he claimed to have been an attack. I wonder who he is…*

Mikal sat down on the grass near his small, brick house. The wind was blowing in from the sea, carrying on it the delicious taste of salt. He stared out past the docks and over the water, the chilling sea breeze whiffling through his ebony hair. Its long strands swept down the back of his neck, barely tickling the tops of his broad shoulders. His solid jaw was speckled with prickly bristles and small, white lines, the result of trying to shave with a five-inch knife.

Mikal was seventeen years old, but his rugged features caused people to mistake him as much older. His skin was tight and sea-worn from years of living by the ocean. His hard, yellow-green eyes scanned the sea front in a cold, calculating way.

After years of being mistreated by the older children in his village, Mikal had grown bitter and hostile. Having no friends, he spent his free time practicing swordsmanship on the beach and had become very skilled with a blade. From years of practice, his arm muscles were taut, and his six foot, two inch frame was large and strong.

He watched the power of the ocean waves as they crashed against the shore, pounding the sand ruthlessly. Mikal admired the ocean. Like him, it didn't care who it crushed and destroyed.

His uncle had tried to warn him that his hatred and rage against the bullies who pestered him would turn him to a cold killer, but Mikal didn't care. In his mind, it had been his Uncle Byran's fault that his parents were killed. He had no respect for his uncle.

Although it hadn't actually been Byran's fault, he had been there. He had done nothing as Mikal's parents were cruelly slaughtered in the street by marauding criminals.

Mikal sneered at the thought of those wretches. If he could, he would track them down and destroy every last one of them for what they had done.

Living peacefully with Byran was hard for Mikal. His uncle was a pious man, dedicated to the prospect of a loving Creator who spoke the world into being with one word. Mikal considered that to be foolish. According to him, there was no loving Creator. How could a loving Creator have allowed his parents to die? In his mind, everyone was on their own.

Suddenly, something interrupted his train of thought. He caught an unusual movement out of the corner of his eye. When he turned his head to find out what had moved, all he could see were the large trees that bordered the beach, shrouding the ground in shadow.

It could have just been someone from town, Mikal thought, though not believing himself.

As he stared at the shadows trying to discern what was there, a small movement once again grabbed his attention. He peered closer and noticed a man dressed in black clothes walking back through the woods, his hands concealed beneath the long cloak he wore.

A bad feeling sunk into Mikal's stomach as he realized why the man must have been there. His brow began to sweat with fear. There could have been many reasons for a stranger walking in the woods, but someone dressed entirely in black? No. The only reason someone dressed like that would be to veil himself in the deep shadows of the trees. He was stalking somebody.

Mikal's face clearly showed his apprehension as he stood up and made his way towards his red brick house, believing that he knew who the man was stalking.

Him.

4

...

A Summons

The bright noonday sun glared down at the world below, scorching the ground with its burning rays. It grinned maliciously, granting no creature asylum from its blinding light and searing heat. The slouching guard in the foremost watchtower of mighty Castle Orthox was no exception. Sweat poured in sheets down his brow and soaked his cotton undershirt with its sticky wetness. His heavy chainmail shirt burned against his skin, offering him no relief. He groaned and shifted position, holding a loose grip on his long, barbed spear. *Guarding is the worst job in the world*, he thought morosely. *I can already feel my skin peeling off from sunburn!*

"D'ya see anything?" A squeaky voice called from behind the guard for what seemed like the thousandth time.

"Malto, would you please be quiet?!" The guard exclaimed, turning angrily on the skinny messenger boy, who was relaxing behind him in the cool shade of the stairwell. "Like I've said before, I'll tell you when I see something! You don't need to ask!"

"Okay, okay!" Malto said, lifting his hands in a placating gesture. "I'm just checkin' how yer doin'."

"Well don't!" The miserable guard turned back and stared down at the brown grass outside the watchtower. He was standing on the outer wall of Aena's capital city,

Kogincheir. Earlier that morning, Commander Yurson, Chief Commander over the Aenian army, had assigned him to this tower. By the king's orders, he was supposed to be watching for unusual characters, specifically men wearing all black. Apparently, they were expected.

Now, why would anyone want to wear black on a day like this? It's bad enough that I have to wear armor! The guard griped and groaned to himself as he stood there, feeling the sting of the sun on his unprotected neck.

Then something caught his eye.

Ghosting across the dry fields towards the gate were five figures that seemed to be made of liquid. Their fluid, black forms stole quickly forward, being warped by the waves of heat coming off the ground.

"Malto," the guard called back, never taking his eyes off of the eerily distorted silhouettes. "Run back to the castle… I think we have our men."

"Is it about time?" A remarkably large man asked in a very deep voice, standing stoically over the stout desk in front of him.

Prime Minister Lithel looked up, his eyes dilated from the darkness of the room. It was illuminated only by the light of two torches flickering on the wall. "The king will meet with you when he sees fit to do so," Lithel stated in a matter-of-fact voice. He looked back down at his papers as if forgetting the man was there.

The brawny man in the black cloak leaned over and looked Lithel directly in the eyes, speaking in a deadly calm voice. "Well, if that's the case, you'd better tell him we're ready."

Lithel gulped and looked hesitantly back up, seeing the daunting blackness in the man's eyes. "But-but sir, I can't defy the king! I could be sent to the dungeon!"

A cold grin crossed his mouth. "I think we'd be better off. Don't you? Now do what I say and get us in there." He glowered at the Prime Minister as he stalked back to his four silent companions.

Lithel, noticing the dangerous looks in the five men's eyes, decided that his best course of action would be to concede. "Very well. I will ask if the king is ready to see you." The slim man stood up gracefully and approached the large, ornate doors that led to the throne room.

Carved into their tough wood was a detailed design, engraved by the most skilled woodworkers. The beautiful etching depicted King Nunor's decorative coat of arms positioned over an elaborate map of the country Aena. The doorknobs were fashioned out of brass and reflected the fluttering torchlight in the room. Inscribed on each knob were the words, "May the line of kings never be broken," Aena's national motto.

Lithel reached for the handles, a hard lump forming in his throat. He grasped them with trembling hands and slowly pushed open the magnificent doors.

The waiting men got a fleeting glimpse of a broad man on an elaborate throne before the doors boomed ominously shut, as if swallowing the Prime Minister whole.

Lithel was built like a bird. His skinny body was surprisingly fit, and he had superb agility. The Prime

Minister's face was narrow and shrewd, his long nose hooking downward like a beak. All this considered, he was an intelligent man, although sometimes very stubborn. His glossy, wooden desk was cluttered with parchment of all sorts, various seals and signatures lining the bottom of each one. Although ignorant bystanders may have considered him messy, Lithel knew exactly what every paper meant and where it was on his desk.

After a few minutes, the doors opened again, and Lithel walked out, fear obvious in his scarlet face and shaking hands. "The king will see you now," he announced, his nasally voice breaking.

The men smirked at each other as they walked into the throne room, staying solemnly in a single-file line.

Upon entering the doors, however, any vestige of humor was gone. They strode down the violet carpet in the center of the room towards the throne, heads lowered in respect and cowls drawn back to reveal their faces. They reached the bejeweled throne and spread out in a semicircle on the white stone of the floor, facing the king.

"Welcome, my most trusted spies!" King Nunor boomed, spreading his arms in greeting. He was a hefty man, his thick belly drooping over his decorated belt, and his dense, black beard hanging down to the center of his chest. The beginnings of age were showing on his face, crow's feet in the corners of his eyes and extra wrinkles on his brow. His graying hair was close-cut and neat, the regal crown of Aena resting lightly atop it.

The men lifted their heads at their monarch's welcome, gazing at the king. These five spies were among the few privileged enough to speak to King Nunor without the thought of punishment.

"I expect you have brought me good news," the king began with a smile in his voice, "for if you haven't... well... let's just say that things would not go pleasantly for you."

The spies curled their lips into forced smiles to patronize their monarch, who always enjoyed a good laugh.

"Now, please step forward and present me with your findings. I assume you are all here for the same reason, yes? Of course you are! Otherwise you wouldn't be here!"

The man on the far left stepped forward and stood at attention, ignoring the king's attempts at humor. His rich, brown hair was draping over his eyes, making him seem dangerous and aloof.

"Creyan! How nice to see you. Have you happened upon a suitable candidate?" The king's green eyes watched the spy curiously.

"Yes, Your Majesty, I have. But I regret to say he's an adolescent. I apologize, but I have convinced these others that the young people of this nation are better suited for the tasks you have in mind. I am sorry if I needed your consent to take this step, but I have already discussed it with my fellow spies, and they agree."

"What are your reasons for this?" Nunor asked, unconsciously stroking his beard as he always did when he was thinking.

"Well, I decided that children, preferably adolescents, have many abilities not present in adults. For example: They are often more athletic, new skills and talents stay fresh in their minds, and they have a natural bravery that comes with their age. We shall train them in the art of being a spy, and when the time comes for us," he gestured to the five spies, "to... you know..."

"Yes." King Nunor nodded his head sadly. The prospect of his favorite spies being replaced was a melancholy one, but there did come a time when even the best grew old and out-of-shape.

"By then," Creyan continued, "they will be ready to take on their new responsibilities as top spies in Aena."

King Nunor pondered this for a moment, resting his head on his hand. "Yes, I suppose you are right. Young people *do* have higher levels of energy than adults and are often better actors during inauspicious circumstances. They will be trained and drilled until they have reached the age to begin work."

Creyan did not show it, but he felt utterly relieved. He had thought that he would be punished for taking something like this into his own hands without leave of the king.

"Continue," Nunor said, leaning back in his heavily adorned throne.

After clearing his throat, the slender spy began once again, looking the king in the eye. "His name is Samuel, son of Marken, and he is fifteen years of age. His parents are simple farmers from Kaltoid Province, and if they do anything else on the side, I am unaware of it. Although he does not have much experience with a common soldier's weapons, he has a good spirit and obvious leadership. He enjoys assisting his parents with various tasks and chores around their farm."

"It sounds like he has good character, but what about this supposed lack of fighting skill?"

"Excuse me for saying so, Your Highness, but I did not say he has no fighting skill. I merely stated that he has no skill with the weapons we use as knights."

"Ah! So he does have some skill?"

"Yes. During my time in Kaltoid Province, I witnessed him engage and defeat an aggressive mountain lion with nothing but a shovel. He wielded it as a mace and beat the beast to death when it attacked his family's chickens. He has very fast reflexes, and it seems to me like he would be a natural with a sword."

"Of course, he sounds fine. I can't wait to meet him." King Nunor waved Creyan back and beckoned for the next spy to step forward.

The second man was short and skinny. His slouched posture and sharp features made him look like a rat. "Nat reporting, Your Highness," he said in a surprisingly deep voice. "I have been observing a young man from Shala Province. His name is Mikal. He has a strong, slender physique and is seventeen years old. One of his pastimes is practicing with a sword on the beach near his home. He is vicious and attacks these practice sessions with ferocity and vigor. Apparently, his parents were killed a few years back, and he wishes to avenge their deaths.

"Despite his constant use of sarcasm and mockery, I think he would be a fine candidate."

"Yes, yes. Of course. He reminds me of my younger self, in fact," the king said morosely, thinking of his parents, who were assassinated by a rogue knight when he was a child. "Next!"

"Hello, Your Highness." An intelligent looking man with a trim goatee stepped forth.

"Vin," the king nodded politely. "Who have you chosen?"

"Her name is Ruth, she's sixteen, and she runs an entire hospital in Farnosh Province. I know that we don't usually allow females to become warriors, but I hope you'll make an exception for this one."

"What's so spectacular about her?"

"She is a gentle soul, but very smart. She knows medicine and was able to assist me when I had an 'accident' with my knife." Vin held up his still-bandaged hand with a sly grin on his face. "When I divulged that it was a knife that had cut me, her expression said she was suspicious. I realized after I inflicted the wound, that a cut on the palm of the hand is not very common." He grinned fully.

"Does she have any skill with weapons, or is she just a nurse?"

"Oh, Your Majesty! She's far more than a nurse; she runs the entire hospital! I couldn't believe it myself when I found out! As for skill with weapons, yes, she is superb with throwing knives and often goes hunting during the time she is not in the hospital."

"Hm." King Nunor pondered it for a moment. *We don't usually have females trained at the castle… well… I guess there have been a couple…* "She sounds like a fine candidate," he announced, beckoning for Vin to move back into the line.

"Wilhelm reporting, Your Kingship," the next spy said as he stepped forward. His face was flat and ordinary, and he spoke with a slight Grudenheim accent, a vestigial remnant of his original nationality.

"Good evening, Wilhelm. Who have *you* found?"

"It's another girl, Your Majesty," Wilhelm replied, squaring his broad shoulders. "Her name is Kari. I found out where she lives with some help from one of our insiders. She is very tolerant of chaos, having fourteen siblings in her household. She is skilled with a sword or a bow, although she prefers a sword. I highly recommend her to Your Majesty."

"You're really sure about her?"

"Indeed."

"Well, then I won't go against your judgment. Who's next?"

Wilhelm retreated, making way for the last and largest spy to step forward. He was a barrel-chested giant, being over seven feet tall, and was feared by all of his enemies.

"Yakob," the king said, nodding respectfully to the towering spy.

"Greetings, my liege," he began in the deepest voice King Nunor had ever heard. "I've been watching an eighteen year old boy named Zane. He works in the mines of Victon Province, and he's very tall. Well, he's shorter than me, but you know what I mean." He gave the king one of his rare half-smiles.

"I asked him a few questions while he was taking a break, and by shaking his hand, I learned that he is massively strong from so many years in the mines. When I asked if he was trained in any sort of combat, he replied that he's 'pretty good at smashing things.'"

King Nunor laughed, a short burst that could have been mistaken for a belch, despite the circumstances. "He sounds like an excellent future knight!"

Yakob nodded his huge head and stepped back, standing with the others, who were watching the king expectantly.

"I think these young people are all fine candidates," he began, standing and spreading his arms. "I want them at my table in a week exactly, so they may all be acquainted with each other at the same time. Also, do not tell them about why they are coming here. Only say that they have been selected to be trained at the castle, nothing more. Just as your existence as spies has been kept strictly confidential, so shall theirs."

"Yes, Your Majesty," Creyan said deferentially, speaking for all the spies. Many years ago, he had been appointed their leader by the king, for his experience was more than theirs. He was respected by all the spies, for although his skill was unmatched, he never flaunted it. Creyan was always polite and gracious, a man that everyone trusted.

"Alright then!" The king exclaimed abruptly, beaming at his trusted spies with pride. "You're dismissed!"

They bowed their heads to the king and simultaneously turned on their heels, marching back through the doors they had come from.

King Nunor leaned back into his chair and closed his eyes, comforted by the thought that his spies had the whole procedure under control. *I can't wait!* He thought excitedly.

In a mere seven days, I get to meet these wonderful prodigies my spies have found! As he sat there, staring off into space, a sharp, metallic odor filled his nostrils.

"Hey! Wha...?" Nunor was cut off by a blot of thick, red mist clouding his vision. He inhaled, gasping for air, but the mist was all that he could breathe and taste. He tried to scream, but he couldn't make a sound. The mist was constricting his throat and penetrating his eyes. Panic set in as Nunor thrashed about, trying to break this thing's hold on him.

Without warning, a searing pain pierced his brain, making him shake convulsively. Nunor grabbed his head, trying to relieve himself of the agony that filled his body. He dug his fingernails into his skull, but it only made the pain more intense.

And then it stopped.

Like a parting of the clouds, a sense of peace filled Nunor's mind, causing him to relax and lean backwards into his seat. *What's going on?* He thought, an odd feeling of calm pervading the atmosphere. *Did something just happen? Is something wrong?*

"Welcome."

5

...

Suspicion Arises

"Hey, mom!" Samuel called to his mother as he ran towards her from the barn.

"Yes?" Lora looked up at him and blew a stray hair out of her face. She was in the process of churning butter and was getting a vigorous workout. Her hair was disheveled, and sweat was trickling down her brow.

"I'm going to go into the forest for a little bit," Samuel announced when he reached her. He shifted a large chunk of bark that was under his arm and set the blade of his father's shovel on the ground. Almost unnoticeable was a slight dent in the metal, an aftereffect of Samuel's early morning battle.

His parents had since discovered what he had done. His mother had not been angry with him for not telling them, only confused as to why he would hold it back. To her, he had done a great deed, a deed to be commended for. His father, on the other hand, understood perfectly why Samuel had held it back. When he had lived in the mountains, there had been many a time when he was forced to face a wild animal in a fight. Those had been traumatizing encounters.

"Why are you holding those things?" She asked, nodding to the shovel and bark with a hand on her hip.

"I'm going to build a pitfall trap. Dad taught me, remember?"

After a few moments' hesitation, she nodded, figuring that it was okay. He had just been taught about trapping a week ago and was eager to test his new skills.

"You sure you'll be careful out there?" She asked, feeling an itch of worry for her son. "You won't get into any trouble?"

"Nope! I know what to watch out for. I'll keep myself safe. See ya later!"

"Okay! Good luck!" She went back to churning, knowing that he would keep his promise at all costs.

Samuel, glad that his mother had approved, walked towards the dirt road that led through the forest. He strolled along the path lined by sunbathed trees until he was about a mile from his house. He plopped down on the pine needle covered ground and stretched his legs. Moments later, Samuel grunted and stood up again, ready to dig his trap.

After ruminating about possible locations for the trap, Samuel decided that he'd best do it in the woods. That way, people wouldn't step on it when they were walking down the path.

After moving into the woods for a few yards, he grabbed the shovel, stabbed it into the ground, and lifted up the meager mound of dirt. *This is going to take a while.*

Hours later, when he had finished excavating a six-foot deep hole, he leaned the shovel against a tree and picked up the slab of thick, grooved bark. In his town, it was customary for a hunter to place a stack of three rocks by the traps or snares that they set to warn passersby. Three stacked rocks was their symbol for danger. For a pitfall trap, the people of his village put a slab of tree bark underneath the stack of rocks and set it near the hole. Samuel carefully placed the rocks on top of the bark, balancing them carefully.

In order to collect fallen branches, dead leaves, and twigs to cover the trap, he set out on a short-lived trek through the forest. When he had located enough debris and brush, the sweating youth brought them back to his pit and laid them over the top, making sure to cover it completely. As a final touch, he spread more leaves, pine needles, and other natural objects over the branches and twigs covering the hole.

Samuel stepped back, admiring his work. *That just about does it.* It was inconspicuously placed and was almost invisible in the dense shadows of the trees.

Samuel sighed loudly and sat down on the ground behind a large tree, the danger sign barely visible from his position. *Well... I hope I catch something.*

Creyan strode out of the throne room, a feeling of satisfaction and relief flooding through him. He was proud that his report had won the king's approval. He hadn't known if King Nunor would approve of a farmer boy.

The limber man strode past the dark, wooden desk where the studious Prime Minister sat.

Lithel looked up as the five men passed. "Goodbye, sirs," he said in a monotone. "Good luck on finding your candidates." He looked back down to his work, intensely focused on the many papers strewn about his desk.

Creyan rolled his eyes at Lithel and marched through the door that led to the magnificent Main Hall, leaving the others behind to converse amongst themselves. He wasn't really a talker. Whenever the rest of the spies started chatting, the quiet man would deliberately avoid them. Creyan's introverted nature caused him to despise getting stuck in a conversation.

As he made his way through the network of hallways towards the front entryway, Creyan fantasized that the king could transform the keep into a giant maze. *No one would ever find their way out,* he smirked, exiting through the wooden doors that led to the outer courtyard.

Around the side of the massive keep, the pungent stables awaited him. He walked in and gave the young groom a few copper shards for his service. Creyan gently pushed open the stall in which his sleek, black steed was waiting.

"Hey, boy. How's it going?" He asked the horse. "We need to ride quickly now, so give it your all." His horse, Diamond, swished his tail and snorted.

After strapping the saddle on, Creyan swung his leg over the horse's body and made himself comfortable. With a slight nudge to his ribs, Diamond took off at a breakneck pace out the entrance of the stables and towards the front gate.

At this rate, Creyan thought, *I'll make it to Kaltoid in a matter of days.* With that optimistic thought, he sped onward through the streets of the capital city, the horse's hooves clattering noisily on the rough, gray cobblestones.

Samuel grabbed another cob of corn from the wooden barrel next to him. He was sitting on a dead stump in front of his house, doing what he considered the most onerous chore in the world.

He grasped the stringy, green top of the corn cob and peeled downward, careful not to hurt the fat kernels. He finished stripping the cob and worked at pulling out the little strings. If he did not eradicate most all of them, they would stick in his teeth at suppertime. Although this was a good incentive to be meticulous, he hated it.

Samuel paused and looked up, another thought crossing his mind. *I should probably check my trap. I could have caught something and not even know about it!* He imagined a plump rabbit trying to escape his pit. It wouldn't be too hard for the little animal to hop right out. *Well, maybe it would be pretty hard... hmm... but I still want to check it, so I can get out of doing this boring chore.* He looked over at his dad, Marken, who was sitting across from him, also shucking corn.

"Hey, dad. Can I go to the woods and check my trap?" Samuel asked.

Marken looked up from his half-shucked cob, his hands covered in green strings and juice from burst kernels. He was oblivious to a stray, green string that hung haphazardly from his tangled beard "Shouldn't you stay until we're finished with the corn?"

Samuel folded his hands across his lap, looking up innocently at his father. "Well, I had a suspicion that I might have caught something already."

"Are you startin' to go all fortune teller?" Marken said, a familiar gleam in his eye. "You aren't gonna start actin' like that old lady who came by once?" He put his hands on his temples and crossed his eyes. "I see a fox... no, wait. That's a rabbit," he joked in a raspy voice. They laughed heartily at his wit.

"Yeah, you can go," his dad said, reverting back to his normal self. "Just be back in time to help finish this up."

"Thanks, dad! And don't count on it!" Samuel jumped up, tossing his unfinished corn cob at his father and running towards the narrow dirt road.

Marken flinched as the corn hit him. "He could have at least finished this one," he mumbled as he ran his hand through his thinning brown hair. He had a nagging suspicion that Samuel had chosen this exact moment to ask because of the corn shucking. He wondered why he had let the boy get away with it.

After he finished Samuel's cob, Marken stood up, stretched his creaking back, and walked inside the house.

"Hey, Lora?" he asked his dark-haired wife. She was sitting in one of the three oak chairs Marken had made, sewing his new pants. "I just let Samuel go check his trap before I could think it all the way through."

"He's probably just edgy about his prey getting away." She looked up from sewing the dark trousers. "He's never actually done this before, you know."

"Yeah, I know. I just promised earlier that I wouldn't let him get out of the corn shuckin'. I guess I messed up this time." He huffed, annoyed at himself.

"Why don't you go after him and help him with his trap?" She asked. "You could wait until he gets back to finish shucking the corn."

Marken paused, mulling it over. "I could... but why waste my energy on catchin' up to him? I'm not as fit as I used to be."

"All the more reason for you to get some exercise." Lora looked back to her sewing, closing the argument.

"All right, all right," Marken gave in. "Whatever you say darlin'. You're the one makin' my pants, anyway." He walked out and closed the door behind him, chuckling at his humor that always seemed to be lost on the others in his family.

6

...

Trapped

Samuel snuck through the forest, careful to move in the hunting style that his father had taught him. Walking heel-toe caused almost no sound to come from his swiftly moving feet, making it the most advantageous way for him to walk.

Samuel had been hunting since he was eight years old. His father had trained him in the ways of the people that lived on Nolai Mountain, such as walking in silence without being seen. His father was a descendant of these people.

Marken had traveled down the mountain away from his family years before Samuel was born. He had been on a mission to sell the pelts he had caught and had happened to come across the town of Vale. While he was bartering furs in the market, he met a young Lora, who soon became his wife.

After having a small wedding in Vale, Marken went back up the mountain one last time to tell his family and friends that he would be moving to the farmlands near the border of Kaltoid Province. They were very happy for him and wished him luck, promising to visit from time to time. When Marken finished his trek into the mountains and back, he settled down with Lora on the land that Samuel now called home.

The young hunter was nearing the spot where he had set his trap, so he began creeping even more quietly than before. He saw the slightly uneven patch of ground with the bark and rocks next to it and crouched low in the shrubbery. What he saw made a shiver of excitement run through his body.

There was a rabbit sitting right next to the pit!

Samuel waited motionlessly for the unsuspecting creature to take one more step forward. The excitement of the catch was already coursing through his veins as Samuel imagined running back home and telling his mother and father of his success.

Suddenly, there was a loud ruckus in the forest beyond his trap. There were twigs snapping and dead leaves crunching noisily. To Samuel's horror, the plump rabbit turned in fright and bounded back the way it had come, disappearing into the forest.

He felt a pang of disappointment at his failure, but then he perked up, wondering what had made so much noise and scared the rabbit away. *Maybe it's an even bigger animal!*

The crashing sounds came closer and closer, until without warning, a cloaked man stumbled out of the brush, groaning when a taut branch snapped back and scored a thin slice on his arm.

Samuel felt his heart pounding intensely as he realized what was happening. The realization hit him like a falling tree, causing his jaw to drop open and his eyes to bulge in surprise.

It was the man from the market!

Marken snuck through the woods, watching for signs of Samuel having been there: A footprint in the grass here, a broken stick there. He remembered his years as an expert hunter, relishing in the chance to experience them once more.

He bent down to check the direction a shallow footprint was facing in. According to the signs, Marken was still going in the right direction.

After examining all there was to see, he stood up slowly, his joints cracking and his back popping deafeningly. *That's going to be real good for staying hidden*, he grimaced.

When he had walked a few more yards, Marken saw something on the forest floor ahead of him. It was a slab of bark with three rocks stacked on top of it.

Samuel's trap! Marken began to move closer, but before he could, he saw something that caused him to freeze.

There was a man in a black cloak standing in front of the trap!

I have to warn him, Marken thought. *Surely Samuel doesn't mean to catch a person!* He broke his cover and stepped out of the shadows, addressing the man casually.

"Hello! I didn't expect to see someone like you in the forest!" He was about to add that the man had better not move forward, but he wasn't fast enough.

The stranger looked up through his long, wavy hair and started to say, "What are you..." but he didn't get any further.

Marken jumped forward to catch the stranger, but he was too late. The man, who was obviously new to hunting in

Kaltoid Province, fell straight down through the mesh of leaves and twigs, landing hard on the floor below.

Marken was surprised by the depth of the pit. *Samuel must have been paranoid about his prey escaping.*

Suddenly, another voice sounded from the bushes right next to Marken. "Hey! Are you alright?"

To his surprise, Samuel seemed to appear from nowhere, stepping out of the shrubbery and looking down at the trapped man with concern on his face.

"Samuel?" The out-of-practice hunter asked. "Have you been hiding there the whole time?"

The disheveled youth looked smugly at his father. "Of course, dad! I was even here when your clumsy backside bumbled by right next to me!"

"Hey! I don't bumble!"

Samuel was about to reply, but the stranger in the trap called out, "Uh, could I have a little help here?"

"Oh. Right," he said sheepishly. "Come on, Dad. Help me with this chunk a' flesh." Together, Samuel and Marken hoisted the helpless man out of the pit.

After they finished filling in the trap and disposing of the bark and rocks, the trio walked back to Samuel's house to tell his mother about this unexpected surprise.

As they conversed with the mysterious man, the two farmers learned that his name was Creyan. According to him, he worked for King Nunor and had been sent to retrieve Samuel for special training. He had left his horse in Vale, for he wished to approach the farm as discreetly as possible.

Samuel was very surprised, but he hid his bewilderment until they arrived back at his house.

When they finally showed up, it was nearly dark and Lora had finished shucking the corn for them. She was currently in the process of boiling the corn for their now late-night meal.

"Who's this?" She asked, looking suspiciously at Creyan. She had not expected a visitor and was in no shape to be keeping company at her house. With a cursory movement, she pushed her unkempt hair behind her head, hiding it from view.

"Hi, Mom. This is Creyan." The darkly clothed man nodded politely in her direction, his blue eyes gleaming brightly beneath the swath of brown hair shadowing his face.

"Hello. I'm Lora." Upon closer inspection, she noticed the dirt covering Creyan's dark clothes and turned towards Marken and Samuel, a hand on each hip. "Did he get caught in the trap?!"

They sat down next to the fire that the cast iron pot was over, and Creyan told them all the whole story, from his departure from the castle to being caught in the pit.

After he had finished, both Lora and Marken stared silently into the flickering flames.

"So, this is the king's messenger," Samuel's mother started slowly, turning towards the lanky man. "Why would you want to take my son?"

"Well, ma'am, I chose Samuel for this because of the remarkable potential he has shown. I can tell that he is a born leader."

Samuel looked up. "I am?"

"Yes, you are. You possess the rare trait of leadership, although you may not even realize it yet."

Lora broke in again. "And what is so urgent that you need to take my son with you?"

"All I'm allowed to tell you is that he has been selected for training at Castle Orthox."

"And why would we let him leave with you?"

"I assure you, ma'am, I am a trustworthy person, and I will take good care of him. Remember, this is the order of the king. Here is my identification as a soldier of the crown, if you need further proof." He produced a brass token that had been hanging on a cord around his neck beneath his shirt. It had the decorative seal of King Nunor depicted on its face, but there was another symbol below that.

I've seen many symbols of rank on these tokens, Lora thought, *but never this one! I've heard rumors that this is the symbol of a man who is very close to the king. He must be very privileged.*

"Well," Lora began hesitantly, realizing that she really only had one choice. "I won't object to his going, as long as he can write to us. His father just has to agree to go with him to the castle." She looked pointedly at Marken.

"He would be able to send you letters. The other part, though, I can't guarantee." He turned to face Marken, who shrunk back a bit.

"So, Dad?" Samuel asked expectantly, raising his eyebrows.

After wavering for several seconds, Marken finally acquiesced. "Fine. I'll go."

Samuel slapped his father on the back joyfully, but Lora turned back to Creyan with worry in her eyes. "Are you sure he'll be safe?"

"Yes, ma'am!" Creyan stated emphatically. "He'll be very safe with us."

"Are you absolutely sure you can protect him?"

"Ma'am," he said, leaning backward and putting his hands behind his head. "After his training is completed, I'll want him protecting me."

7

...

Surprise In The Night

It was the second day of their journey to the castle, and they were sitting around a campfire, eating their dinner. It was after dark, and the stars were twinkling brightly through the trees above their forested campsite. Samuel chewed solemnly on a piece of dried meat, wondering if he would ever finish it.

The first leg of their journey had been spent traveling from Vale to the small town of Filasky. They had taken turns riding on Creyan's horse, Diamond, with the others walking alongside.

The trek on the first day had gone surprisingly well. The only problems had been some light rain and large swarms of pesky gnats.

In Filasky, they had bought a couple of horses for Samuel and Marken, so they could move more swiftly towards the castle. The trio had spent the night at a rundown inn in the town. It was a horrid place, but it was all they had.

Today, they had ridden hard, passing many small towns on the way but not stopping until nightfall. Samuel assumed that they were very near to the border of Mellen Province, judging by how fast they had ridden.

It was peaceful in the forest as they watched the dying fire's orange coals glow. The logs they had built it with were now black and white, their ashes crumbling into gray piles of dust.

"Say," Creyan began, breaking the silence that had blanketed the camp. "Have you ever heard the old folk tale about the Grogger Emperor?"

"Wait!" Marken raised his head, worry apparent in his eyes. "Won't it alert them to our presence? Won't they be able to find us?"

He was referring to a special trait held by every Grogger in existence. If the word "Grogger" was spoken, then they could hear it, even from miles away.

"Don't worry about that," Creyan said reassuringly. "There aren't any gangs of them in this area. Now, please... allow me to tell my story." He cleared his throat and spread his hands dramatically.

"There once lived an old Grogger Emperor who had much wealth and prestige..." Creyan then dove into an elaborate story about how the old Grogger Emperor betrayed the ancient King of Aena centuries ago.

Groggers were nasty creatures. With a pale brown complexion and long spindly arms and legs, they were horrifying to behold. The sickly-looking creatures worked as mercenaries and marauders, living their lives with much cruelty and bloodshed.

According to Creyan's story, the Grogger Emperor had been banished to forever live in the desolate Belsh Desert. His ancestors had survived to pester the lands of Aena with their raids, always trying to exact revenge against the country that had thrown them out.

As he listened to the story, Samuel began to feel melancholy and noticed that his father did too, from his drooping face and glistening eyes.

Unknown to Creyan, Marken and Lora had another son before Samuel. They named him Rosh, and he was a diligent worker around the farm. His blond hair had matched that of Samuel's, and his face was broad like his father's. He had his mother's eyes.

On a cold, autumn day, Rosh was in Vale, buying some supplies for Lora. He was ten years old at the time. He had just come out of a small leather shop, when a vicious band of Groggers attacked.

They pillaged the town's goods, looting and sacking all the shops they could find. Before too long, a group of courageous farmers found them and ran them out of town with pitchforks and scythes. On their way out, the Groggers were driven past the shop Rosh had just come out of.

Not knowing what to do, the young Rosh had stood stock-still and watched the impending wave of shrieking beasts descend upon him. Instead of killing him on the spot, the Groggers roughly grabbed him and, in spite of the efforts of the pursuing farmers, took him.

Marken and Lora were greatly distressed at the tragedy that had befallen them. To ease their suffering, they had another son, whom they named Samuel. Rosh was never seen nor heard from again after that day.

Samuel stared at the coals glumly as he thought of what adventures he could have had with Rosh.

"I heard that one from my father." Creyan said, finishing the tale. "He used to tell it to me when we'd go outside and sit around a fire like this at night." When he looked up, he saw Marken and Samuel's sad faces.

"What's wrong? Why do you look so sad?"

Marken inhaled shudderingly. "I... I had another son." He said in a voice thick with emotion. "He was captured by Groggers."

Creyan studied the ground, suddenly ashamed. "I'm sorry. I shouldn't have told that story."

"It's okay. You couldn't have known."

They sat in silence for a few moments, nobody saying anything.

"I think it's time for bed," Marken said finally, standing up. "It's going to be a long day tomorrow. We should get our sleep."

Samuel nodded and rose to his feet, yawning. His muscles ached from riding a horse all day. He cringed mentally as he thought of how sore he would be tomorrow.

He unrolled his woolen blanket and lay down on one side of it, pulling the other side over him and tucking it in snugly. He closed his drooping eyes, and before long, he was fast asleep.

Samuel's eyes shot open. The sky was dark and the stars were shining. Every once in a while, a lone cricket would chirp.

Samuel laid in the stillness, trying to figure out why he had awoken. Then he heard something. It could have been a slight rustle in the branches, the small crack of a twig... probably nothing important.

He listened vigilantly. There was something different between the sounds he heard now and the sounds he had heard when he went to bed, but he couldn't place it.

Suddenly, there was a series of sharp snaps from deep in the woods behind him.

Samuel's entire body froze. *Is it a... a Grogger?* He closed his eyes to concentrate, trying to discern what it was that he heard moving. His body was trembling from fear and anticipation. He knew that Groggers were able to hear their name from very far away. He took deep breaths, trying to calm himself down. *I'm overreacting. It's probably just a wild animal. Nothing to worry about.*

Samuel had just sufficiently calmed himself, when a light crack sounded nearer than before, sending a fresh shot of panic through his body. He kept his eyes closed and tried to block out all the sounds except what he was trying to hear.

The crack came again, this time a little louder.

Samuel closed his hand around the small knife that was under the blanket with him, feeling the handle slip slightly in his sweaty hand. If there was something dangerous behind him, then he had to be prepared.

As he kept listening, Samuel noticed a subtle change. There was a deep whooshing, almost like a breeze, coming from behind him. He inched his hand out from the blanket and felt the cold, night air. Although it was frigid, there was no wind, whatsoever.

What is that sound? Samuel thought fearfully.

Then, like a smack in the face, it came to him: Heavy breathing!

Samuel gulped silently, his face chilled in the night air. Slowly and carefully, he opened his eyes again.

He sucked in a breath. Standing right above him was a Grogger.

8

...

A New Friend

Instead of moving forward, the hideous Grogger turned back towards where it had come from and whispered in a raspy voice, "Mitho krét nas toseka!"

Samuel heard hissing and horrible laughing. More cracks sounded in the forest behind him.

Don't step forward... don't step forward, Samuel thought, doing his best to remain motionless.

He hoped with all his heart that Creyan was awake. He was the only capable swordsman among them.

Samuel glanced at Creyan's sleeping area and almost jumped. *He's not there!*

The cracks and snaps in the woods moved closer and closer, until a pack of Groggers entered Samuel's vision. They were armed with crude, iron scimitars and axes, which they brandished menacingly.

The horde of creatures rushed past their campsite but unexpectedly came to a halt. There was another grating voice, and then a particularly ugly one at the back of the group turned and sniffed the air.

The campfire smoke! Samuel thought, panicking. *They'll smell the smoke and know where we are!* He tightened his grip on the knife, preparing to use it.

Suddenly, a black-cloaked man jumped into the moonlit scene and slashed his sword down in a deadly arc at the Grogger nearest him.

It screamed in pain as the whistling blade cleaved it cleanly in two. With animalistic snarls and shrieks, the others pulled out their crude weapons and lunged at the shadowy figure.

Samuel, knowing that he needed to help, jumped up from his blanket and shouted at the Groggers. The horses whinnied noisily in the background, adding to the chaos.

One of the horrifying creatures turned and screeched something unintelligible, charging aggressively at Samuel. He ducked beneath its wide swipe and stabbed upwards with his knife. He pierced the Grogger's side, causing black blood to spurt from the wound.

It screamed and stumbled backward into one of its gang, knocking them over.

Samuel looked in awe at his bloodstained knife, shocked at the result of his adrenaline-powered attack. *Maybe I do have some skill!*

Turning back to where Creyan was fighting, Samuel saw that the older man had it under control.

With obvious ease, the nimble spy dispatched every Grogger that faced him, slashing at each with lightning speed.

Out of nowhere, a thin Grogger struck swiftly at Creyan's leg, its flashing sword sinking into him.

"Arghhh!" Creyan yelled in pain, swiping his sword backwards and lopping off its head. He fell to his knees, clutching his calf desperately. The red-faced man haphazardly ripped a section of cloth off of his shirt and bound his leg with it.

Instantly, the blood began soaking through the dark cloth, showing that his makeshift bandage wasn't going to last for long.

After staring at Creyan in fright during this time, Samuel brought his eyes back up and noticed that all the Groggers were dead.

"Creyan," Samuel said, deeply thankful for the spy's intervention. "Thank you for stepping in like that."

Creyan tried to smile, but his mouth twisted into a grimace at the pain. "Y-yeah. It's just my… my job."

As Samuel stood there in silence, he wondered what it would be like when he had sword skills like that. *No one will stand in my way,* he thought, imagining himself as a knight.

"Wha…? What's goin' on?" A tired voice sounded from behind Samuel. A bleary-eyed Marken sat up and looked around at the carnage that surrounded their camp.

"Did I miss something?"

Creyan and Samuel didn't say anything; they were too busy laughing.

<><><><><><><><><><><><><><><><><><><>

They arrived in Mellen Province during the middle of the afternoon, at a small town called Kremul.

After finding an inn, Marken dismounted his horse and walked in, leaving their satchels and the sleeping Creyan with Samuel.

They had redressed the wound multiple times on the road, and Creyan had lost a lot of blood. Both Marken and Samuel knew that if he didn't get proper medical treatment soon, he would die.

"I don't know of any doctors 'round here," answered the robust bartender after Marken had asked him. "Course, I never really leave this here bar. It's kinda my life, ya know? Ya got some sickness or somethin'? 'Cause I don't really want it in my inn." He looked suspiciously at Marken.

"No, that's not what I'm here for," the farmer explained. "I have a friend who's injured and needs medical help. I'll take anyone with experience! Anyone!" He stared at the bartender, hoping that there was somebody the portly man knew.

The bartender opened his mouth to repeat what he had previously said, when he was interrupted by a different voice.

"If you need some help, I know somebody who's skilled in those arts." The man sitting on the seat next to them turned around.

He had a weasely face, with a sharp nose and eyes. His chin was pointed, and there was a layer of dark stubble on his jaw.

Marken looked desperately at the man and asked, "Who is it? Please, I need help!"

"Come with me. I'll take you to her." The man stood up and walked towards the staircase that led to the rooms on the upper floor.

Marken hurried quickly after him, hoping that this stranger was serious.

He followed the man up the stairs and down a short hallway.

At one of the doors on the right side of the hall, he stopped abruptly. He raised his fist and knocked three quick times.

"Hold on, I'm coming." A girl's voice sounded from inside the room. There was some bustling around behind the door, and then it opened.

A petite girl with strawberry blond hair and strikingly blue eyes stood in the doorway.

"Hi, Vin," she said, surprised. "Who's this?"

Without giving Vin a chance to answer, Marken stepped forward and asked, "Can we see the doctor please? It's urgent!"

Vin smirked, trying not to let Marken see it.

The young girl looked around and laughed uncertainly. "My name's Ruth," she offered her hand, which Marken shook, not understanding what was going on. "I could be considered a doctor, but I usually prefer to just be called Ruth."

Marken mentally slapped himself in the forehead. *Why do I have to be so foolish and blurt something out like that? If Samuel had been here, he would've just kicked me in the shin!*

"Excuse me, miss," he said, trying to retain his composure. "I didn't mean to insult you or anything by thinking only trained doctors and surgeons could have skills."

"Wrong again," she said, smiling at him. "I actually am trained, and I run a hospital back in Farnosh Province."

Marken actually slapped himself. "Sorry, sor..." She interrupted his apology.

"It's completely fine. I get that a lot. Most people don't think I'd know that kind of stuff."

Marken sighed in relief, glad that she wasn't offended.

"Now what's your emergency?" Ruth asked, getting back on topic.

Marken's eyes widened as he remembered his purpose for coming to her. "Oh! I have a friend who's very hurt. He needs help quickly! Follow me!" He started back down the hall, Ruth and Vin close behind.

They walked outside, and Marken noticed that it had started raining. They tried to shield themselves from the downpour, but to no avail. The three were soaked to the skin by the time they reached the stables.

Samuel had received permission from the stableboy to put the horses temporarily in the stables so they wouldn't get wet.

Marken could see that he had taken Creyan down and was inspecting the wound, a wet, bloody bandage lying next to him. The slice had opened slightly and was oozing blood.

As soon as she saw the wound, Ruth ran up and crouched down next to Creyan to look at his leg.

The unconscious spy was slowly reviving from his long slumber. He lifted his head groggily and looked at Ruth. "Who are you?"

"Don't worry. I'm going to help you." Ruth reassured him. "Everything is going to be fine."

When Vin walked into the stables and saw Creyan, his surprise was evident. "Oh my goodness!" He shouted. "It's Creyan!" He looked up at Samuel. "You must be one of the kids! Which one..."

Ruth interrupted him. "We have to focus here," she said. "You can find out who everyone is later." She looked closer at the cut. "It doesn't look like infection has set in yet, but it could soon. Have you cleaned it?" She directed her question at Marken.

"Yeah, I guess. We poured water over it and tried to wash some of the blood away."

"Is that the bandage you used?" She asked, pointing at the bloody cloth.

"Yeah. It was all we had."

She grabbed a handful of Creyan's cloak and ripped it off messily. "I need some alcohol," she said to Vin. "It works great for sterilizing wounds." Vin nodded and sprinted into the run-down tavern.

Creyan's subconcious mind was confused. "Drink?" he mumbled with some difficulty. "I'm not...thirsty."

"It's not for you to drink. I need it to kill all the bugs that would like to infect your leg."

Creyan laid his head back, still confused at this answer, but drained enough to not care.

After a few minutes, Vin ran back into the stable with a bottle filled with dark liquid. He handed it to Ruth and stood next to Marken, who had been observing the whole time.

"The bartender was confused by the fact that we needed it in the stable, but I told him that you're a doctor. He was convinced. He said, no offense, but doctors do strange things sometimes."

"That's okay," Ruth said. "It's a true statement." Abruptly ending the conversation, she took the bottle of alcohol and uncorked it. She poured some into the wound itself and a little on the clean part of the bandage. She handed the flask back to Vin.

As he ran it back into the bar, she swabbed the cut gently with a strip of sterilized cloth.

"There's nothing to worry about," Creyan heard her say, as the world around him blurred and darkened. "You're going to be fine."

9

...

The Castle

They arrived at the castle around suppertime the next day.

Creyan's wound was bandaged tightly, and he was awake and talking, feeling much better than he had the day before.

Samuel had become acquainted with Vin and Ruth. He, Ruth, and Marken were having a three-way conversation, discussing what life was like back in their home Provinces.

While they were chatting, Creyan and Vin rode behind them and talked about how they had been. The two friends hadn't had a meaningful conversation in quite some time, so it was good for them to talk.

As they reached the peak of a large, grassy hill, the mountainous fortress of Castle Orthox appeared on the horizon.

Its giant stone turrets shot into the sky like majestic trees of stone, looking down on the inferior humans below. On four large, conical roofs that jutted into the air, the vibrant flag of Aena flapped in the gusting wind. Situated around the base of the citadel were small houses and shops, where the citizens of Kogincheir resided, fenced in from the outside by an extensive wall of wooden stakes. The castle itself was surrounded by a massive, stone wall.

Marken's eyes widened as he beheld the vastness of the castle before him. *I've never seen anything like this! This is amazing!*

The five travelers' horses trotted down the hill into the shallow valley and up to the thick, wooden gate that barred entry to the capital city.

Vin dismounted his steed and limped up to the gate, sore from the hours on horseback. After rapping three short times, he stepped back, waiting patiently for the gatekeeper.

"Yes?" A frail voice called out from inside. "Who's there?" They heard the wooden creaking of a chair, and footsteps coming up to a small peephole.

"It is I, Vin. I have returned."

A bloodshot eye appeared in the peephole, scrutinizing him and the others behind him.

"Vin, eh? Hmm. I don't know who yew are, and I didn't know yew'd been gone." replied the creaky-voiced old man. "What business do yew have here?"

"Samson!" Vin groaned, abandoning his cool demeanor. "It's me, Vin! I work for the king!"

The eye in the hole widened. "Oh! It's yew!" The man ducked down out of sight. There was the sound of clinking metal, and the gate yawned open, producing a bearded old man with crooked eyes wearing a wool jacket.

"Sorry, Vin. I didn't realize it was yew. Glad yer back!" He waved his hand forward, beckoning for them to enter.

The bedraggled party slowly rode into the city, being careful of the bustling citizens. Fortunately, the crowd was light at this time of day. Most were at home, eating supper with their families.

As they reached a crossroad in the winding streets of Kogincheir, Marken called out for them to stop.

"Well, guys, I think it's time for me to be gettin' back," he started, a forlorn expression on his face. "I'd best go home to my wife before she gets too nervous. She's always worryin'." A half-smile appeared on his scruffy face.

Turning to Creyan, he said, "You take good care of my son, d'ya hear? Don't let him get into any trouble, or anythin' of that sort." He winked inconspicuously.

"It was nice meetin' you," he said to Vin and Ruth. "I hope our paths cross again sometime."

Finally, Marken turned and looked at Samuel. "And son," he said with a choking sound in his throat. "Don't die on me or anythin'." He smiled, but Samuel could see the glistening in his eyes.

"I won't, dad," Samuel said, leaning over to hug his father.

With the goodbyes said, Marken turned and spurred his horse in the other direction, waving a hand behind him in farewell.

Samuel gazed up at the huge, stone wall in front of him. The massive bulwark formed a large ring around the inner keep of the castle, built to discourage enemies.

Castle Orthox had been constructed long ago, when the ancient King sat on the throne. The top of the wall was lined with stone battlements, so archers could stand on the wall-walk and fire down at encroaching enemies. At each of its four corners sat a solid turret, from which lookouts could keep an eye on their foes.

The foursome brought their steeds to a halt when they reached the large wooden doors that led to the inner courtyard. The doors were braced with dark iron and had an intricate design carved into them.

Although somewhat dusty from the constant travel on the dirt road adjacent to it, Samuel could make out the king's symbol on the doors: A leopard wearing a crown and sitting in a reclined position, looking out over the capital city with an arrogant expression. This reminded Samuel disturbingly of his recent encounter with the panther.

Inscribed below this depiction was the motto of the country, first put into place after the tragic disappearance of the ancient King. It read: May the line of kings never be broken.

Unbeknownst to many, these had been the last words spoken by the King before he disappeared.

There was some controversy surrounding his last words. Most said that the motto now known to Aena was exactly what he said before his disappearance, but there were some who disagreed with them. The Messengers of Adonai, who most citizens considered a foolish cult, said that there was more to what he had said, that he had given the people of

Aena a dire warning before mysteriously vanishing. Although both sides believed their versions were true, no one really knew.

Vin dismounted his horse once again and strode up to the magnificent doors. As he had expected, they were not barred, for there was currently no active threat to the king's safety. However, there were always archers positioned upon the wall, vigilantly watching for any suspicious characters.

Climbing back on his horse, Vin led the group into the perfectly symmetrical courtyard. Every blade of verdant grass was cut at exactly the same height. Majestic fruit trees dotted the landscape. Directly in front of the small group, there was an ornate staircase that led to a decorative, wooden door in the front of the keep, obviously the main entryway.

Samuel saw a young, fleet-footed messenger dash inside the door, most likely to inform the king of their arrival. The armed knights guarding the door didn't spare him a glance.

Vin and Creyan led the two newcomers around the side of the keep, where the stables were located. They dismounted their horses one by one and led them into the open double doors to find a stall.

"Johan here will take good care of your horses," Creyan told them. He smiled at the skinny stable boy who was opening the stalls for them.

When they were finished making sure their steeds were comfortable, they walked back around to the beautiful stone steps. Vin and Creyan climbed the staircase, while Ruth and Samuel adjusted their satchels and ascended more hesitantly. Visiting a large castle was a very new experience for them, and they were busy taking in all of their surroundings.

When the four of them reached the top, the guards blocked their way, crossing their poleaxes.

"What business have you with the king?" One of them asked gruffly.

Creyan limped forward and presented to them his medallion. Samuel and Ruth watched with wide eyes.

Without hesitating, the two knights nodded curtly and stepped aside, holding their poleaxes in at-ease positions.

Vin and Creyan pushed open both the doors and let Ruth and Samuel step through before closing them.

Directly before them was a simple, stone hallway with what looked like a three-way intersection at the end.

Without hesitating, the two older men led the way down the hall, turning left and right so many times that Samuel became very disoriented.

He was going to ask if they were lost, when a magnificent room seemed to appear out of nowhere.

Samuel's breath caught in his throat.

The room had a high ceiling and banners were hung lavishly on the walls, repeatedly depicting the leopard emblem of Aena. Torches were hung lower on the walls, and crystal chandeliers hung from the ceiling. Gleaming suits of armor stood at attention on either side of the room, holding their razor-sharp swords out in front of them with the tip resting on the ground.

As the awestruck guests slowly walked down the burgundy carpet in the center of the floor, their eyes took in everything around them.

"This is the Main Hall, kids," Creyan said, proud to be showing off what was almost like his home. He pointed toward a pair of regal-looking doors to their left. "That way is to the Great Hall, which is where King Nunor holds his feasts and banquets. It's also where you will be dining."

Creyan gestured to an equally royal set of doors. "That way leads to the towers, latrines, and guest rooms, where you will be staying. Those doors," he said finally, indicating the large, elaborate ones at the end of the Main Hall, "lead through a small vestibule and into the Throne Room, where the king sits now."

As Creyan finished, Vin started walking towards door on the right. "This way to your rooms."

Samuel and Ruth followed Vin, with Creyan limping close behind.

The doors opened into a hallway that looked very similar to the ones in the maze they had just been through. They walked all the way to the very end, where there were two thick, wooden doors leading to the right and left. A sign hung on the wall in front of the group with two arrows carved into it, each pointing at one of the doors. Underneath the arrow that pointed to the left, it read, "Soldier Quarters." The other read, "Guest Quarters."

Without pausing, Creyan pushed open the heavy door on the right and let the others through before he closed it. The group made their way down a claustrophobic hallway, until they reached a point where there were more doors alternating on either side. Samuel could see that at the far end of the hallway, there was a door and then to the side, a staircase leading up. He supposed that the door led to the latrine.

When Vin had walked about halfway down the hall, he stopped and reached into his pocket. Unearthing a crinkled piece of paper with a few numbers written on it, he mumbled, "Yep. Number forty-seven and forty-nine."

He turned to Ruth and Samuel, who were staring at him as if waiting for orders.

"Samuel, you're in room number forty-seven right here," Vin pointed to the door next to him. "And Ruth, you're going to be staying in number forty-nine." He gestured towards another one that was a few feet down the hall.

"Please make yourselves comfortable," Creyan said from behind them. "One of the servants will be around to tell you when it's suppertime. Until then, please stay in your rooms."

As they walked away, Samuel watched Creyan with concern. He was limping quite a bit on his injured leg.

Samuel shook his head. He passed a hand in front of his face, as if to brush the dark thoughts away.

Samuel turned back to the thick door that stood in front of him. He looked to his left and saw that Ruth had already gone into her room and was probably well into unpacking.

Well, here goes, he thought. His hand grasped the tarnished metal handle and twisted. He swung the door open and gazed at the interior of his new room.

10

...

New Discoveries

Rays of the afternoon sun were shining through the solitary window implanted in the wall. They struck the center of the floor, illuminating the sparse furnishings.

The bed was a simple white mattress in a wooden frame, pressed closely against the wall. It was covered by two wool sheets and had a thin pillow at the head. It was a simple bed, but it was better than what Samuel had been sleeping on for the last few days.

On the other side of the room was a chest of drawers for him to store his few garments. Next to that, there was a new innovation that Samuel had heard was becoming popular in multi-storied houses: A laundry chute.

He walked over to it and looked down. Sure enough, there was a wooden container waiting for his dirty clothes down at the bottom. If he craned his neck, he could just barely see the floor of the washroom below him. A faint ringing of bells entered his ears. *I wonder what that is.*

Samuel stood back up and surveyed the rest of the room. There was a torch in a metal grip on the wall and a small desk beneath it. There was a simple chair in front of the desk. He figured that this was for any writing work he might do. Last but not least, there was a smudged mirror with a decorative frame hanging above the dresser.

Samuel unslung the pack from his sore shoulder and set it down on the bed. He sat down slowly, stretching his aching muscles.

I may as well get settled in. He picked up his bag and started to unpack.

Vin and Creyan reentered the Main Hall and sat down on the carpeted floor for a brief moment's rest. Creyan's leg was hurting from the exertion of walking down the halls and back. He was sure Vin thought he was in pain, but he couldn't let it show.

"Those two," Creyan said, gesturing back to the guest rooms, "are the perfect ones. I don't think we could've chosen better."

"Yeah," Vin allowed a grin to tilt his lips. "Especially for what they're going to have to do. I have a feeling that there are big things planned for their lives."

"Well, let's get going to the king. I'm sure little Malto has already informed him of our arrival, so he'll be expecting us." He smiled at the thought of the feisty messenger boy.

Vin nodded and stood up, offering a hand to Creyan. Creyan brushed it away and struggled to his feet on his own. Together, they walked to the vestibule before the Throne Room.

When they opened the doors, Prime Minister Lithel looked up with a tired expression on his face. When he saw who it was, he tried to look happy at their arrival, but the sentiment wasn't compatible with his mood.

"You're back," he said in a monotone voice. "I'll go tell the king." Lithel stood up with stiff legs and disappeared through the door that led to the Throne Room.

Vin looked at Creyan. "He looks worse every time I see him. I wonder if he gets any sleep."

"Personally, I don't know why the king hired him in the first place. It definitely wasn't for his organization skills," Creyan pointed at the cluttered desk in front of them.

After a few more seconds, the Prime Minister opened the door and beckoned for them to enter.

"I'm so glad you've returned," the king said when they reached the throne. "I assume you've brought them with you?"

"Yes, Your Majesty," Vin replied. "Ruth and Samuel are unpacking in their rooms as we speak."

"Good. I expect to see them at suppertime."

Something's wrong here, Vin thought. *He doesn't seem to be himself today. He was as boisterous and fun-loving as ever last time I was here.*

"Yes, Your Majesty. Um… excuse me for saying so, but… is something wrong?"

King Nunor stared blankly for a moment. "Uh… no. I do not believe so. Why do you ask?"

"Well… it's just that you seem a bit… different today. That's all."

A crooked smile crossed King Nunor's face. "Oh, well, I guess everyone has bad days."

Vin glanced at Creyan. "And, uh, one more thing." King Nunor raised an eyebrow. "While Creyan here was on the road with Samuel, he received an unfortunate injury to his leg. He won't admit it, but it needs to be tended to very soon."

"Yes, of course." The king said. "We will definitely have the physicians look at that." He clapped his hands and the tiny Malto ran in from an adjoining room and bowed his head to the king.

"Please take this man to the infirmary, where he may be properly treated." Malto bowed his head again and ran over to Creyan.

Vin looked at Creyan and in an undertone, said, "Sorry, but I noticed you were in pain. I needed *some* way to help you."

Creyan nodded understandingly as Malto led him away. "It's fine. I was going to ask soon, anyway."

Vin, still wary, looked back at the king, who dismissed him with a wave of his hand.

As soon as Vin left, King Nunor arched backwards, and his teeth ground against each other. With a sudden, convulsive movement, he lurched forward, and a red stream of misty light seeped from every pore in his face.

"*Close call,*" it whispered. "*But next time, we'll be ready.*"

With that, it sank into the stones of the floor and vanished, leaving King Nunor slumped in his chair with his eyes glazed over, submitted involuntarily to the will of this mysterious being.

Ruth was lying comfortably in her new bed. She stared up at the stone ceiling, wondering what she should do.

She was thinking about what they might be eating for supper, when a sharp rap sounded on the door. She swung her legs over the side of the bed and walked to the door, opening it. There stood a royally dressed servant waiting for her.

"Yes?" Ruth asked.

"King Nunor has sent me to inform you that supper has been prepared, and you have been summoned to meet him at the Great Hall."

"Alright. I'll be down in a moment." The servant bowed his head to Ruth and walked away.

She walked over to the dirty mirror and looked at her reflection. The glass had obviously not been cleaned recently, so it was hard to tell whether the smudges were on the glass or her face. She ran her fingers through her hair and straightened the shirt she had on. *I wish I had something better to wear than this. Oh, well. I'm not going to die because I don't like the shirt I'm wearing.*

After she was finished getting herself ready, she headed cautiously out her door to the Great Hall.

When Ruth had finished traversing the long stretches of hallway, she slowly approached the large doors on the opposite side of the Main Hall. They had intricate designs carved into them, similar to the other three sets of doors in the immense room. She reached up to the large, bronze handles that protruded from the dark wood. They were so highly set in the doors that they came up to her chin. *I guess they weren't expecting to have someone so short come in here. They're probably just that way to make everything look bigger. He is the king, after all.*

With a grunt of effort, she pushed open the well-oiled doors, revealing a magnificent room. Lit by massive chandeliers even fancier than the ones in the Main Hall, the Great Hall was an architect's dream.

Large tapestries were draped extravagantly on the towering walls, and mighty arches of stone rose up to the ceiling. The arches' bases gently touched the carpeted floor, having become decorative pillars. These pillars landed on either side of an unusually long table in the center of the room.

Sitting at the far end of the table, in a throne that would have paid off the debt of everyone in her town, was the king. Behind him, there was a large banner hanging from the ceiling, on which the royal seal was portrayed.

Among those who were already seated at the table, there was Vin, an average-sized man, an unusually large man, an unusually small man, a man wearing chain mail, a very tall boy, a girl about her age with long, black hair, and a smirking, athletic-looking boy.

Everyone is so solemn, Ruth thought as she approached the table. She didn't want to let her self-consciousness show, so instead, she smiled at everyone.

"Hello!" She tried to make her voice sound as light and carefree as possible.

"Hello, Ruth! I expect it is you, isn't it?" The king said in a booming voice that echoed throughout the hall. "You're definitely not Samuel!"

"Yes, Your Majesty." Her voice sounded tiny in comparison.

"Well! Then, by all means, have a seat!" King Nunor indicated an open chair next to the gigantic boy. Ruth hesitantly walked over to it and sat down.

The boy sitting next to her turned and introduced himself with a genial smile. "Hi! I'm Zane." He offered his immense hand to shake. Ruth watched him uncomfortably, noting that his muscular forearm was almost as thick as her head.

"I'm Ruth." She reached up and grasped the hand warily. She saw who she assumed were the spies look at her with pity in their eyes. Ruth held in a gasp as she painfully shook Zane's hand. In her town, she was one of the few females who had a strong handshake, but this was not like any handshake she had ever felt before. This was a vise!

When he released, Ruth could hardly feel her fingers.

"We're just waiting for one more," the king announced. "Samuel, I believe."

The smirking boy said in a scathing tone, "He should be here by now. Didn't he get the message?"

"That's enough, Mikal," said the man of diminutive stature. "It's probably not his fault, anyway."

Mikal raised his eyebrows sarcastically. "So you're saying it's your fault?"

Ruth was watching this exchange closely. She knew the small man must be a trained spy, and that this Mikal was probably a random youth just like her. She wondered if this arrogant boy would challenge the other to a fight. If so, she was sure he would lose.

Just when Mikal was about to make a sharp retort to something the spy had said, the doors swung open.

Everybody's eyes turned towards the boy that was now standing awkwardly in the doorway.

Samuel looked around shyly. Ruth noticed the blood rising in his cheeks, a sign that he felt as self-conscious as she had, maybe even more. He was a farmer, after all. His exposure to being in front of groups was probably much less than hers.

"Hello, Samuel!" the king boomed once more. "I'm glad you made it. Have a seat." He pointed to the last seat at the table.

"Um, thanks, Your Majesty." He bowed his head stiffly and quickly walked over to take the seat next to Ruth, not wanting to be in the spotlight any more than he had to.

11

...

The Feast

"Now that we're all here," King Nunor began, "we shall introduce ourselves. We'll go around the table saying our names and ages. I'll start." He had a hint of mirth in his eyes as he stood up from his elaborate chair.

"I'm the king, and I'm fifty-seven. You'll obey me, or you'll die. Clear? I hope so." He sat down again and pointed at Vin, a sly grin crossing his aged face. "Your turn."

"I am Vin, and my age is none of your business." He sat down again, looking at the next man in line.

The other spy stood up. "I am Wilhelm," he said with a slight Grudenheim accent. "And I am thirty-four, although why that is important to you is beyond me."

As they went around the table, Samuel learned that the large man was Yakob, and the last, smallest spy was Nat. The man wearing chain mail introduced himself as Commander Yurson. He informed the youths that he was in charge of them for the whole of their training at the castle. He also said that he would be waking them up at precisely seven o'clock in the morning every day. They were to be up and ready immediately after to begin instruction. He sat down and glared at them. Samuel wondered if he was always like this. If so, then they had a long training ahead of them.

Then they started on the minors' side of the table. Each of the recruits said their name, age, and what province they lived in.

It struck Samuel as odd that Ruth was sixteen. He had thought she'd be younger than that. She barely came up to his shoulder!

Then it was Samuel's turn. He stood up, his knees and hands shaking. He could feel the blood rushing to his face as he stammered out his introduction.

"M-my name is Samuel, I'm fifteen, and I'm f-from Kaltoid Province." He sat down as fast as he could, slamming his backside against the chair. Fortunately, there was a cushion that absorbed the sound of his hard landing, so the others didn't hear it.

Samuel hated being up in front of people. Even though he was sitting down, he could feel his red face, and his heart was thudding rapidly. He was always annoyed at how his body reacted to speaking in such small circumstances.

"Good!" King Nunor exclaimed once Samuel was seated. "Now that we all know each other's names, please try not to forget them." He grinned again.

"On another note," he continued, "you may explore the castle after supper, and hopefully get better acquainted with each other."

Having finished his introductions, the king exclaimed in a loud voice, "Let's eat!"

He clapped his hands and a door at the side of the room flew open, spewing forth many servants, laden with pots and platters. They all stood in a line that led back to the door of what must have been the kitchen.

The first few servants sped around the table, laying forth the finest settings that Samuel had ever seen.

The main body of his plate was made of ivory, from the mighty tusked seals of the north. It was inlaid with gold designs, depicting many things that Samuel could not have possibly comprehended. The silverware was literally made of silver, with a gold leaf streak winding around the handle. The napkins were made of a deep red cloth that was woven from silk produced by the desert spiders of Yalaj. These spiders were known to spin large nets that could trap prey. The material is not sticky and is naturally a dark red color.

When the drink glasses came around, Samuel inspected his curiously. It had a gold rim around the top, and was made out of a delicate type of glass that was obviously created by the most skilled of craftsmen. It was transparent, but Samuel still couldn't see through it. To him, it looked like a fog had come inside the glass. He'd never seen anything like it.

The next couple of servants went around the table, asking each person what they would like to drink and writing it down in a small notebook.

After collecting each person's request, they retreated into the royal kitchen to prepare the beverages.

Samuel found a myriad of smells entering his nostrils as he inhaled the bounty that awaited him. The cupbearers returned and filled the glasses with the drinks that each person had asked for.

Samuel watched the others as they surveyed their surroundings, examining everything of interest.

Zane had picked up his fork and was looking at it wonderingly. He had probably never used one before.

Mikal leaned slightly backwards as a servant set down a giant dish in front of him. He looked at it suspiciously, wrinkling his broad nose.

Samuel tentatively raised his hand above his head and looked at the king.

"Yes, Samuel? You have a question?"

"Sorry, Your Majesty, but I was just wondering, what if we don't know what the food is, or if it's something we'll like? Can we ask the chef?"

"Of course! Kymavay!"

"Yes, sir! Coming, sir!" A squeaky voice sounded from beyond the door. Before too long, a skinny man stumbled out of the kitchen, scooting his way past bustling servants going in and out. He was followed by an equally thin woman, who had short, brown hair that was tied in a tangled knot behind her head.

The man and the woman hurried up to King Nunor's seat and bowed their heads. "You called, Your Majesty?" The man asked timidly. "Is there a problem?"

"No! Not at all! My new trainees here were just wondering about some of the dishes you've cooked up today." He smiled easily. "Kids, meet Mr. and Mrs. Kymavay, the royal cooks." The two gangly servants looked up with wide eyes, as if they'd never been introduced to anybody in their lives.

"Um… hi?" Mr. Kymavay said hesitantly. "You have… uh… questions?"

Samuel cleared his throat. "Yeah, uh, could you tell me what this is, right here?" He pointed at the dish directly in front of him, a bright red sphere of something that glistened in the light of the chandeliers.

"Oh! That's a jempetulum!" Mrs. Kymavay said, her eyes suddenly lighting up.

Mr. Kymavay cut in. "It's a fruit that starts out sour but…"

"Turns sweet!" They turned to each other and grinned toothily.

"Um, hey!" Mikal interjected, waving his hand in the air. "What's this thing?" He gestured to the large, meaty dish that was sitting almost right under his nose. "It smells weird."

"That is the roasted hindquarters of the Lanyan water oxen!"

Mikal looked confused. "What's a… hindquarters?"

Both Mr. and Mrs. Kymavay stared blankly at him for a moment and then simultaneously burst into laughter.

"What?" He asked. "What's so funny?"

The king looked as if he was holding in a laugh as well. "Mikal," he began in a strained voice, "It is the, er, *derriere* of this creature, if you get my meaning."

Mikal stared at him blankly.

"You don't know what that is, do you?" When Mikal slowly shook his head, the king sighed, put his hand over his face, and motioned for Vin to continue for him. The two Kymavays were still holding their sides with laughter. Everyone except for Mikal was trying to hide a grin. Even the stoic Yakob had slightly upturned lips.

Mikal, now a bit angry at the unhelpfulness of the king, asked in exasperation, "What is it, Vin?"

The thin spy grinned humorously and explained. "It's the meat off the rump of the animal."

"Oh." That was all that he said, and he slumped back into his seat, his cheeks bright red with embarrasment.

"Well… I hope that… answers your…questions!" Mr. Kymavay said, trying to catch his breath. "I guess we'll be… going now!" He and Mrs. Kymavay turned and walked in sync back to the kitchen, their shoulders still shaking as they entered the door and disappeared from sight.

"Oh, come on!" Mikal said, glaring at all the faces around him. "It wasn't *that* funny!"

Everybody ate their meals in silence from then on, no one else wanting to be embarrassed in front of the king.

Samuel tried most everything. He even tasted the water oxen "derriere" as the king had put it. It wasn't too bad, actually. It had been well cooked, and had sort of a sweet, nutty flavor. There were also some breadsticks that were stuffed with a creamy, white cheese. Samuel asked what Province it came from, for some people in his town sold their milk.

The king replied, with a laugh in his eyes, that it came from the large rats of the Felid archipelago.

After getting over his surprise, Samuel learned that the bread came from Kaltoid Province. He wondered if any of his neighbors had grown the wheat, because his family grew corn, not wheat.

After they had been eating for a while, Samuel cleared his throat and asked King Nunor the question that had been on his mind for some time. "Excuse me, Your Majesty. I have a question."

The king finished chewing and answered. "Yes, Samuel?"

"I've been wondering why you sent for all of us so suddenly, and why we're all just kids."

The king went stiff and sat up straight in his chair. "Uhh... well... I mean..." he stuttered in a strained voice.

Seeing that for some reason, King Nunor was having difficulty saying it, Vin stood up. "You five are here to replace..." He got no further.

"Stop!" The king boomed, jumping to his feet with a look of sudden rage in his eyes. "That is not the reason!"

"Oh... um... I'm sorry, Your Majesty... but I thought..." Vin sat down awkwardly.

"I changed my mind!" He roared.

Samuel shrunk down in his chair. This was becoming an uncomfortable situation.

Suddenly, the king seemed to have a change of attitude and sank back down into his chair with a wearied expression. "I'm sorry," he said. "I'm not myself today." He didn't notice everyone's frightened looks around the table. "I... I've changed my mind."

"You mean you're not going to replace us?" Vin asked hesitantly.

"N-no... I mean... well... I've had some second thoughts about this." Before anyone could say anything, he continued. "The reason I summoned you here is so that I could create a team. I need a group of people that can carry out special tasks for me when the circumstances are dire. And I've chosen *you*." He pointed at each of the five stunned adolescents.

Samuel pondered this for a few moments, letting the king's mood swing pass off as a byproduct of too much stress. He liked the idea of being part of a team, but he still had one more question to ask the king. "Sorry," he apologized, "but I have another question."

"It's fine, it's fine. Go on."

"What, exactly, are we going to be doing in our training?"

King Nunor sat back and smiled. "That, you will find out tomorrow." He saw the disappointed looks on their faces.

"But," he continued, "I'll tell you this. There are many things in this world that you've never heard of before." They looked at each other, wondering what he meant.

"Probably most of your muscles," Vin mumbled, then coughed to cover it up.

Noticing that they had finished eating, the king dismissed them with some final instructions. "I see that you have all finished your supper, so you are free to leave and explore the castle. Just remember, get to bed at a reasonable hour. Tomorrow is going to be a long day."

Before they could leave, however, he added one more thing. "Oh, and if you come across a locked door, don't open it." He smiled at them, but this time it was more of an "I'm-watching-you" smile.

The new team members nervously thanked the king for the meal and left the Great Hall, wanting to forget about their disturbing experience and explore all the rooms and hallways that the magnificent castle had to offer.

12

...

Making Friends

The first thing Samuel did after he returned to his room was sit down at the small desk to write a letter to his parents. He was very disturbed by the king's reaction at supper, so he decided that the best thing to do would be to get his mind off of the subject.

He opened the one drawer in the desk to try to find some parchment or writing utensils. When all he unearthed were a couple of yellowed envelopes, Samuel looked around for a way to summon a servant. *There has to be* some *method of communication with the servants in here.*

After scouring the room for a couple minutes, he finally found it. A small rope with a lead weight tied to the end was poking itself out of the floor next to the laundry chute.

Samuel grasped the weight and yanked on it, hearing a high-pitched bell ring in the room below.

"Just a moment!" He heard a husky female voice call up to him. *That must be why I kept hearing bells ringing earlier,* Samuel thought as he waited for the servant. *I guess it wasn't just my imagination.*

When she finally arrived, the matronly lady looked as if she'd been working very hard. Her servant's gown had dirt and splotches all over it, and her hair was disheveled and unkempt.

"You rang?" She said in a twangy, Lanyan accent, one hand on her hip.

"Do you know if there is any parchment, some ink, and a pen I could use? I would like to write a letter to my mother." Samuel tried to be polite, but it was hard when the other person was so terse.

"Yeah. I'll getcha some." She bustled away, lifting her poorly kept dress above her ankles in order to walk faster.

After a few minutes, she returned, carrying a sheet of parchment, a silver inkwell, and an expertly carved wooden pen. "Here ya are."

Samuel thanked her, shut the door, and walked back over to the desk.

A few years ago, he had taken a writing class from a man in Vale. After six months of intense studying, he had become an adept speller and had expanded his vocabulary immensely. In fact, he had become so skilled at writing that by the end of the six months, he had surpassed his teacher.

Samuel set the inkwell down on the side of the desk, where his arm wouldn't bump it. He smoothed out the finely made parchment, dipped the pen in the ink, and began to write:

Dear Mom and Dad,

This is my first day at the castle. It's very nice. I wish you were here too. I met the King at supper today. I also met some other kids my age who are going to be training with me. The king did not restrict us from telling our parents, so I'm going to. You probably should not spread the word, though. We don't want to make him mad.

He told us that we're here to be a team that will carry out special tasks for him. We begin training tomorrow, but he didn't tell us what we would be doing. It's supposed to be exciting, though.

My room is comfortable, but not royal. I have a few pieces of furniture and a window with a view of Koginshire. Right next to it is a torch that is lighting up this paper. Don't worry, I won't burn anything up.

When you get a chance to write back, I have some questions. Did you have a good time with Valintena? Did Dad make it back okay? How is Margrit doing?

I have to go now. The king said we can explore the castle, and I think that is just what I am going to do. I'll write again tomorrow. Please tell Dad that Crayin is doing better. I hope I can see you again when training is over.

Love,
Samuel

Purposefully leaving out his recent experience, Samuel signed his name on the letter, folded it neatly, and slid it into one of the old envelopes.

Stretching his back, he stood up and walked to the door. He needed to find out where he could get his letter mailed so it could arrive in Vale as soon as possible.

Just as his hand was on the doorknob, he heard a knock. Somewhat surprised, Samuel opened the door.

Standing before him was Ruth.

"Um, yes?" He asked.

"Come on!" She said ebulliently, waving her hand forward for him to walk out.

Struck with a spell of habitual awkwardness, Samuel asked, "Why?" He could feel his cheeks turning pink, which seemed to always happen when he talked to girls. It even happened with the ones he knew in Vale. It wasn't that he *fancied* them or anything. The blood in his face just seemed to be very fond of embarrassing him.

"You were already going to come out of your room, right?" Ruth asked. "I mean, you were going to go explore?"

Samuel nodded slowly, his face still prickling with annoying warmth. "Well, I was going to... but after I got this letter to my parents sent..." He dug the letter out of his pocket and held it up.

"Well come on, then! Let's go!"

Startled by her abruptness, Samuel stepped quickly out the door and closed it behind him. As soon as the door swung shut, Ruth started walking down the corridor towards the Main Hall.

When Samuel didn't follow her at first, she turned around. "Come on!" She coaxed.

Galvanized into action, Samuel strode down the passageway behind her. *Why do I always have to be so awkward?*

When they reached the Main Hall, Ruth paused. Almost slamming into her from behind, Samuel quickly stopped too.

To his surprise, she beckoned for him to walk beside her, looking at him expectantly. Not knowing what else to do, Samuel made his way towards the Throne Room, Ruth at his side.

After he had delivered his letter to the courier, who was stationed in the vestibule leading to the Throne Room, they headed back to the Main Hall to decide their next course of action.

When Samuel closed the giant doors behind him, he noticed Zane wandering aimlessly by himself, looking at the large tapestries hanging on the wall.

"Hey... uh... Zane!" Samuel called to him, remembering his name. "What're you doing?" The oversized miner looked up.

"Hi, Samuel," he said in his immensely deep voice. "I'm not really doin' anything. Just... ya know... explorin'."

"Where are the other two?" Ruth asked. "Mikal and... uh... Kari?"

"Right after supper, you and Samuel went back to your rooms, and they went off to go stir up some trouble or somethin'. I didn't know what ta do, so I've been wanderin' around." He looked down.

Zane was obviously lonely. Samuel could only think of one thing to do. He opened his mouth to say, "You can come with us if you want," but Ruth broke in before he could utter a word.

"Why don't you come with us?" She offered.

Zane's face lit up. "I can? I won't be in your way?" He was used to being a bulky nuisance to most people. Zane fidgeted with his hands, pulling at a necklace that was hanging around his neck. Upon closer observation, Samuel noticed that it was just a leather strap with a thin piece of metal hanging off of it. *Probably a memento from home.*

"Of course you won't be! We're just going to explore the castle a bit. You're welcome to come along." Samuel reassured him.

"Alright! Where are we goin' first?" Zane was much happier now that he had someone to explore with.

"I don't know," Ruth said. "Where do you want to go?" He thought about it for a second.

"How 'bout we go outside to the courtyard?"

"Good idea!" Samuel said. "We just have to be able to find our way through the maze of passages that lead there."

"Oh, don't worry 'bout it!" Zane said. "I got a good mem'ry, an' I r'member the way."

The trio then strolled to the entrance of the passageways in camaraderie, each happy to have new friends.

When they had finished traveling through the network of hallways, the three explorers pulled open the doors that led to the outer courtyard. The guards posted there nodded to them politely as they walked out, maintaining looks of grim indifference.

It was late evening, and the sun was setting behind the hills in the distance. The wall that surrounded Castle Orthox cast an immense shadow on the courtyard, forcing them to watch carefully where they were going.

After they had come down the long flight of steps, they strolled around to the side of the keep, near the stables. They passed by quickly, the rancid stench nearly overpowering them.

The outer courtyard was dotted with a variety of trees and shrubs. There were apple trees, apricot trees, and even fig trees. None of them dared to touch the fruit, however, for who knew what restrictions the king had on his fruit trees.

As they strolled along the side of the keep, each of them told what it was like in their different Provinces.

Eventually, the conversation turned to how they had met the spies for the first time. Samuel and Ruth told their stories, and then Zane told his long and detailed version.

"After I saw that guy's sword," he was saying, "I just had the problem of convincin' my Ma that I had ta go see the king. My Pa never cares what I do. I finally got my Ma convinced, promisin' to write, an' such, and I went off with Yakob to get ta the castle." Zane paused for a moment, as if struggling to remember, and then continued. "Oh, yeah! On the way here, we didn't find much trouble. Only a few bandits here an' there. Ya know, that Yakob guy is pretty good with a sword."

He continued talking about how Yakob had defeated many thieves and bandits on the road, when Ruth tapped his shoulder and pointed up to the top of the keep, her eyes widening and the color draining out of her face. Immediately closing his mouth, Zane beheld what she was indicating.

Looking down into the courtyard from the wall walk on top of the keep was a large black shape. It was hard to tell exactly what it was in the failing light, so Ruth strained her eyes to see it.

Suddenly, two yellow eyes snapped open at the front of the black silhouette, glowing brightly with a savage light.

"Guys," Ruth said, her voice trembling, "I think we'd better go inside. Whatever that is, it doesn't look friendly."

As soon as she said that, much to their awe and disbelief, the creature climbed over the battlements, and began crawling down the wall.

"Run!" Samuel shouted.

During their conversation, they had walked most of the way around the massive keep and were fairly close to the entrance. They bolted as fast as they could towards the corner of the building, not stopping to look back.

Adrenaline raced through Samuel's body as scenes of a horrible and gruesome death by an unknown creature flashed before his eyes.

The long stairway came into view around the corner. The two guards who had been posted there were no longer visible.

Ignoring the stairs, Zane vaulted over the railing and pounded on the doors with all of his might. A latch clicked, and the door swung open, revealing the concerned face of one of the guards.

Realizing their plight, he said, "Quick! In here!" and hurriedly pulled them inside.

They heard a ghastly noise that sounded like a mix between a hiss and a growl coming from the dark shadow behind them. There was the loud clacking of feet on stone, and then the armored soldier slammed the door shut and quickly bolted the lock.

A terrifying screech sounded from outside, and something scratched noisily on the door.

Ruth stood petrified with fear, wringing her sweaty hands in panic.

After a couple more thumps on the door, the sounds diminished, the beast apparently giving up on its would-be prey.

The two knights who had been standing inside led them through the hallways to the king with unsympathetically stern expressions.

When they entered the Throne Room, the king stood up with a confused look on his face and asked, "What are you doing here? Is something wrong?"

The knight answered for them. "They were outside, running from the Night Guard."

The king went pale and slumped back into his chair. "I am so sorry!" He apologized to the traumatized kids with an expression of pity.

"You can go now," he told the sentries. "They're fine." King Nunor dismissed the soldiers with a wave of his hand and then turned back to the three adventurers.

"I can't believe I didn't tell you about the Night Guard! I knew I forgot something!"

"It's okay," Ruth reassured him, her hands shaking slightly from the experience. "What is it?"

"Before I tell you, are you sure Mikal and Kari are safely inside?"

"Yep," replied Zane. "We walked 'round the whole keep and didn't see 'em."

"The whole keep? You must have been out there for a while." He studied them closely. "But never mind that. Back to the Night Guard."

"The Night Guard is from a rare breed called the Spider Hounds. It is believed to be a cross between giant jungle spiders and black mastiffs. It's an excellent watchdog for the castle, and I mean *excellent*.

"Since it's a mix between dogs and spiders," he continued, "it has venomous fangs and a superb sense of smell. It uses the paws on each of its eight legs to rip its prey apart, slicing them with its sharp claws."

Ruth was stunned by this horrific description. She hoped that she would never encounter it again.

"Please warn Mikal and Kari about this when you see them again," he ordered somberly. "I don't want them to get hurt."

King Nunor was about to dismiss them to their rooms, when a courier burst into the room.

"What is it?" He asked in a suddenly wary voice, as if he knew exactly why the man was there.

Without speaking, the straight-backed messenger strode up to the king and handed him a note. The lithe man bowed his head respectfully and retreated back through the doors from which he had come.

Ruth caught a glimpse of his eyes as the man passed by. *Did his eyes just glow… red?* She turned back and watched the king.

As King Nunor read the elegant handwriting on the letter, his face blanched considerably, and he looked like he was about to faint.

"Is… everything alright, Your Majesty?" Ruth asked hesitantly.

The king gazed at them with glassy eyes and mumbled, "Yes, yes. Everything's fine. Please go back to your rooms now."

"Okay… um," Ruth said, unsure as to whether she should leave the Throne Room yet. Not wanting to disobey the king, she turned and led the other two boys out of the lavishly decorated chamber, glancing back over her shoulder apprehensively.

As she closed the door behind her, however, Ruth heard strange sounds coming from the direction of the throne... voices.

The king was talking to someone.

13

...

The Training Commences

Samuel awoke in his new bed, forgetting where he was for a moment. The morning rays of sunshine were streaming through his window and brightening the room. The cold night air was flowing into his chamber, trying to escape the warm sunbeams that were quickly burning it away.

As he lay there, memories of the day before came rushing back. Samuel remembered talking with Ruth and Zane, eating a dinner of strange but delicious food, and being chased by a maniacal hybrid that was trying to eat them. Such fond memories.

Closing his eyes, Samuel wondered if Commander Yurson was going to get them up in a few minutes. He didn't know why, but he often awoke right before somebody else tried to wake him.

Samuel thought back to the strange dream he had. He was sprinting through the courtyard away from the ghastly Spider Hound, but however many times he circled the keep, he could never find the door.

He wondered why his mind enjoyed torturing him like that.

Suddenly, heavy footsteps sounded in the hallway outside his door, breaking his train of thought. Excited for the training to begin, Samuel quietly stepped out of bed and began to dress for the day.

Just as he finished pulling his shirt over his head, Commander Yurson's booming voice shook the hallway. Samuel hoped that there weren't any other visitors sleeping in the guest rooms.

"Time to get up!" Yurson shouted. "Once you're ready, head down to the Great Hall for breakfast. If you're not out of your beds in ten minutes, then I'm comin' in after ya!" His footsteps thundered down the hall again.

Samuel slipped on his leather shoes and quietly opened the door. He crept down the hallway and followed the Commander out.

After exiting the hall to the guest rooms, Commander Yurson went straight to the Throne Room to tell the king that he had woken the trainees.

Samuel went into the Great Hall to wait for the others. He was the only one there, so he stood next to the same seat he sat in before.

Samuel had been waiting by the padded chair for a couple minutes, when the king pushed open the large doors and strode over to his bejeweled seat at the head of the table.

"Good morning, Samuel." He said cheerfully, a hint of sleep still in his voice. "It's a beautiful day to begin training!"

"Good morning, Your Highness," Samuel bowed, remembering the disturbing episodes of the previous day. "How are you doing this morning?"

"Very well, thank you," the king answered, yawning and stretching his arms above his head. "Feel free to have a seat."

They only had to wait a few more minutes before the others came in and took their places at the table.

Once the last person arrived, which happened to be Mikal, the king greeted them all.

"Good morning, everyone! I trust you all slept well?" He was answered by multiple nods and yes's.

Samuel looked around the table at the other trainees. It was apparent that they had prepared hastily, for Mikal was wearing his shirt backwards, Kari's hair was disheveled and hanging down in her face, and Zane looked as if he had only gotten a couple hours of sleep. *He probably didn't fit on the bed!* The only one who actually looked ready to go was Ruth. Her clothes and hair were in perfect order, and her eyes were bright and shining.

"Wonderful!" King Nunor continued. "Let us not delay any longer and begin breakfast." He clapped his hands, which Samuel thought he did much too often, and the servants filed out of the kitchen to serve them breakfast.

It was a breakfast just as flamboyant as dinner the previous night. They had large bowls of eggs, what kind of eggs, Samuel wasn't sure, platters of perfectly shaped sausages, and many other things, such as fruit and cheese.

Samuel didn't eat as much as he normally would, for he was too excited to discover what training they would be doing. He looked around at the others and noticed that they, too, were not eating very much.

When King Nunor saw that they were all waiting patiently for him to finish eating, he said, "I guess it's time we started your training." They looked at him expectantly. "I will be observing you during your battle training to make sure that you are properly suited with the right weapons, but don't let that make you nervous. Just do your very best, and you will get along fine."

As he said this, a familiar-looking servant walked through door towards the king. *That's the same man that delivered the weird letter last night!* His straight-backed posture reminded Samuel of a man who was used to being in charge.

Not surprisingly, he handed the confused king another note.

King Nunor skimmed the crisp paper, becoming paler and paler with each line he read.

What's going on? Samuel thought. *King Nunor must have more on his mind than meets the eye.*

The king crumpled the letter shakily and gazed at the servant, nodding his head.

The slender man turned and strode out of the throne room, averting his eyes from those in the room.

King Nunor turned to the Commander. "Commander Yurson, you may lead them outside. Please let the instructors know that I will not be observing the weapons practice. I have an urgent matter to attend to."

"Yes, sir!" Yurson said in his gruff voice, abruptly standing at attention before the king.

He takes everything too seriously, Samuel thought.

"Follow me to the training grounds!" He marched stiffly out the door. The young trainees quickly jumped up and trooped out behind him.

They eventually reached the "training grounds," which turned out to be the courtyard around the back of the keep.

Commander Yurson stopped in the center of the large open area and turned around to face them.

"This is the training area where you will be taught the various skills necessary for survival as a member of this team," he explained succinctly. "I will now show you where the different classes will be held. They will be in the same place, at the same time, and with the same instructor every day."

He proceeded to list off the various subjects they would be learning throughout their training, pointing at different sections of the courtyard as he spoke.

After he finished, Commander Yurson barked, "The instructors will now introduce themselves." As he walked towards the small back door of the keep, Samuel wondered why the Commander always told them what was going to happen before it did. He deduced that it must have been the result of too many years in the country's military.

The strict Commander walked back out of the building with five adults, who were obviously the instructors. They fanned out in a line opposite the cadets. Yurson stood on the end between the two lines and gestured for the first instructor to introduce himself.

The thin man stepped forward. From his looks, Samuel could tell that he was only slightly older than Zane. His dark brown hair was cut short on top, and his angular jaw twitched intermittently.

"Hi, guys!" He said in a breezy voice. "I'm Daniel. I'll be your instructor for how to survive in the wilderness. Not dying is going to be one of our priorities." He stepped back, smiling slyly, and the next instructor stepped forward

"I'm Brusall," the heavily-built man rumbled with a thick accent. "I'll be teaching you combat skills." His features were rugged, strong, and hairy. A long, black ponytail dangled from the back of his head.

Mikal inspected him shrewdly, as if he were sizing him up for a fight.

A feeble-looking old man stepped forward and introduced himself as Shem. Although he was small and had white hair on his head, he held himself with a strong dignity that impressed Samuel. He explained that he would teach them the colorful history and ancient legends of Aena.

The next man was called Jamis. He had shoulder-length black hair, a battle-scarred face, and the looks of a toughened warrior. He said that they would be learning physical fitness from him, and that in the field of battle, there was no mercy.

Samuel surmised that this would be a difficult class.

The last one in line was a pretty young woman with dark brown hair. She introduced herself as Eyla and said she would be teaching them stealth and other spying skills.

Mikal winked at her as she stepped back into line, but she ignored it completely. Ruth rolled her eyes in exasperation.

With the introductions concluded, the instructors walked off, and Yurson informed the trainees that he and a couple of other high-ranking knights would be watching their every move from inside the keep.

In a rough voice, the Commander announced, "The training may begin!"

14

...

Eating Plants

The five trainees walked over to the first station on the right. The instructor, Daniel, was sitting on the ground, waiting for them. The other teachers were relaxing at their areas, loitering until it was their turn to teach.

"Have a seat," he said pleasantly, motioning to the verdant grass on the ground.

Once they had made themselves comfortable, he began his lesson. "Today we're going to learn about plants."

Zane thought that this would be interesting to learn. There were so many plants he didn't know about.

Mikal obviously thought the opposite. He had a bored expression on his face, and was slumped forwards with his chin in his hands.

"I can see some of you think this will not be a very exciting class," Daniel began, glancing at Mikal. "You probably want to get on to a more exciting subject, like fighting. Believe me, though, this can be much more interesting than beating on each other with weapons."

Daniel reached behind himself, pulled out a handful of leaves and berries, and set them in front of him. He organized them into two categories, in a way that they could all be seen.

"Okay. We'll start with the leaves." He pointed to a bright green leaf that had so many bright yellow veins running through it that it looked as if it was glowing. "Do any of you know what this one is?"

"I know what that is!" Ruth exclaimed immediately. "That's Shining Star! I've used it for healing people before."

"You're absolutely right! It is said that this helpful vine can cure almost any sickness or injury." He enjoyed the look of awe on some of their faces.

"What's this next one here?" He pointed to a black leaf very similar to the Shining Star, except for the fact that it had bright red veins running through it. "Both of these vines are rare," he hinted.

Zane didn't know, so he watched Daniel expectantly.

"This is the Dragon Fire vine," the young instructor explained. "It's the opposite of Shining Star. Instead of bringing healing, it brings death or extreme illness. If you touch it, you must wash your hands before eating, because it will poison you. However, it can only affect you if it enters your mouth or bloodstream."

Zane peered at the dark leaf nervously. He made a mental note to stay away from any plant that was black and red.

"There is a unique myth about both Shining Star and Dragon Fire," Daniel was saying. "Some people think that Shining Star grows in places close to something pure. When something evil is near, however, the Dragon Fire vine thrives." He saw their questioning looks and expounded. "These are just myths, though. I don't know if they're true or not." He

133

decided that history was Shem's job and changed to a different subject.

"Let's continue on to the other leaves." He proceeded to describe all sorts of leaves that were edible, inedible, poisonous, and used for healing.

Finishing this topic, he began focusing on the berries.

"We're going to play a little game," Daniel said. He pawed through the pile of berries and sorted them into categories.

When he finished, there were five piles lying in the grass, one for each trainee.

"Here's what you're going to do," he began. "You'll each take one type of berry and hold on to it. On my mark, you'll eat them." Zane wore an uncertain look on his face, as did the others, so Daniel reassured them.

"Don't worry, none of them are poisonous. Are you ready?"

Zane reached for a tiny, green berry from the pile in front of him and held it in his hands nervously. He was uneasy about eating something that he couldn't identify, but he forced himself to trust Daniel and nodded.

"Ready... go!"

Zane popped the small berry into his mouth and chewed, waiting for the juice reach his taste buds.

When it hit his tongue, a disgusting flavor flooded his mouth, an indescribably nasty taste that lingered even after he had swallowed it. Zane had only experienced something as horrid as this once before.

When he was a young boy, his mother had given him an apple for an afternoon snack. He had been thrilled with the idea of eating an apple whole, because his parents had always cut it up for him before.

When he was about halfway through, he took a large bite. As he chewed it, Zane realized that it tasted different than normal. In fact, a revolting flavor was filling his mouth as he munched.

Spitting the nasty-tasting apple out of his mouth, Zane looked where he had bitten and nearly threw up.

There was half of a moth inside his apple.

After that terrible experience, Zane had vowed to always cut his apples open before he ate them.

He spit the remains of the berry out onto the grass next to him and wiped his mouth on his sleeve. He spit a few more times to get the taste out of his mouth and looked around at the others.

Their reactions were far different from his.

Samuel had a confused expression on his face, as if he was not quite sure what he tasted. Mikal had already finished his berry, and it had apparently been much better than Zane's. Kari's reaction was similar to Zane's. She grimaced horribly as she swallowed what must have been the remains of her berry. Ruth had swallowed hers and was sucking in gulps of air.

Zane wondered if she was choking, but then concluded that her berry had most likely been very spicy.

Daniel was watching all this happen with an amused expression on his face. It was obvious that he had already known what the berries would do to each person beforehand.

"Each of these are edible, and will keep you alive," the mischievous instructor explained when they had finished. "Don't complain about what they taste like. If you're out starving in the wilderness, you'll eat anything."

"There is only one berry that I will touch on briefly at the moment, for it has some… let's say *interesting* properties." He reached down and picked up the whitish type of berry Samuel had eaten.

The curious student recognized it and said, "I ate that one! It didn't taste like anything!" He sounded somewhat disappointed, although Zane thought that he should have been glad he didn't get anything nasty like the rest of them.

"You're absolutely right! This type of berry tastes like nothing at all. However, the main thing I would like you to learn is what this berry does." He saw their interested, albeit annoyed, looks and continued.

"If Samuel here had eaten this berry at nighttime, he would have been more surprised than he was when he tasted it." Daniel paused enigmatically.

"These are generally known as Spellberries." He rolled the berry around in his palm. "They are named as such for their peculiar reaction when eaten. If ingested between the periods of sunset and sunrise, it will grant the person a special ability. If a second berry is eaten in the same night, however, the power will be extinguished. The abilities we have observed are inhuman strength, invisibility, and the power of flight."

Their jaws dropped. The thought of possessing such abilities was mind-blowing. Zane began wondering if he could try one at night, until Daniel's next words discouraged the idea.

"I know what you're thinking. You probably want to test them out. However much I may want to let you, I can't. They are highly expensive if bought, and are very rare. They usually grow in heavily moist areas, like dense jungles or bogs. So don't even think about trying to steal them from me. You will be punished in most unpleasant ways, and I really would hate to see that." He slipped all the berries back into a leather pouch he had been holding, and pulled the drawstring tight.

"Although it seems to be random what ability one might attain, there is a way to tell. Most people don't take the risk, however." Daniel continued talking to them as he cleaned up the leaves.

"Each berry contains a certain number of seeds. These seeds are small and darkly colored. Some time ago, an alchemist was fiddling with some of these, and noticed that the berries that gave massive strength had three seeds, the invisibility berry had four seeds, and the one that granted flight had five. Many soldiers and criminals have used this knowledge to find the one they need." He finished packing up and made himself comfortable on the grass again.

"I said it was risky, and I'll tell you why. The berry has to be intact when you eat it, and the seeds are inside." Daniel saw understanding begin to dawn on their faces.

"The way to find out about the amount of seeds is very dangerous. You must swim to the bottom of a lake and place the berry on the ground. Something having to do with the water pressure will cause the seeds inside to glow, and you can count them. Most people don't risk it, though, for fear of drowning."

Kari spoke. "How is it possible that the berries will give you special abilities?"

Daniel shrugged. "There's a myth that says there was an old Elf enchantress who found a new species of berry. She wanted to have some fun with us humans, and put a spell on the berries, causing them to give us different powers. I don't know how much of that story is true, but there are many who believe it."

Zane wasn't even sure what an "Elf enchantress" was. *It sounds like some sort of children's story*, he thought.

Daniel stood up and brushed off the seat of his pants, which were slightly moist from the morning dew. "I'm sure you guys have had your fair share of me talking. You can head over to the next instructor now. Tomorrow, we will be talking about the properties of various tree barks.

The five of them stood and began to leave. "Be nice to Brusall, will you?" Daniel said as they walked away. "He can be gruff sometimes, but he's a good guy."

As if on cue, the wooden door on the great, stone building swung open, revealing Brusall, the most muscular man Zane had ever seen.

15

...

Combat

Mikal watched Brusall's muscled arms ripple as he carried a tall, leather sack over to the kids. Poking out of the bag were the handles of swords, axes, and other deadly weapons. Slung over his back were multiple quivers of arrows that were tangling in his long, black ponytail.

As he made his way across the courtyard, the other instructors came towards them. Samuel wondered if they were going to be helping Brusall teach.

"A'right kids," the powerfully-built man bellowed. "Le's see a straight line!"

Startled by this unexpected outburst, everyone froze for a moment before hastily forming a crooked line facing him.

"Today we're going to be assessing your skill in combat," Brusall began, pacing along the length of the line. "We'll be finding out just how skilled you are. I expect no backtalk, no rebelliousness, and complete and utter obedience. If you do not heed my warning, you will be punished severely." He glared at each of them in turn, letting the words sink in.

"My assistants here," he gestured to the other instructors, "will be helping me demonstrate combat and determine *your* ability levels. Now follow me!" He marched towards the outer wall on the right of the keep.

Standing in front of it were multiple large bales of hay. In front of each bale, there was a dummy wearing old, beat-up armor. Their bodies were made out of what looked like tough, battered wood.

Brusall dropped all the weapons in a patch of bare ground.

On the way there, the once-straight line of team members had become a blob, and Brusall saw to correcting that immediately.

"What is this!?" He yelled, talking about the blob. "I said a straight line!" The trainees bumped into each other, trying to form a line again. "When I say a straight line, I mean a straight line! Do you understand?"

This guy needs to tone it down a bit, Samuel thought.

When they had arranged themselves into a sufficient line, he glared at them once more and began lecturing on weapons.

Brusall reached into the burlap bag and pulled out a long, sheathed sword. "This is a longsword," he said, turning it over in his hands. "It is the standard weapon that all knights train with." He drew the sword from its scabbard and brandished it, turning towards Daniel, who was now wearing a suit of armor and holding a sword and a shield.

"It is a double-edged weapon, and has a cross guard at the hilt to protect your hand." Without warning, Brusall swung the sword at Daniel, who instantly brought his weapon up to block it.

At the last moment, however, the whistling blade changed direction and slammed into Daniel's side. With blinding speed, Brusall flicked the blade effortlessly through the air and proceeded to batter Daniel with a series of flourishing blows.

Mikal almost laughed at how badly Daniel was getting beaten. *He must not be very good at swordfighting,* the smirking boy thought. As much as he tried to hold in his laughter, a sharp snort broke through his tight lips.

In less than a second, Brusall had whipped around and was bringing his sword down toward Mikal's head, a look of battle rage shining in his dark eyes.

Mikal ducked in fright and held his arms above his head in a futile attempt to ward off the impending blow. Instead of feeling the searing pain of a sword in his neck, though, he felt something lightly touching the top of his hair. He slowly looked up, straight into the ruthless eyes of Brusall, who was holding his longsword mere centimeters from Mikal's head.

"Was something funny about that?" He asked in a deceptively calm voice. Mikal shook his head fearfully.

Confident that the sarcastic youngster had learned his lesson, he leaned the longsword back against his shoulder and gave Mikal a simple aphorism.

"Here's a life lesson: Never laugh at someone else's misfortune." Brusall slid the sword back into the brown, leather sheath.

As he prepared to talk about the next weapon, Kari spoke up timidly. "What if you had missed and accidentally hit him?"

The beefy instructor looked down at Mikal, who was just standing up shakily.

"I never miss."

Brusall continued to demonstrate the uses of the other close-combat weapons, never once hitting Daniel too hard. Some of these were: a broadsword, a battleax, a flanged mace, a flail, a poleax, a war-hammer, a glaive, a halberd, and a long dirk. He showed them the special properties of each one and how to use them in battle.

When he had finished battering Daniel thoroughly, he motioned for the bruised instructor to go change out of his dented armor. Daniel gratefully obliged.

"Now that we've finished the close-combat weapons," the instructor said, setting down a long mace on the large pile of battle paraphernalia, "we'll move on to the long-range ones."

Mikal checked to make sure they were still standing in a straight line and focused his attention on Brusall. His legs were starting to ache from standing this long, so he hoped that the brawny man would be finished soon.

Brusall pulled a long, powerful-looking bow out of the bag and strung it. "This is a longbow," he explained. "It's for the people who are more experienced with shooting. You kids will most likely start with a recurve." He said, pulling a smaller bow out of his bag.

This one was shaped much differently than the last. It was made of light-colored wood and was curved the opposite direction on both tips.

"Although it may not look like much compared to the longbow, it has a good draw-weight." He flexed the string.

"Another thing about recurves is that the ones our arms-makers produce have sharpened tips coated thinly in metal. They are excellent for close-combat, if the bow is unstrung." He set it down and picked up the longbow and a quiver of arrows.

"Now I will demonstrate how to shoot. Pay close attention."

Brusall drew an arrow from his hip-quiver and placed it on the bow, moving slowly to show them the steps of shooting.

The arrow had a black shaft and white fletches on the back-end. The head was a sharpened triangle that was slightly barbed at the lower tips.

Brusall drew it back, the tendons in his forearms bulging. He reached the maximum point of the draw and exhaled. Using his innate sense of aiming, he released.

The arrow flew true and smacked into the center of the helmet on the dummy directly in front of him. The arrowhead was buried deeply in the wood, planted there by the immense power of the superior bow.

Brusall slid the bow back into the bag and addressed the trainees, asking a question: "Have any of you shot a bow before?"

Mikal said he had, and Ruth and Kari echoed his response. Zane and Samuel, however, had never seen a bow shot.

"Good," said Brusall. "That way you three can teach them how to shoot in your free time," he motioned to Zane and Samuel. "Let's move on to knives." He lifted the leather jerkin he was wearing, revealing a belt that held many sheathed knives. "Most of these can be used for close-combat, but since we're talking about long-ranged weapons, we'll work on throwing them."

As Brusall demonstrated how to throw knives, Mikal mentally prepared himself for the assessment. He had practiced swordfighting before leaving for the castle but hadn't had time since then to hone his skills. He would hate to be humiliated in front of his new team partners.

Brusall was now talking about javelins and long spears. By this time, all of the kids were becoming antsy, each of them ready to try out the weapons and prove their skills to the instructors.

"We have a lot of time for this class, so we'll assess you each one by one," Brusall said finally, finishing his discussion about spear throwing. "Who wants to go first?" They tried to hide their looks of relief. No one in Brusall's past had ever liked listening to his lectures on weapons.

Right after he said this, Mikal shot his hand into the air and volunteered. He hoped that if he went first, the others would admire his skills. No one had admired him before.

"I figured so much," Brusall muttered to himself. Earlier, he had noticed that this boy was the most arrogant one in the group. He looked at Mikal. "What is your weapon of choice?"

"Longsword," Mikal quickly answered, very aware that the others were watching his every move. He tried to straighten his back so he would look as tall and strong as possible. Mikal had grown up showing off what he could do to others. It was his way of life. Nobody had paid any attention to him as a child, so he always tried his best to impress the others into liking him.

Brusall reached into the beat-up leather sack and pulled out the sword he had been using earlier. He handed the hilt to the confident young man, watching him closely.

Mikal took the sword and drew it from its scabbard. The balance was good, but it was heavier than the sword he used at home. *I guess I'll have to get used to it.*

"Demonstrate your skill against that dummy over there," Brusall said, pointing to the one closest to the group. He was about to say something else, when Mikal interrupted him.

"Yeah, I got it. You don't need to tell me anything else. I'm not a dimwit, you know." He wanted them to know that *he* was in control of himself, not the weapons instructor.

Brusall closed his mouth reluctantly and nodded at Mikal. *If he's not going to take instructions, then he's going to have to learn for himself.*

Flippantly, Mikal swaggered off to the targeted figure, swinging the sword in tight circles at his side. *Why am I not being tested against a real opponent?* He thought. *That would be a better way to measure my skill.* He shrugged mentally and swung the sword in a fast overhead cut at the dummy's sword arm.

To his surprise, the blade swished past the dummy and embedded itself in the ground, all the momentum of the powerful swing sinking it in deeply.

Before he could wonder about what had just happened, Mikal felt a sharp thump on his forearm. He looked up from where he stood, tugging at the sword in the ground.

To his further bewilderment, the dummy was flailing about, swinging its crude, wooden sword at him. Shocked, he jumped out of the way before the weapon could smack him again, his sword jerking out of the ground in the process.

Mikal stared at the dummy, confused beyond comprehension. Sweat streamed down his face already, the result of the adrenaline that had just been coursing through his body. The odd, wooden mannequin in front of him was swinging its arms and turning its body as if it had a mind of its own!

With a newly imbued rage at being tricked, Mikal attacked the mechanical beast ferociously. He hacked at its head, trying to decapitate it, but before he could, the arm came up and parried his sword.

His iron blade sunk into the wood and stuck there, unmoving. Mikal yanked at it, but before he could pull it free, the other arm came up under his guard and punched him in the stomach, twisting the sword from his grip in the process.

Mikal sank to the ground, his breath lost. He gasped for a moment before just lying still.

Brusall called out an order. "A'right. That's enough. I've seen what I need to see." He walked over, helping Mikal unwillingly to his feet and bringing him back to the others.

"What… just… happened… there?" Mikal asked angrily, while desperately trying to catch his breath.

Brusall held back a smile as he explained. "We have a few adroit engineers that live here in Castle Orthox. They designed these harmless-looking dummies to have more in store for the trainees than expected."

He walked toward the backside of the hay bales, beckoning for his students to follow him.

Sitting innocently on a wood stool behind the bales was Daniel. Although the group hadn't seen him, he had walked behind the dummies and hidden there after changing out of the suit of armor.

In his hand was a pole that descended downward into the earth. There was a curved line dug into the ground that the long dowel could apparently move around.

"What are *you* doing back here?" Mikal asked, now more confused than angry.

Brusall spoke, gesturing towards the dowel. "This pole controls the movements of the dummy in front of the hay bales. When Daniel moves it from side to side, the dummy rotates slightly, swingin' its arms in the process. This creates the illusion that it's fightin' you."

Mikal had to admit that it was an ingenious idea, though he still felt some anger towards the combat instructor. "Why didn't you tell us about this before we started?" He asked, looking suspiciously at Brusall.

"I was about to," the large instructor said, spreading his hands, "but you didn't give me the chance. You were a bit touchy about me tellin' you anythin' else, if I remember correctly."

"Oh. Yeah." Mikal took a mental note not to interrupt the instructors anymore.

"Enough of this talk!" Brusall exclaimed suddenly, making them jump. "We've got work to do! Who's next?"

The others went through their assessments fairly quickly. Kari was good with a sword and was better than she would have been, because she knew about the trick with the dummy. She also proved her skill with a bow by hitting mere inches from Brusall's demonstrative shot.

Ruth was an expert knife thrower. It was obvious that she had practiced many times. The instructors were very impressed. Brusall commented that she had excellent hand-eye coordination, probably the best among them.

Zane picked the flanged mace and mauled the dummy he was assigned to. Brusall had to tell him to stop, because there wouldn't be any dummy left when Zane was finished. When asked where he had learned to use a mace, he just smiled.

Then it was Samuel's turn.

16

...

A New Trainee

"A'right, Samuel. You're up." Brusall beckoned for him to pick his weapon.

Samuel's heart beat rapidly as he surveyed the conglomeration of weapons in front of him. His hands were slick with sweat, and his knees were trembling. Normally, he wouldn't be this nervous, but this was a test. He'd never held a sword in his life, and now he was being asked to fight with one!

It was true that he *could* pick another weapon from the pile, but Creyan had told him on the road that he would be a natural with a sword. He didn't want to disappoint the friendly spy.

Samuel bent down and lifted the dented longsword out of the pile, gripping its wooden handle tightly.

Its weight surprised him. He had thought that it would be uncomfortably heavy, but it seemed to weigh about as much as the axe he used to chop wood back home. It was also better balanced.

Samuel held it up in front of himself, staring at the battered blade, but then he remembered that everyone else was watching and waiting for him to start.

Samuel, wary of the strange engineering of the dummy, approached cautiously. He held the sword in what he felt like was a defensive stance. When he got near enough for it to hit him, Samuel decided to take a risk and lunged forward. He figured that a quick thrust forward would be more direct and harder to parry than a wild swing.

He was right. The blade shot forward and hit the mannequin in the chest with a low thump.

Unfortunately, Samuel didn't have quite enough power behind the jab, so his sword bounced off its chest and fell away. In retaliation, the dummy swung back and smacked him in the shoulder.

Samuel yelped and jumped away, bringing the sword with him. Time and practice would make his attacks more effective.

He tried stabbing a few more times, until Brusall said he could stop. Even after such a short time holding the sword, it felt much heavier in Samuel's hand than it had when he first picked it up.

The tired trainee walked back to his team members and dropped the sword into the pile with a loud clang. He took his place in the line and looked at Brusall, waiting for instructions.

The large instructor nodded his head at them respectfully, his black ponytail bobbing. "I commend you all on your work today. You have given us a sufficient summary of your skills." The other instructors nodded their agreement. "We will inform you of your next tasks tomorrow."

Brusall looked up into the sky, judging the time. The sun was bright and blazing overhead, signifying that it was nearing noon.

"It looks like it's about midday, so you may head to lunch. Meet near that grove of trees over there for your lesson with Shem after you finish." He indicated a small, grassy area that sat next to a jumble of exotic trees.

Hungry, they ran back into the castle, feeling that they had done well in their first combat lesson.

Slowing down to a dignified walk before entering the Great Hall, Samuel was somewhat nervous about what exotic dishes they would be served for lunch. He hoped that they weren't *too* strange.

Mikal's voice came from behind him as they walked through the Main Hall. "I'm gonna go to the latrine, so don't none of you miss me!" He smirked and sprinted away towards the entrance on the opposite side of the room.

Samuel rolled his eyes and opened the giant doors for the other three. As he looked in, he noticed that the king was already waiting for them and looked as if he had been there quite a while.

Samuel had been known back home for his good vision. The people of Vale had said that he could see a deer coming from a mile away. While that was an exaggeration, it was true that he could see better than most people.

The moment Samuel walked into the Great Hall, he could tell that something was wrong. Even from far away, he could see that the king's head was drooping, and his eyes were glazed.

"Your majesty?" He asked slowly. "Is everything okay?"

"Yes, Samuel," King Nunor said, shaking his head as if to clear a fog and looking up. "Everything is perfectly fine. How about you and your friends have a seat." He motioned for the guards to close the doors behind them. Samuel sat down, keeping his eyes fixed on the king.

Then he saw her.

Sitting next to the king was a girl of diminutive stature. Her skin was as white as the full moon, and her long, dark hair fell down her shoulders to her waist. It was so black that it appeared to be almost purple. She was garbed in simple wool clothes that were as black as her deep, searching eyes, which scanned the room in a cold, calculating way.

Despite her unsettling appearance, the king seemed unconcerned. She stood next to him with the demeanor of one who had control of the situation.

The trainees glanced at each other in bewilderment. *Who is that creepy girl?* Samuel thought.

King Nunor rose from his bejeweled throne and addressed the assembled students. "My young prodigies, before we begin our noonday meal, I would like to introduce a new member of the team." He turned to the girl. "Please introduce yourself."

She took one small step forward and spoke in a haunting voice that Samuel would remember for years to come.

152

"Hello." Her voice washed over their minds like a dry wind. "I am Ticha. I will be joining you for your training." She nodded her head at them.

With that slight movement, every feeling of unease vanished from Samuel's mind. His brain was cleared of nervous tension, and he felt completely at ease in the company of this mysterious girl.

"There you go!" said the king as she sat down next to him. "Now that you've been introduced, let's eat!" He clapped his hands for what seemed like the billionth time, and the servants poured through the doors, bearing platters of strange delicacies.

Relishing the meal, Samuel was not worried about the unusual looks and tastes of the food. As he ate, a nagging feeling floated in the back of his mind that something was not right. He was missing something very important.

Unnoticed by Samuel, he was in a daze. His ears were clogged, and everything he looked at seemed to be shrouded by mist. He ate his food, but didn't taste it. The aroma of the meal didn't reach his nose. The only thing he smelled was the faint scent of metal. He figured that it must have been from the silverware.

He looked up at the girl with dark shadows under her eyes and seemed to recall that she was now part of their team. *I wonder where she's from*, he thought, not at all disturbed by her unsettling appearance. *I guess it won't hurt to ask.*

Samuel sat up and addressed the girl. "So it's Ticha, right? Where're you from?" He looked at her expectantly. When she didn't answer, he tried again. "Hello! Do you see me over here? Yeah, you!" She turned towards him with an annoyed expression. "I asked, 'Where're you from?'"

Ever so slowly, a thin smile crossed her face, never reaching her eyes. "You want to know where I'm from?"

Samuel nodded.

"Then let me show you." She tilted her head forward, and her black eyes turned a fiery red.

Like a cold splash of freezing water, Samuel was snapped back to reality. He stood out of his chair and stumbled backwards, a sharp sense of imminent danger searing through his veins. The others just sat where they were, still entranced by this girl, whoever she was.

With a laugh that chilled him straight to the bones, Ticha brought her hand into the air and wrenched it sideways.

Feeling a blow as if someone had kicked him in the head, Samuel was knocked backwards and hit the ground with a painful thud. In mere seconds, a wave of darkness had covered his eyes, and everything went black.

17

...

Rebellion

Samuel awoke groggily to the sharp scent of mildew and rot, his eyes fluttering slowly open. His head throbbed painfully, and he felt cold, rough stones pressing into his back. Everything surrounding him was shrouded in darkness, except for a single square of dim light seeming to float in a void in front of him.

Samuel tried to sit up, then winced as an excruciating throb pulsed through his skull. He lifted his hands, but as he moved, he felt the biting cold of frozen metal weighing down on his wrists.

What is this? He mused sleepily. *Where am I?*

Vaguely, he remembered a strange girl next to the king and that something had shoved him backwards, apparently knocking him unconscious.

I... I must be in the dungeon, Samuel thought. He tried to turn to look to the side, and a rock protruding from the wall jabbed into his shoulder.

"Ow!" He yelled in surprise.

"So you *are* awake," a soft voice echoed from the far side of the room. "I was wondering when you might wake up."

Samuel scanned the darkness and tried unsuccessfully to push himself up. There were heavy manacles around his wrists and ankles, which hindered his efforts.

"Who's there?" He asked.

"I am your conscience," it whispered.

Samuel paused for a moment. "Really?"

There was no answer but a light cackle. "Ha! I can't believe you fell for *that* one!" The unknown person continued laughing.

"Wait... so you're not my conscience?"

"Of course not! Why would I be your conscience? Ha!"

Samuel was starting to become angry. "Who are you *really*?"

The voice stopped its laughter and went very silent. "I am Shem," it said after a moment's pause.

Shem, Shem... Oh yeah! The history instructor! Samuel finally managed to push himself to a sitting position. He vaguely remembered an old man with a white, scraggly beard. "What are you doing here?"

"Well," he cleared his throat. "I was at that fateful meal too, if I recall correctly."

Samuel didn't remember. He had been in too much of a daze to take in any details.

"When you were knocked unconscious," Shem continued, "it kinda shook us back to reality, and we tried to stop that wretched brat. It was no use, though; she was too strong."

"What do you mean she was *too strong*? She was just a girl, for crying out loud!"

Shem was silent for a moment. "A very powerful girl," he replied softly.

"Yes... I guess you do have a point there." Samuel's eyes were beginning to adjust to the dim light of the room. He could just make out the stone wall in front of him, and in the furthest corner, a dark figure. "What about the others? Are they all right?" Ominous thoughts of death filled his mind.

"Oh yeah! They're fine. I think they're prob'ly in the cells next door."

A massive surge of relief flooded Samuel's body. *They're still alive!*

They were quiet for a few minutes, musing over the recent happenings. Then Shem broke the silence.

"Would you like to know what I believe may be the reason for her power?"

"Wait... you *know* who she is? How!?"

"Alright!" Shem said with apparent delight. "Let's begin!" There was a clinking of chains as the old instructor repositioned himself.

"I'll start with the history of the elves... actually... I'll just give ya a short summary: They live in a city on the clouds, they're super smart, etcetera. What I'm really goin' to talk about is what happens when one of them elves starts messin' with the wrong people. An example I'm goin' to use is one particular Elf who was named Prosperity."

"She lived in a time long ago, when the elves were fighting a massive war against the evil Xortahn." He spread his hands dramatically. "For your information, a Xortah is the opposite of an Elf. Elves are named for good feelin's and characteristics, while the Xortahn are named for downright nasty things, like hatred and such.

"So... the elves were fightin' this war against the Xortahn," he explained, "and it lasted for many years. One of the battle commanders was this Elf, Prosperity. She was in control of all the armies of Melyn Toche, the Elven kingdom.

"There was one battle that they were losing dreadfully The Elven king wanted to send a spy into the Xortahn headquarters to discover their plans. No one was willing to do this, until Prosperity herself volunteered.

"She stole into the Xortah fortress, which is mighty big, mind you, and attempted a theft of the plans. Unfortunately, she was caught."

Samuel hadn't expected this. He had thought there would be some sort of showdown with an evil person, such as Ticha, but he decided not to make any assumptions until Shem was finished.

"The Xortahn imprisoned the Elven commander and tortured her, trying to wheedle the location of the Elven base out of her. So strong was her resolve, though, that she never gave in.

"The Xortahn could not get any information out of her, so they tried one last trick.

"Their leader, Destruction by name, had a talent for chemistry. He carefully mixed an immensely powerful potion, and with some difficulty, forced her to swallow it.

"The instant results: Her face turned pale, her hair turned black, and her voice was transformed into horrible, raspy-soundin' noises.

"From then on, she went about Domilia, cursing hundreds and bringing evil upon many more, her mind havin' been twisted by the potion. This creature that the Xortahn created was known as an enchantress. This particular enchantress called herself 'Ciath,' or 'wicked' in the Elven language. And the name Ciath mixed around makes... you guess it! Ticha."

"How do you know this?"

"I *am* a history instructor..."

"Oh. Yeah. Well, I guess I should know my enemy." *So that's why she has so many weird powers!* "Is there any way to stop her?" Samuel asked.

"She *can* be killed, but there's no way you're going to get out of this cell. Whatever you're thinking isn't going to work."

"You don't think so?" Samuel said, leaning back against the rough wall. "Well, I know just the way."

Mikal crouched down behind the old door and remained motionless. His eyes were wide with fear, and his palms were sticky with sweat. He could usually keep his cool in times of stress, but this was too much for his mind to handle.

He was hiding in a small room that had happened to be unlocked when he went running past. Surrounded by darkness, Mikal squeezed his eyes shut as memories of the most recent events flashed through his brain.

When he had returned to the Great Hall from the latrine, he had heard strange sounds coming from behind the doors. Instead of bursting in, he had decided to listen and find out what was going on. He had heard an unfamiliar voice that made him shiver. It sounded somewhat like a girl, but it seemed too deep and throaty to be feminine.

Hey! That sounded like Samuel! Mikal thought when another voice spoke up. Suddenly, there was a crash, and Samuel cried out in pain. The eavesdropping trainee leapt up in fright and ran away as fast as he could. He found the first unlocked door, the closet he was in currently, and dove inside.

Mikal shivered at the terrifying memory. As he sat trembling in the darkness, a thought came into his head. *Wait... why didn't I stand and fight?* A twinge of regret pinched his mind. *Aren't I brave? Aren't I up to this?* Some of his past confidence began seeping its way into his soul. *I'm a warrior! There's no evil lady that can stand against me!*

Mikal stood shakily to his feet and put his hand on the door, ready to push it open. A loud shout from the hallway beyond made him step backwards and crouch down again. He gently put his ear to the door to listen.

"Hey! Don't touch me! Stop it! When I get free I'm gonna... ow! Watch it!" *That's Daniel!* Mikal thought with surprise. *Whoever's out there must have captured him! I have to go save him!*

Testing his courage, the reckless boy stood up once again, wanting to leap out of the door and save the day. When he heard something that chilled his bones and made his hair stand up on end, Mikal changed his mind.

"**You will pay for your defiance**!" The voice that spoke was hideous and slithering, making his heart drop to his feet. *Wh-what is that? Is it...?* Mikal's thoughts were cut off by Daniel's bloodcurdling scream. After the menacing "boom" of a door slamming shut, the horrible noises ceased abruptly.

M-maybe I sh-should get some help.

Zane paced back and forth in his cramped prison cell, loosely attached to the wall by the iron manacles.

After Samuel had been knocked to the ground in the Great Hall, Zane had snapped out of the daze and attacked the evil girl. She had been too strong, and in no time, he was lying unconscious on the ground. When he woke up, he had been in this dingy cell with no one but himself. Fortunately for him, he had a barred window with which to look down on the kingdom below.

Zane walked over to the small opening and peered down at the ground, breathing in the fresh air. It was summertime, so the sun was still shining brightly in the late hours of the afternoon. He could see the peaceful city of Kogincheir bustling around merrily, completely oblivious to the threat that loomed overhead.

Something he noticed startled him.

Ticha's small form was sprinting across the lush grass towards the front side of the castle wall. The thing that was surprising was her speed. She was running much too fast for a girl her size. Her legs pounded the ground with supernatural force, sometimes kicking up thick clumps of grass.

Zane pressed his face against the bars to get a last glimpse of her before she was out of his sight, but she was already gone.

I wonder what she's up to, he thought. *Prob'ly nothin' good.*

The sharp bite of despair began nipping at his heart as he sat down on the rough ground of the cell. He rested his head in his hands morosely and sighed one deep, sad sigh. *We're doomed. There's no hope for us now. Ticha's gonna kill us all or make us slaves. I don't even know which one's worse.*

As he sat there gloomily, soft footsteps sounded outside of his door. A sun-tanned, angular face with wavy, black hair moved in front of the barred window on the door, but Zane was so caught up in his brooding that he didn't notice.

"Psst! Hey! Zane!" A voice whispered.

Zane instantly snapped out of his thoughts. "What?!" He exclaimed. "Who...?" He was cut off by a loud shushing sound.

"Shhhh! There are guards just around the corner over there!"

"Mikal?!" Zane said in a more quiet voice. "But... how? How did ya git out?"

"They never caught me. I went to the... uh... latrine, remember?"

"Oh yeah! So can ya help *us* git out?"

"Yes, but I'm going to need a distraction. I have to steal the keys."

"Not a problem, my friend!" Zane replied, beaming. He was beginning to feel hopeful after all!

"Shhh! When I go away, just start doing whatever you're gonna do, alright?" Zane nodded. "Well, I'll see you in a bit!" With that, Mikal's face disappeared from the door, and his light footsteps trailed off down the hall.

Now what am I gonna do as a distraction? He shrugged and answered his own question. *I guess whatever comes ta mind.*

Zane drew in a deep breath and then let it out in one massive bellow. "BLAZOOGA! BLAZOOGA! BLAZOOGA!"

The effect was immediate. In chaos and confusion, the guards rushed down the hall to see what was the matter. There was a clatter of weapons and armor as they clambered in front of the door, trying to see into Zane's cell.

When the first bearded face appeared at the window, Zane put his face up to the bars and yelled at the top of his lungs, "BLAZOOGA!"

The sheer volume of the nonsense word sent the guards reeling backwards and cursing dirtily.

"It's nothin'!" One of them spat. "E's jest messin' with us!" The boisterous soldiers scowled at Zane and stalked back the way they had come, grumbling amongst themselves.

When they were all gone from the room, Zane heard the quiet pattering of footsteps and saw Mikal's grinning face in the window of his cell again.

"What did you say?" The free youth asked.

"Never mind about that. Did you get the keys?"

Mikal held up his hand and gave the large ring of keys a jingle.

He was about to reply, when someone from down the hall interrupted him.

"Was that Zane?" Samuel's voice called from the end of the corridor.

Mikal grinned again and searched through the many keys until he found one that fit snugly into the keyhole on Zane's cell.

<><><><><><><><><><><><><><><><><>

In no time, they had gathered the rest of the trainees together. They also released the five instructors, who had been incarcerated as well. Daniel, who was holding his arm the whole time with a pained expression, suggested that the instructors go back in the direction of the Throne Room to look for the girl.

Shem interjected. "She was not just a girl!" He then retold the story about the enchantress, Ciath, and that she may possibly be the one disguised as Ticha.

The five highly trained instructors went after the guards, since they were more experienced in fighting.

Left alone, the trainees agreed unanimously to head to the armory for weapons, despite the fears of their instructors. They knew where it was located because one of the bows had shattered during training that day, and Brusall had taken them with him to retrieve another. However, they hadn't been allowed inside.

The five trainees crept warily through the hallway that led to the armory, carefully watching for any guards that were under the enchantress's spell.

As they walked around one corner, Samuel was very surprised by what he saw. A guard had been posted in front of a door in the hall, but he wasn't standing up. Instead, he was lying on the floor, unconscious.

"Guys! C'mere!" The others abandoned all caution and ran to the unmoving man, their eyes opened wide. Samuel checked the fallen soldier's pulse and felt a faint heartbeat.

"He's still alive!" They sighed in relief. "I bet this is the work of Ticha!" Samuel examined the man's armor. "He's got the royal symbol right here on his helmet."

Ruth nodded her agreement, as did the others. "She probably knocked out all of the guards loyal to the king. If she can do that, then she's very capable of causing much more harm than we expected. We should move on."

After walking through many more passages, fearful at every corner, they eventually arrived at what Samuel believed was the armory. Although it was the only door in the hallway, it was fairly inconspicuously placed and hard to find.

Samuel looked both ways for guards and tried the handle.

It was locked.

He stepped back and tried to think of a solution.

"Does anyone here know how to pick locks?" He asked, looking around at the four youthful faces surrounding him.

Zane tentatively put his hand in the air. "I do." For some reason, he looked sheepish, almost embarrassed by saying this.

Samuel wondered where he had picked up that skill in Victon Province. *He seems shy about it,* he thought, *or else he wouldn't be acting so self-conscious. I wonder if people who can pick locks are looked down on in his Province.*

"Well, by all means, go ahead!" Samuel said, gesturing to the door and watching carefully.

Zane tentatively walked up to the door and began examining the hinges.

"Why are you looking at the hinges?" Mikal was curious as to how one picks a lock, but his reasons were less than honorable.

"Oh, I jest need to figure out how strong it is." He went back to looking at the hinges and then started scrutinizing the handle.

Samuel was wondering why the hinges were important, when he suddenly realized the big boy's intent.

"Wait...!" Samuel exclaimed just as Zane rammed his shoulder into the iron-reinforced door, breaking it off its hinges and leaving it in shambles on the floor of the armory.

166

Maintaining his look of sheepishness, Zane motioned to the empty frame. "Weapons, anybody?"

18

...

Transformation

Having lost the option of stealth, Samuel led the others through the mangled doorway.

As they entered the large room, the cadets looked around in wonder, awed by the massive chamber before them.

When Brusall said "armory," Samuel had envisioned a hundred by two hundred foot room that had weapon racks lining the walls. He thought that there might be a few hundred individual weapons on those and another couple racks for shields.

That picture, however, was nothing compared to what he saw before him now.

The size of the room was incomprehensible. It must have been a thousand feet long! At the far end of the room near the ceiling, there were large, unelaborate windows that let in the light of the afternoon sun. The walls of the room were constructed of gray slabs of stone stacked higher than Samuel could see in the dim light.

The weapon racks started at the door they had come through and went most of the way down the room. Nearest to the trainees were simple weapons, such as swords, spears, and bows. The shield racks came after those. This group was obviously for the ordinary knights that had no special training.

As the group slowly strolled between the racks of assorted, metal implements, Samuel began seeing unique weapons that Brusall had not shown them.

Held in their own custom racks were weapons of all different shapes and sizes. There were a few that piqued his curiosity.

First there was something strange that had a normal axe handle, but at the top, there were four blades sticking out at different angles. *That's very brutal-looking,* he thought.

One rack had a large assortment of exotic knives. There were long-bladed ones, thin-bladed ones, and a couple that had blades that wrapped all the way around the knuckles of the user. *There are so many of those, I wouldn't know what to do with them... though I bet Ruth would*, Samuel chuckled to himself, thinking of her knife-throwing performance earlier.

He looked away from the weapon racks along the sides of the room and turned his attention towards what lay at the back of the room.

Standing in front of them in frightful splendor were several massive war machines.

"Holy cow!" Mikal exclaimed, his eyes wide with awe.

Samuel looked over at him, confused. "Cows are not holy."

"Hey, it's just an expression."

There were various sizes of catapults, siege towers, and other implements of destruction sitting unused at the back of the armory. At the far end of the room, shrouded in shadows, was a pair of massive doors that stretched all the way to the ceiling.

Samuel wondered why he hadn't seen them when he'd walked around the building the other day. He must have been too absorbed in conversation to notice.

Mikal's voice shook them out of their stupor and brought them back to the situation at hand.

"Are we just going to stand here gaping the whole time, or what?"

"Right!" Samuel replied, breaking his gaze away from the battle machines. "Everyone, arm yourselves and be ready to move in five minutes!" They all nodded and moved to the weapon racks. *Did I really just say that?* Samuel thought, feeling a thrill of pleasure. *And they listened to me!* His mind drifted back to Kaltoid Province, when Creyan had said he was a born leader. *I guess he was right! Maybe I really* can *lead!*

Snapping out of his daydreams, Samuel walked over to one of the longsword racks to look for a suitable weapon. As he scanned the rows of blades, his gaze lighted on one that looked about the right size for him. He reached up and pulled it off of its holder.

The blade was encased in a leather sheath with a strap he could wrap around his waist. It was mildly heavy, but that's what Samuel expected of a sword. When he drew it out of the sheath to look at it, the blade became much lighter. *Wow! This is even lighter than the training sword I used today!*

Samuel brandished it around his head a couple times to test the feel of it. He wasn't a weapons expert, but it seemed like it would do for a short battle.

As Samuel continued examining his weapon, Zane found a satisfactory fit for his large build. He held a mace that was as tall as Ruth. Its iron handle had a soft leather strip wrapped around it for ease of handling.

At the business end of the mace were many smaller blades jutting outward, forming a ring of blades around the top. Although they looked somewhat flimsy, Zane was sure that they would withstand a large amount of battering.

Both Kari and Mikal had grabbed a couple swords similar to Samuel's, but with slightly different hilt designs and blade sizes.

While they were testing them, Ruth selected a variety of different knives that were hanging on the knife rack. She tied the sheaths to her belt and cinched them tightly.

Samuel slid the sword into its scabbard and wrapped the belt around his waist. He looked around at the others and saw that they were properly outfitted and ready to go, each of them looking at him.

Well, here goes nothing.

"Alright, guys! Is everyone ready?" They nodded their heads in assent, so Samuel continued. "Before we leave, I'd like to remind you that we're a team now. We've got to watch each others' backs. From this moment on, we must be able to trust each other. We need to work together in order to succeed... now and in the future. Oh, one more thing: If we don't work together today, we won't *have* a future. Are we in agreement here?" They responded with a hearty cheer.

Encouraged, Samuel became conscious that his face wasn't bright red as it usually was when he talked in front of people. His hands weren't even shaking. In fact, they were resting comfortably at his sides. *This is amazing! I feel perfectly calm!*

Samuel looked around at the faces before him, each one dreading the imminent fight, but in a way, they were excited too. Samuel's short speech had caused them to feel united, like they had been bound together, and whatever would happen, they would stay together forever.

Samuel raised his fist in the air, a shiver of exhilaration running through his body. "Let's go show that ugly lady who's in control of Aena!" They cheered again, brandishing their weapons, and Samuel marched out the door, ready for whatever happened next.

Ticha rounded the corner of the massive keep, running as fast as her supernatural legs could carry her. She didn't care who saw any of her abilities now. The time for attack had come.

As she sped past the long front stairway, the guard who was posted there yelled after her.

"Hey, you!" He shouted incredulously. "What are you doing?!"

Ticha smiled to herself. *Oh, he'll find out soon enough.*

She barreled through the front gate, slamming aside a guard that was standing in her way and knocking him over.

He shouted in surprise and put his hands out to brace himself. The evil enchantress turned on him and grinned wickedly. However, before she could do anything to harm him, a powerful voice echoed in her mind.

"NO! Do not tarry!"

With extreme willpower, Ticha pulled herself away from the man and grumbled in frustration. *Why am I not allowed to do* anything *without approval?*

Muttering obscenely, she sped through the empty streets, watching for the house she had designated as the meeting spot.

There it was! Ticha slowed down to a brisk jog and stopped as she reached the front steps of the small cottage. She burst through the small door.

"Hey! Hey! Watch it!" A man brusquely shoved her back and started to draw his sword.

"Bratt!" She yelled, recognizing the man. "What do you think you're doing?"

"Oh!" His eyes widened as he realized who she was. "My lady! I-I'm sorry!"

Ticha walked in, sighing resentfully. *These soldiers are worthless. I wish I could have hired a better army than this mob.*

All the men in the room looked up when she strode in. Fumbling with their weapons, they immediately stood from what they were doing and saluted, trying hard to keep their slouching backs straight.

"Have you ever heard me tell you to look before you threaten somebody?" Ticha shouted at Bratt, looking to make a display of it. "I expect to be welcomed, not shunned!" *Maybe I can gain some respect from this.* "I do *not* expect to be yelled at by some blundering oaf like you! Do you understand?!" She drew up her five foot body as tall as she could and scowled at him.

"Y-yes, ma'am." He stammered, backing away.

No one could win an argument with Ticha. However small she might be, she was downright frightening when she was mad.

Bratt, apparently not the brightest in the room, started talking again.

"B-but it's awfully hard to know if it's you," he said pathetically. The other soldiers in the room turned and stared at him, marveling at his lack of self-preservation.

Ticha turned back slowly and glared at him, her cold, black eyes seeming to bore into his flesh.

Trying to save himself from another scolding, Bratt said, "I mean, with you being such a small girl, we can't tell if it's you or some other kid." Unfortunately for him, Bratt's attempt to save himself only made things worse.

Not saying anything, but keeping her eyes trained on his, Ticha began to grow. Her long, black hair shriveled and twisted until it became one long, disheveled mass at the back of her head. Her skin turned white, and her eyes sunk deeper into her head. Her nails turned into black claws, and her teeth sharpened into fangs. Her body kept growing until it was nearly seven feet tall, her knotted hair brushing the ceiling. The only things still the same were her stony, black eyes.

When she spoke, it was in a raspy, hissing tone. "***How about this? Better***?" She flexed her fingers, feeling their power once more.

Bratt, now petrified with fear, could only manage a high-pitched squeak.

The other soldiers pressed back against the walls of the room, trying to get as far away as possible from the horrific enchantress.

Now in her true form, she grabbed Bratt by the throat and lifted him off the ground. He didn't move a muscle, terror paralyzing him.

"*Little Bratt.*" She laughed a terrible laugh and looked him directly in the eyes. "*I'm sorry, but I have no time for disrespect.*" The unfortunate soldier's eyes became large. He squirmed about, trying to break free from her concrete grip, but to no avail.

"*Goodbye.*" She twisted her hand and dug her talons into his neck, puncturing all the way through. She withdrew her fingers and dropped him to the ground, landing him in a pool of his own blood.

He convulsed violently and then lay still.

She turned back to the other, cowering soldiers and addressed them. "*Go outside the city walls and gather your brethren. I've already poisoned most of the guards at the castle. We attack within the hour.*"

"Yes, Ticha, ma'am." The soldiers filed hurriedly out the door.

"*Call me Ciath.*"

19

...

Undermining The Enemy

The battle-ready escapees snuck towards the corner of the keep, treading softly on the bright green grass. It was nearly sunset, and they were becoming anxious. Earlier, Zane had informed them of the enchantress's sprinting out of the keep towards the city.

The five of them had made it outside with almost no incidents. Right as they reached the outer door, however, a guard roughly approached them and demanded to know what they were doing. Upon a cursory inspection, Samuel noted that the symbol of Aena was not on his armor.

Conveniently, there had been a small room next to his post where they stowed his now-unconscious body.

Samuel poked his head around the corner, careful to be slow and deliberate so anyone who was out there wouldn't notice him.

When he didn't see Ciath or anyone else suspicious, he pulled back and informed the others.

"She's not out front. There are only a couple unconscious guards on the stairs. We've already checked both sides and the back. The only other places she could be are in the city or somewhere inside the keep. We know she went into the city at least once, but we haven't seen her come back.

176

Then again, we haven't been watching the entire time, either." There was a moment of silence as they pondered the possibilities.

"From what Zane described, she was running pretty fast," Kari said. "I think that it's most likely she was planning to stay in the city for quite some time. She may have even gone to retrieve *more* rebellious soldiers! You remember the one we found inside… maybe she's planning an invasion!" Their eyes widened as they realized what they could be dealing with in the very near future.

Suddenly, Mikal had an inspiration. "Wait a minute! Listen to this, guys: We think that she's probably gone to get some soldiers to help her fight, soldiers are generally men, and men like to eat. A lot." A sly grin began forming on his face.

Samuel, catching on to what he was thinking, started as well. "Especially when that food is from a castle they think they've defeated."

Ruth, Zane, and Kari were still in the dark about the whole subject.

"Soooo… what's your big epiphany?" Ruth asked.

Mikal began making motions with his hands, really getting into the explanation. "I say we set out a whole bunch of food in the Great Hall and make it look like we left in a hurry! The soldiers will be so busy eating that they won't even see us sneaking up behind them!" Mikal grinned excitedly at his genius.

"But wait! The plan isn't complete yet." Ruth put in, an idea popping into her head. "We need something else for it, and I know just the thing!" She waited for the others to take the bait and ask.

"What?" Zane asked, to get it over with.

"There's a certain tree that I saw when we were walking in the courtyard. It's a laxative."

Following this announcement, there was a simultaneous chorus of "ohh's" and "eww's" from the others in the group.

"Wow, Ruth," Samuel remarked. "That's pretty rough... but I guess they *would* be trying to pillage the castle. What's this plant called?"

"It's called cascara, and I've used it before. Don't ask."

"Guys," Zane whispered, a warning tone in his voice. "There's somebody there!"

While they had been conversing, an unseen soldier had wandered through the front gate of the castle and was quickly ascending the stairway to the keep. As he paused in front of the double doors at the top of the steps, the man noticed something strange. Poking out from behind the corner of the keep was something small and brown. He leaned in closer to see what it was, when all of a sudden it moved out of sight.

The soldier only saw it for a fleeting moment, but in those few short seconds, he had been able to identify it: A sheath. His heart began to thump as thoughts of the unknown raced through his head. The soldier turned on his heel and dashed back down the steps, leaping over an unconscious guard in the process. His arms pumping wildly, he sprinted out of the gate and disappeared.

Samuel relaxed against the rough stone he had been pressing his back into. "Great. He saw us. Well, we'd better be *very* fast in setting this whole thing up." He felt his leadership beginning to show its face once more. "Ruth, you take Kari and go get the plant. The three of us will go to the Main Hall and set up our 'abandoned meal.' We're boys, so we know how to be messy." Ruth grinned and stood up, Kari following her example. They turned and began running towards the jumble of trees at the back of the keep.

"Well guys, its time to make a mess."

Ciath slowly walked in front of the few lines of men she had ready to storm the castle. She had positioned them in a dark alley behind her large, hidden headquarters. They were amateur fighters but would work for what she had in mind.

The enchantress planned to send them into the huge keep ahead of her to kill anyone she had missed with the sleeping poison. Then, she would seek out the king and kill him, taking his throne for herself. A crooked smile stretched across her deathly pale face.

Suddenly, a malicious voice broke into her thoughts. *"You will not be the one on the throne, Ciath!"* It spat. *"Without me, you would not even be in this position!"*

The enchantress harumpphed. It was useless to reason with the voice. It always won.

As she was griping to herself, a soldier reeled into the alley, redfaced and gasping for air.

"**What? What is it?!**" She shouted, taking out her annoyance on the ignorant man.

"Mah lady... huh huh... it was at da castle... huh huh... thar were people still awok!"

"**Ughh! Your incompetence amazes me sometimes! Skyrcoh, Garimec!**" She yelled the names of the two captains.

The two armored men rushed forward, ready to carry out her bidding.

"**Are your men ready to march?**"

"Yes, ma'am!" They replied simultaneously.

"**Good. Lead them to the front entrance of the castle and ignore any citizens. Most of them should be inside at this hour. I will be following behind.**"

Ciath watched distractedly as the captains organized their troops and marched forward into the streets of Kogincheir. She was thinking of what the scout had said about people still awake. *The only ones that I didn't poison were the ones in the dungeon and the king! There couldn't have been... wait a minute... they must have escaped! Rrrr! Those... kids! I will have them dead by the end of this day, I swear!*

Samuel set a strange pot of meat on the table, leaving it tipped haphazardly to the side. He stepped back to survey their work. Food was spread all over the table, some of it untouched, but most of it spilled sloppily. He and the other two boys had found a stockpile of various dishes of food in the back of the kitchen that had probably been prepared for supper that night. Hopefully, they would still have a supper.

180

The girls should be back any moment now, he thought to himself.

As if on cue, Ruth and Kari ran through the doors, panting and holding two sacks filled with leaves.

"Where'd you find the sacks?" Mikal asked curiously.

"There was an unconscious servant holding them," Kari replied, trying to catch her breath. "He was probably picking fruit."

"How are we going to use the leaves?" Ruth inquired. Although she had come up with the idea, she was unsure as to how they would make them unnoticeable among the food.

Samuel took the bags from her and said, "We'll crush them into small bits and sprinkle them over the food. The soldiers will hopefully think they're herbs." He handed the sacks to Zane, who had just come out of the kitchen to put more settings on the table.

"Zane, can you crush these leaves into small pieces? They need to be tiny enough to look like seasonings."

Zane nodded, set the bowl he was carrying on the table, and unstrapped the gigantic mace from his back. "I found the two cooks in the kichun and I put 'em in a closet so they wouldn't be hurt." With that, he dumped the two bags on the floor and began pounding the green leaves ruthlessly with his weapon.

Well, whatever works, Samuel thought.

After they had finished sprinkling the smashed bits of cascara over the food, Mikal asked Samuel what they should do next. Samuel was surprised that even *Mikal* deferred to his judgement. He vowed silently to do his best at leading the group.

"We need to get ready for an ambush," Samuel began. "Once they've found the food and eaten it, we may have to wait an hour or so for the laxative to set in. When that happens, we should be hidden near the latrines. We can attack them as they run past us. Anyone have any questions?"

Kari raised her hand. "I have one: Why are we being so crude?"

Samuel shrugged, grinning. "Well... would you rather be taken prisoner and tortured, or give our enemies digestive issues?"

"Yeah... good point."

"Then let's go!" They tromped out of the room, nervous but also excited for the impending skirmish.

"Halt!"

The order rang through the evening air as the small battalion came to a standstill in front of the towering keep.

Garimec and Skyrcoh walked up the front steps and pushed the motionless guards out of their way with their feet. Skyrcoh, a stocky brute with a long, white scar on his arm, turned around to face the assembly of soldiers standing motionless in the fading light. A thrill of excitement shot through his body as he hefted his massive battleaxe and gazed at the legion of men.

The sun was just disappearing behind the trees that protruded off of the many hills outside the city, casting an orange glow over the valley.

"Men!" Skyrcoh yelled at the top of his lungs, not caring who heard him. Most of the knights in the keep were incapacitated, anyway.

"Your orders are to kill anyone you come across!" He shouted. "The only exception is the king! If you see the king, let him alone. He is not to be touched by any one of you! You must leave his demise to our mistress, Ciath. Do you understand?" His men roared their assent, ready for the attack to begin.

Skyrcoh cleared his throat and lifted his huge axe into the air. "CHARGE!" The mob of soldiers cheered, brandishing their weapons. He motioned to Garimec, who rushed towards the the closed doors, slamming his beefy shoulder against them. Shattering instantly, they flew off their hinges and landed on the floor in a heap of wood and iron. He flexed his powerful biceps, made a feral snarling noise, and stomped into the halls of the castle, a gleaming broadsword clutched in his powerful grip.

The band of soldiers rushed through the disfigured doorframe, thirsty for blood. They left the servants and knights that were already unconscious where they lay as they stormed through the castle, searching for their prey.

Ngylin, a mercenary from Racous, led a gang of men from his country through the maze of hallways. He burst through a small door and found himself in a magnificent chamber. It was lined with ornate banners and had chandeliers hanging from the ceiling. There were three doors in the room, each on a different wall.

"Le's go dis way!" One of his men shouted. He was pointing at the door to Ngylin's left.

"Yeh! Get de uders!" Ngylin yelled for all his men to follow him through the tall doors. To his surprise, they were unlocked.

When the scraggly group of mercenaries shoved them open and burst in, they were astounded at what they saw.

Before them were what looked to be the remains of a great feast. There was food all over the table, much of it spilled every which way. The chairs were pushed out, as if whoever had been sitting in them left in a hurry.

"Men, we got arrselves a feast!" Ngylin exclaimed. "Le's eat!" He and his soldiers rushed to the table and grabbed whatever food they could find, stuffing it indiscriminately into their mouths.

"Dose hard rations are nutin' compar'd ta dis!" One of his men declared.

Before long, more soldiers began barging into the room and devouring the food. The meal on the table disappeared quickly.

Some of the men found the door to the kitchen, and shortly afterwards, the cooking area was overrun with sweaty soldiers.

Ngylin and his friends thought that this was their best expedition ever. They had never found this much food left behind before.

Soon, however, they would discover that the huge feast was not exactly what it seemed.

20

...

Confrontation

"They should be here any moment," Ruth said impatiently. "In the *past* it wasn't very long before the plant took effect."

They had been waiting for at least an hour. The sun was fully down now, and it was completely dark outside. Ruth's legs were getting tired from standing, so she paced back and forth across the step she was on.

They were hiding a little way up the stairs to the right of the bathroom. If they had gone all the way up, then they would be on the wall walk that stretched around the top of the keep. Samuel guessed that this staircase led up to one of the four turrets.

"Here they come," Ruth whispered, hearing footsteps pounding down the hall. "I almost feel sorry for them... but I *am* glad they found the latrines."

Samuel peeked around the corner, moving slowly and inconspicuously so the men wouldn't see him. Fortunately, they were in too much of a rush to notice.

Soldiers were racing into the tiny room, each one trying to sit on the privy before the others. Although utterly disgusting, it was entertaining in some aspects.

No more soldiers were running down the hall. They were all in the small bathroom, fighting amongst themselves for their turn on the privy. Shouts and curses sounded from the room, and a rancid smell began seeping out of the open doorway.

In a moment of inspiration, Samuel stood up from his hiding place and walked to the door. Shutting it behind the clamorous mob, he picked up a large slab of wood that was usually used to prop it open. He stuck it in front of the door, securing the wood between it and the floor, which made it extremely difficult to escape.

"Great idea, Samuel!" Zane said, understanding his tactics. "Now they won't be able to git out!"

"And it'll also be a while before they find out that they're locked in," Mikal commented, approving Samuel's stroke of genius.

"Well," said Ruth, surveying the blocked door. "It's cruel, but effective."

Wondering where the king was and what hovel he had taken refuge in, Ciath watched men in full battle armor rush past her.

Before the attack started, she had infiltrated the king's mind. She warned him of his coming fate, and had convinced him that resistance was futile. She chose not to poison him because she wanted the privilege of killing him while he was awake.

Being the coward that she knew he was, King Nunor had shrunk away from her and eventually fled to a safer place in the keep. She had searched many rooms already, but the one in which he was currently hiding she had yet to find.

The enchantress walked around a corner and peered carefully down the long hall in front of her. As she slowly traversed its length, Ciath sensed a presence behind one of the many doors. She followed her supernatural instinct and turned towards the entryway directly to her left.

With inhuman strength, she bashed the heel of her grotesque palm into the center of the door, punching a hole through its wood. She reached through the opening she had made and opened the door from the inside. Ciath scrutinized the interior of the room.

It was a fairly large chamber, although smaller than the vast halls at the foremost part of the keep. In front of her was a large, metal gate that was implanted in the center of the back wall. Behind the iron bars was a dark, cave-like room, the interior of which she could not see.

As she observed her surroundings, a cowering man who was hiding in the corner of the dark room lifted a short crossbow to his shoulder. He took aim at the enchantress's pale face, let out his breath, and fired.

Ciath sensed movement to her left and swiveled on her heel with extreme speed. She heard a familiar click and ducked down to the ground. There was a clattering sound above her. The shooter of the crossbow had missed and hit the stone wall.

She stood up quickly and strode towards the huddled figure in the corner, filled with rage at the incompetent archer's attempt at assassination. She pulled a small vial out of her belt and threw it against the wall, shattering it.

A ball of fire erupted from the wall and hung in the air, illuminating the room.

In the new light, she could see that the character in front of her was, in fact, King Nunor.

"**Well, well, Nunor**," she chuckled throatily. "***I'd say you need to brush up on your shooting skills.***"

The terrified monarch stood up to his full height in a burst of reckless courage.

"Get away from here! This is *my* kingdom, and YOU WON'T TAKE IT FROM ME!" He yelled the last words in her face and used her surprise to dart away to the other side of the room, near the barred gate.

Unfortunately, Ciath was still partly blocking the door, deeming any escape attempt futile.

"***Nunor, do you realize that you have no hope? There is no hero who will foil my plan and stop me.***" She strode closer to him with every word. "***I will take control of this land, making your subjects into slaves. Your wife and daughter will be my personal servants, and they will be tortured at any sign of rebellion.***" King Nunor tried to keep a look of defiance on his face, but as she spoke, it slowly melted away, replaced by an expression of pure terror.

"***Don't you get it, Nunor? You are hopeless! There is no one who can save you now! Not even those worthless children you were training!***"

Ciath slowly raised her hand into the air, a black potion held between her fingers. She constricted her hand around it and crushed it, the glass shards tinkling onto the floor. The black fluid slowly dripped out of her clenched fist.

Before any drops could fall, however, the liquid hardened into an ebony, rock-like substance, taking the form of a razor-edged knife. Ciath grinned, eager to complete her bloodthirsty task.

The king sank to the floor and scooted as far away from her as possible. He knew that his end was near, but there was nothing he could do about it.

Before the execrable enchantress could plunge her blade downward, she sensed something behind her. Ciath whirled around to face whoever it was, when something smacked her hand and knocked her newly-created knife onto the floor. It shattered instantly.

Standing defiantly in front of her, was a little, old man. He had a mere wisp of white hair atop his head and a short, scraggly beard.

"Ya don't touch 'im, ya hear? "E's *my* king, and I won't let no scum like you meddle with *my* king!"

Letting out a rage-filled scream, Ciath slashed downwards with her black talons... but the old man wasn't there.

With unnatural coordination and flexibility, Shem leapt into the air, flipping over the enchantress's head and chopping backwards with his foot, striking her in the side of the head.

Ciath cried out in pain and lunged at her foe, deadly talons extended threateningly.

Shem bent his back, watching the enchantress's gnarled hands fly over his head, and kicked upward, hitting her wrist with a sickly crack.

She screamed and withdrew her arm. With white-hot anger, she struck down at the short man with her claws, pulling back and lunging with the other hand at the last moment.

Shem, not expecting this turn of events, leapt directly into Ciath's grasp, feeling her razor-sharp talons slide into his torso. He gasped and shuddered at the uncommon warmth that was filling his body. He fell backwards and hit the ground with a thud, a red stain soaking through his plain, white shirt.

"Noooo!" A voice yelled from the doorway to the room.

Ciath whipped around and snarled. Standing aghast in front of her were the five wretched children. *"So you've decided to reveal yourselves! How wonderful!"*

She yanked a dagger from her belt and slashed it from side to side, threatening the attackers to keep them away from her, while she fished in her belt for a potion. Her hand closed around one that was producing a small amount of heat.

She pushed the fallen Shem aside with her monstrous foot and pulled the vial out of its holder, flinging its contents at the encroaching youths.

It splattered the ground in front of Zane, emitting an eerie, orange glow.

Within seconds, it erupted into a massive pillar of flames.

The large boy was thrown back by the power of the explosion and hit his head on the floor. He lay on the ground, unmoving.

"Zane!" Samuel yelled. His friend's body lay motionless. With a newly imbued anger, Samuel lashed out at Ciath with his sword.

She dodged the swipe and backed up to where Zane was lying, blocking his body from them. She faced the four of them and cackled maniacally, tossing another potion at them.

They scattered quickly as a blue ooze sizzled on the floor where the bottle had shattered. Samuel backed up against the iron gate, watching the bubbling pool.

Steam rose from the blue substance as the stone slabs underneath it dissolved into a gritty mush. The remnants of the sludge fell through the floor and into the room below with a disgusting splat.

As Samuel turned his attention back to the enchantress, he heard a very familiar noise behind him, like a mix between a hiss and a snarl.

He leapt from the gate and gaped at what was now standing in front of him.

The king, who had been hiding by the bars, also scrambled away hurriedly.

Even Ciath was staring in horror at the monstrosity behind the gate.

Before them stood the Night Guard, the horrific Spider Hound that had chased them into the keep just yesterday.

The creature screeched in wrath and slammed its body into the metal bars, excited by the smell of Shem's blood.

Using the Spider Hound as a distraction, Ciath jerked another chemical solution out of her belt and cast it at Kari, who was standing nearest to the enchantress.

Fortunately, Kari had excellent ears, and she heard the slight clinking of the glass bottle against Ciath's belt.

She pivoted on her heel and, in a moment of instinctive reflexes, snatched the whirling bottle out of the air.

Ciath swore under her breath and watched the hand Kari now held the bottle in. Everyone else had overcome their awe at the screeching Spider Hound and was trying to surround the enchantress.

She lashed out at them with her gleaming claws.

They leapt nimbly out of the way of the whistling knife each time she struck. Slowly circling Ciath, each warrior was devising a plan of attack.

One by one, the team of combatants struck out at her with their weapons.

As if on some unspoken command, the line in front of her split apart. Ciath wondered why they had opened a way for her to escape. That seemed foolish.

Before she could bolt through the narrow gap towards the crouching king, Ciath felt a heavy impact on her backside, which launched her into the air, screaming.

Zane, who she thought was unconscious, had been awake the whole time. He had planted himself in a position where he could use both his feet to hurl the enchantress into the air. Since she had her back to him most of the time, he used those moments to his advantage and signaled to the king.

Although he was a terrible warrior, King Nunor realized that he could play a part in this battle too.

Slowly, the king snuck over to the wooden crank on the wall and using all of his strength, turned it, causing the heavy iron bars to rise creakily. The Spider Hound screeched and snarled, trying to fit its ugly head underneath the rising gate.

It was in that moment that Zane had kicked Ciath into the air, launching her straight under the bars and into the gruesome Night Guard's cage. King Nunor let go of the crank, which spun backwards and slammed the huge gate shut.

Ciath screamed in a terror she had never felt before, scrambling to get away.

The malnourished Spider Hound pounced on her viciously and sunk its fangs into her flesh, tearing at her body.

The enchantress let out an ear-piercing shriek and looked up at the young warriors, her mangled body falling limp.

To their utter astonishment, a bright red mist streamed out of her eyes, mouth, and every pore on her body. It congealed together to form a floating mass of red, hovering mysteriously in the air.

There was a dazzling flash of light, and a slithering voice unlike anything they had ever heard echoed through the air.

"You wretched children! Beware! Your time is coming!"

With those horrible words, there was another bright flash, and it was gone.

21

...

The First Mission

It had been many months since the "Battle of the Enchantress."

King Nunor had passed off her strange demise as "her life essence dissolving and dispersing, letting her final thoughts flow free." Whether or not this was an accurate description, Samuel didn't know.

In the months that followed their victory, the actual facts of the battle had become skewed. People told the tale in a way that made it seem like the king had won the fight single-handedly. King Nunor was perfectly comfortable with this version, although when he had insisted that they be a larger part of the story, every one of them, even Mikal, had refused.

Samuel thought that being the hero in a tale would only cause the citizens of Aena to lionize him excessively, which was definitely not what he wanted. He could only imagine the embarrassment that would come with that kind of recognition. He was sure the others concurred.

In the aftermath of the battle, a feeling of gloominess had surrounded them. Yes, they had slain the wicked Ciath and saved the kingdom from impending anarchy, but there had been many losses.

Samuel thought back to the dark night of the confrontation. He remembered seeing her black talons piercing Shem's body. He was filled with anguish as he thought of the kind, old man he had met so recently. Through it all, one bold maxim seemed to stand out among all their victories: "In battle, there is always death."

He remembered kneeling next to the gaunt old man and hearing his breath rasping in his throat, the red stain on his shirt growing much too large. He had held Shem's head in his lap, ignoring the sounds of the others' voices around him. The feeble warrior had peered up as if looking through a thick fog. His eyes had focused on Samuel's face, sharpening suddenly and glinting a color so vivid human words could not describe it. He had grasped Samuel's hand in one of his and had spoken two, distinct words, "Mesabach Ochal." Then he breathed no more.

Samuel had asked many people what these words meant, but no one could tell him. It was as if the language in which they had been spoken did not exist. After months of trying to discern the meaning, he eventually gave up.

Following the battle, Samuel's parents had sent letters asking about his involvement in the now-famous story. He had told them the simple truth: His involvement was limited to only a few encounters with the enchantress, and in the end, it *was* the king who had opened the gate.

Directly after the skirmish, there had been a small ceremony honoring the five youth for their bravery and prowess in the battle. As a reward, they had each received a weapon of their choice, made specially by the castle armorers. Samuel had chosen a simple but sturdy longsword that had a balanced weight, a comfortable grip, and a hilt with a delicate gold sheen. It was the perfect weapon for him.

As life at the castle returned to normal, the young warriors' training continued. Each one of them grew in strength and ability, learning the tricks of the trade from their mentors. They learned the local history and folklore from the king himself, who willingly filled the empty hole that Shem had left. They spent almost an entire year fighting together, eating together, and learning together, all the while becoming closer as a team. Even more importantly, they became the best of friends.

Samuel was sitting in the Great Hall with his friends, digging into a steaming plate of roasted turnips and boiled turkey. They had just come inside and sat down to hear that this was to be their final meal in the castle. Their training was complete. The next morning, they would be setting out on their first mission for the king. Keeping to his usual tendencies, King Nunor abstained from revealing the details until after they finished eating.

He had also informed them that messages would be sent to their parents to explain the situation, but those missives would not include any explicit information.

It was now nearing the end of the meal, and all of them were eager for the announcement of their first mission.

Samuel had a feeling of nostalgia as he remembered the night almost a year ago when they had been excited and ready to begin their training. He smiled to himself. If only he had known the mental and physical exertion that lay ahead of him, maybe he would have been less so.

Wiping his face with a scarlet napkin, King Nunor stood and addressed his trainees. "You have all come a long way since you arrived here at the castle, and I am very proud of you." He smiled at them fondly. "But let's cut all the fluff and get down to business."

Samuel hid a grin at the king's characteristic colloquial attitude.

"Since you are my specialty team, I am going to be assigning you to important missions that only *you* can accomplish. This first mission has to do with the brewing rebellion in Yamal. I assume I've told you about that before?"

They nodded their heads.

"Good, because your task has to do with snuffing this rebellion." He began to go into greater detail.

"The, shall we say, "country" of Yamal is one gigantic fortress. The original Province was much bigger than it is now, but the new country is covered by the massive fortifications they call "Ratkon Fortress." It's huge and almost completely indestructible. Behind its gate sit many legions of trained warriors that their king, Ogrion, has amassed over the years. The problem is, the gate can only be opened from the inside. It was crafted thousands of years ago out of a very strong combination of minerals, and the first Ogrion took this knowledge to his grave."

Zane interrupted. "So you want us to break in?"

"Oh no!" King Nunor said, shaking his head. "I would never ask you to do such a thing. You'd be killed before you even made it to the gate! Now... let's see... ah yes! The front gate is not the only entrance. There is rumor of a secret passageway that leads straight into the fortress's keep. The unfortunate thing, however, is that the location of this secret entrance is unknown." He saw their looks of confusion and explained.

"The door to Ratkon Fortress must be opened by a key, and there is only one key that can do that. It is called 'the key to Yamal.'" King Nunor rubbed his eyes and then continued. "From facts I've obtained from various spies, I learned that this key is split into two halves, each half hidden in a different place."

As the king explained everything, Samuel watched his face. There was something not quite right about what the king was telling them, but he just couldn't place it.

Mikal, who was starting to understand, asked, "You want us to get the key?"

"Precisely!" King Nunor exclaimed. "I want you to get the key and bring it back to the castle so we have the means to enter Ratkon Fortress." He nodded at Mikal and then rubbed his eye again.

Wait a minute... that eye-rubbing he's doing... is he... lying? Samuel watched the king's face closely.

"But where are the halves hidden?" Ruth asked.

"I was just getting to that." Nunor sat down again, for his legs were starting to ache from standing for so long.

"The first half is hidden somewhere in the Evis Ocean, on a mysterious island. This island is extremely hard to find, and only the natives of Velendaw know its location. The citizens of that country call it the Realm of Y. It is said that an ancient being, who gives sage advice to anyone who asks, lives there." King Nunor's hands were unmoving in his lap.

"The second half is said to be kept by the Dragons of the North, three magnificent creatures that live at the peak of Vanguard Mountain."

The king hadn't moved his hands at all during this short lecture, so he must have been telling the truth.

While he watched the king's face, Samuel realized that King Nunor was nervous. Creases marked the monarch's forehead and unobtrusive drops of sweat dotted his face.

"I don't know how you're going to do it, but I suppose you'll figure something out." The king said, rubbing his eye again.

Wow. How flattering.

"Well... are you up for it?" King Nunor looked around at the youthful faces in front of him. "I mean, if you aren't, you still have to go, but that's beside the point. How about this: Are you ready?"

Samuel couldn't help feeling excited, despite the king's mood. He stood up and pushed his chair back. "I think I need to pack."

Samuel sat on his bed, looking around at the room that had been his home for the past ten months. The torch flickered on the wall, casting a soft glow throughout the room. The sounds of the bustling citizens outside had long since faded away with the fall of night. Everything was still and peaceful, and for that, Samuel was glad.

Here he was, sitting on his bed, with his first mission for the king the next day. It seemed as if the whole world had opened up before him, as if he was going to be truly free. The sadness of leaving this home behind drew upon his soul, but the excitement of setting out into the unknown world pushed away that sorrow.

Sighing to himself, Samuel stood up and walked slowly over to the dancing flames of the torch. He stared at their ethereal beauty, each tongue of flame lasting for a fraction of a second. It made him melancholy to think of how pointless the short life of a flame must be... only a flash of light and heat before it was gone forever. But then he realized that, when working together, the multitude of flames is transformed into a burning blaze, providing heat and light for the benefit of others.

That's what we are, Samuel thought philosophically. *Flames. We are all small in the overall scheme of things, but together we can make a difference.*

He solemnly lifted a rag soaked in water and laid it gently over the torch, extinguishing it. Samuel felt his way back to his bed and sat down, pulling the two wool blankets over his body. He laid his head back on the thin pillow and stared up at the ceiling, thoughts of the day ahead of him whirling through his mind.

Unnoticed by Samuel, a light breeze picked up outside of his window. It brushed across the stones outside, making quiet noises. The sounds picked up as it blew harder, forming an unnatural whispering cadence.

Samuel became restless with the increasing noise, as the hairs on the back of his neck prickled with unease. He closed his eyes and turned towards the wall, trying to block out the disturbing sounds of the eerie gusts.

The wind gushed rhythmically into his room, until its low intonation formed the recognizable pattern of a haunting voice, speaking one, hair-raising word that was emblazoned into Samuel's mind for the remainder of the night:

"*Beware.*"

And then it was gone.

Part 2

The Realm of Y

22

...

Ambush

The horses plodded along the rutted path, walking at an easy pace. The five tired warriors could not see any end to the winding road, and it was nearing nighttime.

They had been riding through a section of woods known as the Crimson Forest. Back at the castle, King Nunor had told them that this particular area had a reputation for housing thieves and murderers. Nevertheless, the eager cadets had been confident that they could handle a few bands of robbers. So far, all had been quiet.

Kari shifted in the saddle. Before they left, the king had instructed them to ride to Shala Province, where they could find a ship to take them to Velendaw. They had been riding almost nonstop since then and were exhausted.

Although the poor horses were doing most of the work, Kari's legs burned as if she had been walking the whole way. The hard, leather saddle dug into her backside, making her feel sore all over. Her shoulders were also aching, for she had been carrying her small satchel on her back the entire time. The king had not been able to spare a pack mule.

Another discomfort they had to endure was the food. Besides berries and the occasional rabbit or squirrel, they had been surviving on dried fruit, dried meat, and hard bread that tasted like leather.

"Ohh," Mikal groaned. "I wonder if we'll *ever* make it to civilization."

"I know," Samuel agreed, letting his head droop down. "We've been riding for days, and I haven't seen anybody except for that wagon we passed a few hours ago."

Ruth, who didn't want the boys' complaining to dampen their spirits, exclaimed, "Would you please stop whining?! We'll get there soon enough!"

They shut up, and the group rode in silence for a while.

As they rounded a corner, Mikal smelled something that he had not smelled in many months, something that excited his nerves and awakened his senses.

"Hey, guys, do you smell that?" He asked, a light of anticipation shining in his eyes.

Kari sniffed the air. It smelled different than normal, but she couldn't tell why. "Yeah. What is it?"

"That, my friends," Mikal said, spreading his hands dramatically, "is the smell of seawater! We're in Shala, my home Province! I don't recognize this road, but there might be a town around the next bend!"

His guess proved to be incorrect, however. All they saw were more trees. Not discouraged, Mikal kept a sharp eye out for civilization.

After many other twists and turns, they finally came upon the first signs of life.

"Look!" said Zane suddenly, pointing down the road. "There's a house!"

Sure enough, a small shack was nestled in the forest a little way off the road. Although it looked abandoned from afar, they could make out the faint puffs of smoke seeping from the cracked chimney as they rode closer.

"Let's ask how far it is to the nearest town," Samuel suggested when they arrived next to the shanty. He dismounted his dappled mare and strode up a small trail that led to the house, not waiting for the others.

Kari told the others to stay put and ran to catch up with Samuel. When she reached him, they strolled casually up to the dilapidated cabin.

Kari stepped up on the creaking porch and knocked firmly on the old door, the soft wood flexing unnaturally beneath her knuckles. She felt a sharp stab of pain as a stray splinter embedded itself in her finger. She pulled out the sliver of wood, threw it aside, and folded her hands behind her back, waiting for the owner of the house.

After a couple moments of waiting in the chilly autumn air, the door swung open, revealing a short man with a scruffy beard and a suspicious look on his face. His bald head reflected the light of a warm fire blazing inside. When Kari looked at him, she noticed a black tattoo inscribed on the man's forehead. It depicted an eye-like shape with one horizontal and two vertical lines slashing through it.

When the man saw who was at his door, his expression turned dour and gruff.

"Whad'ya want?" He barked menacingly, closing the door so only a small crack remained.

"Excuse me, sir. I just wanted to ask how far it is to the next town." Kari tried her best to be polite to the rude stranger.

"'Bout a mile, as the hawk flies." The heavyset man slammed the door in their faces, evidently wanting to get back to his own business.

Samuel and Kari turned away and walked quickly down the path to the others. When they returned, they told Zane, Mikal, and Ruth about the brusque man and his comment on the distance to the next town.

"Is everyone here like that?" Kari asked Mikal after they had remounted.

He shrugged. "It depends. Some are, some aren't."

Great, she thought sarcastically. *This is going to be a fun trip.*

As the horses plodded steadily down the dusty road, Kari was immersed in her own thoughts and neglected to notice several sets of beady eyes peering out at the small party from the brush.

It had been about an hour since they found the cabin. The rough man had obviously lied to them, and their muscles were aching.

The horses were approaching a sharp bend, and Samuel was beginning to wonder if there were any towns around.

An odd chill suddenly ran down his spine, and the hair on the back of his neck prickled, standing on end. Samuel had the unnerving sensation they were being watched, as a cold feeling washed over him.

He turned around in his saddle and motioned for the others to stop, scanning his surroundings. *There's something here... I can feel it.*

"Wha...?" Zane began, but Samuel quickly shushed him and scrutinized the forest.

As he stared at the dense shadows underneath the trees, something caught his eye: A glimmer of light on metal.

Without warning, the forest erupted, and a dozen men garbed in dark clothing leapt at the small group.

Startled, Samuel leapt off of his horse and drew his sword, adrenaline beginning to course through his body.

The bandits attacking them were obviously amateurs looking for easy prey. Samuel could tell by the clumsy way they wielded their weapons. He and the others had only been given about a year of training, which wouldn't seem like much to an inexperienced eye. However, they had one advantage. They had been trained by experts.

With the battle reflexes Brusall had hammered into him, Samuel whipped his sword around and slashed at the bandit nearest to him. His quick strike scored a thin slice on his adversary's arm.

Samuel heard him shout in surprise at the unexpected blow. In retaliation, the man swung his small battle-axe.

Knowing that a sword could not counter a battle-axe, Samuel swayed his body to the side so the man's weapon would fall short.

With powerful momentum behind the swing, the battle-axe buzzed through the air and was deeply embedded in the ground. As the bandit tugged at his weapon, Samuel swung his sword downward for the killing blow.

When he withdrew his sword and looked towards the other bandits that were running around, Samuel felt a wave of nausea sweep over him. He stared shakily at the corpse at his feet, at the scarlet liquid staining his sword. With a shudder of complete revulsion at what he had done, Samuel threw up.

He wiped his mouth and looked at the battle raging before him. The others seemed completely fine. They were fighting with all their might, never letting the enemy gain an advantage.

As he watched his friends battle, Samuel decided that if he was going to keep his life, he was going to have to fight.

With a feeling of regret in his heart, Samuel leapt into the wild fray, slashing, dodging, and swiping with finesse that couldn't be taught.

The skills he had practiced for many months came to him naturally, and he put them to use. Although repulsed, he fought expertly, deflecting any blow the bandits attacked him with and instantly reacting with a swipe or stab of his own.

With a sixth sense, Samuel whirled around in time to see an unexpected sight that aroused a feeling of dread in the pit of his stomach.

There, standing on the side of the road and taking shelter under a tree, was a crossbowman aiming a quarrel directly at Samuel.

The frightened boy stood frozen in place, his panicked mind not knowing what to do.

For the sake of self-preservation, he willed himself to move. Samuel lunged to the side in a feeble attempt to avoid the aim of the deadly bolt.

Instead of landing solidly on the ground, however, Samuel felt a sharp jolt of pain as his foot twisted beneath him, getting caught underneath the body of a fallen bandit.

He landed heavily on his back, knives of pain streaking through his hurt ankle. Out of the corner of his eye, Samuel saw the man with the crossbow adjust his aim slightly.

Trying desperately to evade the coming shot, Samuel struggled to heave himself behind the bodies of a couple dead bandits. Although pain was shooting through his twisted ankle, he managed to roll in a way that placed a black-cloaked corpse between him and the archer.

A tall, muscular thief screamed in fury at Ruth, who was battling him skillfully with a long dirk. The man stepped backwards to avoid one of her blows and landed his foot directly on Samuel's hurt ankle.

The unfortunate youth cried out in agony as the heavy man slipped on his ankle and fell to the ground. His huge boot had twisted Samuel's foot the other way, causing Samuel unbearable agony.

Ruth took his fall to her advantage and pounced on the large man, driving her knife into his heart.

At that moment, when Samuel was in utmost anguish, the man with the crossbow pulled the trigger.

23

...

The Town

In slow motion, the bolt traveled its deadly path towards Samuel's chest. Incapacitated, he tried ineffectively to evade the shot, knowing all the while that it was useless.

As his life flashed before him, Samuel hoped that his parents would get over their grief of his passing. His wide eyes were plastered on the finger of death streaking through the air in his direction. He braced himself, waiting for the inevitable.

Suddenly, a flashing object whizzed through the air and intercepted the lethal projectile. The quarrel was knocked off course, falling harmlessly to the ground.

The object that had deflected the crossbow bolt stuck quivering, deeply embedded in a large fir tree.

It was a knife.

Ruth jogged calmly to the tree and retrieved her weapon. Samuel watched as the crossbowman kneeling near the edge of the forest struggled to cock his weapon again, heaving on the tense cord.

With deadly accuracy, Ruth pivoted on her heel and slung her knife end over end at the panicked man. He emitted a quickly silenced yelp of pain as the razor-sharp blade slammed into his chest, killing him.

After she had retrieved her weapon a second time, Ruth hurried over to Samuel, who was lying on the ground, clenching his teeth in agony.

"Thanks," he managed to spit out before a sudden throb of pain streaked through his leg. He rolled over awkwardly onto his front and tried to stand up. He was unsuccessful and fell back to the ground in a heap.

"Lie still and don't move," Ruth said gently, kneeling down next to him. She pressed lightly on his ankle, and he shouted in surprise. "Your ankle is strained. It should be healed enough by tomorrow, but I need to make a splint so you can walk. It's going to hurt."

"Be careful!" Samuel managed to grunt.

"Yeah, yeah." She rummaged among the bodies for a moment, looking for something.

Finding what she was searching for, Ruth extracted a short javelin from the heap and snapped off two small sections of the shaft. She opened the small container that held her medical supplies and took out a long strip of cloth. Ruth placed the broken spear shafts on each side of Samuel's leg and wrapped the cloth around them and his ankle, being sure to keep it tight but comfortable.

Once she had finished securing the bandage to his leg, Ruth stood Samuel up carefully and helped him hobble slowly to his horse. He couldn't bend his foot because of the splint, making it hard for him to get saddled. However, with some help from the others, he was able to mount.

Mikal, Kari, and Zane had dragged the bodies off the road and laid them in a small pile in the woods next to the trail.

Although the bandits had been enemies, Samuel was sad that they had to die. He had always thought that being a knight would be honorable and filled with chivalry, that he would feel proud after defeating his opponents.

What he felt now, though, was not pride. Samuel's heart was heavy for the men's lives he had just destroyed. He wondered if he would ever overcome that guilty feeling. It was doubtful.

Mikal, who was feeling the same remorse as Samuel, said glumly, "Let's move on, guys."

With that, the tired horses started slowly plodding down the trail.

After several minutes of silent riding, Samuel looked up from his thoughts and peered down the long stretch of road in front of him. There was something there, something that was not part of the seemingly endless forest.

He strained his eyes to see what lay there. Although it was very far away, Samuel had good vision, and he could just make out a patch of stout buildings. They had obviously been there a while, for they were overgrown with vines and shrubbery.

"Hey, guys!" Samuel exclaimed, a feeling of excitement growing inside him. "I see a town!"

"I'll have an ale! And put it on Flen's tab!"

The lanky man behind the bar acknowledged the boisterous customer and grabbed a tankard from the shelf. After filling it to the brim with a brown, foamy liquid, he handed it to the beefy man, who drank deeply.

The tavern was loud this afternoon. All the off-duty stevedores had gathered there during their break to have a drink before the next round of cargo hauling.

However, not all of the people sitting in the room were working men. Some were the regulars. They were known around town to spend hours upon hours drinking themselves into oblivion every day, leaving their poor wives and children to fend for themselves.

The blond-haired bartender looked up as he heard a louder than normal ruckus in the corner of the room, disturbing the comfortable atmosphere of his tavern. Two of the burly dock workers had risen and were yelling curses at each other, shaking their fists in rage. One of them started with a tiny shove, then the other with a bigger shove, until it slowly progressed to an all out, rolling on the floor fistfight.

"Hey, you!" Someone pointed at the bartender, who was wiping down the counter with a ragged cloth. The slim but sturdy man was used to being addressed this way; not many people knew his real name. "You gonna do somethin' about this, or what?" The alcohol-toting customer gestured toward the squabble going on in the corner of the room.

With a sigh of annoyance, the muscled bartender reached down below the wooden counter and pulled out a huge, wooden club spotted with iron studs.

Hefting it over his shoulder, he strode through the throngs of yelling people until he reached the fight. Heaving in a deep breath, he shouted at the top of his lungs, his voice booming surprisingly loud for a man of his size.

"ENOUGH!"

With that one, powerful word, the entire room became as silent as night. Even the two fighters had the rage startled out of them by this unexpected outburst.

"There will be no fighting in my tavern! D'ya hear me?" The angry bartender yelled. "I said NO FIGHTING!" He shouted the last toward the faces of the two men who were still lying on the ground, stunned.

They jumped up from where they had been brawling and apologized sincerely, their eyes darting apprehensively toward the gigantic club.

"Good. Now go back to your drinking." The slender man returned to the bar and rolled his eyes. The aggressive drinkers who came to his tavern never seemed to remember the rules. Fortunately, he always had his club handy.

What his customers did not know was that he was a warrior. The club he had hidden under the bar was only for show. If there was ever a real fight, he had a secret cupboard on the wall behind him that held a razor-sharp sword. That was only if things turned really ugly.

Shaking his mop of blond hair out of his face, he went back to the menial tasks of a bartender. As he wiped some spilled ale off the counter, the front door to the inn opened. Hearing the creak of its hinges, he looked up to survey the newcomers.

When the bartender laid eyes upon them, he stared in disbelief at what he saw.

24

...

The Bartender

Mikal led the small group into the crowded tavern, scrutinizing the throngs of people clustered around various tables.

The bartender looked up from what he was doing, his eyes widening when he saw them. Mikal wondered if he was suspicious of their age. One didn't normally see people so young walking into a bar.

The confident youth made his way to the counter and addressed the bartender, who was a slim young man with a shaggy mop of blond hair and a pair of slightly crooked eyes.

"Excuse me, sir?" Samuel had made it very clear that Mikal must be polite. If he was rude to the people of this town, then the possibility of them being shunned would increase. Mikal had reluctantly agreed.

"Do you have a place where we can spend the night?" The tall warrior asked. "We can pay."

The man leaned against the counter and looked at them shrewdly. Mikal hoped with all his heart that he would relent and give them a room.

"What business are you kids on that led ya to here?" The bartender asked, studying their faces. He looked up at

Zane, whistling silently. *Dang.* When he saw Samuel, however, the slim man narrowed his eyes.

Mikal instantly replied, having been prepared for this sort of question. "We would like to keep that to ourselves, if you don't mind," he said mysteriously. "Now, do you have a room for us, or should we go ask elsewhere?"

The man smiled. It wasn't a warm smile, however. The expression on his face was more of a how-much-money-can-I-get-these-kids-to-pay-me look.

"I got rooms, but they're expensive," he began, confirming Mikal's suspicions. "I'll accept ten silver shards for a one-night's stay."

Mikal stepped back and allowed Kari to move forward. They had already established that she would do the bartering. When she was a small child, haggling over prices had been a game for her.

"We can't pay that much, and we're only staying for one night. Make it three."

"Sorry, but my deal stands at ten, and it's not moving." The bartender began wiping down his counter again.

She turned towards the others and said, "I guess we can't pay then. Come on, guys. Let's go find someplace cheaper." They followed her lead and began to walk through the crowd to the door.

Mikal felt a pang of disappointment. They had lost the bargain. There probably weren't any other inns in the town. They might end up sleeping in a shed somewhere!

Before he could think any more negative thoughts, however, a voice shouted from behind them.

"I'll make it six!"

To Mikal's surprise, Kari turned around and walked back to him, her face impassive. "Make it four."

"Five."

"Deal." Mikal watched her as she reached into a pouch on her belt and pulled out five silver shards. He marveled at her bartering ability. Even though he could be very disagreeable at times, he would never have been able to cut a deal in half by arguing for a couple minutes. He was very impressed at Kari's ability.

The shrewd girl placed the shards on the counter, but before the bartender could take them, she covered them with her hand and said, "Show us the room first. Then you get the money."

Mikal was once again in awe of her knowledge of how these sorts of things worked. *If the room is bad, then the bartender won't get the money!* He thought. *This way, he has to give us a good room! Wow, she's thought of everything!*

The bartender reluctantly agreed, realizing the willowy girl's motives. He walked from behind the counter to lead the five travelers up to the second floor of the inn, appointing one of his friends to monitor the tavern.

After making his way up the rickety staircase, the bartender opened one of the doors in the short hallway of the second floor.

"This is it!" he announced. "Satisfied?"

Kari inspected the medium-sized room, examining every detail. It was fairly clean for a roadside inn, and it looked the right size for the five of them to sleep in.

"Good enough." Kari placed the five silver shards in the bartender's hand, walked into the room, and set her satchel down on the bed.

Mikal and the other three followed her lead, walking into the room and setting their bags wherever there was space.

Ruth began taking the sheets off of the bed and creating a partition that would separate the girls from the boys, for privacy's sake.

The three boys began laying their blankets on the section of the floor closest to the door, while the girls took the back section of the room. No one wanted the bed. One never knows what lives there.

As he laid his sleeping blankets out on the floor, Samuel pondered the day's events. At the foremost of his brain was the bartender. He thought that he had recognized the slender man's voice, but he couldn't figure out why. He decided that he would go talk to him for a bit before going to bed.

Samuel looked up. The others had finished with their beds and were chatting about the long day's affairs.

"I'm going to go talk to the bartender," Samuel announced. "See if I can learn anything about where we are."

That was partly true, but he didn't want to tell them about the strange feeling he had until he was absolutely sure it was correct.

Samuel pushed open the thick door and walked down the creaking steps that led to the tavern below. His twisted ankle was still hurting, though not as badly as it had before. He could now walk comfortably with only a slight limp. Ruth's splint was working well.

Samuel pushed open a door at the bottom of the steps and walked through, shutting it quietly behind him.

Many people had left since he had gone upstairs. The bartender was still there, talking with a few customers and refilling drinks. The number of drinkers in the tavern was slowly decreasing.

Samuel sat at the bar for a while, observing the bartender and waiting until the last people had gone.

"See ya tomorrow, Flen!" The bartender waved at the last man leaving the building. He began wiping down the counter with his ever-present washrag, drying up puddles of spilled beer.

"Excuse me, sir," Samuel began, but the bartender interrupted him.

"I'm no sir, so don't say that. You can call me bartender, Mr. Bartender, or even 'hey you.' Just don't call me sir."

"Um, Mr. Bartender?" Samuel grimaced at the clumsiness of the name.

"Yeah?" He looked up from his scrubbing.

"My name is Samuel," he began, "and I was wondering if I could ask you a few questions." The bartender nodded his consent, still watching him closely.

"Where are you from?"

"And why would you need to know that?"

"I was just curious. Your voice sounds familiar to me, but I can't place where I might know you from."

"Well, curiosity kills the cat, and if it can kill a cat, it might kill you." He continued scrubbing the counter vigorously.

Samuel pondered this in silence for a moment. He wondered why the man was being so touchy. Then he had an epiphany. *What if the bartender recognizes me too?*

Keeping this thought to himself, Samuel tried again. "Why are you agitated?"

The bartender looked up from his work, annoyance plain on his face. "Why are you asking so many personal questions? If we knew each other, then I would recognize you, but I don't! So stop asking me!" He went back to wiping furiously.

Hearing a doubtful tone in the man's voice, Samuel asked a different question. "Are we in Shala Province?"

"Yeah." The bartender wondered why this was relevant.

"How far are we from the coast?"

He figured that this was a harmless question. "You've got probably two leagues until you reach it, continuing on this road."

That simple statement gave Samuel a feeling of triumph. With victory in his heart, he asked another question, completely sure that he was correct in his suspicion. This interrogation had become somewhat of a game.

"You're not from Aena, are you?"

"I thought you weren't going to ask personal questions!"

"Well, it doesn't matter anymore, because I already know you're not from Aena, or you at least spent a long time out of the country."

"What?" The bartender asked, shaking his long, blond hair out of his face. He was very confused now.

"In that last comment, you used the measurement of leagues, and in Aena we use miles. It was changed about ten years ago."

Samuel felt the thrill of success as the bartender cursed silently.

The man looked up and surveyed the intelligent boy in front of him. "Are you able to keep a secret?"

Samuel nodded, wondering what the man was getting at. "You seem like a good, trustworthy person, so I think it's safe for me to tell you my story. Besides, you'd probably figure it out anyway." They laughed, alleviating the tension they both felt. Samuel guessed that he must not have been angry with him; he was just nervous.

The now relaxed bartender held out his hand to Samuel, who shook it, grateful that they were able to act friendly towards each other.

With a smile, the man brushed his hair out of his face and introduced himself.

"My name is Rosh."

25

...

A Surprising Revelation

Samuel was shocked. He stared at the young bartender who was unaware of the importance of what he had said.

"Is something wrong?" Rosh asked when he noticed Samuel's open-mouthed expression.

"Is your name really Rosh?!" Samuel exclaimed.

"Um, yeah." The young man looked confused. He wondered if the kid in front of him had figured out how they knew each other.

"Did you use to live in Kaltoid Province?"

Rosh was taken aback. "How did you know that?!" This youth was really starting to unnerve him.

Samuel started pacing around the room, muttering to himself. He stopped in front of Rosh and studied his face.

"Yes, you do look like them!"

"Who? Who do I look like?! Why are you saying these things when I hardly even know you?!" Rosh stepped back and put a hand on the cupboard where he kept his sword.

Samuel realized that he had to explain himself to Rosh, who was obviously frightened and had no clue as to what was going on.

"My name is Samuel. I come from Kaltoid Province, and my parents' names are Marken and Lora. Sound familiar?"

Rosh's eyes widened as he realized the extent of what Samuel was saying. "You mean that we're… you know… like…?"

"Yes!" Samuel grasped Rosh's shoulders and started talking rapid-fire. "We're brothers! My parents told me that they had another child, but he was kidnapped by Groggers and was never seen again. They said his name was Rosh and he was taken when he was just ten years old, and…"

Rosh held out his shaking hands, trying to placate the enthusiastic boy. "Slow down there, Samuel. I know you're excited, but it's really late, and I… I need time to process everything you've told me. You should go to bed. Don't tell your friends about me. Wait until morning, when I can tell all of you my story." Rosh turned away and headed to the back of the tavern, where his sleeping quarters were.

Samuel reluctantly conceded and headed back up the stairs to his room for the night. Excited from his new discovery, he had a hard time sleeping, but his tired body eventually drifted off into a deep slumber, not to awaken until sunrise.

Rosh opened his eyes and sat up. It was morning, and rays of sunlight were shining through the crack underneath the door that led outside. The crisp morning air nipped at his ears and nose.

Rosh stood from his simple bed of blankets on the floor and quickly changed into his everyday clothes. He walked to the door and opened it, squinting in the bright sunlight.

From the position of the sun, he judged that it was about six o'clock in the morning. His bar opened at noon, so he would have plenty of time to talk to Samuel and his friends.

Through the night, Rosh had thought about all that had happened the previous day. *I have a brother!* Just thinking about that sent shivers running through his body. *And Mother and Father are alive!* During his travels, he wondered if they had survived all those years he had been gone. Now he knew that they had felt happiness again with the birth of Samuel.

Rosh heard the door to the second floor open behind him, and muffled footsteps padded towards where he had slept. Closing the door to the outside, he turned around and opened the one that led into the bar from his room. He made his way to the counter, where a bleary-eyed Samuel waited, yawning wide.

"Hello, *brother*," Rosh said, relishing in the pleasure of the word. "How did you sleep?"

"Just fine. My friends are only stirring upstairs, so it'll be a few minutes until we see them."

Rosh led Samuel to one of the tables in the bar and sat down. "While we have some time to ourselves, tell me what's going on back home. Are Mother and Father well?" He knew they were alive due to their previous conversation, but he didn't know if they were in good health.

Samuel assured him that they had been doing just fine the last time he saw them. He then began filling Rosh in on all the things that had happened at home in the time that the young man was gone.

By the time Samuel finished, the others had come downstairs and were milling about.

Rosh stood up from the wooden stool on which he had been sitting and addressed Samuel's friends.

"I don't have much food, but I think it will be enough to fill all of our bellies." He walked behind the counter and unlocked a small cupboard next to the racks of alcohol. Inside were various types of vegetables and bread, stacked in an organized fashion.

"This is what I've been living on. It will have to do. I don't often have boarders, so I don't keep extra on hand."

"It looks better than what *we've* been eating for the past week." Mikal stared at the food hungrily, already tasting it.

Rosh withdrew a loaf of bread and a few heads of cabbage out of the cupboard, setting them on the counter. He pointed at Samuel. "You, come divvy this out to your friends." He purposely didn't use the term "brother." He was waiting for the right moment to break the news to the others.

Samuel walked over to the loaf of bread and began digging in his pockets for his small knife. He had apparently misplaced it, for it was nowhere to be found.

Ruth, seeing his dilemma, whipped a dagger out of her belt and handed it to him.

"Has this been cleaned?" He asked, turning it over in his hands.

"Of course! Otherwise I wouldn't have handed it to you." She stood next to him as he sliced the bread and bounced lightly on her toes, waiting for him to finish.

While Samuel was slicing up the bread, Mikal noticed a problem. "Don't you have any meat?" He asked Rosh.

The young bartender smiled and shook his head. "I never keep meat around here. I can't stand it. I live on vegetables, bread, nuts, and the occasional piece of fruit. I can never handle the thought of eating another living creature."

"But it's not living anymore. It's dead."

"I just don't like the thought of it, okay?"

Mikal shrugged, although he was still somewhat disappointed over the loss of meat in his diet.

After they sat down to eat, Rosh and Samuel told them their news.

The effect was immediate. Zane stared, wide-eyed. Kari nearly choked on her bread.

"You guys are *brothers*?!" Ruth exclaimed. She looked back and forth between the two of them. "I guess there are some similarities, although I never would have suspected you to be related!"

After the four others recovered from the initial shock, Rosh asked them the question that had been on his mind for some time.

"What are you five doing out here in Shala all by yourselves?" He had been wondering about this ever since they walked through the doors. He had thought about asking Samuel but decided that if he asked all of them, he would get a more detailed answer.

"We're on a mission!" Zane exclaimed, instantly trusting this new friend. "We need to get a key that opens a secret door in Yamal, so the king can get his men in there to attack Ogrion!" He beamed at Rosh.

"Whoa," Rosh said, surprised that the five in front of him were doing something so important. "That's a pretty big task to assign to youngsters like you. I assume the king had a good reason?"

A little insulted by being labeled as a youngster, Samuel interjected. "He had a perfectly good reason! We were all brought to Castle Orthox to be trained in preparation for carrying out missions like this."

"Alright then." He was still somewhat doubtful about their skills. *Well, only time will reveal the truth,* he thought.

"Now that I know about you guys, let me tell you my story." He leaned back against a table and looked off into the distance, as if he was reliving events that occurred long ago.

"After I was captured by Groggers in Kaltoid, I was taken across the countryside until we reached the edge of the Belsh Desert, which is where they live.

"We hiked across the desert for weeks. The heat was so intense I almost died! They forced me to eat scorpions and snakes, and they used some sort of crude faucet to drain the water out of cacti. The only break I had from drinking cactus water was when we came upon the occasional oasis. At these stops, we would load our canteens with fresh spring water and fill our small packs with edible leaves.

"We finally reached their home after about three weeks of traveling through the desert. I don't know how they found their way over all those sand dunes. They must have some sort of internal navigation system they use.

"I first realized that we had reached our destination when our entire caravan began disappearing through the sand one by one. When it was my turn to follow them, the Grogger behind me pushed me towards the ground, but instead of hitting it, I went through and landed in a dark tunnel without a speck of sand on my clothes. I have no idea what happened, but I have to say, it was one of the weirdest experiences of my entire life.

"When all the Groggers had fallen into the tunnel, my kidnappers took me to their emperor. I couldn't understand much of their language, but I did learn his name after many times of hearing it. They call him 'Emperor Nasgatar.'

"I was appointed to be his servant, which meant that I was forced to serve him food and clean up any messes he made, which were many, I assure you. I kept time by scratching marks into the wall of my prison cell.

"On the day of my escape, I counted those scratches and learned that I had been there for fourteen years. I was much stronger than I was when I started, so I was able to overpower my guards and break out of the prison.

"I went back to the same room that I had appeared in when they first brought me there and looked for some sort of hole in the ceiling. I eventually found a tube and climbed through it until I reached the desert above.

"Using the same methods I learned on my first trip, I just barely survived my journey through the desert and reached Shala Province in about three weeks.

"From then on, I've been going from town to town, looking for jobs to help me make enough money to travel back to Kaltoid. I've been running this place for about two months."

"Wow," said Zane. "You've been through a lot."

Rosh laughed. "Yes, I have, but my job-searching has now come to an end."

"How's that?" Zane asked curiously.

With a sense of finality in his voice, Rosh stood up and announced what had been on his mind since the previous night.

"I'm coming with you."

26

...

Setting Out

"Hey you! Get over here!" The heavyset man pointed at Flen, who was in the middle of unloading a large crate from the ship currently in the harbor.

"Be right there!" Flen set down his load and hurried towards the pile of crates on the dock, confused as to why his boss needed him. He was afraid that it had to do with his behavior the previous day.

Yesterday during his shift, a couple of the other dock-workers, one of whom was his supervisor, asked him to do something that he did not want to be a part of.

They had wanted him to deliver a shipment to someone who lived in his town, which was only a couple miles away from the harbor. Normally, he would have been finc with this task. They often asked him to take things there.

This time, however, they had asked him to deliver a package that contained an illegal substance called Vrotimir. It was highly addictive, and in the past, it had caused many prestigious people to fall into the dregs of society.

Upon hearing what the package contained, Flen refused to deliver it. This made his boss very angry. Flen was given a leave of absence for the rest of that day.

As he now approached his hefty employer, Flen dreaded what was to come.

The man, whose name was Kiyel, watched his subordinate as he walked slowly towards him.

"I hear you've been causin' some trouble lately," Kiyel began. "Been defyin' orders."

Flen drew his body up, knowing for sure that his brawny superior was talking about the previous day, and replied, "I would have delivered the item if it had not been against the king's law!"

"Let me get something straight with you," Kiyel said, glaring menacingly at the shorter man. "Your job is to unload and deliver packages that ships bring in to our docks. You have no right to refuse orders, illegal or not."

"It's against my moral values, and I will not..."

"Oh, don't worry. You won't have any problems with that anymore. Ya know why? Because you're not allowed to work here anymore!" Kiyel yelled at Flen. The other stevedores turned to see what was happening.

As if he was expecting it, Flen hid his dismay and nodded, saying, "I guess I'll just be off, then." He walked towards the road that led to the town, picking up his lunch satchel and water skin as he went. He made his walk a brisk one, so his former coworkers wouldn't see his hands shaking.

"What?!" Zane exclaimed.

Rosh nodded his head. "You heard me. I'm coming with you. You kids need an adult along on this expedition of yours." He stood up and walked over to the counter. Reaching down behind it, he pulled up a bag that looked like it was fully packed.

"As you can see, I've given this some thought. I've decided that coming with you on your quest would be much more beneficial to my health than standing all day in this bar of mine."

"But who will take over the tavern?" Samuel queried.

Rosh opened his mouth to answer, but before he could, the door swung open. A man that Zane had seen the bartender talking to the other night rushed through the door.

"Why, hello, Flen!" Rosh said in a surprised voice. "What are you doing here? You know the bar isn't open 'til noon."

"Sorry," he said, panting, "but I had to tell you! I was just fired from my job at the docks for refusing to deliver a box of Vrotimir to someone in the town! I ran all the way here to tell you!"

"Wow. I can't believe that they would fire you for refusing to break the law!" Rosh shook his head in bewilderment and then looked back at Flen. "Why did you need to tell *me*?"

"I was wondering if you might... um... have a job for me here at your inn?" Flen asked, shuffling his feet.

Rosh winked at Samuel and said, "Of course I do!" Zane watched him walk over to the former stevedore and pat him on the back. "How would you feel about being the owner?"

Flen was stunned. "Wha-what about you? Don't you need a job?"

"Here, Flen. Let me introduce you to somebody." Rosh led Flen to Samuel, who stood up and offered his hand. "Flen, meet my brother, Samuel." They shook hands.

"I didn't know you had a brother."

Rosh laughed. "Me neither, until just last night!"

Still confused, Flen asked, "Has your brother offered you a job?" He surveyed Samuel up and down. He certainly didn't look old enough to be an employer.

Rosh waved a hand towards the group. "He and his friends here are on a trip, and I've decided that I'm going to join them."

Still taken aback by his new acquisition of rank, Flen nodded his head slowly. "Will you ever come back?"

"Of course I'll come and visit you!" He turned towards the others, who were sitting down and watching this exchange. "We're gonna get going soon, so let me give you some instructions as to how you run this place."

As he led Flen around the bar, showing him the works, Zane and the others went up to the room to retrieve their belongings in preparation to leave.

Zane grabbed his satchel and slung it over his back. After he finished checking the floor for any other belongings, he picked up his giant mace from where it was leaning against the wall and tried to attach it to the strap that wrapped around his upper body.

Unfortunately, he was unsuccessful and proceeded to drop it on the floor with a loud crash.

Huffing in annoyance, he bent over and yanked the large implement from where it had fallen on the floor. He tried again to attach it, and this time he succeeded.

Ruth was waiting for him at the door, and they walked downstairs together.

Meanwhile, Flen had been set to work behind the bar, wiping out mugs with a cleaning rag.

Rosh was sitting with the rest of the group at a table near the door. He looked up as Ruth and Zane approached.

"I see that you're all ready. We should be going now." Rosh stood up and waved goodbye to Flen, who casually waved back. The lithe man cinched his sword belt tightly around his waist and pushed open the door.

When they were all outside, Zane started to move towards the stables, but Rosh stopped him.

"We only have a couple of leag... I mean miles to walk. You may as well leave your horses here. Flen will take care of them until we get back." He figured that, since he was the only adult among them, he was now in charge of the group. Rosh started to walk down the road but noticed that none of the others were following him.

"I'm in charge now, aren't I? I *am* the oldest."

Zane was becoming annoyed with Samuel's brother. He didn't seem to have any sense of respect for the others in the group. He had even made the assumption that he was their *leader*! That could not go unchecked.

"No." Zane's deep voice broke the silence that followed Rosh's question. "You're not our leader any more than those horses in the stables are."

Echoing the big boy, Ruth stepped forward and said, "Yeah. You're not even an official part of our team!"

"Now, wait a minute, guys," Samuel began. "Don't pick on my brother. He can be in charge if he wants to." Having a complaisant personality, Samuel only wanted everybody to get along. He didn't care who was in charge.

"They're right, Samuel." Kari looked him in the eyes. "He's not our leader. You are."

Swallowing his pride for what he knew was right, Mikal stepped forward. "Well, Sam? You're the boss. What are we gonna do with this guy?"

Rosh suddenly realized that he had no control over them, no matter how old he was. Samuel was their leader, and they respected him.

Sighing, Rosh backed off, putting his hands in the air. "Alright, Samuel... lead on." He walked to the back of the line, sufficiently humbled by the loyalty of the youths to their leader.

Perceiving that they were all waiting for his word, Samuel spoke up. "We'll leave the horses here, because when we get on a ship, they're not going to be able to come anyway."

They nodded in agreement, watching him closely. "And I think it's time to go."

With firm resolution, Samuel stepped forward and began walking down the road, the others following behind. He felt a twinge of pain in his ankle, but ignored it.

Rosh quickened his pace until he was walking next to Samuel.

"What did you do to deserve such loyalty?" It wasn't a mean comment, but Samuel thought he detected a tinge of envy in his brother's voice.

Grinning, Samuel replied, "I guess they all respect me. I did sort of take charge when we battled an enchantress at Castle Orthox. That might have done it."

"You battled an enchantress?! But I thought the *king* defeated her! I never heard any mention of *you* being there!" Because of Rosh's confusion, Samuel began telling the true version of the story that had been circulating Aena.

By the end of the tale, the other four were adding bits to the story, making it as factual as possible. They had converged around Rosh, feeling better towards him now that he had ceded leadership to Samuel.

It had been an hour since they left the town, and they could hear waves crashing in the distance. They were nearing the harbor where Flen had worked.

They walked around a bend in the road, and there, lying peacefully before them, was a small, tranquil fishing village and beyond that, the mighty Evis Ocean.

27

...

Getting A Ride

"Bring 'er in, boys!" The swarthy captain called to his busily working crew.

The huge cargo ship slid over the foamy waves towards the shore, where the stoic stevedores were waiting to unload it. Its captain stood at the stern, waving a hand to the men standing along the shoreline. The graceful vessel swung about as they brought it in to dock. A couple of the crew heaved the anchor over the side and into the water with a thundering splash.

The ship was painted a deep hue of green, with large, gold letters emblazoned on its side. Its name was the *Campekter*, and its captain, Chan, was very proud of it. He had named it after a town in Velendaw that had brought him in when he shipwrecked once on the coast of that country. The natives there had been very kind to him. They even helped him rebuild the wrecked pieces of his old craft into this new ship, which had been his favorite ever since.

After that experience, Chan decided to become a trader between Aena and Velendaw. He would bring goods from his home country to give to the Velendians in exchange for their valuables and homemade items. It was a job he had come to enjoy. He had old friends in that country, who he always loved to see when he traveled there.

His crew slid a long, wooden plank out of the ship and onto the dock so the stevedores could board. Once they were on the ship, the workers were directed to the cargo hold by the captain.

As Captain Chan now looked upon the shore from the bow of his ship, he saw some figures walking toward him. There appeared to be three of them, and they were obviously there for a reason. One of them had a very large build, which was not a good sign.

"Permission to board?" One of them yelled.

He shivered, wondering what he had done wrong *this* time. Hopefully he didn't owe them any money.

"Sure! Come aboard!" He hid his anxiety and beckoned for them to come up the ramp.

When they approached him, he was very surprised to find that all three of them were young men, not even adults.

"Can I help ya?" He asked, not sure as to whom he should address the question. To his surprise, it was the one who looked the youngest that answered.

"Hi, I'm Samuel."

"Cap'n Chan," the weathered sailor replied. They shook hands.

"I was wondering if I might request a favor." The captain nodded warily, wondering what he was getting himself into. "I asked around town, and I eventually learned that your esteemed vessel makes regular trips to the country of Velendaw."

"Yeah, we do." He was being even more cautious now. Chan wondered if this kid was going to ask to hitch a ride with him.

"My friends and I are on a journey, and it's important that we reach Velendaw very quickly. Would you and your crew be willing to have us on board for your next crossing?"

Chan thought about it for a moment, realizing that his assumption had been correct. "I don't s'pose that would be a problem," he replied, after mulling it over. "As long as you and your friends ain't meanin' to cause any trouble. I have a rule aboard my ship, an' that's 'No violence.'" Samuel reassured him that they would never even think about it.

"How many people are you plannin' to bring? Three?" He looked at the two others standing solemnly behind Samuel.

"I have us three and three more waiting back on shore." The blond-haired boy pointed to the beach behind him. Chan noticed the muscles that rippled in Samuel's arms and realized that this was not an ordinary young man.

"You'll have to bring your own supplies," Captain Chan said slowly, wondering if this kid and his friends had enough money to provide for themselves.

"Got that handled."

Captain Chan stroked his beard thoughtfully, trying to recall anything he may have missed.

"Ah!" He said. "One more thing. There is the matter of your payment. It'll be five copper shards per person for the ride. Will you be wantin' ta come back, 's well?"

"No. We'll be staying in the country for a while. Anything else we need to be aware of?"

Captain Chan considered the question and then shook his head. "Nope. I think that's about it. You can deliver your payment when ya board. We'll be leavin' tomorrow morning at seven o'clock precisely. If you and yer buddies aren't here, then we're leavin' without ya. Got it?"

"Yes, sir. Thank you, sir. Seven o'clock. We'll be here." Samuel shook hands with the captain one last time before walking down the ramp and back to shore with his two friends.

"He seems like a nice kid," Chan said to his first mate, Marcus, who had come to stand next to the captain. "Let's hope he's that nice while he's aboard."

"We leave at exactly seven in the morning, and there are no exceptions." Samuel was standing on the side of the road, briefing the others on what the captain of the *Campekter* had told him. "You guys all need to be on your best behavior while we're sailing on this ship. The one we'll be taking is the big, green one at the dock second to left over there." He pointed towards the *Campekter*, which was slowly bobbing up and down in the tide.

Kari listened closely to what he said. She had heard stories about what some cruel sailors did to passengers who disobeyed the rules of their ship, and she definitely did not want that to happen.

Earlier, when they had arrived at the harbor, they had chosen to stay at an inn called the White Swan. Although the name sounded pleasant, the bedrooms on the second floor were hideous hovels infested with roaches and mice.

As in Rosh's inn, the others had elected her to barter with the owner for a room. She had successfully taken the price down to two silver shards, but even that was too much for the dank, smelly caves they called rooms.

When she was a child, Kari's mother had taken her to the market many times. She had first decided that Kari had the natural skill of haggling when she traded a set of deer antlers for a beautiful bearskin rug at thirteen years old. From then on, her mother, Delba, took her to the market every week to practice that skill.

Kari had enjoyed haggling, until her mother said that it was a skill all proper ladies should practice. That just about killed it for her. She hated it when her mother called things she did for fun, "skills of a proper lady."

Now, after she thought she would never need it again, her long-forgotten talent as a bargainer had come to life.

Samuel had finished giving them the instructions for the next day, so they decided to head back to the inn. Discussions of their impending journey were kept outdoors, where there were less ears to hear their plans.

As they approached the front door of the White Swan, it swung open, and a large man wearing a hooded cloak strode out. He headed to their little group, but they couldn't see his face, due to the setting sun and looming shadows.

Samuel, who was trying his best to not look intimidated by the size of the stranger, took a couple of steps forward. "Can we help you?" He asked.

Kari watched the cloaked figure closely, her hand wavering over where her sword should have been. With a pang of panic, she realized that they had all left their weapons in their room at the inn.

Instead of replying to Samuel's question, the burly man drew back his cloak and pulled a long sword out of a sheath hidden by his side.

The sound of rasping metal twinged an instinctive reaction in Samuel. He reached for his sword, but when his hand swiped empty air, the frightened warrior felt a mounting anxiety in his chest.

The aggressive man in front of him drew back his sword and lunged at Samuel. The nimble youth leapt out of the way just in the nick of time, the long blade whizzing safely by.

"Samuel! Catch!" He turned around and saw a knife soaring through the air towards him. With a flick of his wrist, Samuel caught it by the handle and jumped backwards into a ready position.

Good ol' Ruth, he thought, the corner of his mouth tilting up in a slight grin as he watched the others grab the daggers she tossed them. *Never leaves home without a beltfull of knives.*

As the man swung again, Samuel instantly retaliated, lunging in with the borrowed knife.

In a desperate attempt to ward off the blows that struck at him, the stranger swung his sword around him, slashing at the sharp offenders.

As he fought, Samuel had a sinking feeling that sent a shiver of dread coursing through his body. The man was obviously not skilled enough to fight the six warriors. His stance was clumsy, and his movements were uncoordinated. He would not have been sent to attack them unless there were others in the area to back him up.

He whipped around, scanning the buildings behind him, from which pale, frightened faces watched the ensuing battle. Standing at the corner of a civilian's house, a man cloaked in black solemnly observed the fight. The lone stranger drew back his arm, as if preparing to throw something.

Samuel's face blanched and his heart dropped into his stomach as he realized that the man, whoever he was, was aiming for him.

Kari, who had been striking at the bulky man in front of her, saw Samuel's face pale. She turned to where he was looking and gasped, forgetting all about the clumsy assassin the others were battling.

Kari watched as the figure whipped his arm back and flung something at the group. In slow motion, she saw a black dart streaking through the air toward Samuel's head.

Not knowing what else to do, Kari took a deep breath and threw herself in front of him, shielding her face with her hands. As she waited for the dart to penetrate her body, the words, *"Better me than him,"* crossed her mind.

Kari heard the whistling noise of a projectile zipping through the air, and felt a sudden, searing pain as it pierced her arm. Its sharpened tip sunk deep into her flesh and grated against her bone.

Kari screamed in agony, and with pain roaring through her body, she fell to the ground and blacked out.

28

...

The Doctor

Counterattack was immediate.

With a lightning-fast movement, Ruth flipped her dagger end over end towards the man who had cast the dart.

Not expecting such sudden retaliation, he gasped as he felt a heavy impact on his chest. A burning sensation spread through his body and the world around him went red. The assassin collapsed, dead before he hit the ground.

The larger man who had originally attacked them was unconscious, Zane having dealt a solid blow to his jaw.

Ruth rushed over to Kari, who wasn't moving. She had passed out from the shock and pain.

The people that had been watching in fright from their windows now receded deeper into their houses, not wanting any part of the violence that had just occurred in the narrow street below.

The dart was about a foot long. Its shaft was colored black, and its fletching was white: The colors of death.

Ruth gently picked up Kari's arm and examined the other side, being careful not to touch the dart. It had gone halfway through, its barbed end drooping slightly on the backside of Kari's forearm.

"I'm going to have to push it through," Ruth announced in a shaky voice. "Mikal and Samuel, you two hold her down. Zane and Rosh, keep watch for more assassins." The two boys knelt down and held her legs and her uninjured arm.

"Alright. Here goes nothing." Ruth grasped the fletched end of the arrow and snapped it off. She then slowly pushed until it came free of Kari's arm.

The wounded girl woke up and screamed, thrashing and wriggling against the two boys' grips. Once the dart was fully out, Samuel and Mikal let go. Kari's ear-piercing shrieks lessened into soft moans as she passed out again. Blood was now oozing freely from the wound.

After binding the other girl's arm tightly with a strip of cloth she had found in her pocket, Ruth examined the dart.

A feeling of despair made its way into her heart when the young medic saw something that she hadn't expected.

"Oh, no! No, no, no!" Ruth drew her hands through her tousled hair, dropping the dart in the process.

"What? What is it?" Mikal looked concerned as he studied her face.

"There's a darkened part of the shaft here," Ruth explained, trying to contain her panic, "and it's not blood." The others looked at her questioningly.

Taking a deep, shuddering breath, Ruth delivered the bad news. "I believe the dart was poisoned." She heard an intake of breath. "I don't have the skill to treat this wound. We have to find a doctor as fast as possible!"

As the others stood up and spread out to find someone with medical expertise, Samuel sat very still and stared at Kari's pallid face.

"I-I'm sorry," he said, feeling a deep sense of remorse. "I should have taken that dart. It was meant for me, but you took it!" A tear ran down his face as he watched her shoulders move up and down slightly with the cadence of her breath.

As he gazed upon the pale girl, Samuel realized something. He had always thought that conceding to others was a noble act, and it was, in a way. But this... this was what true sacrifice looked like: Laying down one's life for another.

With a shaky voice, Samuel spoke again to the unconscious Kari. "From now on, I will follow your example of sacrifice."

Samuel stood up and wiped his moist eyes. "I promise that we will find a way to save you. You *will* be healed."

"Tarius! There's somebody at our door!"

The doctor looked up from where he was organizing his instruments and called back, "It's okay, honey! Let them in!" His wife directed them to his workroom. Footsteps approached the door. A gentle knock sounded on its hard wood.

"Come in," Tarius said, covering his tools with a white cloth.

The door swung open, admitting two girls and a boy. One of the girls was very pale and was being supported by the other two. Her arm was wrapped in a cloth that must have once been white, but was now red with blood.

"Here, lay her down on my table," Tarius said quickly, realizing the urgency in their expressions.

The girl with strawberry blond hair and the muscled boy laid the wounded girl on his long, wooden operating table.

"Let's have a look at this." He bent over and looked at her arm.

"I see you've made an effort to stop the blood flow. That's good, but now I'm going to need to take the bandage off." He looked at the injured girl for consent. It was unnecessary, but it was also procedure for the doctor to ask his patients' permission to work on them.

She nodded slowly and then clenched her teeth together, awaiting the pain that was surely to follow. She moaned as he peeled the sticky cloth away from her arm. The area around the wound was swollen and pink, the hole which the arrow had pierced deep red and clotted.

"Ooh. That's a nasty one. What did it? An arrow?"

"It was a dart. A poisoned dart." The boy gave this answer. He looked defiantly at Tarius, as if he was denying the fact that his friend had been wounded.

"Do you still have the dart?" The doctor asked.

The blond girl had been holding it in her hand. She handed it to him, being careful not to touch pointed end.

Tarius turned the dart over in his hands, examining it. He lifted the tip to his nose, sniffing deeply.

"I recognize this scent. The poison smells like burning flesh, which can only mean one thing." He turned around and started searching through his shelves and cupboards for something.

"And what is that?" The girl asked, irked at his silence.

"Oh, oh yes!" He said in a flustered voice. "The poison is Dragon Fire. I wish it wasn't, but it is." He continued searching through the cupboards frantically.

"Dragon Fire?! Are you serious?!" The short girl exclaimed. "There's only one cure for that. We need Shining Star, and you would know if you had some! Well? Do you?"

Tarius sat heavily on his stool and held his head. "No! I don't have any!" Dragon Fire is immensely painful for a couple weeks before causing a horrible death.

The girl seemed to have an idea. "Do you know any places where it might grow?"

"Yes, yes!" Tarius said. "I've seen it growing abundantly on the eastern side of the ocean. But why does that matter? You'll never make it in time!"

"Yes we will." She grabbed a cloth bandage from the counter and began wrapping the wound again.

Tarius stood from his chair and watched her work. "What are you going to do?"

"We're going to Velendaw tomorrow. Hopefully we can find some Shining Star while we're there." She finished tying the bandage, and the boy picked the girl up, being careful not to touch her wound.

"What's going on?" The wounded girl mumbled. "Why are we leaving?"

"It's gonna be okay," the sturdy boy said. "We're going to go get medicine to make you better."

"You should rest now," the other girl told her. "You've lost a lot of blood. All you should do now is sleep."

Tarius stepped forward. "How are you going to get to Velendaw?"

"We're going with Captain Chan, who takes regular trips there. Hopefully his ship is fast enough to make it in time."

"Well," Tarius said as he ushered them out the door, "I wish you luck and good fortune on your journey. May you make it in time to get the plants and heal your friend. Goodbye." He waved a friendly hand to the three companions as they made their way through the darkened streets.

He watched them until they rounded the corner and then walked back inside, closing the door behind him.

"It's all right! You can come out now!" He called into the small room.

Some rustling and clunking sounded from behind the wall, before a hidden door opened in the shelves. Three men stumbled out from the dark room in which they had been hiding. They gathered around the operating table, forming a semicircle facing Tarius.

The doctor placed his hands facedown, revealing a black tattoo he had previously hidden from the three visitors. It was a pointed oval with two vertical lines slashed through it and one horizontal line crossing through the whole symbol.

One of the men spoke with a deep, rumbling voice. "What's the news, Tarius? Where are they headed?"

"They're going to Velendaw with a man called Captain Chan." He pointed to one of the cloaked men standing before him.

"You own a ship, do you not?" When the cloaked man nodded, Tarius gave him an order. "You and your crew can follow them. Make sure you're not seen, and when you catch them, be certain to make it look like an accident. Got it?" The man nodded, a slight grin breaking through his stoic face.

"You two," Tarius said, pointing to the brawny men, "take word to our lord. Tell him of our current plans, and inform him that Nunor's brats will soon be no longer among the living." He smiled wickedly. "Now get out of here."

The men silently left through the secret room, avoiding suspicious eyes.

Tarius chuckled to himself as he wiped the girl's blood off the operating table. "We'll see if you save your friend. Oh, yes. We'll see."

29

...

A Sea Tale

It had been a week since they left the coast of Aena. The initial seasickness from one's first time on a ship had struck Samuel and Zane, but by now they had mostly recovered. Unfortunately, Ruth still spent most of her time heaving over the rail.

The only people not affected by the strength of the sea were Rosh and Mikal. Mikal had grown up around the ocean, so he was quite used to its effects. Rosh was the strange case. He had never even been on a ship before, but he hadn't felt a pinch of seasickness since they boarded.

Kari's condition had worsened with the addition of sea travel. She spent her days in a ratty bed, white-faced and groaning in pain at the constant rocking of the ship. No matter how much they wanted to help, there was nothing that Ruth or the ship's medic could do about her wound until they reached Velendaw. They could only try to keep Kari warm and comfortable.

The swollen area around the wound had spread, now covering most of her forearm. It was pink and moist with a slight tinge of sickly orange to it. The effects of the Dragon Fire were beginning to set in.

There was not much for the others to do aboard the *Campekter*. Many of the crew kept their distance from the passengers, each group minding their own business as much as possible. The team members who were not sick spent a lot of time sitting in their quarters and reminiscing about life at the castle.

Mikal spent much time with Kari, reassuring her that she would be okay. He didn't know when they would reach Velendaw, but he felt in his heart that they would find the plant, and she would survive.

He was growing attached to her. She was the only person he felt like he could relate to. That first night at Castle Orthox, she had courageously approached him and asked him how he was. At the time, his demeanor had been grumpy and malicious. Reluctantly, he started talking to her, and they eventually came upon the subject of their lives back home.

Mikal only had one relative he lived with, which was his Uncle Byran. His uncle was considered a fanatic in their town. He had been dubbed an outcast from society for his beliefs. He was part of a special organization that called themselves "Messengers of Adonai." This group believed that there was a higher power in the universe, a being that had created all life in Domilia.

Although he had grown up with this in his household, Mikal had never truly believed in his uncle's stories. Byran had told him many times that whenever he had a feeling of guilt or remorse in his heart, that was Adonai speaking to him, warning him about doing something wrong. Mikal had experienced these feelings before, though he had never stopped to wonder what they meant.

Presently, they were sitting in the large mess hall of the *Campekter*, and Marcus, Captain Chan's first mate, was showing them a map of Domilia, giving them an impromptu geography lesson.

Ruth was currently in a state of reduced seasickness, so she was able to be there with them. Mikal was not present, however; he was keeping Kari company in the infirmary.

"This is Aena." Marcus pointed to their home country, situated in the lower left corner of the map. "As you know, Aena is split into five Provinces, Shala being here." He pointed to the coast of the country. "We are currently in the middle of the Evis Ocean, which is the expanse of water that separates us from Velendaw and her neighbors. As I assume you've already figured out, Velendaw is here, on the opposite side."

Zane raised his hand. "How d'ya know we're in the middle of the ocean?"

"I can tell 'cause of the position of the stars in the night sky. We sailors have known how to do that for generations."

Marcus was becoming fond of the young passengers. He had spent some time with them during the past week and had grown used to their constant questions. He was actually beginning to enjoy answering them!

Samuel peered at the map on the table, studying the country of Aena. "Where's Kaltoid Province?" he asked. He had never taken a lesson such as this before and was curious as to where his parents lived.

"It's right here." Marcus pointed to the upper, left-hand corner of Aena. Figuring that the others would ask where their home Provinces were too, he pointed to each of them, including Yamal, even though it was technically no longer a Province.

"Wow," Rosh said after Marcus was finished. "Yamal was one big Province. I wonder why Ogrion wasn't satisfied with what he had." Although he was twenty-seven years old,

Rosh had never been taught anything about geography. He had spent too much time in the horrid tunnels of the Groggers.

"I don't know. Frankly, that guy was a fool. He should have kept what he already had instead of losing most of it. Some people are just like that. Never satisfied. Always greedy for more." They sat quietly for a few moments, caught up in the history of their country.

"D'ya guys wanna hear a Velendian sea tale?" Marcus asked, breaking the silence.

"As long as it doesn't involve any enchantresses," Samuel said under his breath. The other three hid smirks.

Deciding that he meant yes, Marcus began his story.

"A very long time ago there was a breed of sea monsters that lived in the Evis Ocean. They were very large and were blue-green, the color of the sea. In addition to a thick layer of sticky mucus, they were covered in tentacles that they used to pull trading ships into their mouths. These monsters were known as the 'Phanoia', which is the Velendian word for 'Destroyers.'

"The Phanoia would prey upon any ship that sailed across the Evis Ocean. This made it very hard for Aena and Velendaw to trade.

"This destruction went on for many decades, until finally, a man stepped up and pledged to kill off the Destroyers once and for all. His name was Yanonelias.

"Yanonelias was a famous warrior who lived in Velendaw. He was brave almost to the point of recklessness, and he always took on the most difficult challenges. When he said he would destroy the Phanoia, he wouldn't stop until he did.

"To begin his quest, he hired two ships to bring him to the middle of the ocean, where the attacks were most frequent. Upon reaching his destination, he ordered the captain to stop and leave on the other ship. Yanonelias was kind of a harsh guy. He forced the crew to pack into the other vessel sail back until they reached Velendaw.

"Not having any other choice, the captain went with the rest of his crew back to Velendaw.

"After they left, Yanonelias stayed on the ship and watched the waters around him, armed only with his sword and shield. After a couple days of waiting, the first Phanoe surfaced.

"They say it attacked him like a raging storm, the mighty beast throwing water everywhere, making it seem like rain was pouring down from the heavens. The great creature lunged for the ship, but before it could make contact, Yanonelias leapt from the deck to the Phanoe's head. He drove his sword through its skull, killing it.

"He battled many of these creatures for days. After a week of silence, he believed that he had killed the last one. He sailed the ship singlehandedly back to Velendaw in triumph, and for several years, there were no more attacks.

"But one day, Yanonelias's home town was attacked and utterly destroyed by a Phanoe larger than any that had ever been seen. All the citizens saw of it was one gigantic tentacle, and then both the city and the monster were gone.

"Yanonelias kept searching for the beast until he had some bad luck and became a statue on a deserted island in the middle of the ocean. That's a different story, however.

"All of this is true, and some say that the giant Phanoe, which they named Pheno, made a deal with Yanonelias, and it stands guard near the island that his statue is on. That island is called the Realm of Y, after Yanonelias. They also say that the only thing he ever desired from Pheno was one of her majestic teeth as a trophy."

Samuel decided to keep it to himself about their attempt to reach the Realm of Y. He hoped the others would do the same.

"To this day, it is said that Pheno still lurks in the waters and eats any ships that come too close to her." Marcus sat back, putting his hands behind his head. "So how was it?"

"Great!" Zane said. "Is this story true or made-up?"

"As far as I know, it's true. But don't quote me on that." He smiled at them, the crow's feet in the corners of his eyes wrinkling.

Suddenly, a panting sailor burst through the door that led to the upper deck.

"Marcus!" He said, his eyes wild. "The captain needs you! There's another ship following us!"

30

...

The Duel

"Marcus!"

"Yes, sir?" The first-mate jogged over to Captain Chan, who was standing at the stern, watching the oncoming ship.

From what he could see, the unknown vessel was colored midnight black, with flesh-colored sails flapping in the wind. Mounted on its prow like a looming threat was a carving of a vicious-looking viper, its fangs bared menacingly.

"Use your good eyes an' tell me somethin'," the captain said to Marcus. "What flag is that ship flyin'?" He pointed towards the fluttering banner in the distance.

Samuel had followed Marcus up the stairs and was now standing next to the captain as well. He could just make out the flag's color: White, with no emblems or symbols printed on it. This hit a chord in his memory, but he couldn't remember why the flag was familiar.

Marcus peered at it, straining his eyes to see. "It's... it's a white flag! A white flag of truce!"

Oh, yeah! Samuel thought. *Now I remember learning about that!*

"Good," Captain Chan said, keeping an eye on the strange craft. "Tell the rowers to slow down so it can catch up with us." Before Marcus could run off to deliver the message, though, Captain Chan added one more thing. "Even though they're comin' to us under a flag of truce, make sure the crew has their weapons ready. Also, tell our passengers to prepare their arms just in case." Marcus nodded and ran off.

After a few minutes had passed, the ship behind them had gained until it was right next to the *Campekter*. Captain Chan could see the man who was obviously in charge yelling at his crewmembers. Upon finishing his reprimanding, the man, who was cloaked in black, turned and addressed Chan.

"Greetings! May I have permission to board?" The man called in a loud voice.

Although Captain Chan was sure that this was no chance meeting, he called the order to bring the man in.

Once the stranger was on board, he asked a question. When it reached Samuel's ears, a cold shiver went down his spine. He suddenly became more alert and watched the other ship's captain closely, observing his every move.

"I have been informed by my superiors that you have passengers aboard your ship. Is this true?"

In a wary voice, Captain Chan replied, "And why would ya need to know that?"

With a dangerous look in his eyes, the man introduced himself. "My name is Gorix, and I have been sent to retrieve your passengers and take them back to the mainland. They have committed a capital crime and are to be executed. If you refuse to give them up, then we will have to settle this in the old-fashioned way."

By the man's expression, Chan deduced what that meant. This stranger, Gorix, was saying that if he didn't turn over his six young passengers, then he would be subjecting himself to a ship's duel.

As he thought about it, Chan realized that he liked the group of friendly kids that were on his ship. With firm intent, he decided that he would never get over the guilt of betraying his passengers. Destroying the other ship, however... *that* he could get over quite easily.

"Be that as it will," Captain Chan stated simply. "I'll never give 'em over to you."

"Is this your final decision?" Gorix watched him closely, a deadly look in his eyes.

"Yes. Let us have a duel."

Gorix sneered at the crew that was watching and leapt backwards over the railing into the sea. He hit with a minimal splash, but instead of sinking, he began climbing up the side of his own ship with the agility of an acrobat. The arrogant man flipped over the side of the craft and landed on his feet, immediately calling to prepare for battle.

Captain Chan was annoyed by this delay in his plan, but he knew that his men were all seasoned fighters, and they could easily overpower the challenging crew.

"Marcus!" He yelled. "Are the men ready?"

"Yes, sir. They're awaiting your orders."

"Good. Did you warn our passengers?"

"All except for the sick one."

"Oh, yeah. Her." He thought for a moment. "Bring her to the upper deck. Make sure a longboat is ready, so she can get away if needs be." He turned back and looked towards the other ship, which was slowly drawing away from them. A hand tapped his shoulder.

"Hey, captain," Samuel said casually. "I guess you have to relinquish that rule about no violence."

"Yeah." He laughed. "I'm glad to see yer in good spirits. I assume you and yer friends are fighters?"

"Yes. Although we're still amateurs, we've been trained enough for this sort of battle."

"Good. Is your hurt friend safe?"

"Yes. We brought her up to the deck and laid her in one of your longboats."

"If we start to lose," the captain said, "get your friends and escape in that boat. I wouldn't want any harm to come to ya." Captain Chan didn't know the details about Samuel and his friends' mission, but he did know that it was very important.

As the other ship backed away from the *Campekter,* Samuel could make out the golden words painted on its side: *Viper Fang.* It was a name that instilled fear in the hearts of its victims.

While he was watching, Samuel saw the white flag of truce being lowered. In its place, a new flag was hoisted. This flag had an ominous symbol decorating it. Sewn onto the black background of the banner was an eye-like shape with two vertical lines and one horizontal line slicing through it. The entire depiction was colored the bright red color of blood.

"Look at that!" Mikal pointed at the flag, which was fluttering furiously in the strong wind.

"It must be their country's flag! I saw the same thing on that rude guy's head back in Shala!" Samuel shouted over the noise of the sea, which was becoming rougher by the second. "Maybe they're from Yamal!"

During this exchange, the bright sea had turned dark and gloomy. Clouds thundered overhead, signaling that a storm was approaching. In the distance, bolts of white lightning struck the water, thunder following like a roaring beast.

"Get ready to fight!" The Captain shouted to his crew. Before he could say more, there was a thundering explosion, and an iron cannonball whistled over their heads.

"They have a cannon! Prepare to come in close! The only way we're gonna win this thing is by boardin' their ship!" Captain Chan scurried up to the steering platform and adjusted the rudder, trying desperately to keep them on course in the wind, which was howling across the turbulent waters.

Ruth, seeing that they needed help, obtained a bow from a passing sailor and nocked an arrow. They were about a hundred yards from the *Viper Fang* and moving in fast. She shook her damp hair out of her face, focusing on her arrow, not on the target. If she focused on the target, her shot would be off.

She waited until the *Campekter* was about fifty yards from the *Viper Fang*, and then released.

One of the crewmembers manning the cannon let out a strangled yell and fell to the deck, Ruth's arrow hitting true to its mark.

None of the others could do anything but stand and watch, waiting until they were near enough to board. Ruth kept picking off people that she thought were important, rarely missing.

Before long, the *Campekter* was so close to the *Viper Fang* that they could hear its crew screaming curses above the wind. Most of the people who had been working the cannons were lying still on the deck, one of Ruth's arrows transfixing each of them. It was apparent that none of the other men knew how to operate a cannon, for they were making no move towards the large weapon.

The waves crashed over the deck, soaking everyone on the ship. Mikal rushed over to where Kari lay groaning in the longboat. Her wet, black hair stuck to her face, which was pale and sweaty. All her clothes were soaked, and she was shivering terribly.

"Are you okay?!" He yelled. Shivering violently, she shook her head. Mikal scanned the tilting deck for something to warm her.

His eye eventually lighted upon a soaked wool blanket that was draped haphazardly over a railing. He staggered over and picked it up, bringing it back to Kari. He had heard that wool kept one's body heat in, even if it was wet.

"Here, use this!" He shouted. "It'll keep you warm!" He laid it over her and turned back to the others, watching them through the rain.

Some of the enemy had tried boarding the ship, but Samuel and Rosh were holding them off. The men were obviously skilled fighters, for the two brothers were having some difficulty.

The rain was pouring down in sheets now, and the wind was so strong it was driving the water droplets sideways. There didn't seem to be much lightning in this part of the storm, for all was dark and gloomy. This had better not get any worse, Mikal thought, feeling the cold rain soak through his thin garments.

As if reading his mind, the clouds in the sky boiled and peeled away, letting in the sunlight that had abandoned them.

The last rolling waves crashed over the ships and then fell back into the suddenly calm sea, sending up a spray of water.

The rain stopped instantly, giving way to a moment of pure silence as the men on both ships looked around in bewilderment.

It was then, in this surprising moment of eerie stillness, that they heard it.

31

...

Amidst The Calm

It was almost like a deep humming, a melodious sound emanating from an unknown source.

As they listened, the sound clarified and became stronger. The mellifluous noise thrummed like a giant heartbeat and began forming words. The vibrating syllables wafted over the sailors' minds, soothing their nervous thoughts.

Zane stood on the deck of the *Campekter*, slowly swaying back and forth with the movement of the ship.

Strange words flowed into his mind, singing his praises and filling him with pride. With a change of tact, they began warbling in his ears, trying to persuade him of something, but he could not discern what. Oddly, the words became increasingly garbled and unclear, as if something else was interfering with his thoughts. Listening intently, he attempted to make sense of it, until the noise in his head decreased into an incessant hum that he could not decipher.

Zane looked around at the others. They apparently knew what the words were saying, for they were caught in a trance, staring blankly forward.

In the silence, he realized that the hum was gone! Everything was quiet and calm, the soft lapping of the waves against the hull the only sound he could hear.

A deeper, gentler voice penetrated the depths of his mind. It was not like the other; it was authoritative, but kind.

"*Zane,*" the voice said. "*You must awaken your friends from their slumber. Prevent the beast from destroying.*" It faded away, leaving Zane with those perplexing words.

"Wha'?" He said out loud. This voice was obviously instructing him. He shuddered at the thought of someone else entering his mind. It was unfathomable!

"Hello?" Zane asked tentatively. "Is thar someone else here?" When no one answered he shrugged and then looked at his friends. When he saw them standing stock still, he realized that they were still frozen, listening to the voice.

Something bad is 'bout to happen, he thought. *I can jest feel it!*

With panic rising in his chest, he ran over to Samuel and Rosh, who were standing closest to him, their swords still drawn.

"WAKE UP, GUYS!" He grabbed their shoulders and shook them as he shouted.

The violent movement and the sound of Zane's booming voice knocked them back into reality. Samuel wagged his head and pressed his hands against his temples.

"Whoa! What was that?" Rosh looked around in a frightened manner, seeming slightly off-balance. "That... that voice was telling me to jump overboard! I... I almost did, too!" He noticed that everyone else was still entranced. "We need to wake the others! Quickly!"

As he spoke, everyone on each ship began slowly and simultaneously walking towards the water.

Zane, Samuel, and Rosh were panicking now. They ran to all the people who were part of Captain Chan's crew, shaking them vigorously. Soon everybody was awake and moving.

"We need to get out of here!" Marcus yelled.

The other crewmembers agreed and hustled to their separate posts, preparing to leave the site of the disturbing occurrence.

Unfortunately, before they could leave, a sailor from the *Viper Fang*'s crew reached the rail and leapt overboard.

Everything went quiet as the poor man fell silently into the tranquil sea. He hit the water with a small splash and disappeared, the ocean becoming serene once again.

The water exploded.

A massive, blue tentacle burst from the previously calm sea, writhing and shaking seawater everywhere.

Men on both ships screamed, having been yanked out of their hypnotized state.

The tentacle lashed around, slamming into the two vessels. Zane recalled the beast the mysterious voice had talked about. *I guess I'd better prevent it from destroyin',* he thought, remembering the voice's warning.

The warriors aboard Captain Chan's ship were galvanized into action as the vessel surged over the foamy waves.

Ruth drew another arrow from her dwindling supply and loosed it at the flailing creature. The projectile flew true and penetrated the beast's thick, mucus-covered hide.

Trumpeting in rage, it turned to seek out its attacker. When it whipped around towards the *Campekter*, Zane saw its face for the first time.

The thing was hideous. Its mouth was full of hundreds of spiny teeth, each looking as sharp as a saber. Its eyes were beady and intelligent, and it had no nose as far as Zane could tell. Every way it turned, mucous slime was slung from its dripping skin. Its smooth, blue-green hide was the color of the sea.

As the beast thrashed from side to side, the noonday sun shone down on its flesh. Bright, rippling lines zigzagged across it, forming the illusion that it was made of water.

The creature felt another stinging jab in its side. It swung towards the source, focusing on Ruth. As it struck down at her, she leapt to the side, barely avoiding the attack. It streaked past her, roaring.

The beast's huge head smashed through the center of the *Campekter*, ripping it into two halves, each of which creaked ominously and began to sink, water pouring through the cavernous fissure.

Samuel, who was standing on one of the halves, looked over his shoulder, searching for his friends. To his relief, there was a longboat floating amidst the wreckage, and it held Mikal, Kari, and Zane.

As he watched the small craft, a soaked Ruth pulled herself out of the water and fell haphazardly into the longboat, shivering intensely.

Glancing to the opposite half of the ship, he noticed a lone figure standing near the prow, brandishing a long cutlass and trying to keep his balance: Captain Chan.

Meanwhile, the *Viper Fang* was in much worse condition. The worm-like creature was smashing it to bits, knocking many of the enemy sailors on a high-flying journey through the air and eventually back down to the water, where they hit so hard their bodies were broken.

Samuel watched all this in awe, as the mighty beast raged before him. Without a doubt, he knew that this creature was the mighty Pheno he had learned about a mere half-hour ago. *No wonder Yanonelias hadn't been able to defeat it.*

He turned to the captain on the opposite half of the ship and shouted, "Hey! Captain Chan!"

The muscular man turned to Samuel and shouted back, "What?!"

"Let's take 'er down!"

Getting the general message, the captain nodded and turned to face the enraged monster. Taking a deep breath, Samuel jumped off the wrecked ship into the water.

He hit the ice-cold ocean with a stinging splash. He didn't know how to swim, but he was close enough to Pheno that he was able to latch onto it with his arms. The distracted beast didn't notice him, so Samuel climbed its body, digging his hands into its sticky mucus for support.

After reaching a considerable height, he looked down and saw that Captain Chan was still standing in the destroyed ship. He waved his sword at Samuel, who obviously couldn't wave back, and started yelling at Pheno.

Amidst the cacophonic noises, the creature heard a buzzing sound from behind it. Pheno turned from the wreckage of the other ship and looked upon the one it had cleaved in half.

There, standing defiantly on the deck, was a small person yelling and throwing something. Pheno felt a jab as a small knife punctured its skin.

It screeched and lunged at the figure, who jumped aside just before the infuriated serpent shot past, destroying another section of the ship.

The mucus adhering him to its body, Samuel used that violent motion to his advantage and climbed faster up to the head, trying his best not to fall off.

Once he reached the top, he drew his sword, and holding on with one hand, plunged it into Pheno's skull.

Feeling a piercing jab, Pheno writhed around, trying to shake the annoying human off its head. Trumpeting furiously, it managed to knock the irritating thing off, casting it into the water, along with the offending spike.

Pheno shook itself, trying to get rid of the pain that was flooding through its body. It started moving slower and slower, until it stopped wriggling all together.

With a dying scream, the towering body of Pheno fell into the water, making an immense wave cascade over the remains of both ships.

As the beast sank, green blood drifted up from the deep gash in its head, staining the blue waters.

Samuel, who still could not swim, floundered around in the water, looking for something to grasp so he wouldn't drown.

With waves crashing over him, Samuel flailed about, but the weight of his sword was pulling him down. In this absent-minded moment, he didn't think to unhook the heavy implement.

As the cold started setting in, he thrashed slower, feeling his body give in to the ocean. He felt his eyes starting to close and tried to force them open again, ignoring the warm, buzzing sensation that was spreading through his limbs.

Struggling to stay afloat, Samuel's hands hit a large board from the wrecked ship, and he clutched it desperately, digging his fingernails into its saturated wood.

Although he was no longer sinking, Samuel's eyes started closing again. He strained to keep them open, the fear of death coursing through him.

"*Samuel,*" something spoke into his mind. "*Look up, for your deliverers draw near.*" The euphonious voice faded away.

Samuel forced his drooping eyelids opened and pushed his wet, brown hair away from his face with a numb hand.

Drifting silently on the water, a wide boat floated next to him. The board he was holding scraped against its hull.

"Look!" A familiar voice shouted. "There he is!" Strong arms grabbed Samuel's limp body and heaved him over the side of the longboat.

He looked up, seeing the concerned faces of his friends. The world began to go dark, as the sweet relief of unconsciousness came to take him away. However, that didn't stop one last thought from plaguing his mind.

Wasn't Pheno supposed to be covered with tentacles?

32

...

A Voice

Samuel awoke leaning against the side of a boat.

It took him a moment to remember what had happened and where he was. Then, with a flash of memories, he suddenly recalled the battle, the slimy serpent-like creature, and the icy water he fell into. He remembered being pulled out of the water by his friends and then everything had gone black.

Samuel looked at his surroundings, but they weren't much. There was water as far as the eye could see. He turned his head and noticed the others sitting in the prow of the longboat, talking quietly amongst themselves.

All their weapons, including his sword, were lying in the center of the boat, along with a couple of water skins that had been saved from the wreckage.

He looked down at his clothes. There was no sign of the ooze that had coated him from climbing the creature, but his shirt and pants *were* covered in a layer of crusty, green stuff.

Samuel brushed some of it off his sleeve. To his surprise, it crumbled into a fine dust and blew away in the wind like flour. He figured that the slime must have dried and become this odd substance.

"Hey, guys!" He called to the others after he had finished wiping the dust from his jerkin.

They turned and greeted him, forcing smiles.

"Hi, Samuel. It's good to see you awake again," Ruth said somberly.

He instantly knew that something wasn't right. He'd never seen Ruth this forlorn before. She was always cheerful and excited.

"Why's everyone so serious?" Samuel asked. "I mean, I know we're lost at sea, but you don't have to be so gloomy about it." He looked around at the faces surrounding him. Ruth, Mikal, and Zane were all there, and Kari was lying down, sick. Everything looked all right to him.

Then it dawned on him.

With a bad feeling rising in his chest, Samuel asked, "Where's Rosh?"

They looked down. "I'm sorry, Samuel," Ruth said. "We looked everywhere, but there was no sign of him."

Samuel's eyes stung, the beginnings of tears glittering in them. He had only just found his brother, and now he was gone. He couldn't help but start sobbing. The four of them cried together, mourning the loss of a brother and a friend.

While the others were commiserating with Samuel, Kari was shivering on one of the benches of the longboat. Her face was an unhealthy white, her eyes were bloodshot, and her skin was clammy. Every once in a while, she would cry out in pain.

Her wounded limb had the same dirty bandage wrapped around it from the doctor's house in Shala. Her arm was puffy and still slightly orange. In a futile attempt to keep her warm, she had the damp, woolen blanket wrapped around her. She shivered, pain shooting once again through her body.

Zane wiped his eyes and moved away from the small group. He sat down on a bench and looked off into the distance.

He kept thinking about the voice that had spoken to him while he was in the trance. It was such a weird but somewhat comforting experience that he felt like he needed to hear it again.

Zane closed his eyes and concentrated on what the voice had sounded like, the cold sea breeze blowing across his face. With his eyes closed, his senses of smell, hearing, and touch were enhanced. He could hear seabirds cawing in the distance, the scent of salt drifting into his nose. He could feel tiny droplets of water kicked up by the rocking of the boat.

Even with all of his concentration, however, he did not hear the voice.

Huffing in annoyance at his failure, Zane kept his eyes closed and spoke with his mind, hoping to elicit an answer.

"Hullo?"

Nothing happened, so he tried again. *"I know yer thar somewhere, voice in my head. Ya talked ta me when I was standin' on the deck a' that ship. If ya wouldn't mind, I'd like ta know who ya are."* He listened closely.

278

After not hearing anything for several seconds, Zane felt defeated.

However, just before he opened his eyes, a voice vibrated deeply throughout his mind.

"Hello, Zane."

"Wha'?!" Zane mentally shouted, very surprised. *"Did you jest say somethin'?!"*

"Yes, I did." The voice was calm and patient.

Hoping that he would be able to have an actual conversation this time, Zane spat out a hasty "thank you." *"Wal, hi! Thank ya fer savin' me back thar. I prob'ly wouldn't 'ave lived if it wasn't fer you."*

"You must stay alive, Zane. You are very important."

"I am?" Zane had sufficiently calmed down by now, but he was confused by this statement. *"How am I important? Who are ya, anyway?"*

"My name is Adonai." As the voice said that name, a tingle ran through Zane's body. He could feel the immense power that it held.

"Adonai?" He had the tingly feeling again when he said the name. *"Why are you, Adonai, talkin' ta me?"*

"Well, Zane, I created you."

This confused Zane beyond measure, for he had always thought he had come from his parents. *"Wha'd'ya mean? My Ma an' Pa made me, didn't they?"*

"Of course they did. But before they conceived you here in Domilia, I created you."

"So, you're sayin' that you created everybody, then?"

"Yes, Zane. I created everyone and everything."

This was very surprising to Zane, who'd thought that the world had always just been there. *"If yer so powerful, why're ya talkin' ta me? I mean, I know ya said I'm important, but what does that even mean?"*

"Allow me to explain. I have a plan for everything in the universe. Although you think you are not anything special in this world, everyone is valuable in my eyes. There is no person alive that does not have a purpose in my ultimate plan for Domilia."

"But why do ya need a plan? If yer so powerful, can't ya jest make everyone do what ya want?"

"I could, Zane. I could. But there is greater meaning in life for those who find their own way. I allow you to discern what you lack, so you rely on me to supply your needs. Some people have searched for their own importance, and they have found what they thought was their life's goal. These people, however, do not listen to my voice and are sucked into the evils of life."

"So yer sayin' that people like... Ogrion went on the wrong path? Ya talked to him, but he didn't listen ta you?"

"Yes. I have talked to every one of my creations in different ways, and not all of them have listened. You are a wise person, Zane, to listen to me."

"Should I tell my friends about you, or do you want ta be a secret?" A lot had just been poured into Zane's mind, and he wasn't sure if this "Adonai" would like being exposed to people other than who he chose.

"I definitely do not want to be a secret, Zane." The voice reassured him. "You may tell anyone you want about me. The more people that believe and listen to me, the more people that will come to live with me when they die."

"We get to live with you when we die?!" He was talking to the One who created everything, and he just found out that he was allowed to live with Him. It was almost too much to comprehend!

"Yes. You must go and tell your friends about me now, for you are approaching your next destination. Just remember, any time you need guidance, you may always talk to me." The voice faded away.

Zane opened his eyes and looked around. He must have dozed away while he was talking to this Adonai, for he felt good and rested. Everything was still the same as it had been before the conversation. There was water everywhere.

"Hey, guys!" Zane called to his friends, who were once again engaged in a light conversation. "You'll never guess what I jest found out!"

Without waiting for them to guess, Zane began telling them of his experience.

Although the entire story was true, doubt still shone on at least one of their faces.

"Are you sure this wasn't just a dream?" Mikal asked, a frown crossing his features.

"Yes! I heard the same voice right before the sea monster attacked us! That's how I was able to wake up and help everyone else wake up!"

"Yeah!" Samuel exclaimed. "I heard a voice too, while I was in the water!"

Mikal doubted it. Even though he had grown to like Zane, this was the nonsense he had grown up with. Hearing one of his new friends say it just made it worse. He hated it when people tried to convince him to believe stuff that he didn't believe was true.

"It must have been a dream. There's no such person as Adonai!" Mikal stated scornfully.

The others looked at him in surprise. Although he had started out rude and inconsiderate, Mikal had changed a lot since their first day at Castle Orthox. Everyone knew that he had become kinder and slow to anger. This must be a problem that went far deeper than adolescent defiance.

"You don't have to be rude, Mikal," Ruth said softly. "He makes a valid point. How could he have woken from the trance while we were still stuck?"

"Maybe it didn't work on him or something!"

"Why do you deny this Adonai's existence?"

They kept arguing, but Ruth kept the upper hand throughout. Eventually, Mikal gave in and told them the reason for his resistance.

"It's the same thing my uncle says. 'There's some Adonai who created us all and loves us!' How can someone like that love me, yet still cause me to go through pain?!"

Zane interrupted. "He told me that we're all important, and we all need ta find our own way through our troubles. That way, He allows us ta see what we need and ta rely on Him for it."

Mikal shut his mouth at this. Such a profound statement from Zane was not normal.

Realizing that they were all against him and would never understand his issues, he apologized. "Sorry for arguing. I never thought of it that way, but it's hard for me to believe it after having it forced on me all my life."

Everyone was silent for a few moments, feelings of guilt and shame weighing on their shoulders, due to the argument.

Then Samuel hesitantly broke in. "Hey, guys. This is kind of off-topic, but I see land!"

33

...

The Island

The sturdy longboat scraped against the shore with a horrible grating sound.

The three boys jumped out of the boat into the cold water and pushed until the small craft was fully beached.

Ruth and Mikal gently lifted Kari's limp body and carried her ashore, being careful not to touch her wounded arm. They walked to a spot on the white beach and laid her down on the soft sand.

Ruth checked her temperature. Kari's forehead was damp with perspiration and very warm, despite the biting wind.

She stood up and gazed for the first time at the landscape of the island. Not expecting what she saw, Ruth stepped back and slapped a hand over her mouth.

Towering over them was a dark, daunting jungle. Massive trees leaned over the beach, bright green moss hanging down from them. The shrubs and undergrowth, although smaller than the giant trees, still came up to the young warriors' necks. Intermittent rustles shook the canopy and the floor of this foreboding forest, giving signs of unknown wildlife.

"Well... this doesn't look promising," Samuel commented, turning to see if Rosh agreed. Then he remembered, grief stabbing his soul once again.

Ruth clapped her hands together and ordered, "Guys! I'm pretty sure we're not in Velendaw, but this is good enough. Go look for Shining Star! Remember what it looks like? Daniel showed us some on our first day of training." She beckoned for them to leave. "I'll stay here with Kari." The boys ran off down the beach, searching along the edge of the jungle for the star-shaped leaves.

"It's going to be all right, Kari," Ruth softly reassured the comatose girl. "The boys will be back with your medicine soon. You'll see." Ruth tucked the ratty wool blanket around Kari, who moaned in her sleep.

The cut was orange, blistering, and increasingly painful. Ruth knew that every minute, Kari inched closer and closer to death. The maximum time for someone to survive a Dragon Fire poisoning was two weeks, and it had been about one since the wound was inflicted.

It had been two days since the five of them had eaten a meal. They were all very hungry, making scavenging for food one of Ruth's priorities. That and finding some Shining Star were top in her mind.

Ruth heard fast footsteps padding across the sand behind her and turned around.

Mikal had just arrived and was panting in exhaustion from the run. "Ruth... bring... Kari," he said between breaths. "We found... a house!"

Ruth stood up. "Where?" She knew that any sort of civilization was a good sign.

He pointed in the direction the others had gone. "Back... there!"

"Alright," Ruth said, bending down next to Kari. "Help me with her." Together, they managed to pick up the sick girl and carry her down the long stretch of sand.

The ramshackle shanty made out of boards and driftwood obviously hadn't been there long. There was no greenery growing on it, and the wooden boards were crusty and parched from the sea air.

Zane and Samuel couldn't see a way to help, so they stood on the sand and watched as Ruth and Mikal carried Kari into the hut and laid her on the makeshift bed.

After setting her down, Ruth stood up and surveyed the interior of the shack.

It was very simple. The bed was made out of a couple of boards with some large, cushioning leaves scattered over the top. Besides that piece of furniture, there was nothing else of interest. She wondered who lived there. Whoever-it-was was probably still on the island somewhere.

Ruth walked out and saw that the boys were loitering by the house as if they didn't know what to do. "What are you guys doing?" She yelled in frustration. "Go look for the plant!" She made a sharp shooing motion and walked back into the hut.

Ruth leaned over and examined one of the boards that made up the wall. She traced her finger over it lightly. When she reached the middle of the plank, she saw something that made her heart leap.

There, where her finger was lying, was a fleck of green paint.

Her heart thundering with excitement, Ruth wondered if someone from the *Campekter* had survived, since the ship had been painted green.

As she examined the wood and mulled over the possibilities, an unseen figure approached from behind her. She felt a light tap on her shoulder, jolting her already frayed nerves.

In a lightning-fast movement, Ruth whirled around and whipped a knife out of her belt.

Standing in front of her, with amazement plain in his eyes, was the last person she expected to see.

"I don't know if we'll ever find it!" Samuel exclaimed, kicking a clump of sand, which scattered into a million grains and blew away in the wind.

They had been walking along the beach for about a half hour with no success. Samuel and Zane were getting tired, but Mikal was as energetic as ever.

"Aw, come on!" He said. "Don't be a pessimist!"

Although the other two were worried about her, they had come a long way from the hut, and it was growing darker. Samuel didn't know what came out of the jungle at night, and he didn't want to find out.

He was just about to turn back, when a rustling sounded in the bushes. The leaves of the exotic plants shook slightly as something unidentified scrambled through the dense undergrowth.

Being the inquisitive person he was, Samuel followed the unseen creature on its path along the edge of the shore.

When it suddenly stopped, he crouched down and tried to catch a glimpse of it. Zane and Mikal had seen it too and were now standing beside him, watching.

The sun was slowly setting, and the afternoon light was fading. After watching the bush for a few minutes, Mikal gave in and decided that they needed to head back to the girls. He leaned over and tapped Samuel on the shoulder.

"We need to go back now. We don't know what's going on with the girls, and we might have more time to find the plant tomorrow."

"Wait!" Samuel exclaimed, brushing his hand away. "I see something!" He moved in closer to the bushes.

"What? What is it?" The other two boys leaned in, trying to spot what he had seen.

"It's... it's light!" Taking a step of courage, Samuel closed his eyes and reached into the unknown bush, pulling out a bright green vine covered in star-shaped leaves.

Holding it with trembling hands, he turned one over and revealed an intricate network of glowing veins.

"Is this what I think it is?" Samuel asked in a quiet voice. He yanked on the vine, hoping to uproot it, but it kept coming.

When he reached the end of the long tendril, Samuel pulled it from the ground. He coiled it around his arm and held it tightly, for fear of losing it.

"We've finally found it!" He exclaimed. "Let's go, guys!" They turned around and started sprinting back across the beach towards the primitive shanty they had left.

When they finally came in sight of the hut, there was a roaring fire outside the doorway, illuminating its interior.

"There's the house!" Mikal shouted.

Ruth, hearing him yell, ran out and waved to them, beckoning for them to come quickly.

To their surprise, someone else walked out behind her. They could tell it was a man from his build, but in the darkness of the evening, they couldn't make out his features. He and Ruth had obviously become acquainted already, for they acted at ease around each other. The others wondered if he had built the shanty.

After observing the incoming boys, the man walked back inside the house, but Ruth stayed out, waiting for them.

Samuel picked up speed as he ran towards the hut, pumping his legs as fast as he could. As he thought about who the man could be, a spark of hope began growing in his mind.

Samuel let that thought power his rapid steps, running faster than he ever had before.

When he reached the door, he was moving so fast that he nearly slid past the house altogether. Having unwrapped the vine as he ran, Samuel tossed it into Ruth's arms.

She grinned excitedly at their success and led him inside.

Hope washed through Samuel's body as he saw the man turn around.

Then it dawned on him. The man's black hair, his sea-green eyes, and his familiar half-grin made the expectation in Samuel leak out of him like a bleeding gash in his chest.

Zane and Mikal puffed in behind them and gasped when they saw the newcomer.

"Marcus?!"

34

...

The Healer

"What are you doing here?!" Samuel asked the first-mate of the *Campekter*.

"Hello to you, too," Marcus muttered under his breath.

"How did you get here?" Samuel asked, extremely disappointed over the fact that it was not his brother.

"Well, when we were attacked by Pheno, the ship was destroyed, and all of us sailors fell into the ocean. Fortunately, I know how to swim, and I swam until I found a big chunk of the ship to grab onto. I sat on that board for the longest time, and I eventually floated to this island. I used driftwood and pieces of the ship to build this hut so I could be safe from the weather and whatever other dangers lurk here."

"How long have you been staying here?"

"Just since this morning. I've had just about enough time to build this little shack and gather some food." Marcus turned back to Kari and changed the subject. "You guys had better start treating your hurt friend here, before she dies."

That one simple sentence jolted them back into action after Marcus's surprise appearance.

Ruth had already ripped most of the leaves off of the vine, and she was currently grinding them into smaller pieces with an oval-shaped rock she had found on the beach.

She vigorously broke them apart on a wooden board that had once been part of the shack. The minute pieces of Shining Star stuck to the wood, mixing with the sticky liquid that seeped out of the veins of the leaves.

"What can we do to help?" Mikal asked, bending over next to Ruth. She turned and looked up at him, brushing unkempt hair off her sweaty brow.

"Can you go get some seawater? I just need a small amount to make pulp."

Marcus interrupted, pointing towards the jungle. "I found a small spring of fresh water not a hundred meters from here."

Mikal nodded and ran in the direction Marcus had indicated.

While the others were helping Ruth prepare the Shining Star, Kari's status had declined rapidly. She was coughing now, horrid racking coughs that came from the bottom of her lungs. Her eyes were painfully bloodshot, and her wound was swelling so much that Ruth had taken the bandage off. Her skin was sticky with sweat, but she was also shivering violently.

For some time now, she had been in a state of unconsciousness, her body twitching intermittently with pain. Ruth feared that she wouldn't last much longer. The Dragon Fire now coursed through her veins, and if they couldn't procure the antidote soon enough, she would be lost.

This was a fact that Ruth had not told the others. There was no sense in causing them more worry.

The young healer finished grinding the leaves and scraped most of them into a small pouch she carried on her belt.

The rest she put in a compact, wooden bowl that had come out of her medical kit. Its only purpose was for mixing remedies.

Right on cue, Mikal ran into the shack with a curved leaf filled with water. The leaf was firm and rigid, obviously a species native to this island. He handed it to Ruth, being careful not to spill any on the ground.

As she stared at the clear, but slightly dirty water, the healer's thirst was overwhelming, but she forced herself to make Kari her priority.

Ruth poured some of the water into a special cloth that she had Samuel hold over the wooden bowl. It strained the water, making sure that as little debris as possible filtered through.

When she felt that she had enough water, she stopped pouring and gave the bowl-shaped leaf back to Mikal.

Ruth picked up the ovular rock she had found earlier and began using it to mix the sticky leaf bits and water. After her mixture was a nice, gloopy mush, she called to Zane and Mikal.

"Help me hold her down. This is going to hurt very badly, and I don't want her moving."

Ruth walked over to Kari, who was still unconscious, and sat down next to her. She reached into her medical kit and extracted a small spatula-like object. She smeared some of the Shining Star mixture on its end, and while Mikal and Zane held Kari, Ruth began dabbing the poultice on the infected area of her arm.

Kari immediately started thrashing. She tried to wriggle away from the strong hands that were holding her down and escape the burning pain in her arm, but she was too weak to succeed. Her breaths came in quick spasms now, due to the pain of the pulp entering her wound.

When Ruth finished coating the injured area with the dull green solution, she set her spreading tool to the side and brought the bowl up to Kari's mouth.

"You need to drink this, Kari," she said in a gentle voice, hoping to break into her friend's comatose mind. "It tastes nasty, but it will help the infection subside."

Without hesitating, Ruth tipped the bowl slowly until the mushy mixture began oozing into Kari's mouth. The wounded girl gagged subconsciously, but Ruth leaned her head backward, forcing her to swallow it.

The boys grimaced and looked away at the sight of the disgusting glop disappearing down Kari's throat.

Ruth rolled her eyes at them. She had seen things much more revolting than this during her life.

After she finished cleaning and putting away her tools, she came back to watch Kari with the rest of them. She hoped that her Shining Star mixture was a fast-acting remedy.

The girl had grown quieter since the pulp was administered. She was still shivering, and the swelling in her arm seemed to be the same, although it was hard to tell underneath the wet, green mixture.

The blanket that had been wrapped around her since being on the ship had stiffened from the salty air, but it still kept the heat close to Kari's body.

"It's going to work," Ruth commented, "but I don't know how fast. It might be a while before it takes effect." She leaned over and put her hand near Kari's mouth to check for breath. Ruth's eyes widened.

"What is it, Ruth? What's wrong?" Samuel asked uneasily.

"Her... her breath. It... it's not there!"

"What?" Mikal asked, fearing the worst. "What do you mean?"

"She's not breathing!"

Ruth was panicking, not knowing what to do now that her poultice had seemingly failed. Ruth put her head down and began sobbing in frustration.

"I... I thought it would work, b-but it didn't!" The boys comforted her, tears beginning to run down their faces.

All this time, they had figured that it would turn out all right, that the Shining Star would work, and Kari would be okay. They had never thought that it might not work, and that Kari might die! It had all just been a fantasy in their heads.

Marcus, who had been standing in the corner watching this whole time, came forward and put his hand on Kari's neck, where her main artery was, frowning suspiciously.

"Her heart is beating faintly," he announced, "but I don't know if it will prevail." He looked pityingly at the four sorrowful companions and then back at Kari.

Watching quietly, Marcus's eyes fell upon Kari's arm. He leaned closer to examine the swollen wound.

"Hey!" He yelled. "Come look at this!" Ruth lifted her red eyes and looked where Marcus was pointing, sand sticking to the tear trails on her face.

"The swelling's going away!" She shouted, standing up.

The three boys quickly made their way to the wooden bed and looked at Kari's arm as well.

To their surprise, the puffy, orange wound was visibly decreasing, the poultice having soaked in completely.

Mikal reached for Kari's shoulder, but Ruth stopped him.

"Wait! Let her wake on her own." They continued watching the slumbering girl. As they gazed upon her, sweat broke out on her brow, and she convulsed.

A small stream of a sickly-looking, orange fluid spurted from the puncture wound in her arm, falling to the sand and soaking in. The unhealthy tinge that had once covered her arm faded away, leaving nothing but pink skin with a dark scar.

With a gasping intake of breath, Kari's eyes shot open and she sat straight up.

She blinked a few times, looked around at the faces surrounding her, and punctually vomited green mash all over the ground.

35

...

Into The Jungle

The morning sun peeked through the cracks of the wooden shanty, shining its pale light upon the six sleeping figures.

Two of them, the girls, were sleeping on a crude bed made out of wooden planks and thick leaves. The boys had the privilege of sleeping on the floor, which consisted of a messy mix of sand and dirt.

Samuel's eyes opened, and as usual, it took him a second to remember where he was. With a sudden flashback, he recalled the excitement of the day before: Arriving on the island and Kari nearly dying. He groaned and sat up, stretching his arms.

After Kari had a sudden change in condition and threw up, Ruth immediately told her to lie down and checked her temperature. With joyous eyes, Ruth pronounced Kari fully healed from the poison, although she would be weak for a while afterward.

Following Kari's revival, the boys were sent to fill up the few water skins they had with fresh water from the spring. They had a simple celebration feast of water and the edible plants Marcus had gathered.

Samuel's sleeping arrangements had not been very comfortable. He never would have guessed it, but Marcus snored louder than his father. In addition to that, Mikal seemed to have dreams that were quite violent. Throughout the night, he had jerked his arms and legs in a seemingly random manner, repeatedly hitting Samuel.

The only other problems he had were the temperature, which was very cold due to the nearby ocean, and the constant biting of the pesky sand fleas. There were so many of them that Samuel had to cover his mouth, nose, and ears to be able to sleep.

Now that it was morning, the tired youth stood up, carefully stepping over his companions to get outside.

Walking out the door, he shook his head and combed his hands through his hair, trying to rid his scalp of the tiny sand fleas that had left small, red sores on his body during the night.

When he thought that all the bugs were gone, Samuel looked out across the water, squinting in the bright light of the morning sun. Surveying the vast ocean, he felt the beginnings of despair and wondered how in the world they would get back to the mainland.

Samuel heard footsteps padding behind him. He turned around.

Ruth walked up and stood next to him, her eyes bleary and her long hair disheveled.

"Good morning," she said, yawning.

"Hi. How are you doing?" She had been tending Kari for most of the night and hadn't had much sleep.

"Very tired," she replied, nodding. "It took me forever to fall asleep, with all the excitement, you know."

"Yeah. And Marcus's snoring." They laughed.

"Where do you think we are?" Ruth asked, changing the subject. The question had been on her mind since they landed.

"I think we may have landed on the Realm of Y."

"Do you really think so?"

"Yeah. I mean, we're on a big island in the middle of the Evis Ocean. The sea monster that's supposed to be guarding it attacked us. I'd say there's a pretty good chance that we landed right where we needed to be."

Ruth asked a different question. "Do you remember all that stuff Zane was telling us about?"

"Yeah…"

"What if it's true, and there really *is* someone watching us right now?"

"I'm guessing that Zane is right. This Adonai he told us about might have led us straight to the island we needed to reach." They stood in silence for a moment, watching the waves crash against the shore.

"Since this is most likely the Realm of Y, we should go wake the others and prepare to find the statue King Nunor told us about. The earlier we start, the better. You never know how long it will take us."

With that they turned and walked back toward the hut to wake the others and get ready to find the mysterious Y.

Everyone was up now, and they had eaten a small, but nourishing meal.

Samuel informed the others of his deduction about their location. Marcus had concurred, saying that from his years of using maps and charts, it was very likely.

Moving quickly so they wouldn't lose any time, the six energized people finished packing up their weapons, water skins, and food in preparation to leave.

When the shelter was vacant the previous day, Marcus had been foraging for edible plants and animals. He had found some berries and leaves that he could identify, so he brought those back to his hut for consumption. However, he hadn't counted on having more than one mouth to feed, so he suggested that they look for some more food while they hiked through the jungle.

Kari's arm was hardly swollen anymore, and her skin regained its healthy hue. She said she felt very energetic, although she had not moved in a while. She was eager to go, but before they set off into the jungle, she spent a few minutes exercising her muscles. A couple weeks without using them had not helped her retain her strength. They would have to take frequent rest stops.

"Alright, guys!" Marcus exclaimed in his loud sailor's voice. "Time to leave! Let's go!" He marched towards the edge of the jungle, beckoning for them to follow.

Samuel hiked up the beach to where the jungle started, watching the back of Marcus's sun-tanned head, his short, black hair rippling in the sea breeze.

As the group approached the jungle, the trees seemed to tower dauntingly, threatening to smash them at any moment. Fortunately, Samuel was smart enough to know that if they were weak enough to fall, they would have fallen a long time ago.

Upon passing the barrier of trees, the temperature rose drastically. When they had been on the beach with the wind blowing on them, the heat hadn't seemed very bad.

Now, with no wind, the climate affected them. Within the first fifteen minutes of hiking, sweat was already pouring down their faces.

In addition to the extreme temperature, the humidity was very high. Although oxygen was plentiful due to all the plant life, Samuel felt as if he was getting very little air with each breath. Kari was breathing heavily, so Ruth was helping her along the tangled path.

They encountered other hazards as they trekked deeper into the jungle. Roots bulging out of the ground made it hard to walk without tripping, and large, almost invisible spiderwebs regularly crossed the path.

Swarms of small, biting insects also flew irritatingly around the travelers' heads. These creatures were everywhere, flying in huge masses that made incredibly annoying whining sounds. If someone accidentally ran into one, the bugs would scatter and go every which way, causing them to fly into mouths and up noses.

Another interesting phenomenon that Samuel noticed was the texture of the ground. Instead of consisting of moist dirt and rocks like a normal jungle, the ground was quite smooth. Even more fascinating was that a network of cracks ran through it, forming scales of smooth ground everwhere.

The plants that grew from the ground seemed to come only from these strange cracks. The lines were not very noticeable, though, because they were colored a dull bluish-green. Samuel kept this abnormality to himself and pondered it as he hiked.

Earlier that day, Samuel had told Marcus of their mission to find the key half that lay with the mysterious statue of Y.

Having studied the Realm of Y frequently as a child, Marcus believed that he knew almost everything about it. He considered himself to be an expert.

After pondering which direction to go to reach the statue, he decided to alter their course slightly to the north. He knew that the statue of Y was said to be somewhere near the north center section of the island.

Firm in his resolution, Marcus marched recklessly through the masses of plant life, not taking precautions as simple as looking down.

The stocky sailor jumped over a large root that was impeding his path and landed heavily on the other side. When he tried to move his feet again, however, he realized that they were stuck tight.

He had landed in a pile of something strange. It was light brown in color and looked smooth and runny. However, its consistency was exactly the opposite of that. As Marcus yanked on his leg, he realized that it was doing no good. He was stuck.

"Hey! Can I get some help here? I seem to be stuck!" He yanked at his legs violently, trying to loosen them from the sticky goo.

Samuel climbed over the root and stopped suddenly, barely avoiding the pile of muck.

"What is this stuff?" He asked, talking to no one in particular.

As if answering his question, a large, squirrel-like creature scrambled up a tree to Samuel's left and sat on one of the gnarled branches. It stared at the trapped sailor and emitted a high-pitched, gurgling sound. A stream of light brown gunk fell from behind the animal and landed in a steaming pile on the ground.

Samuel grimaced and turned back to Marcus. "That," he said in an low voice, "was disgusting."

"Yes, yes, I know! Now can you please help me?!" Marcus yelled, exasperated.

"Here, grab my hand." Samuel reached out to the unmoving guide, who twisted his body in order to grab the offered hand.

The strong boy yanked hard, but he could not seem to free his friend. Soon, all five of them were grabbing Marcus's clothes, pulling with all their strength to free him. However, the harder they pulled, the stronger the substance seemed.

Samuel let go for a moment and gasped. Marcus had budged a small bit, but he was still very stuck. As he was about to draw his sword to cut Marcus out of the gunk, a deep voice spoke into his head.

"*Samuel, grab hold of your friend!*" Astounded, Samuel wondered if this was the Adonai he had heard once before.

"*What?*" He thought back.

"*Grab your friend and hold on to something!*" Adonai's tone was urgent, so Samuel shook himself out of his surprise and grabbed Marcus's hand, not stopping to question.

"Hold on to something, guys!" He yelled to his friends. "Don't ask why, just do it!"

Heeding his advice, they grabbed on to the trees that were closest to them, grasping the moist bark and heaving themselves off the ground. Samuel wrapped his other arm around a thick tree branch that was above him and dug his fingers in.

Moments later, the ground began rumbling. The trees and plants shook violently. Samuel held on to the tree branch as tight as he could, sensing that if he let go, something very bad would happen.

Before any of them knew what was going on, a large crack split through the ground beneath their feet, and a gigantic chasm yawned open.

36

...

Discoveries

Everyone screamed, hugging their trees tighter.

"Help me!" Marcus yelled, his fingernails digging into Samuel's bulging arm. He was dangling precariously over the pit, his face red and dripping with sweat.

"I think that gross stuff is gone!" Samuel said, wincing at the sharp pain in his forearm. When the chasm had opened, the pile of muck peeled away from Marcus and fell into the depths below.

"Hold on tight!" Samuel yelled. He bent his body until his legs reached the tree branch his hand was clutching. Now upside down, he wrapped them around it and grabbed Marcus with his other hand, hoisting the heavy man up. Fortunately the branch was strong, and it held both of them as Samuel heaved Marcus high enough to grab on to the tree.

The guide breathed heavily as he hung on to the branch. "Thank you, Samuel! I don't know how I can repay you, but..."

"Marcus!" Samuel reprimanded. "Don't even think about repaying me! We have more important things to worry about right now."

Trusting his toned arm muscles, Samuel let go of the branch with his legs and began inching toward the main tree trunk.

As he did this, he looked around at his other friends, who were still hanging on to various trees and branches. In the dim light of the jungle, he could barely see their faces and hands, contrasted against the dark trees.

He reached the trunk and dropped to the ground at the rim of the gorge.

"Hey, guys!" Samuel yelled to the others. "I'm over here! Start climbing to this side of the pit, but be careful!" He watched as his friends slowly advanced through the tangle of branches and moss, creeping their way from tree to tree. One by one, they dropped to the ground next to him, very frightened but safe.

Samuel counted them as they came through to make sure they were all there. He saw Mikal, Kari, Zane, and Marcus, but no Ruth.

"Ruth! Where are you?" He called out.

"Right here!" She was crawling through the twisted branches just over the pit, being careful to only step on the ones that looked strong enough to hold her weight.

"I'm almost there!" Ruth scooted herself through a hole in the mass of wood and dropped towards the ground.

To everyone's surprise, however, the chasm grumbled open just a bit wider, and Ruth fell screaming into the blackness.

A scream streaked through the heavy air of the island.

The sound waves rippled through the air until they penetrated the ears of a tall, stone statue.

This statue was carved in the likeness of a man, his face intense, with a narrow nose and sharp, piercing eyes. His hair was long and windswept, the corners of his mouth equal, forming an expression of placid indifference. A long cape was draped over his back, curving slightly to give the impression of a breeze blowing through. His clothes were elegant but simple, a long sword hanging in a sheath at his side. The man's posture was straight and nearly eight feet tall.

The statue, once dull and lifeless, creaked and groaned, shaking dust and rubble to the ground. Its joints cracked and heaved, until it moved, stepping awkwardly off its stone pedestal and thundering to the ground.

The statue reached behind itself and peeled a long strip of moss off its back, flinging it into the brush.

It had been a long time since Y was awakened, but now he rose again, seeking to aid those in need.

He lifted his heavy foot and slammed it to the ground. In moments, the ponderous statue was speeding into the jungle, his resounding footsteps shaking the island as he went.

Samuel reacted the instant he saw the ground begin to move. He lunged forward, grabbed Ruth's arm, and hooked his leg around a tree root all in one fluid movement.

Ruth screamed in terror, dangling undsteadily over the black void below her.

"Hold on, Ruth!" Samuel yelled, fighting to keep a grip on her sweaty arm.

"Well I'm not going to let go!" She yelled back.

Samuel felt his legs being yanked, as Zane slowly pulled him and Ruth out of the pit.

Samuel fell to the ground, exhausted. Ruth also dropped next to him, the terror dissipating and leaving only pain and fatigue.

"Thank you, Samuel!" She said, grabbing his arm and looking into his eyes with pure gratitude.

"Uh... you're welcome." Samuel looked up and realized all the others were staring at them.

"Oh!" Ruth said, letting go of his arm and standing up. "You'll never guess what I saw down there!"

Relieved that they could change the subject, Samuel heaved himself to his feet and asked, "What did you see?"

"The walls of the chasm! I think they're lined with... with teeth!"

"Teeth?!" Mikal asked incredulously. "Why would there be teeth down there?"

"I don't know! Maybe there's some sort of creature that lives under the ground. Maybe it's even part of the ground!" Ruth looked at the chasm, then followed the large crack all the way into the distance with her eyes.

"Wow! That pit goes a long way! Whatever this thing is, it's huge!"

Right after she said that, a familiar voice penetrated their thoughts and seeped into their minds.

It began a familiar pattern: Praising them and coaxing them to the edge.

"W-wait. Don't I kn-now this voice?" Ruth asked dazedly. She knew she had heard it before, but couldn't place where. The words were making her mind fuzzy, causing her to lose her train of thought.

"*Ruth*," another voice said. "*Wake up.*" Those simple words revived her brain and sharpened her senses.

Is this... Adonai? She asked tentatively with her thoughts.

"*Yes, child. Now wake your friends, for the wise warrior approaches.*" Adonai's soothing voice melted away, leaving her with feelings of peace and completeness.

"Wake my friends!" she exclaimed, coming back to the present. "Right!" She ran over to the others, shaking their shoulders and yelling in their faces, anything to break their concentration on the eerie voice.

Samuel shook his head, trying to clear his thoughts. "That's the same voice I heard on the ship! Right before Pheno attacked!"

"Yeah, I know! That's really weird!" Ruth paused for a moment to think. "Wait... what if that *was* Pheno?"

"What?" Mikal asked, perplexed. The others gathered around Ruth, listening with interest.

"I mean, what if Pheno can speak into our minds like that and try to influence us towards her? Maybe so she can eat us?"

"I've never thought of it that way. Maybe we didn't kill her, and she's somewhere on this island." Samuel looked down into the chasm. "Maybe she's down there."

"But Samuel! I saw teeth down there! Remember?"

The realization of what was going on suddenly dawned on them.

Samuel bent down and stroked the scaly ground, his eyes widening with understanding.

"You know what?" He said softly. "I'll bet this island *is* Pheno, and we just happened to stumble upon her mouth!"

The others froze and stood in silence, trying to comprehend the size of the sea monster they must be standing on if Samuel's assumption was correct.

Then, a thought hit Samuel like a meteor. "You know how she's supposed to guard the Realm of Y?" They nodded. "If this pit is her mouth, then maybe she *is* the Realm of Y!"

Before they could say anything else, however, the jungle began shaking. A thundering sound approached from behind them, vibrating like giant footsteps.

They hastily retreated into the shrubs and waited with tense muscles as the footsteps grew louder. Moments later, a tall, stone statue burst through the thick greenery.

37

...

The Statue

The bounding statue halted directly in front of their hiding spot and looked down condescendingly.

"WHO ARE YOU AND WHAT ARE YOU DOING ON MY ISLAND?" It spoke in a deep, gravelly voice that vibrated into their skulls. Its lips didn't move when it talked, forming the illusion that there was something else living in the statue.

I wonder who this guy is, Samuel thought cautiously as he stepped out of the bushes to address the statue. "Um, we're looking for someone called Y."

As he said that, Samuel took a good, long look at the tall statue standing in front of him. He contemplated the way its dull, gray eyes stared piercingly at him. "You are Y, aren't you?"

"WHO ASKS THIS?" It questioned, looking around at the small people that stood before it.

I may as well tell him, Samuel thought. *He definitely looks like Y, although the king didn't tell us he could actually move.*

Samuel cleared his throat, nervous at being in the presence of such a creature. "Uh... my name is Samuel, and I was sent from King Nunor of Aena to ask you a favor."

The statue stared down at him for a long time. The feeling of being watched by a living chunk of stone was quite unnerving for the six people standing there.

"YOU SPEAK THE TRUTH," it rumbled, after examining Samuel and his friends for several minutes. "I DO NOT CARE FOR THIS KING, BUT THE LIGHT OF ADONAI FLUTTERS WITHIN YOU, SO I WILL DEIGN TO PROVIDE ASSISTANCE. WHAT MAY A BOY SUCH AS YOU ASK OF ME?" Y spoke very slowly. A minute passed as they listened patiently. Samuel hoped this conversation would be short.

"I have been sent to retrieve the key to Yamal. I was told that it was split into two halves, and you are the keeper of one of those." Samuel hoped that this creature was up for bargaining. It would be problematic if Y was not willing to give them the key half.

Y stood very still, mulling over this request. Finally, he seemed to come to a decision.

"YOU HAVE ASKED FOR THE KEY TO YAMAL, AND I WILL GIVE IT TO YOU." Samuel sighed in relief, but before he could revel in his good fortune, Y continued.

"BUT BEFORE YOU RECEIVE IT, YOU MUST CARRY OUT TWO TASKS." Samuel looked around at his friends. He had a good idea of what Y was going to ask, for he remembered the tale about Yanonelias that Marcus had told them.

"FIRST, YOU MUST TELL ME THE PURPOSE FOR WHICH THIS KEY IS NEEDED. SECOND, YOU MUST OBTAIN FOR ME AN ITEM. I SEE THAT YOU HAVE CAUSED THE MOUTH OF PHENO TO BE OPENED. THUS, I WILL ASSIGN YOU THE TASK OF RETRIEVING ONE OF HER LUSTROUS TEETH. THIS MUST BE ACCOMPLISHED BEFORE SUNDOWN

TODAY. I WILL STAY WITH YOU AND MAKE SURE YOU DO NOT ABSCOND WITH THIS PRECIOUS ITEM, BUT I WILL NOT INTERVENE IN ANY WAY. IF I DO NOT HAVE THE TOOTH, THEN YOU MAY NOT HAVE THE KEY. HAVE I MADE THIS CLEAR?" The large statue looked down at Samuel questioningly.

This whole conversation had taken well over five minutes, and Samuel's legs were getting sore from standing still. *I may as well agree and make him quit talking,* he thought. *At least we know that this island really is Pheno. Although, I'm not sure if that's a good thing.*

"Very well. We will abide by your terms and deliver the tooth to you in time." He nodded at the tall statue, which dipped its head slowly, closing the deal.

"NOW... FOR WHAT DO YOU WISH TO USE THE KEY?" Y questioned.

"The king told us that it would be used to open a secret door that leads into Yamal." Samuel said. That was all the king had told him. If the key had any other use, then he wasn't aware of it.

Y stood motionless in thought for a moment. He did that frequently. Samuel wondered if it was his slow brain trying to process everything.

"YOU ARE TELLING THE TRUTH. IF YOUR INTENTIONS HAD BEEN EVIL, I WOULD NOT BE WILLING TO BESTOW THE KEY UPON YOU. HOWEVER, I SEE THAT THIS KING HAS NOT TOLD YOU ITS REAL PURPOSE." Y said mysteriously. "I AM ALMOST CERTAIN THAT HE INTENDS TO USE IT DIFFERENTLY THAN YOU MAY EXPECT."

"What do you mean by that?" Samuel asked, confused. He hadn't thought about it having another use.

"AS OF NOW, THE KING ON HIGH FORBIDS ME TO INFORM YOU OF ITS REAL PURPOSE. JUST KNOW THAT YOUR KING MAY HAVE AN ALTERNATE PLAN IN MIND. ONE YOU WOULD NOT EXPECT." He paused for a moment. "YOUR ANSWER IS SUITABLE. CONTINUE WITH THE FINAL CONSTITUENT OF OUR BARGAIN." Y walked a few paces away and turned back, standing as still as only a statue can.

"Alright!" Samuel said to the others, glad that the long conversation was over. "Let's get to work!"

"Lower me down, now. Slowly!" Ruth dangled from a vine that hung over the cavernous maw of Pheno. Since she was the lightest, Ruth had been elected to be the one to retrieve the tooth for Y.

"Keep it going!" She yelled up to the others. Marcus had claimed that the vine they were using was extremely strong and wouldn't break from so little tension. She hoped he was right.

Ruth placed her feet on the moist walls of the mouth, slowly rappelling into the depths below. She hadn't been very thrilled about coming back in here after her close call, but she figured that it wasn't the worst thing she would do in her life.

Pheno's teeth were located just below a section that was covered with slime and ooze. If she craned her neck, she could just see the spiny protrusions. Unfortunately, the goo reminded her of the tentacle that had attacked them at sea. That was a dreadful memory.

After being swatted into the air, nearly drowning, and living on a boat for two days with soaking wet clothes, Ruth was not excited to discover that what they killed wasn't even the real thing.

"Are you almost there?" Samuel called down to her. She smiled.

"Almost! Just a little bit more, I think!"

Samuel had been protective of her, since she had almost died multiple times. He had been against her going down in the mouth, offering to do it instead. Fortunately, she had convinced him that she was the lightest, even with a belt full of knives on, and it would be much easier if she retrieved the tooth.

Ruth looked at where she was and determined that she was low enough. "You can stop now!" She yelled up to the others.

"Alright!" She heard Samuel's voice call down. The descent of the vine stopped abruptly.

Ruth surveyed the lines of teeth that protruded from Pheno's mouth. She had wondered why the statue hadn't come down to get one for himself. She realized that he must be too heavy and would probably just fall.

Ruth swung her body forward, trying to reach one of the teeth she saw before her.

Suddenly, she heard yells and swords being drawn up above. The sounds of a battle echoed into the pit from the surface.

Ruth looked up anxiously, her heart pounding. Before she could do anything, there was a hard jerk on the vine around her waist and a sudden loosening of tension. With nothing to hold her up, Ruth fell screaming into the depths of Pheno's mouth.

38

...

Completion

"You can stop now!" Samuel heard Ruth yell up to him.

"Alright!" Samuel called back. He wrapped the vine tightly around a gnarled tree root, making sure his knot was secure.

They all stood up. All five of them had been cautiously lowering the vine, their every movement being supervised by the statuesque Y.

"Well, I hope it doesn't take her too long to get that tooth," Marcus said. "I don't like the way Mr. Y over there is watch... aagh!"

Marcus suddenly fell to the ground on his back, struggling with something that the other boys could not see. Samuel drew his sword and beckoned for the others to do the same.

Then there was a strangled gasp, and Marcus stopped moving.

"Marcus?" Kari asked tentatively. "Are you okay?" She walked over to the unmoving man and knelt down next to him. She felt Marcus's pulse. There was no heartbeat.

Kari stood up and looked around, wondering what in the world had just happened. "Guys," she said, choking on bile. "I think he's dead." They stared, stunned, at the still body.

Suddenly, Marcus lurched and flipped to the side. Blood had pooled where he had been lying, oozing from a deep gash in his back.

Everyone, except Y, gasped.

Despite the gruesomeness of the wound, that was not why they were surprised. Everyone was staring at the small creature that had killed Marcus.

It was about three feet tall with a long, flexible tail. It was obviously a reptile of some sort, but it stood on two legs, walking like a human. The many scales that covered its thin body were the same color as the bright moss that hung from every tree, providing it with excellent camouflage.

Each of its hands had three fingers, one that looked as if it might be an opposable thumb. On its feet there were five toes that would look humanoid, except for the scales and sharp talons.

The creature bared its fangs and hissed at the humans standing in front of it, its forked tongue flickering out from its mouth.

"What is that thing?" Samuel asked Y. Unfortunately for them, the statue kept its word and did not say anything.

"Well, whatever it is, it killed Marcus, so we need to kill it!" Kari exclaimed. She rushed forward with her sword drawn back to strike.

"Wait!" Mikal yelled, but it was too late.

Kari swung her sword at the creature, but before she could hit it, the strange reptile leapt into the air, landing on the flat of her blade. Using its powerful hind legs, it bounded straight over the aggressive warrior's head and onto the ground near the vine that held Ruth. With a clever look in its eyes, it swiped its foot forward so fast that they couldn't even see it happening. The large claw on a thumb-like toe slashed through the vine as if it were paper.

"No!" Mikal leapt for the vine, but before he could grab it, it disappeared into the deep blackness of Pheno's mouth.

Ruth screamed as she fell, flailing for something to grab on to. Her hand hit a bulky tooth, and she grasped it tightly, holding on with all her strength.

The end of the broken vine whipped past her and disappeared into the darkness.

Trying not to panic, Ruth paused a moment to catch her breath. Figuring that the vine would just be a hindrance, she carefully drew a knife with her unoccupied hand and cut it away from her waist.

Her breath was coming in quick gasps now, a feeling of hopelessness rising within her. Her shoulder was straining against her arm. Free of the vine, she grabbed the thick tooth with her other hand and shifted her grip.

Ruth was frightened beyond all comprehension, dangling over the throat of a gigantic beast while holding on to one of its teeth.

Realizing that her main goal had to be climbing out, she reached up with her right hand, grasping at another tooth. She grabbed hold of one and tightened her grip fiercely. She then put her feet on two other teeth and began climbing. Fortunately for her, the teeth curved upwards, ready to slice anything that fell in, or to provide handholds, whichever the circumstances required.

"Here I go," she muttered to herself. "Let's just hope I make it out of this place." As she was climbing, she remembered the voice that had woken her from Pheno's paralysis. Zane had told her that Adonai said anyone could call on Him at any time if they needed help.

"Hey, Adonai?" Ruth whispered shakily into the blackness. "Could you please help me while I try to get out of this? Please?" She looked up at the crack of light far above her head and suddenly felt an overwhelming sense of peace. It was as if someone had picked her up and held her close after a frightening tribulation.

With a newly imbued resolution, Ruth grabbed the next tooth above her and began climbing again.

After about five minutes, she had reached the section of Pheno's mouth that was covered in the sticky slime. Her hands were cut and bloodied from the multiple times she had slipped. Strangely, however, she did not feel much pain. Adonai was supporting her.

She resolved to get to know this mysterious Adonai better. He seemed like He could be a good friend, whoever He was.

Sweat streaked down her face, tracing lines in the dirt and dust that coated it. She stared at the wall of slime ahead of her. *Well, here goes nothing.* She reached up with her left hand and plunged it into the goo.

The sensation was surprisingly soothing, like a cold balm spread over her hands. Although it was somewhat disgusting, Ruth knew that this was the only way up, so she had to go.

Before she started climbing the rest of the way to the top, Ruth remembered the reason she had been sent down in the first place. She pulled her hand out of the clinging gel. The gooey substance bounced back into place, as if her hand had never been in it.

Cautiously reaching down with her slimy hand, Ruth grasped the tooth that was closest to her. It was a big, pearly white fang that glistened from the small amount of sunlight shining in from above.

Ruth held on to the goo tightly with her other hand as she yanked on the selected tooth. *Oh, gross!* She thought, as the root of the tooth cracked and snapped. She jerked it one last time, and it came free with a final "pop."

When she had pulled it out, an ear-shattering roar, louder than anything she had ever heard, thundered from the abyss below. The walls of Pheno's mouth started shaking, and ever so slowly, they began sliding closed.

"No!" Ruth shouted, panicking.

She began frantically climbing through the goop, not caring how much got on her clothes or her face. She could see the daylight above, getting closer and closer as she raced upward. She could clearly hear the sounds of swords slashing and something hissing and growling from the battle above.

The gap between the two sides of the monster's mouth inched together, rumbling and groaning.

Just when Ruth thought that she would never make it, her hand hit the top of the mouth. She hurriedly pulled herself up, breathing heavily with fear. She swung her leg over the side and clambered to the ground right as the chasm slammed shut with a earth-rattling boom.

Ruth laid her head on the scaly ground and breathed in shuddering gasps, trying to catch her breath.

Suddenly, a small green creature flew over her head, swinging from branch to branch with a long, flexible tail. Ruth jumped to her feet.

Samuel, Zane, Mikal, and Kari were fighting small, green creatures that were climbing nimbly up and down the gnarled trees of the jungle.

To her great surprise, Marcus was on the ground, lying motionless in a pool of blood. She ran over to him and checked his pulse. It was nonexistent. Marcus was dead.

Ruth looked up, angry at the small creatures for what they obviously must have done. Before she could react in her anger, a quiet voice in her head reminded her not to attack in rage.

Thanks, Adonai, she thought.

Ruth looked around the battle scene and suddenly had a brilliant idea. She ran over to the statue of Y, ducking a flying lizard.

The stoic statue was standing in the exact same place he had been when she descended. When she reached him, Ruth lifted her hand and shoved the shiny tooth in his face.

"Here you go, Y!"
With a slow hand, he reached up almost reverently and took the tooth out of her palm, staring at it incredulously.

"Now, can you please help us with this?" She asked, gesturing to the snarling reptiles.

The stolid statue gazed at the tooth, which he had longed for since Pheno attacked his hometown. He looked back at the mere children who had finally managed to bring it to him.

"YES, I WILL HELP YOU." The giant statue leaned his head backwards with the noises of stone grinding against stone and uttered a long, rippling cry that blasted through the jungle, piercing the ears and hearts of every being that heard it.

39

...

The First Half

The hissing creatures stopped suddenly and stared at Y.

The thundering bugle faded away, and the tall statue tilted his head back down and glared at the frozen creatures. If a statue could look disdainful, then Y did.

In an equally loud voice, he bellowed, "BEGONE!"

The small lizards were still for a moment, before turning around and swinging through the trees, using their tails, hands, and feet to move.

"Why didn't you just do that before?!" Samuel exclaimed indignantly. "One of our friends died, and you could have done something to stop it!"

"I DO NOT INTERFERE IN YOUR HUMAN MATTERS." Y said slowly. "YOUR FRIEND IS GONE, AND THAT IS NONE OF MY CONCERN." Before they could protest more, the statue continued. "NOW THAT I HAVE THE TOOTH I LONGED FOR, YOU WILL RECEIVE THE KEY. MANY PEOPLE HAVE TRIED TO GET IT, BUT ALL OF THEM HAVE FAILED. I AM GLAD THAT YOU HAVE DELIVERED TO ME MY PRIZE." Samuel thought he didn't look very glad.

Y turned around and headed to the place from where he had come.

"Wait!" Samuel said. "Let us bury our friend first!" The ponderous statue turned around and looked at him.

"YOUR FRIEND NO LONGER NEEDS YOUR ASSISTANCE. HE HAS PASSED ON INTO ANOTHER WORLD. YOU MUST FOLLOW ME NOW." Y turned back and continued walking.

Reluctantly Samuel followed. His thoughts traveled to Rosh. A deep aching filled his chest as he realized that his brother wouldn't be here to see them complete their mission, or to reunite with their long-lost parents.

Becoming truly aware of his thoughts, Samuel shook his head violently. *Why am I thinking this? Rosh is gone, and I need to stop brooding over it! It's just like Y said: He no longer needs our assistance, so I don't need to feel so downcast about it. I can let it go.* With this silent declaration, he felt a comforting wave of peace wash through his soul, and he marched on.

After hiking for several minutes, the group of tired warriors came upon a small clearing in which the jungle trees did not grow. In the center of this bare spot was a massive stone block. Samuel figured it must be the pedestal he stood on as a statue.

As they drew closer to it, Samuel could make out an inscription engraved on the side. It said:

Blessed are those who heed wisdom's instruction.

Samuel remembered that Y was known for giving wisdom to people who could find the Realm of Y.

The plodding figure stopped when he reached the block.

Y bent over and placed his hand on the stone. Samuel pondered how he could bend. *I wonder what he's made of. I've never seen anything like it before.*

As soon as Y's massive hand made contact with the stone, a buzzing sound echoed in their ears. It soon evolved into a loud rumbling that shook the ground.

To everyone's surprise, the stone block slid across Pheno's blue-green scales with a horrid grinding sound, revealing a compact chamber. Samuel mused how Pheno felt about a chunk being carved out of her skin.

In the pit, there was a wooden box that looked like it had been sitting there for ages.

Y turned back toward them and motioned to the box. "HERE IS YOUR KEY. BE CAREFUL WITH IT, AND REMEMBER WHAT I SAID. OPENING A PATH INTO THIS EARTHLY MONARCH'S FORTRESS MAY NOT BE THE ONLY REASON IT IS WANTED. THE KING ON HIGH PETITIONS ME TO WARN YOU: BEWARE! A DIFFERENT EVIL STIRS BENEATH THE GROUND. WOE TO HE WHO WAKES IT!"

Something about what Y had just said rang a bell in Samuel's mind. He recalled back when the king was assigning their mission, and with jarring certainty, he knew that this was why King Nunor had been so nervous. He was keeping something from them. Something very important.

Samuel reached into the pit and extracted the crusty, old box. As soon as he had taken it, the stone pedestal slid back, sealing the chamber shut.

Y stepped up onto his stand and gave them one last piece of advice, pointing to the right. "YOU MUST TRAVEL THAT WAY TO REACH YOUR NEXT DESTINATION. THE KING ON HIGH HAS PROVIDED YOU WITH A VESSEL. REMEMBER, TRUST IN ADONAI, AND YOU WILL BE KEPT FROM HARM." With that, Y struck a heroic pose, his arm still outstretched, pointing towards the east. There was a cracking and grinding noise, and then the tall statue was still.

"Well," Mikal stated. "I guess we don't get to hear any more from him."

Samuel sat down on the rough, scaly ground and wiped some slime off of the old container. He slowly lifted the lid, and the outer box immediately crumbled into pieces.

"That must have been sitting there for a long time," Kari commented.

Now lying in Samuel's hand was another box. This one was made of a hard, dark wood and looked like it was built to last. Samuel opened this one's lid and revealed what they had all been waiting for.

Sitting on a black cushion that rested comfortably in the container was a key, or half of one, anyway.

Its body was made of solid gold, and the blade of the key looked like a sharp point. If the two halves were put together, then Samuel knew it would look like a crown. Along its edge, where the two halves were supposed to fit together, were small marks that looked like rough scratches.

The most fascinating part of the key, however, was the bow. At the end of the long stalk that separated the blade and the bow, there was a half-circle. On this shape was a peculiar decoration. There was half of a deep blue, diamond-shaped jewel implanted in it. Samuel had never seen anything like it before. Not even the many gemstones in Castle Orthox were this beautiful.

The strange thing about the blue jewel was the effect it had on light. When a glint of sunlight struck the interior of the box around the key, the reflection that should have shown up on its glossy surface was nonexistent. Its blue color was so deep and dark that it absorbed all light that shone upon it.

"I think this is it." Samuel said.

"Well, duh." Mikal replied.

The shorter youth gently removed it from the box.

The key was surprisingly light. It felt like a dry twig that had just fallen from a rotting tree.

"Who's going to carry it?" Kari asked. One of them had to keep it, but she wasn't sure who could handle the responsibility.

"I think *you* should, Kari." The others nodded their heads in agreement.

"Me?!" She exclaimed skeptically. "Why me?" Everyone answered confidently.

"Because you're trustworthy."

"You know how to be organized."

"You can hide really well when someone's trying to find you."

Kari stared at the key as Samuel handed it to her.

"I think it's unanimous," he said.

She held it reverently, gazing at its elegance. Pulling herself out of her awe, she took the small box from Samuel. Kari gently laid the key back on the pillow, closed the lid, and placed it delicately in her satchel.

"I'll keep it safe. You can count on me."

"I know we can," Samuel said, smiling at her.

"Alright!" Ruth exclaimed. "I think it's about time we get off this island." The others agreed heartily, and with joy in their hearts, they began walking east, their minds full of thoughts about the adventures that lay ahead.

Part 3

The Dragons of the North

40

...

A Fateful Bath

The bright sun was shining overhead, and it was going to be a beautiful day.

They'd experienced a lot since they left Castle Orthox, and they looked the part. Their clothes were dirty and ragged, and their skin was filthy. Anyone who saw them probably would have thought they were an incompetent band of urchins looking to cause trouble. No one would guess they were on a mission for the king of Aena himself.

The five travelers had just landed on the coast of Velendaw, after sailing east for two weeks in a fishing boat that was given to them by the mysterious Adonai.

When they found it on the shore of the Realm of Y, it had been stocked with food and provisions, everything they needed to survive their trip to the next country.

Minutes earlier, they had sold it to a rich fisherman at the docks for eight gold shards. They had had a bit of trouble making the deal, because the man only spoke fragments of the common tongue. However, after many signs and gestures, they were eventually able to sell it.

The journey had been relatively uneventful. The only problems they had come across had been moldy mouse dung and a large, carnivorous fish that wanted to eat their ship.

Their next and final destination was Vanguard Mountain, which had the tallest peak known to man. Unfortunately, they were two countries away from it.

The other four left the planning up to Samuel, and he had decided that they needed to find a place in town where they could clean up and replenish their energy for the next, long journey. Back at Castle Orthox, he had learned that Velendaw was famous for its hot baths. Samuel had only ever experienced cold baths, and right now, a hot one sounded too good to be true.

"Look!" Zane exclaimed, pointing at one of the buildings along the side of the street. "Thar's an inn!" It was a neat-looking establishment, but as the small group had learned, you should never judge an inn by its front door.

A swinging wooden sign hung above the entrance. It had the words, "The Fowl Inn," printed on it, with a fat hen depicted underneath.

"I hope they didn't misspell that middle word, there," Ruth commented sarcastically. "It had better not be like that other inn we stayed at back in Shala." She was referring to the "White Swan", which should have been called the "Dusty Maggot."

"I guess there's only one way to find out," Samuel said, as he strode through the door.

The interior of "The Fowl Inn" was actually quite clean. There were circular tables placed evenly throughout the room, and there was enough space to walk easily up to the front counter.

It's probably because they're Velendians, Samuel thought to himself. People from that country are known to be cleaner and more proper than the citizens of other countries.

As they approached the polished counter, the proprietor of the hotel looked at them suspiciously. A pang of heartache hit Samuel as he remembered when his brother, unknown to him at the time, had done the same thing.

"You street rats need to leave!" The man said in a slightly accented, nasally voice. He looked down his long nose at them. "I'll have no stray rascals like yourselves ruining the atmosphere of my inn!"

Ignoring the man's warnings, Samuel said, "We need a room, a bath, and some fresh clothes." Before he could protest further, Samuel revealed the bag of coins he had been holding in his hand. "And we can pay." Kari had taught him a few tricks.

"You shouldn't be here! Get out of here!" The man said, although more hesitantly than last time. His eyes flicked to the bag Samuel was holding.

Not giving the man any reaction, Samuel opened the sack and pulled out one gold shard, turning it between his fingers. The man's eyes widened as he beheld the great sum of money that was laid before him. It was a week's wages!

"I-I think we may be able to make accommodations for you," the owner said reluctantly, deciding that obtaining the money would be the best course of action.

The man accepted the valuable coin in exchange for a slip of paper showing their room number on it, but then he had second thoughts when he saw the weapons strapped to the young warriors' belts.

"Wait a moment, please!" The man shouted to them. "You're going to have to leave those weapons here!" His eyes were trained mostly on the gigantic mace the very large youth was carrying.

Samuel sighed and ignored the yelling owner. He wasn't going to leave his weapon *anywhere*, after what had happened back in Shala Province.

Compared to battling a giant sea monster, the screaming bartender's threats were nothing more than an annoying mouse squeaking in their ears.

After finding their room, they set down their things, except the weapons of course, and left the building to purchase new clothes.

With clean garments to wear, the group reentered the inn and made their way to the baths.

At the end of the hall on the second floor, there were two doors: One for men and one for women. The words on the door were written in the Velendian language, but there were carvings to help those not native to Velendaw.

When he entered the room, he saw another, shorter hallway that seemed to be a dead end. It was decorated with the unique art of Velendaw.

There were four doors on one side of the narrow room and a blank wall on the other. Trying the handle on one of them, he found it unlocked. Samuel opened the door and walked in, tucking the bundle of clean clothes under his arm.

On the floor before him was a smooth, stone, bowl-like structure. Poised over this bowl was a shiny, metal pump.

Barring the door behind him, Samuel undressed and put his new clothes on a rack that stood against the wall. He wadded up his old, nasty ones and threw them on the floor.

Shivering from the cold air wafting over his body, Samuel stepped into the bowl and started hand-pumping water into it.

After scalding himself with the near boiling liquid, Samuel found that relaxing in a tub of hot water was quite comfortable.

A unique but pleasant odor drifted up from the water as he sat there, probably some sort of perfume they added to make their patrons smell better.

When he had spent a considerable amount of time soaking, Samuel climbed out and pulled a wooden plug that drained the water. He grabbed a thin towel that was hanging on the wall and dried himself off.

His eyes were feeling very heavy. He couldn't believe how tired he felt. It must have been the long journey combined with the relaxing bath.

After he was dressed and ready, Samuel went back to the room they had rented and waited for the others to return.

Yawning, he looked out a small window and observed the little town. Since it was getting close to suppertime, many people were bustling around outside, heading back to their homes for the night.

Samuel lay back on one of the two beds that were in their room, his fatigue overwhelming him. He tried to keep his eyes open as the setting sun covered him in a blanket of soft warmth.

Before long, however, his eyes closed, and he fell asleep, the fragrant scent of the bath still tingling in his nostrils.

Samuel's eyes popped open.

He didn't know how long he had been sleeping, but the sun had long since gone down. Everything was still and quiet. *I didn't realize I was* this *tired,* he thought.

To his surprise, his friends hadn't returned yet. A shiver of panic snaked through his body. *They should be back by now! Where are they?!*

Samuel reached for his sword with unsteady hands, knowing that something was amiss. He peered into the cracks and crevices of the room, trying to discern any possible threats. All he saw were the two plump beds, their shadows flickering from the light cast by a solitary torch on the wall.

That simple observation awoke something in his memory, something from a few hours ago, when he had been awake.

He hadn't lit the torch.

Samuel stood from the bed, his weariness replaced with adrenaline. He looked around warily, his senses prickling. He slowly took one step towards the door, scanning the darkness that the torchlight did not reach.

Samuel stopped suddenly.

In front of him, the old, wooden door was ajar. Past that, the ebony darkness of night made it so that he couldn't see a thing. The hallway beyond the door was cloaked in blackness, as if a multitude of shadows had cast themselves upon it.

That's strange, he thought, as he turned back to look at the beds. *Shouldn't the torchlight be hitting the door across the hall?*

Before he could think any more about it, a flicker of movement made him flinch and spin towards the door again. He stared into the blackness beyond, adrenaline racing through his body.

With his keen vision, he discerned another slight movement. Before he could react, a gleaming object flashed through the air, flying straight at his head!

41

...

In The Moonlight

Acting purely on instinct, Samuel hit the floor. The whistling blade flew over his head and slammed into the wall, quivering from the impact. It was a strange looking knife, resembling a curved cat's claw.

At that instant, a cloaked figure leapt out of the shadows, a serpent-shaped dagger in hand.

Samuel staggered to his feet and jabbed his sword clumsily at the attacker. The mysterious person dodged the attack and struck speedily at Samuel with the deadly knife.

Samuel just managed to parry the blade and in retaliation, brought his sword over his head in a downward arc. The cloaked assailant raised the dagger in a defensive position, but at the last moment, Samuel twisted his hand and brought the blade in a sharp swipe under the attacker's defense.

With a deep yelp of pain, the attacker, that Samuel now knew to be a man, collapsed to the floor, blood pouring from a deep gash in his side.

The man clutched at his wound and writhed until his movements slowed, and his hands dropped to the ground, moving no more.

Samuel yanked the torch out of its holder on the wall and shoved it into the hallway. When he saw nobody else, he walked back to the man and knelt down by his side. He pulled the hood back and gazed at his pale face.

He had a closely cropped beard and bushy eyebrows, but other than that, he was completely bald. What really caught Samuel's attention, however, was the peculiar tattoo on the man's forehead. Sketched in black ink was a symbol that Samuel had seen before. He strained his memory, trying to remember where he had seen it.

Oh, yeah! That's the same symbol that was on the Viper Fang*! This* must *be the symbol of Yamal.*

His thoughts returned to his missing friends and he wondered where they might be. He hoped they hadn't been captured, or worse. After searching the man's clothes for anything that might provide information, Samuel stood up and pushed the dead body to the side with his foot. All he had found were the accoutrements of an assassin, nothing more.

Being very cautious, Samuel crept out the door, looking both ways before he continued down the hallway. He decided to check the baths first, which was where he had last seen his friends.

He turned the doorknob to the men's baths slowly and carefully, grimacing when it emitted a high-pitched squeak.

Assuming no one had heard the door open, Samuel walked slowly forward, gripping his sword tightly. Sweat was beading on his brow, and his heart was beating rapidly. He peered into each room, his muscles tense and dread knotting within him.

So far, all of the small rooms were empty. However, he had one more to check.

Opening the door carefully, he hoped to see the same sight as the other rooms. Samuel peered into the darkness, trying to discern if there was anything of interest.

His heart leapt when he saw it.

There, lying unmoving in the tub, was a body.

Kari looked around the room and shivered.

She was clothed in her new garments and was huddled in a ball in the corner of the bath. She clutched a sharp knife close to her chest.

While bathing, a strange smell had permeated her senses and caused her to fall asleep in the bowl, despite the desperate warnings her brain had sent her.

When she had awoken, Kari hadn't known how long she'd been in there, but the water was cold and the sky outside the window was dark.

She had quickly dressed herself in the new clothes. As she started to walk out the door, she had found herself pinned to the floor with a knife at her throat.

Kari reacted instantly, pushing her attacker off and elbowing him in the jaw. The thin man had been knocked out cold, obviously not prepared for her reaction.

Kari had taken his knife and kept it, because her sword was back in the room. She had intended to walk out into the main hallway and look for the others, but had heard voices speaking in low tones.

While retracing her footsteps back into the washing room, Kari had seen two men huddling in the bathroom corridor.

After secretly listening to their conversation, she had learned that they were planning to hunt her down! They obviously thought she had run away and hid after taking down their comrade.

Wary, Kari had slunk back to the room in which she took her bath. She thought they wouldn't look for her there. So far, she had been right, but that did nothing to ease her apprehension.

Wondering if she had waited long enough, Kari slowly stood up. She walked carefully into the hallway, keeping her ears and eyes wide open.

As she stepped out into the main hall of the second floor, the tense warrior looked in all directions. Sensing movement up ahead, she froze, keeping her body as still as possible.

After a few moments of silence, the frightened girl started moving forward again.

A rough hand unexpectedly slapped over her mouth as someone tackled her to the ground.

The body was very still, so Samuel approached stealthily. In the moonlight that shone through the small window, he saw the figure's slumbering face.

It was Zane!

Forgoing all caution, Samuel dashed to the big boy's side. He patted Zane's damp shoulder, trying to wake him.

The water in the bowl had since gone cold, so Zane woke up, shivering violently.

"S-s-samuel?!" He said, utterly confused.

"Shhh!" Samuel put a finger to his lips. Zane took the cue and spoke in more hushed tones.

"W-what are you d-doing here S-s-samuel? Why is it n-nighttime all of a s-sudden? W-what's going on?!" Zane stepped out of the water, and Samuel turned his back, giving the very muscled youth some privacy.

"I think a substance to make us fall asleep was put in the bath water. As far as I can tell, it affected all of us.

"Also, there are people in the building that are trying to kill us. I've already dealt with one, but who knows how many more there are?"

Zane finished getting his clothes on and tapped Samuel on the shoulder.

"Do you have my mace?"

"No, I only have my sword. I didn't see any more weapons in the room."

"I put it under the bed for safekeeping. Just in case we had any trouble."

"Well, then I don't think anyone's found it yet." Samuel beckoned for the door and crouched low, sneaking out as quietly as he came. Zane walked beside him, his huge bicep brushing against Samuel's shoulder.

"We need to go back and find everyone else," Samuel whispered. "You were the first person I came across."

Zane was just about to agree, when a scream echoed through the inn.

42

...

Gone

Kari yelled, but the strong hand that was pressed against her mouth muffled the noise. She was about to bite her attacker, but before she could, somebody whispered in her ear.

"Kari?! Is that you?" The hand pulled away from her face.

"Mikal?!" She exclaimed softly, recognizing the voice. "What are you doing attacking me like that?"

"I'm so sorry!" In the moonlight that shone through the inn, she could see him. He looked truthfully penitent and very frightened, clutching his sword with white knuckles. "I didn't know it was you. I thought you were one of *them*." By his tone, she could tell that he meant the cloaked men that were hunting them.

"It's okay. I thought you were one of them too." She turned her head and examined the hallway behind where they were crouching. "It looks like there's none back there." She looked back at Mikal as a dark shadow loomed up behind him.

Kari screamed.

Mikal instantly took action. He whipped around and, seeing the threat, jumped to the side, slicing his sword at his attacker.

The cloaked man parried it expertly with a swipe from his long dagger. The assassin was obviously a skilled warrior. He blocked, struck, and dodged speedily, always managing to evade Mikal's flashing blade.

"Kari!" Mikal yelled, barely avoiding a jab to the stomach. "Run! Get out of here!"

The terrified girl stood petrified for a moment and then turned and raced down the hall. Mikal was relieved that she would get away, even if *he* was stuck with the assassin.

Kari ran around the corner and slammed into someone, whose face was hidden by the darkness.

The unknown person whispered in a quiet voice, "Everything's going to be okay."

"Is that Samuel?" She whispered back.

All of a sudden, a canvas bag was pulled over her head and she was grabbed from behind, someone binding her arms and legs with a rough rope. She wriggled and took in a breath to scream.

Before she could, however, something hard slammed into the side of her head, and she blacked out.

Mikal slashed and parried, never seeming to gain any ground on the quick man in front of him. He wondered if he would make it out of this battle alive. With this man's speed and agility, he wasn't so sure.

Applying a fast backhand swipe to the hilt of the sword, Mikal's assailant knocked the blade out of his grasp. The long implement stuck quivering into the soft wood of the hallway, leaving Mikal defenseless.

The wild-eyed boy began slowly backing up to the end of the hall, where the stairway to the first floor was.

The assassin approached, confident that he had won the fight. He spun his long dagger around in his fingers and chuckled throatily.

That was the last sound he would make.

Without warning, a shining blade emerged from the man's chest. He arched his back and then collapsed to the ground in a heap, still as only a dead man could be.

Standing behind the would-be assassin, face pale in the darkness, was Mikal's benefactor: Samuel, the shadowed body of Zane towering behind him.

"Boy, am I glad to see you guys!" Mikal exclaimed, still in a whisper.

"Yeah, you too," Samuel replied. "Did you hear that scream?" He wiped his blade on the dead man's clothes and sheathed it silently.

"That was Kari. She was with me just a minute ago, but I told her to run away. She went that way." He pointed behind him, to the staircase that led to the floor below.

"Have you heard anything from her since?"

"No. We should probably go check on her." Mikal walked over to the wall and yanked out his sword. *I need to work on my swordsmanship*, he thought, criticizing himself harshly. *I can't believe that guy defeated me so fast!*

Mikal followed Samuel to the stairs. Zane trailed behind, having retrieving his mace.

By the time they reached the dark lower floor, Mikal was becoming apprehensive. *We should have found her by now! Where is she?!*

Above the obnoxious snoring of who he thought must be the innkeeper, Mikal heard something different: Wagon wheels on cobblestones.

Throwing caution to the wind, Mikal raced to the door and looked out. A small, black-colored wagon was rumbling down the street, two sleek horses in the lead.

Knowing for sure that Kari was in it, Mikal sprinted towards its shadowy silhouette, his heart thundering in his chest.

Unfortunately, the wagon was too fast. Before long, it disappeared from sight down the long road that led out of the town.

Aghast, Mikal slowed to a stop, staring into the blackness that covered the small village.

Samuel and Zane ran up behind him, breathing hard. "What're you doin'?" Zane asked. "Where'd they go?"

The two others followed his line of sight down the road and guessed what had happened, a dark feeling sinking into their hearts.

"Is she gone?" Samuel asked tentatively.

"Yes!" Mikal exploded. "And I could have stopped them! If I just knew they would do that..." He fell to the ground miserably, not caring about the hard stones of the street digging into his knees.

Samuel laid a hand on Mikal's back, comforting his friend, and looked down the road in the direction the carriage had gone.

As he stared forlornly, something caught his eye, glinting in the moonlight. He left Mikal's side and walked over to investigate. It was a knife, pointing in the direction the carriage had gone. Samuel picked it up carefully.

"Guys, this is... was Ruth's." They stared at him as they realized the gravity of what he had said. "I think she was kidnapped too." Samuel suddenly felt the weight of extreme anxiety weighing on his soul. Two of their friends had been taken to somewhere unknown, and on top of that, they had lost the key half!

He and the other two started walking back toward the inn, knowing that there was nothing they could do this late at night.

When they opened the door and stepped inside, Samuel heard voices above them. He closed the door, which fortunately was well-oiled, and beckoned for the others to follow him to the side of the large main room.

The voices began moving closer, so he crouched down behind one of the tables and watched, the others following his example.

Two men walked down the staircase, talking in lowered voices. One was tall and broad, and the other was slightly shorter and slim. They were moving slowly, so Samuel was able to hear a good portion of their conversation.

"What'll we do with 'em, Raga?" The shorter one asked in a raspy whisper.

"I had Hugo take them to the compound," the larger man's voice was a deep bass, echoing throughout the room even if he tried to whisper. "They'll stay there until we can get them to tell us where the others are."

"What'll we do then?" The broad man, who must have been Raga, chuckled.

"Then, Nostal, we'll kill them." Both of the sadistic assassins laughed quietly.

Something about the conversation disturbed Samuel. It was the way they were talking, like they were being forced to dialogue.

The smaller one, Nostal, asked another question. "How're we gonna get the key?"

"That's why we took the female ones. They can tell us where their friends are going, and then we can go get them. They'll try to find us, but they won't succeed." Samuel breathed a silent sigh of relief. They didn't know that Kari had the key half.

"What base did you have them taken to? Was it the..." Raga cut him off.

"Shhh! You never know if they're listening."

"It's fine! I saw them upstairs. They were unconscious."

"Fine," the man said reluctantly. "But don't tell anyone else like you did last time."

"Yeah, yeah. I'm not doin' that again!" Nostal replied.

Something about that string of words made Samuel's heart skip a beat, but not in a good way. It was highly doubtful that someone would give in to telling a secret like that in a public place, nighttime or not. Something suspicious was going on, but Samuel just couldn't put his finger on it.

"Hugo's taking them to the swamp," the big man stated. "Hopefully, the other ones won't think to look there." The two men snuck out the door, being as silent as when they came in.

Samuel stood up shakily and put aside his suspicions for the time being, resolving to talk to the others in the morning.

Knowing that Adonai would help them find the girls, Samuel stood up and headed back to their room.

43

...

The Bard

Ruth had been walking down the hall in the dark after leaving the bath, wondering why she had fallen asleep, when someone roughly grabbed her from behind, tying her hands and feet and yanking a bag over her head.

Whoever-it-was didn't stop to search her, and that was a good thing, for she had a knife strapped to her back, hidden by her woolen shirt.

Ruth had no idea what was happening except that she was being kidnapped by big, smelly men. She wriggled and thrashed, trying to break free, but it was no use. Her captors were too strong.

She tried to scream, but couldn't because the bag was tied too tightly around her throat. She could barely breath.

After being carried through rooms and down steps, she was thrown on a hard surface. With the bag over her head, she couldn't tell where it was, but she could feel drafts of cold air blowing over her.

Then she heard the creaking of hinges and a slam. Clicks sounded as a door locked... the door to her prison, whatever that was.

Ruth had been waiting in silence for a few minutes, when she heard the door open again. Something else was thrown in with her. She tried to feel what it was, when her hands hit soft flesh.

Ruth tried to talk to the person, but the bag was too tight. It came out as a strangled, "Hehhhg!"

To try to loosen the choking bag, Ruth stretched her arms up behind her back. She had always thought she was flexible, but now her ability was being truly tested.

Suddenly, the small room jerked, and Ruth fell backwards, her head hitting the floor. With her ear pressed against the ground, she felt the grating of wheels against stone.

She was in a wagon.

Panicking that the others wouldn't know where she and the other captive were, Ruth scooted herself to where she thought the entrance was.

Taking a deep breath, as best she could with her neck constricted, she slammed her body against the door.

Any passersby may have thought she was trying to break out, but when she threw her body against it another time, the small dagger slipped out from her shirt and fell clattering to the road.

There, she thought. *I hope they get the message.* Her hands were shaking behind her back, and her heart was racing. Under the bag, she closed her eyes and tried to calm herself down, taking in as deep breaths as she could. *Come on, Ruth. Get yourself together!*

That wasn't working, so she tried reaching out to Adonai with her mind. *Adonai! Can you* please *help me with this? Please make me calm!*

Nothing happened for a moment, and she wondered if He didn't hear her. Then she realized that wasn't accurate. He had promised that she could call on Him whenever she needed him, and He would help.

After waiting a bit longer, Ruth received her answer.

The wagon hit a bump in the road, and her head whipped back and slammed against the side of the cell.

Seeing the blessing in disguise, Ruth thanked Adonai as she slipped off into unconsciousness, free from the worries that had previously plagued her.

They had been hiking for six hours now.

The morning following that dreadful night, Samuel, Mikal and Zane had been ready to go before the sun was even up. They collected a quick breakfast from the innkeeper, who was oblivious to what had happened, and left at the break of dawn.

The three boys were eager to continue the mission, and they felt the loss of the girls weighing heavily on their hearts. They *had* to find them.

Once they were past the town, the trees that had surrounded them before seemed thicker, forming large barriers on either side of the road. Branches leaned over the path, keeping a watchful eye on travelers and providing relief from the sun.

Samuel was very sure that the wagon had gone this way. He had learned some tracking skills from Kari back in Aena, so every once in a while, he would examine the ground, looking for signs of a wagon. When he stooped down, he could see shallow ruts in the ground, signs that confirmed the passage of the black wagon.

The three boys were not very talkative. As they hiked along the road, they were absorbed in their own thoughts about what the girls might be going through and how they were going to save them.

After a while, they reached a bend in the road. The path curved in a gradual, ninety-degree angle, so Samuel guessed that it was turning to the north. That was the direction they needed to go to get the second half of the key, but he was doubtful it would continue in that direction.

Samuel wondered how the girls were doing. He hoped that the kidnappers hadn't discovered that Kari had the key half. If they learned that she had been appointed the keeper of the key, then the mission would fail and the girls' lives would be forfeit.

Samuel was so absorbed in thought that he didn't notice a change in the landscape.

The tall, looming evergreen trees slowly evolved into shorter, sickly snags. The hard, dry ground under his feet was now moist soil that squished when he stepped. On both sides of the road, there were many small ponds, green in color and covered with scum. Long, pale lichen hung from the sagging branches of the dark trees, their groping tendrils swaying in the wind.

"Um, guys," Zane said, breaking into Samuel's thoughts. He looked up from the muddy ground and heard an intake of breath from Mikal next to him.

"I think we've reached that swamp."

"Hugo! You're back! And with guests! How delightful!" The slim man in green clothes smiled wickedly, exposing his crooked, yellow teeth.

He had a sharp nose that pointed out from his face like a spear, and his eyebrows were virtually nonexistent. The most striking features of his face were his eyes. They glowed with a mad light, the light of insanity.

He positioned himself in a simple chair in the center of a slightly raised dais. His satin clothes were expensive and rare. A regal-looking hat sat tilted on his head. Although the room was utilitarian, he acted as if he were a king.

"Yes, m'lord," the brawny man replied, his rough voice grating along their spines. "These are the two females that were traveling with the group you were told about." The kidnapper pushed forward two people who were bound hand and foot with bags tied over their heads. They fell to their knees from the force of the shove.

"Hello!" The man in charge said. "How are you? Did you have a pleasant ride?"

They didn't answer.

"Why aren't they answering?" The skinny man asked in a whiny voice. "They should be answering my questions!"

"Sorry, m'lord. The bags on their heads are tied too tightly for them to speak."

"Well loosen them, by all means!"

Hugo walked forward, roughly untied the ropes around the captives' necks, and yanked off the bags.

The long hair of the two girls fell behind them, tangled and disheveled. They gasped for breath, sucking in mouthfuls of air.

Recovering their breath, they looked at each other in surprise. A moment of understanding seemed to pass between them, and they both turned back to the man in the bright green suit.

"I would say we certainly did not have a pleasant ride!" The one with black hair said disparagingly. "Although I missed most of it because I was unconscious!"

The man looked at them and grinned. "Then I'm guessing that comfort didn't matter during your incapacitation!" Reverting to a more serious expression, he continued.

"Now... what are your names?" After they stared stubbornly for a few moments, he repeated the question. "Oh, come on! Just tell me your names! You can trust me!" He looked at them and smiled much too widely to be sane.

"We can *trust* you?!" The other one exclaimed. "After you tied us up and hauled us off to your little hideout? I don't think so!"

"Ooh, you have attitude!" He rubbed his hands together. "Well, if you won't tell me your names, then I guess

I'll have to give you new ones. Let's see…" He stroked his nonexistent beard, something he did rather often. "I'll call *you* Number 1 and *you* Number 2!" He pointed to each of the girls respectively.

The blonde one rolled her eyes. "Wow. How creative."

"Why thank you!" The sarcasm of the statement seemed to go right over his head.

"And what can we call you?" The black-haired one asked patronizingly, hoping to gain information.

"I guess I'll tell you, since I *know* I can trust you. After all, you are my prisoners." He grinned again, that scary, insane glint flashing in his eyes, proving to them that something was definitely wrong with his brain.

"You may call me Vincent the Bard."

44

...

The Swamp

"Whoa." Samuel stared at the murky water and gnarled trees on either side of the road. "Zane... I think you're right."

After looking around at the swamp for a few moments, Samuel turned his gaze to the ground. Crouching down, he studied the road for wagon ruts to make sure they were still on the right track.

Sure enough, there were thin lines that traced through the mud and along the trail.

Before he stood up, though, Samuel noticed something else. A small wood splinter was lying embedded in the road. He picked it up and examined it, turning it over in his fingers. It was very likely a piece of the wagon.

"They're still heading this way," Samuel informed the others. "I'm guessing it won't be long until the tracks lead off into the swamp. It won't be obvious, though. These are pretty smart people we're dealing with."

Mikal and Zane nodded, promising Samuel that they would keep an eye out for any change in direction, and they marched on, albeit slowly, down the long, sticky path.

As they walked, Zane noticed a flash of movement in the bushes to his right. He turned quickly and surveyed the murky undergrowth.

Nothing moved now, but he was sure he had seen something... or someone.

After another half-hour of trekking through the gloppy mud, the ruts in the road made a slight change in direction. They veered off to the side almost unnoticeably, but it was a change.

"C'mere, guys! Look at this!" Samuel pointed to the ruts, which were now heading into the swamp at a slight angle.

Before he stepped into the bog, however, Zane stopped him. "Wait, Samuel!"

The confident warrior turned and looked at Zane, raising his eyebrows in a questioning manner. "Yeah?"

"What if they meant fer us ta find the girls? What if it's a trap?" Zane had a bad feeling about following these men. His mind wandered back to the movement he had recently seen in the underbrush. *What if that was one of them?* He thought to himself. *They could have been tracking us this whole way, maybe leading us into a trap!*

Samuel's expression told him that the young leader wasn't ready to consider postponing their search for the girls. "That is possible," he said, "but if they're waiting for us, then we'll be ready."

Zane shrugged nonchalantly, hiding his real feelings. He wasn't about to go against Samuel's judgment, but he was wary. It seemed to him as if the men at the inn had been a little too open with their conversation. Maybe they had meant for the boys to find them. He put his hand on the solid handle of his mace, a small comfort to boost his confidence.

Putting his fears aside for the moment, Zane marched on, following Samuel and Mikal through the murky water.

The girls had been there overnight. The rough man that kidnapped them had thrown them in a dank cell, giving them no food or water. They had slept fitfully in the company of water rats and other unidentified swamp creatures.

"They're coming, m'lord." One of Vincent's men burst through the door, panting for breath.

"Who's coming?" Vincent asked. His mind was elsewhere, as usual. He plucked a random string on the small, wooden lute he was holding, sending a note reverberating throughout the room.

Vincent liked playing music. That was why he called himself "Vincent the Bard." With no regard for his hobbies, his men just called him "m'lord."

"The others from the group of our enemies, m'lord. I saw them turn off the road and come towards our base. They have to get past the trolls, but they might reach us.

"Good," Vincent said. "Let them come. You and your buddies can bring them to me after those pesky creatures are finished with them. I figure you have this under control." Vincent looked back at the lute, continuing to play random notes that obviously had no correlation to each other.

The man bowed his head, although in reality, he had little respect for the odd man. He turned and left, wondering when Vincent would die so they would be able to get a new commander. The cacophony of tuneless notes made him wince in agony.

The skinny bard suddenly called after him, "Oh! And tell Borgla to bring me an apple!" But the man was gone, so Vincent went back to strumming his lute.

In truth, Vincent was an excellent musician... when he chose to be. None of his men appreciated it, though. All they appreciated was brute force and violence.

They identified better with Vincent's sadistic nature. The only thing he loved more than music was hearing people scream as he tortured them in ways utterly unnatural. This was the true reason he was in charge. He ruled by fear, and that fear was rampant as rumors of his cruelty spread among his men.

Vincent stopped playing the instrument and looked up, absorbed in his own thoughts. His face suddenly broke into a wicked grin as he imagined what those three boys must have been going through right then.

Those trolls were nasty creatures.

Samuel's shoes squished and squashed as he made his way through the mucky swamp.

They had been traveling for about fifteen minutes since entering the mud, and all three of the boys were soaked and covered in grime up to their knees, besides Mikal, whose entire body was covered.

When they had first started into the swamp, Mikal had tried to jump to and from patches of grass, stabilizing himself by holding on to tree branches.

When a dry branch broke and he tumbled into the water, Mikal decided that walking like the others would be best.

Zane was probably having the hardest time. Because of his size, he sank further into the mud than the others. Eventually, he unstrapped his giant mace from his back and held it so it wouldn't drag through the muck.

They had been pretty quiet since they started out, each of them concentrating on their next strenuous step through the quagmire while trying to keep their weapons out of it.

Before long, Samuel felt a change in the surface of the ground. Instead of being soft and gross like the other mud they had just walked through, it felt like he was actually standing on solid ground, despite his feet being covered up to the ankles in sludge.

Eventually, Samuel spotted a large patch of earth. He beckoned for the others to stop and surveyed the island they had come across.

It was covered with tall grass and crooked trees that had murky green lichen hanging down from them. Small frogs and whining mosquitoes populated this island, just like they did the rest of the bog.

The most fascinating thing about the island, however, was not the flora or the fauna, but in fact, a large mound of dirt that rested in the center of the land formation. A small wooden door was embedded in the dirt, forming the impression that something lived there.

"What is that?" Mikal asked.

"I have no idea," replied Samuel. "It looks like some sort of dirt house. Let's just hope that whatever lives in it is friendly."

"I wonder…" Zane started, but Samuel cut him off.

"Wait!" Samuel put a hand to his ear, listening for something.

"What is it?" Zane whispered.

"I don't know," Samuel whispered back. "It sounds like a rumbling or something like that." He started walking closer to the hut. He put his ear right next to the wall, concentrating on the noise.

"Can you hear it better?" Mikal asked quietly.

"Yes…"

"Can you tell what it is?"

"I think it's… voices."

45

...

Hearing Voices

After this surprising revelation, both Mikal and Zane leaned closer to the house to listen as well.

Mikal was just barely able to make out the voices, until they suddenly clarified. *That was weird,* he thought. However, he could now hear the strange conversation loud and clear.

"Eh, Bofe," said a slimy-sounding voice.

Another voice, equally as wet and sticky, replied, "Yeh?"

"What you got on da stick?"

"Ees nuteen."

"No, really! What you got? Ees it toad or rat?"

"I sed nuteen!"

"Eh, you calm down. Eef you no want to tell me, you no have to tell me."

"Me no tell you! Ees mine!" Mikal grimaced as he heard a horrid crunching sound, obviously the creature, Bofe, eating whatever he had. There was silence for a few moments, and then they started talking again.

"Lurd, you pass da worms?"

"Me no have worms! Gave dem to Chemp!"

"Me have da worms, Chemp?"

The voice that answered was indescribably nasty. "Yeh, me got it." There was a clinking of something and then a disgusting squishing sound. These creatures, whatever they were, were apparently eating a meal, and judging by their choice of food, they were not human.

"Ees goot!" The first one exclaimed. There was some silent munching for a moment. "Me try you idea, Gund!"

"Wha' idea?" A deeper, gritty voice asked.

"Da worm an' toad! Ees so goot, but me want sumteen else."

"Wha'?" Gund answered.

Mikal had been listening to the whole conversation, and it seemed completely pointless. However, his thoughts about it changed when the next statement made him jump.

"Me want to eat snoopeen boys outside house." At this declaration, a cold shiver ran down Mikal's body. He slowly backed away from the mound.

Imagining the possibilities of what horrible creatures lived in that clump of dirt and what they would do to the three of them, Mikal let go of all caution and sprinted past the house and in the direction the wagon had gone.

He looked behind him and saw that the others were running as fast as him, their feet squishing in the cold swamp mud.

Remembering to look where he was running, Mikal turned his head forward and ran smack dab into the ugliest creature he had ever seen.

Ruth adjusted her position in the dingy prison cell. The two girls had been in here for a full day now, and all they had eaten was a chunk of hard, crusty bread hardly fit for worms. They washed it down with a bowl of dirty water.

From her observations, Ruth had concluded that there was no guard for their cell. The crazy man, Vincent, must have thought they weren't very formidable enemies.

Boy was he wrong.

Ruth and Kari, now that the bags had been taken off their heads, had spent the last few hours formulating a plan to escape the murky prison.

Ready to exact their plan, Ruth laid down on the floor in a fetal position, ignoring the thin layer of water that enveloped her ear and soaked into her hair. She slowed her breathing as much as she could and tried to make herself look dead.

Kari, seeing that Ruth was ready, took immediate action and screamed at the top of her lungs.

A high-pitched shriek echoed throughout the dark halls and corridors of the small swamp fortress.

It reached the ears of a soldier named Borgla, who thought it necessary to check on the two prisoners. Something might be happening, and he had been assigned to guard them loosely. He assumed it was his duty to find out what was going on.

The overweight guard made his way down the flight of steps that led to the dungeon. Cobwebs drooped lazily from the ceiling, and drops of moisture fell to the stone steps, plinking when they hit.

Borgla didn't like the dungeon any more than the prisoners did. He thought it was a disgusting place. In his mind, captives should be given the best treatment and good food, until someone pays a ransom to get them back. That was the right way to do it.

Unfortunately, Vincent's way was anything but right.

Borgla reached the bottom of the staircase and pulled a key from his belt to unlock the door that led to the cells. The key clicked in the lock, and he swung it open.

The screaming was still echoing through the dank room, but it was more of a suppressed wailing at this point. He sauntered down the rows of cells and eventually found the one where the two girls were being held.

The sight that met his eyes was quite unexpected.

One of the girls, the black-haired one, was making the awful noises. The other was lying on the floor, unmoving.

"What's goin' on in there?" He asked in a loud, gruff voice, peering through the bars.

The wailing girl stopped her horrible sounds and looked up at Borgla with big, teary eyes.

"It-it's her!" She moaned. "She j-just fell d-down and stopped m-moving!" She started sobbing miserably.

Borgla assumed that this was a problem, since Vincent had wanted them to be alive, but he didn't know what to do about it.

"And what do you expect me to do about it?" He asked indignantly.

She gazed at him again, very pleadingly. "W-would you please c-come in and see if... if she's alive?"

Borgla rolled his eyes and bent to unlock the barred door. He figured that it wouldn't hurt to check. *This girl's pretty fragile. I can handle her if anything goes wrong.*

He stepped inside. As soon as he stooped down next to the crying girl, the seemingly unconscious one leapt up and pushed the door all the way shut.

"Hey... !" Borgla started to yell, but a sharp blow to the head from the black-haired girl sent him reeling into the wall.

He shook his head, his thoughts fuzzy. *I didn't know girls had such sharp elbows*, he thought, wincing at the pain in his skull. He took in a deep breath to call for help, but before he could, another blow hit him in the stomach and he fell to the floor, gasping for breath.

Ruth looked down disdainfully at the helpless guard and hit him with one more blow to the temple. The man lurched and fell on his side, knocked unconscious by a couple of "fragile" girls.

Kari's eyes immediately dried, and she drew the man's short sword to use as her temporary weapon.

Ruth retrieved the man's keys, opened the door to their cell, and closed it with a clang, locking him in.

"Well," Kari said, a grin breaking out on her face. "That was fun."

46

...

A Slimy Scuffle

Mikal yelled in surprise and slapped at his face. The creature he had run into grabbed at his hair, squealing psychotically.

"Aah! Get it off!" He shouted. The whatever-it-was squealed one last time and jumped off Mikal's face, catching one of the overhanging tree branches and dangling on it.

The disgusted boy wiped the sticky slime off his face and stared in bewilderment at the creature.

It looked like somebody had just blown it out of their nose.

The wretched thing had dark green, slimy skin that was stretched tight over its body, making it look emaciated. Its eyes were a dull yellow with dark slits for pupils, and its nose looked like that of a bare skull, cartilaginous nostrils flaring menacingly.

From the bottom, its ears looked like normal, human ears. The tops, however, evolved into pointy spikes that stuck straight into the air, twitching intermittently. A single streak of dark gray hair ran from the center of its scalp all the way down its back.

It crouched in a defensive position, its putrid lips curled into a snarl.

The creature hissed at Mikal and opened its mouth. He thought it was going to spit at him, but instead, the voice that belonged to Bofe, sounded from behind Mikal.

"Eh, leetle boy. You want play?"

Thinking that he was about to be ambushed, Mikal whipped around. Instead of seeing something about to attack him, he saw Samuel and Zane struggling with two other creatures of equal appearance.

Just then, something wet and slimy hit him from behind. Mikal struggled with the small creature that was now on his back, trying desperately to wrench it off. It bared its yellow fangs and tried to bite the helpless boy on the neck.

Right as it struck downwards, Mikal jutted his shoulder backward, hitting the creature in the jaw and knocking it free of his body. Mikal rolled over and stood up, drawing his sword in preparation for another attack.

A voice came from his right, but this time he was prepared for that trick.

Mikal lunged out with his sword, and the creature had just enough time to leap into a tree before the blade would have driven it through.

Suddenly, another one of the creatures flew threw the air and smacked the one Mikal was battling off the tree branch.

"Thanks, Zane!" Mikal said, not having to look at who had thrown it. "Do you have any idea what these things are?"

"Yeah!" Zane was struggling with yet another of the creatures, trying to knock it unconscious against a tree. "I think they're swamp trolls! Someone told me 'bout 'em once! Nasty little things, aren't they?"

Samuel, who was trying to get a little troll off his back, gave another helpful tidbit. "I think they use voice projection to lure their prey in and kill it!"

Yeah, like I hadn't figured that *out yet,* Mikal thought as he swiped at another troll. *They must not be very good fighters. I seem to be getting the best of them.*

Before he knew what was happening, a gross-looking troll jumped at his face and tackled him to the ground. Instantly, another one climbed onto him and started scratching at his leg.

Before he knew what was happening, there was a familiar snap, and something whistled through the air.

The troll that was on Mikal's face went rigid. Its eyes popped wide open and it emitted a gurgling squeal. It fell sideways off of Mikal and hit the muddy ground, a black crossbow bolt embedded in its back.

An unsuspecting guard stood against the wall, his eyes drooping with fatigue.

Something hard hit him in the head, and he slumped to the ground, instantly unconscious.

Ruth beckoned for Kari to follow her around the corner. They snuck through the shadowed hallways, always vigilant for more soldiers.

Since Ruth didn't have her knife anymore, she resorted to her fists and an occasional sword swipe from a blade she had retrieved from an incapacitated guard.

Another of Vincent's men walked around the corner, making his rounds for the afternoon. He never saw the swift punch that caused him to fall backwards and hit the ground.

Before they moved on to the next section of the swamp lair, Kari mused, "I wonder if there are any more prisoners being kept here."

"Yeah, we should go back down and check the dungeons," Ruth replied.

They snuck back the way they had come, stepping over unconscious guards in the narrow passageways and avoiding large spider webs that hung throughout.

When they finally reached the door that led to the dungeon, it was slightly ajar, still in the position it had been when they first opened it.

Moving quickly so as to not lose any more time than they already had, Ruth and Kari jogged past the dingy chambers, checking to see if there were any other people that had been captured.

They didn't see anyone until they reached the last cell.

Ruth stopped in front of it and peered inside. To her great surprise, there was a body lying on the floor. It was a man, who was apparently sleeping.

"Hey, Kari!" She yelled to the other girl. "I think I found someone!"

"Let's get this cell open and wake him up." Kari ran over and gazed in at the slumbering figure.

After Ruth had unlocked the door with the guard's keys, it swung open, making a rusty creaking noise, which roused the imprisoned man.

Stirring, he opened his eyes and sat up. His face was covered in grime, as if he had been there for a long time.

"Hi," she said. "We're breaking you out. Your option is to help us, and we won't kill you." She was trying to be strict, just in case the man was a rebel from Vincent's men and didn't want to work with the two girls.

The man squinted at her. "Do... do I know you?"

"How would you know me?"

Not giving her an answer, the man stood up from the muddy ground and stepped into the dim torchlight.

<><><><><><><><><><><><><><><><><><><>

More crossbow bolts shot through the air, impaling the creatures that had attacked Samuel and his friends.

After pushing the dead body of the swamp troll to the side, Samuel drew his sword, ready for whatever came next.

The shots stopped, and the air went quiet. The remaining beasts scampered into the woods, shrieking in dismay.

Zane called out, "Thanks, whoever ya are!"

Before he could say more, another crossbow bolt sped from the shrubs and stuck quivering in the handle of Zane's giant mace.

Zane flinched. "Hey! Why'd ya do that!" Samuel turned to him and shushed him, but before he could turn back around, camouflaged men leapt from the tall grass and ran towards them.

Samuel's battle training kicked in, and he leapt out of the way as one beefy man barreled past him.

The cloaked assailant whipped around and slid a long sword out of a hidden sheath. He snarled menacingly, brandishing his sword deftly.

With a rush of adrenaline, Samuel surged towards him, his sword slashing forward for the kill.

Unexpectedly, the man's blade came up, deflecting the rash warrior's blade in such an awkward way that it flew out of Samuel's grasp. He jumped back, barely avoiding a swipe to the midsection. The man struck again and again, gaining ground with every pace.

With lightning fast movements, the man tackled Samuel to the ground and planted his foot on the boy's chest. He drew his sword up and above his head, ready to strike.

Out of nowhere, there was a swooshing noise, and the sword was knocked from the attacker's grip, flying off and splashing into a pool of water.

With mace in hand, Zane stood heroically next to the man's side.

"You got it from 'ere, Samuel." He charged off to help Mikal.

Not waiting a moment longer, Samuel lifted his knee and slammed it into the burly man's backside, knocking him forward. Lifting up his hands, he caught the man by the collar and threw him to the side.

Samuel leapt to his feet and posed in a ready position, waiting for the other man to make a move.

As soon as the stranger stood up again, the young warrior struck, slicing his hand toward the man's neck and at the same time, kicking his leg against the other's ribcage.

Before Samuel could hit him, however, the trained man twisted backwards and snatched Samuel's foot out of the air, throwing him off balance. Catching himself, Samuel dodged a swift punch, flipped onto his back, and kicked forward, hitting his opponent in the groin.

The man fell backward, moaning in pain.

Samuel leapt to his feet once again and chopped downward with his fist, hitting him in the solar plexus.

He groaned again, the wind knocked out of him.

Samuel made ready to strike again, but before he could, he felt a sharp pain in the side of the neck, and he fell over, still coherent but temporarily paralyzed.

With despair washing over his unmoving body, he watched as Mikal and Zane were disarmed and pinned to the ground by a new swarm of men.

Another hulking brute stepped out from behind a tree, motioning for the attackers to get up. "You are now our prisoners," he bellowed. "We will bring you to the base!"

47

...

An Old Friend

"Hello, girls," the familiar-looking man said.

"Rosh!" Ruth shouted, his identity dawning on her. "You're alive?! But how?"

"Yep. I'm alive." The dirty man shook his blond hair and mud sprayed everywhere. "But that freedom was hard-earned."

"What do you mean?" Kari asked, stunned.

"I mean surviving wasn't easy." He looked down the dim hallway and seeing no guards, said, "I see you've cleared the way. Shall we get going?"

"Of course!" Ruth exclaimed.

They traipsed through the passageways, not caring about guards. As she jogged, Ruth imagined Samuel's overjoyed expression when he discovered that his brother wasn't really dead! She could hardly believe it herself. It made her heart leap with joy and excitement.

She paused in her tracks, realizing that they had reached an unexplored hall. At the end of the short corridor in front of them, a normal-sized, wooden door sat modestly. As

Ruth looked at it closely, she noticed a tiny sliver of light peeking out from underneath.

Beckoning for the others to stay right behind her, she crept down the hall and put her head to the door, listening to what was happening on the other side.

Ruth could tell that there were a couple of men having a conversation. She recognized that one of them was Vincent, but she couldn't discern who the other was. *It must be one of the guards,* she thought.

"Are you sure they escaped?" A nasally voice asked.

That was definitely Vincent. No one could mistake his whiny tones.

"Yes, m'lord," the other man said. "The guards are all unconscious. I don't know how they did it, but when I checked, the two girls were not in their cell. It must have been them."

"It might have been, but those two didn't strike me as tough. It could have been that other fellow, the one we caught last week."

"I checked him, m'lord. He was still in his cell when I went down there."

The silence that followed was punctuated with brief twanging sounds, as if someone in that room was playing a lute. Ruth wondered if it was Vincent. He *had* called himself "Vincent the Bard."

"Go check again. If he's not there now, then we know they must be allied with him. If it really was them, then we have to get some guards down there."

The other man voiced his agreement and footsteps made their way towards the door where the eavesdroppers were standing.

Hearing him coming, Ruth wildly gesticulated for the other two to hide in the shadows. When the door swung open, letting in the bright torchlight of Vincent's "throne room," she backed against the wall and made herself as still as possible.

The man muttered to himself, saying things about Vincent that shouldn't be said. After closing the door behind him he turned around and walked past the hidden escapees, unsuspicious.

The hapless soldier felt a sharp pain in his jaw and everything went dark.

Kari reacted quickly and caught his body, gasping at the weight of the hefty man. After setting him down gently, she reached to his belt and drew a short sword, giving it to Rosh.

Ruth gestured to indicate she wanted to attack Vincent. The others seemed to understand, so she slowly turned the doorknob.

Kari and Rosh kept their weapons at the ready, preparing to jump in as soon as the door was opened. Rosh was still covered in filth, but he looked ready enough to fight.

Taking a deep breath, Ruth flung the door open and leapt in, ready for retaliation from any sort of "royal" guards.

To her surprise, the only person in the room was Vincent, who was sitting comfortably in his chair.

He grinned at them when they walked in, strumming a lute that he held in his lap.

"Hey!" He said nonchalantly. "I've been expecting you!" He set the lute to the side and pulled out another small instrument. It looked like a smaller version of the lute, with a sharp-looking spike protruding from the end of the body.

Vincent pulled the bow across its strings, which emitted a vibrant, melodious tune. This man was obviously not new to musical instruments. He played it expertly, hitting every note perfectly.

"What are you going to do now?" Vincent asked. "You can see that I'm an unarmed man. Would you hurt such a fellow?" He looked at them questioningly, lifting one eyebrow. "You know, you are going to be my key to promotion one of these days." He grinned. "When my master finds out I have you in custody, oh boy! He's gonna be so happy!"

"Wait," Ruth said. "Your master? Is that…"

"King Ogrion, of course! He will soon be the ruler over all the world! And I, Vincent the Bard, shall be his second-in-command!" He stared off into space and sighed.

Ruth was about to respond that she didn't care about his daydreams, when he flicked his wrist and sent the small lute flying straight at her, its spike gleaming silver.

Reacting with pure instinct, Ruth slashed her short sword upwards, impaling the deadly instrument. She stared at it and realized that if she hadn't caught it, the sharp point would have pierced her face.

Vincent didn't wait for the lute to hit. Instantly after throwing it, he leapt out of his chair and charged at Rosh, swinging the bow with both hands.

Rosh managed to lift his sword and slice through the taut cord, sending it whipping back into Vincent's face.

"Ow! Hey! You broke it!" The bard exclaimed. Instead of throwing it away, though, he swung the bow back at Rosh, who wasn't expecting the blow. It caught him right in the side of the head.

Stunned, Rosh stumbled backwards and braced himself against the wall, shaking his head to clear his vision.

Vincent leapt at him with astounding speed, uttering a horrible cry. Rosh lifted his sword and just managed to parry the oncoming piece of wood. With a thunk, his sword stuck into it and didn't move. The bard yanked, but the weapon was stuck too tightly for him to pull it out.

Instead of using his fists to fight, Vincent lunged at Rosh, biting at the helpless man's face with his yellowed teeth, while at the same time, pushing the sword away, which was still stuck fast in the ruined bow.

Resorting to crude methods of fighting, Rosh brought his knee up and into Vincent's pelvis.

The older man winced and groaned in pain, backing off from the fight. He retreated quickly to his simple throne, hobbling from the pain.

From behind the chair, the Bard pulled out another musical implement. This one was a lute of massive proportions. It was roughly as tall as Ruth! He played a couple dramatic chords with a new bow he had picked up and then threw the bow at Kari, who barely managed to evade it.

Rosh was still a bit dazed from the miniature lute's bow hitting him in the head. He was stabilizing himself against the wall of the room. Though he tried to rejoin the fight, the most he could do was take a few steps forward and fall to his knees.

Vincent swung the giant instrument at Kari. She ducked, and it swished over her head, the momentum of the instrument making Vincent spin. Unsurprisingly, he seemed to think it was fun.

Kari struck swiftly at him with her sword, and Ruth did the same from the other side. Somehow, he managed to block both of the blows with the lute by swinging it around in a circle.

The thin musician was very strong, handling the large instrument like it was nothing. He swung it around viciously, striking at the two girls left and right.

Although it seemed impossible, the battle was turning in Vincent's favor. He had gained the upper hand and was now standing on the dais, swiping his improvised weapon at the girls.

"Are you giving up yet?" He asked them mockingly, slicing downward with an overhead cut.

"Never," Ruth replied, barely dodging the swing. "Not to someone like you." She struck with the most ferocity she could muster, hacking and stabbing, but it still wasn't enough.

Ruth and Kari were beginning to lose strength. She feared that he was getting the better of them.

Rosh was sitting against the wall, his head spinning. He couldn't focus on anything, much less fight.

Just when they were thinking that the battle was lost, the door that they had come through earlier banged open. A group of guards walked through, followed by three unlikely prisoners.

48

...

Reunion

"Hey!" One of the guards yelled at the two girls. "What do you think yer doin'?" The other three drew their swords and snarled menacingly at Ruth and Kari.

Those two, however, weren't looking at the guards. They were staring at the three prisoners standing in front of them with their hands bound.

Vincent shrieked, "Get them! They attacked me, so they must be put to death!" His men leapt into action at once, the queer musician in the lead.

Although they were bound, Samuel, Zane, and Mikal were prepared. They ran at the guards from behind, using their hands and feet as weapons. The soldiers had forgotten about the boys, being too preoccupied with recapturing the girls.

Samuel swung his elbow at a man's head and knocked him away. This was the guard who was holding all their confiscated weapons. He stumbled backwards, trying to retain his grip on the implements.

Panicking, the man managed to draw Mikal's sword from the bundle and swing it at Samuel. The adrenalized captive ducked quickly and brought his fists up sharply into the guard's elbow.

There was a horrible cracking sound, and the man screamed in pain, cradling his injured arm, until a fist struck him on the point of his jaw and knocked him unconscious. The man slumped to the floor, Samuel relieving him of the weapons.

Samuel crouched down and sliced his bonds on the razor sharp edge of one of the swords. Standing up, he examined the raging battle. Upon entering the room, Zane had snapped the thick rope around his hands as if it were string, instantly engaging the largest of Vincent's soldiers. Mikal's hands were still bound, but he was holding his own.

"Hey, Zane!" Samuel yelled across the room to where Zane had engaged the massive guard. "Catch!" Using all of his strength, Samuel heaved the mace towards Zane. The gigantic weapon flew through the air and smashed into the back of the muscular guard. The unfortunate man was knocked to the ground with a heavy "thud."

Zane picked the mace up off the floor and brandished it. He inhaled deeply and let his breath loose, yelling one clear, memorable word. "BLAZOOGA!"

Although the word was complete nonsense, it made everyone hesitate for a moment, giving Zane the chance he needed.

The huge boy lunged at the remaining guard nearest him and sent him flying into the wall. Zane continued to charge around the spacious room, attacking any guard he met. Each one that faced him ended up the same way as their comrades: Twitching on the floor.

During this time, the other four had taken the slight pause to their advantage, beating back the weary guards. When each one had defeated their opponent, there wasn't much left to do, since Zane was rampaging through the room. In no time at all, almost every single one of the guards was either unconscious or dead, each one having met Zane's mace.

Seeing that his work was done, the big warrior breathed out deeply. He let his mace rest on the ground and turned towards the small throne in the center of the room.

Hiding conspicuously behind it was Vincent. He peeked out and saw the towering body of Zane glaring at him. He uttered an unmanly whimper and crawled farther back into the corner of the room.

Zane sighed in exasperation and looked at the others, the rage gone out of him. "What're we gonna do with this guy?"

Not stopping to answer his question, the others rushed together in a huge display of affection, clustering around each other in one giant group hug.

After they had finished expressing how worried they had been, Ruth turned her head towards the sniveling wretch huddling in the corner. She had originally wanted to kill Vincent herself, but she decided to leave his fate up to Zane. He seemed like he had it under control.

"I don't care what you do with him," she said, referring to his previous question. "Do whatever you want." Zane nodded his head and sauntered towards Vincent, his footsteps echoing on the stone floor.

The musician held out his hands as the muscular warrior approached and protested, "Wait! I can play good music! I can entertain you on your... your... your journeys!" He tried to form his mouth into a smile, but it ended up looking like a pathetic grimace.

"An' why would I need a musician?" Zane asked, keeping his expression deadly serious. As he said this, he noticed something on Vincent's hand, something that looked rather familiar. "Wha's that?" He asked, walking closer to the shaking bard. He roughly grabbed the trembling hand and lifted it up to observe it. Sure enough, there was the black, eye-shaped tattoo they had seen so many times before.

"Wha's this?" Zane asked out of curiosity. "Is this the symbol of Yamal?"

"I don't know!" The terrified man wailed. "I guess so! We... we were forced to have it... and... and... please don't hurt me!" Zane glared down at the nerve-wracked commander. Suddenly, a brilliant idea popped into his head.

"I've got it!" He exclaimed. "I know jest the people that're gonna want ya." He grinned maliciously at Vincent, who promptly fainted.

When they had finished tying up the comatose bard, Samuel noticed a figure not dressed in the vestments of Vincent's guards, who was sitting on the floor, leaning against the wall of the room; someone the girls had forgotten about.

Samuel walked over and peered at the man, wondering who he was. As he stared at the unconscious face, a jubilant wave of recognition washed over him.

"Rosh?" He asked tentatively, his heart thudding with excitement.

The blond-haired man blinked his eyes open. He looked up at the face staring down at him.

"Samuel?" He replied, still looking woozy.

"Rosh!" Samuel exclaimed. "It's really you! And you're here! How did you survive? Did they capture you? How did you get here?"

Rosh stood to his feet. "So many questions," he said slowly. A sly grin broke out on his face. "I'm just glad to be back with you guys."

Samuel pulled him into an embrace, each pounding the other heartily on the back with joy.

Rosh pulled away from Samuel and looked around. "I see I wasn't needed much in this fight. I think I blacked out."

"Zane took pretty good care of them."

"I can see that." He turned towards Zane and saw the unconscious body of Vincent slung over his shoulder. "I also see that we have someone to dispose of."

"Yep," Zane said. "And I know jest the place."

Zane sloshed through the swamp, Vincent thrown haphazardly over his shoulder.

They had been walking for a little while now and were nearing the spot Zane was looking for. The sun had already set, and night was shrouding the swamp in darkness. A few torches they had taken lit their way.

Zane determined that they had arrived when the ground under his feet solidified a bit and a small island in the water appeared among the trees. A familiar mound of dirt lay on it, but they couldn't see the door. It was on the other side.

"We're here!" Zane said happily. Vincent groggily lifted his head. He tried to squirm out of the big boy's grip, but he couldn't.

"Where?! Where are we?" He asked in a muffled voice, due to the thick cloth tied around his head.

Kari was going to ask the same question. She, Ruth, and Rosh hadn't been through here the first time.

"Hello!" Zane called out, ignoring the question for the moment. "Are you little guys in there?"

There was silence for a moment, and then a voice sounded from the mound.

"Who's askeen?" It was a disgusting little voice, just like Zane remembered it. Fortunately, he was already attuned to the trolls' vocal tricks and turned around.

There, hanging on a branch behind him, was a tiny creature that looked like a tailless monkey, if monkeys were green and covered with slime.

"Found ya!" Zane said.

The little creature snarled and moved farther up the tree.

Zane decided to be friendly about it. "I brought ya a present!"

The swamp troll stopped its noises and stared down at him. "What ees eet?" It asked, giving in to curiosity.

"Him!" Zane said. He picked Vincent off his shoulder and threw him on the ground next to the dirt lump. The skinny man yelped when he hit and struggled with the tight bonds ensnaring his wrists.

"He's the one who ordered the men ta kill ya!"

The troll immediately leapt down ten feet from the tree, seeing Zane as a friend now. It crawled over to Vincent and sniffed him. Lifting its head, the creature uttered a horrible screech.

With that sound, a dozen more small trolls clambered down from the trees and clustered around Vincent, chattering in their own, gurgling language.

"I think we can go now," Rosh said. "We don't need to stay here any longer. The more we linger, the faster the Yamal rebels get to... well... rebelling."

Samuel nodded his head and led the others through the swamp in the direction of the road.

We did it! He thought. *I can't believe we actually did it! We stormed a fortress... well, I guess we were captured and then stormed it... sort of.*

He looked around at the determined faces of his friends as they sloshed through the water and realized how close they had grown since leaving Castle Orthox. *These are my friends,* he thought, a feeling of pride growing in his chest. *My only friends. My best friends. When we're together, we can do anything.*

49

...

Belief

After spending a night sleeping fitfully in the branches of the trees, the six friends rose early and once again began their northward trek.

It seemed as if the swamp went on forever. Mikal's legs were tired from walking through the mud, and he was aching all over.

"Hey, guys?" He said, pausing in his tracks. "Let's take a break. My legs are killing me." They voiced their assent and stopped marching.

Mikal rested his hand on a misshapen tree, noticing his swollen tongue and dry mouth. *I really wish I had some water*, he thought, *and I don't really want to drink this swamp stuff.*

Then he had an idea.

Mikal grabbed the branch that was above him and pulled down on it. It groaned slightly but didn't break. *Good. I don't want another "episode" like earlier.*

He wrapped both arms around a couple of lower branches and pulled himself up, swinging his legs over and wrapping them around the trunk.

"What are you doing, Mikal?" He heard Samuel ask as he climbed.

Mikal grunted, trying to get a foothold in a fork between two branches. "I'm going to see what's ahead. See if we have much further to go 'til we reach civilization or a lake or something."

Samuel mulled over the idea for a moment and then acquiesced. *It's* sounds *like a good plan,* he thought. *I just hope he doesn't fall. That would be a pain in the neck.* He snickered silently at his unintentional pun.

Meanwhile, Mikal was just nearing the top of the tree. The branches were becoming thinner, making it harder for him to find places to hold on to.

After a few more moments of struggling through the poky twigs, Mikal's head emerged from the top of the tree. He gazed down at the landscape as a feeling of discouragement rose in his chest.

Most of what he saw were the gray tops of the trees, and occasionally, he caught a glimpse of the miry ground below.

In each direction, he could see for what he estimated to be a mile. Although most of it was uninteresting bog, there *was* something that caught his eye.

Roughly a quarter of a mile to the north, there was a small clearing that looked slightly circular in shape.

Mikal put his foot on a skinny branch and tried to lift himself higher to see what was in the peculiar opening. *I just need to get a little bit higher,* he thought. *Just a little bit.*

Right when he was almost high enough to see, his heart leapt into his throat as the weak branch under his foot snapped, and he went crashing down through the spiky branches, hurtling chaotically towards the muddy ground below.

The other five had been watching him as he climbed, ready to catch him at a moment's notice. When they saw him begin to tumble down, they instantly clustered beneath him and held out their arms in a net.

"Whoooaaaa!" Mikal yelled, flailing his hands. His arm hit a particularly thick branch, and the bark dug into his skin. He winced. *That's gonna leave a bruise.*

He hit their spread-out arms hard. His momentum was too much for them to catch, and he fell straight through their makeshift net, landing on his back in the mud.

"Ohhh," he groaned. Opening his eyes, he saw that everyone was looking down at him. Samuel was trying to stifle a laugh.

"Be quiet, you," he said to Samuel. He pulled himself up and shook off his wool jacket that was now covered in even more mud. "Great. Now I'll be sore *and* cold."

"Did you see anything?" Kari asked him.

Mikal remembered himself trying to get a better view, and seeing the silver glistening of something in the distance right before he fell.

"We need to move," he told Samuel. "There's a lake."

After about fifteen minutes of walking, they found the lake.

It was located off the side of the road, just visible to tired travelers in need of a drink.

Mikal figured that a break to fill their water skins wouldn't cause much of a time loss. He made a mental note to remember in which direction they were heading, so they wouldn't get lost.

"There it is!" Samuel exclaimed, pointing. "The lake!" He beckoned for the others to follow him and slogged through the swamp towards it.

Mikal was just about to follow him off the path, but something awoke in the back of his mind, a small warning signal. *It's nothing,* he reassured himself. *This is just a lake.*

He started to walk towards the group, who were already refilling the water skins they had taken from the fortress.

Nothing's wrong with that. It's just a simple lake.

As he made his way through the muck, however, he started to get second thoughts. For some reason, that persistent nagging feeling that something was wrong wouldn't quit. This lake was a little too unnatural for the swamp setting they were in. He dispelled these thoughts as his cautious side getting the better of him and continued walking.

A wave of emotions surged over him, so powerful that he stumbled backwards. It was like no other sensation he had ever experienced. He tried to move his legs forward, but found that he was frozen in place. The sunlight seemed to dim and his friends' actions moved in slow motion.

Before he could wonder any more about what in the world was happening, a voice spoke.

It was so strong and filled with power that it made Mikal want to curl into a ball and hide.

"*Mikal,*" it thundered, "*you have failed to heed my instructions before, so I have chosen to speak to you in this method.*" A bright light flashed before him and shone with a brilliance that surpassed even the sun. Streaks of luminescence jutted out from the hovering sphere, tendrils of pure light curling every which way.

"*I am Adonai.*" It boomed. The magnitude of the voice shook Mikal to his core.

"*He who heeds my commands will be given life for eternity and will ascend into the Realm beyond Realms at the end of times.*" The sphere flashed brighter. "*But he who rejects my words and my people will be cast into the depths of the Flaming Sea!*"

Mikal shuddered and fell to his knees, suddenly able to move. "Adonai... ?" He asked timidly, every muscle in his body shaking in fear.

"*You, my child, are one of the fallen, one of my people who is headed into darkness. But I am giving you a chance. Acknowledge me and live. My Presence will live in you, my holy light surrounding all that you do. My words will echo in your head, reminding you of the One who was, who is, and is yet to come.*"

"I-I know you!" Mikal croaked, his voice hoarse. "My uncle talked about You, but I thought... I thought he was wrong! I thought he was lying!" He squinted in the bright light. "But he's not! You're not! You're real!" Mikal was incredulous.

"Yes, my child. I am Adonai. And I will shield you and guide you, if only you will believe. Do you believe?" The question was asked with such force and power that Mikal crumpled to the ground and whimpered.

"I... I don't know! Why did you let my parents die?" He asked in a choking voice. "If you love me, then why didn't you save them?"

"I allow every human being to exercise free will... it is their choice whether they will be righteous or turn away. Your parents' deaths occurred because there is evil in this world. Rhubin and Friada of Shala are with me, in the Realm beyond Realms. Although tragic, their fate had a purpose. I will use each and every wrongdoing to bring about good in the end. If the thieves had not murdered them, they would have come for you. And I have great plans for you."

Mikal held his head in his hands. All his life he had rejected the idea of Adonai. He had hated it when people talked about Him as if He were real, because in Mikal's mind, He couldn't be! But now, when his parents' deaths were explained, he felt like a huge burden had been lifted off of his shoulders.

"Yes!" He shouted. "I believe! I will no longer ignore you! You are all-powerful! Be in me, like you said, and guide me through my tribulations!" The words just came out of his mouth. He hadn't even planned on saying them. It was like they had always been there, just waiting for him to let them out.

"*Then rise. You, Mikal of Shala, have been made new.*" The power in those words warmed Mikal's soul, and he stood up, feeling the energy of Adonai beginning to flow through him.

The light dimmed slightly and began to fade away. "*Now go! Rescue your companions, for they have been blinded, and they do not see the danger that awaits them in the lake!*" It faded away and was gone.

Mikal stood up slowly, still shaking from his overwhelming experience. He couldn't quite believe what he had just done. He had seen Adonai! *He... He wasn't real! But... He is! This is amazing!*

Remembering his predicament, Mikal snapped back to reality, feeling reinvigorated and ready to go.

The others! He thought. *They're in danger!* He looked to where they were messing around near the lake and felt a sinking feeling in his chest.

There's only one person who can save them from whatever's out there, he thought. *And it's me.*

50

...

The Lake

"Samuel!" Mikal yelled.

A bad feeling started rising in his chest when his friend didn't answer. Samuel just kept talking to Ruth like he had been before Mikal called.

"Samuel!" Mikal shouted as loud as he could. "Get your backside over here!" He stared in horror at them when they didn't respond. It was as if they were deaf to his voice!

He started to take a step forward onto the white rocks of the beach but stopped before he could. There was that same insistent foreboding in the back of his mind, which he now knew to be Adonai warning him.

What is it? He asked. As he waited for an answer, Mikal started thinking about how much he had changed in the last few weeks. When he had started training, he had been rebellious and belligerent. Now he was having conversations with Adonai! It was like he had switched to the complete opposite of who he had been before. The funny thing was that he was glad!

The voice that answered him was the same melodious tone that spoke to him earlier, but it sounded less wrathful than it had previously.

"*If your feet fall on the white stones of the beach, your mind will be trapped by the evil that lingers here.*"

At first, Adonai's words didn't make sense to Mikal. As he considered them, though, a new clarity came to his mind.

If I go onto the beach, he thought, *something evil will take control of my mind. That must be why they can't hear me.*

Fabricating a new plan, he picked up a small chunk of wood that had fallen off one of the old trees in the swamp. He stepped back a pace and lobbed it at his friends.

Mikal had a good throwing arm.

The wood sailed through the air and hit Samuel square in the back. The unsuspicious youth turned around and peered towards the dark swamp.

Mikal waved his arms and jumped up and down, shouting at the top of his lungs. "Samuel! Zane! Kari! Rosh! Anybody! Over here!"

Samuel gazed into the trees for a long time but eventually turned back and shrugged his shoulders as if he was confused.

"No!" Mikal shouted. "No! Look over here!" He stopped dejectedly, realizing that there was no hope of them hearing him.

He had to solve this dilemma some other way. He looked at the ground, examining the white stones that littered the shore.

An idea began forming in his head, when something triggered his senses. He looked up at the lake. Rippling sounds filled his ears. Small waves splashed upon the shore, seeming to come out of nowhere.

Mikal looked up at the sky. *That's funny. There's no wind.*

Then there was laughter.

Samuel looked to his left and saw a slight, silver glint. "There it is!" He exclaimed. "The lake!"

He marched into the trees by the side of the road, lifting his feet high to avoid getting stuck in the murky mud underneath the water.

Now that he was closer, he could see the afternoon sun reflecting off the glistening lake. All was calm on its surface; there was not a ripple to be seen.

Without hesitating, Samuel bounded forward onto the white stones that covered the beach. Something tickled the back of his mind, but it stopped as he crossed onto the rocks.

As soon as his foot hit the ground, a strange sensation swept over him. It was like he was experiencing the best day of his life! A feeling of blissful happiness shot through his body, making him want to jump into the air and soar away.

He walked along the beach and started babbling about anything to the person next to him, who happened to be Ruth. His mind was in a haze, and all he could think about was how happy he was, although he somehow remembered the reason they came to the lake. He took the water skin off his shoulder to fill it.

Slinging the full skin over his shoulder, he looked around. The strange feeling persisted. He still felt as if he could just float away with happiness.

The reasonable part of his mind started to wonder why he was feeling so happy, but his suspicion was promptly dispelled. It was as if some other force was interfering with his thoughts and not allowing him to think freely.

Since he had nothing else to do at the moment, he started talking to Ruth again.

"So how's your day been?" He asked.

She turned and looked at him brightly. "Oh, it's been just wonderful! I've been walking through a terrible swamp, and... " her face became dark for a moment, but the joy came back immediately. "I can't seem to remember! I guess it doesn't really matter, now that we're here. How was your day?"

"I can't really remember either! Isn't that weird? I feel like I should be doing something else, but this lake is so beautiful that I... "

"Isn't it! I just love how the light sparkles on it like that!"

Samuel was about to answer, but before he could, something hard hit him in the back. He turned around and spotted a small piece of wood on the ground.

"I wonder where that came from." He shaded his eyes with his hand and peered into the swamp. Everything was hazy, like a sheet of fog had been pulled in front of him. Samuel strained his eyes, trying to see what was back there. He knew that there must be something or somebody, or he wouldn't have been hit with a piece of wood.

Through the mist, he was able to see something moving slightly, but then it disappeared. A small sound, almost like a voice, reached his ears.

"Hm." He said to himself. "Must be an animal or something." He turned back to where the others were talking incessantly and shrugged.

"Something hit me in the back, guys." Samuel said. "It must have been dropped by a bird, because there's nothing back there." He gestured towards the swamp behind him.

"Yeah, that's weird," said Kari. "I didn't know birds pick up wood and drop it on people." She seemed to be considering the probability of such a thing happening, but eventually shook her head.

"No. It couldn't have been anything but a bird. I wonder if they have wood-eating birds here in this swamp."

"Swamp?" Zane asked. "What swamp? Is there a swamp around here? All I see is a lake."

"What?" Samuel questioned. He turned around and looked back to where he had thought the wood came from. To his surprise, all he could see were white rocks that led off into the distance.

"I guess I must have been mistaken." He said. "There's no swamp back there. Only beach." They began walking away from the lake, along the long, white beach.

A new sound caught his attention.

Samuel twisted his head and peered at the lake. Ripples undulated across the surface, emanating from the center of the lake.

That's funny, he thought dazedly. *There weren't any ripples earlier.*

He was pondering this oddity, when a great sound reverberated through the air and the ground, making the rocks beneath his feet vibrate.

It was laughter.

51

...

Desperation

"Ha ha ha! Heh heh heh! Hee hee hee!"

Mikal looked around, trying to locate the source of the gleeful voice. *What* is *that?* He thought. Is there some sort of insane creature around here somewhere? He turned his gaze back to his friends. To his surprise, they were holding their sides and heaving with laughter, as if sharing a hilarious joke with the vibrating voice in the air.

As the ceaseless laughter echoed everywhere, Mikal put it out of his mind and brought himself back to his current problem: How to get the others out of there.

Before the voice started laughing, a plan had begun to form in his mind. He surveyed the area, trying to locate some big leaves or pieces of wood.

According to Adonai, his mind would be overtaken if he touched the white stones. Using this information, he formed the theory that by making a path out of other materials that led to his friends, he could walk along it and be safe. The only problem with this plan was that if he accidentally touched the white stones, he and his friends would be dead.

Well, he thought, shrugging. *I'd take dying while trying to save my friends over leaving my friends to die any day.*

After gathering a lot of large, mud-covered materials, Mikal started his trail. He carefully laid the first item, a large section of tree bark, in front of him on the white stones.

Holding his breath in apprehension, Mikal stepped out onto the bark.

He waited for a few moments, but nothing happened, and he didn't feel any different. He sighed in relief, knowing that if all went well, his plan would work.

With renewed confidence, Mikal looked up at the sky and realized that it was getting dark fast. If he didn't hurry, there was no telling what might happen.

Mikal threw a large leaf onto the ground in front of him and prepared to step onto it. He had fallen into a rhythm of laying and stepping, laying and stepping.

This time, however, as he was moving forward, a gust of wind breezed through and pushed the leaf out from underneath Mikal's foot.

"Whoa!" He exclaimed, reeling backwards, away from the stones. He looked behind him and dread began coursing through his body.

As he watched, the wind began knocking pieces of his path away, one by one. Even the heavy chunks of bark soaked with water were blown away. Mikal was sure that this was no ordinary wind, for it gusted with the cadence of the now evil-sounding laughter.

Acting quickly, Mikal leapt back towards the swamp, making sure that there was something for him to land on before each jump.

At one point, he jumped right as the leaf he was aiming for blew away in the wind. Before he could hit the ground, Mikal whipped one of the pieces of bark he was carrying out from under his arm and tossed it desperately in front of him. He hit it hard and wobbled for a moment, trying to catch his balance. Breathing quickly, his heart thudded ominously as he resolved to move faster.

After he successfully made it back to the swamp, Mikal looked back in frustration as the remnants of his trail were blown away in the breeze.

"Argh!" He yelled and stomped his foot on the soft ground. When he tried to pull it back up, though, he realized that it was tangled in some vine-like branches. Bending down to extricate his foot, he noticed that the vines were covered with small, white berries.

Wait a minute.

Mikal stopped struggling with his foot and examined the berries closer. Something he had heard before echoed in his head above the obnoxious laughing:

"They usually grow in heavily moist areas, like dense jungles or bogs."

Mikal picked one of the berries off a branch and gazed at it in the fading light.

"Spellberries."

The laughing echoed through the air, penetrating Zane's mind.

After just a few moments of listening to this unknown person giggle and guffaw, Zane couldn't help but start laughing too.

It started as a tiny tickle in his stomach, and before long, he was laughing so hard his sides were aching and tears trickled down his cheeks.

Absorbed in his merriment, he didn't notice the others breaking into laughter as well. He wasn't sure how long he had been laughing, and he didn't care.

A voice spoke into his head.

Usually, Zane would have been very uncomfortable with this mental interference. The only voices he had ever had in his head were Adonai's and Pheno's. If he had been fully conscious of what was happening, the voice would have reminded him too much of Pheno.

"Hello, my dears! Haw haw haw! You're very welcome in my home, tee hee!"

Zane barely managed a, "Who're you?" before he couldn't help but start laughing again.

"Why, thank you for asking! Haha! You may call me, hee hee, Myrth!"

Zane felt words on his tongue that were not his, but he was too busy laughing to be able to catch a breath to stop them.

"May I, heh, meet you?"

"How thoughtful of you! Hee hee!" The voice sang. "Why, if you want to meet me, haw haw, just hop on into the lake!"

Zane tried to stop himself, but he couldn't seem to keep his legs in one place. They moved forward of their own accord, walking towards the edge of the lake. His confused mind battled against Myrth's power.

Zane was panicking. *There's no one who can save me now!* He thought. *Pheno didn't get me, but now I'm gonna die the same way!*

Then, right before he walked into the water, he remembered who could help.

"Adonai!"

Mikal rapidly defoliated the vine of its berries, stuffing them into the money pouch at his side.

After making sure that he had all of them, he pulled one out and examined it, trying to discern what sort of ability it would give him. What he really needed at the moment was flight. If only he could be able to tell between them!

He remembered Daniel saying something about the number of seeds and that you could only see them at the bottom of a lake.

Well, I have a lake. The problem is, if I'm able to reach it, then I wouldn't need the berries! He groaned in frustration at the paradox.

"What am I going to do?!" He cried out at the sky. "Adonai! If you're there, please help me!"

The warm voice immediately seeped into Mikal's mind, blocking out the laughing that rang in his ears and filling him with confidence.

"Mikal, I recognize your dilemma, so I will assist you this one time. The berry you hold will grant you the power needed to rescue your companions. Now go! For time is of essence, and dusk is upon you!" The voice was gone just as suddenly as it had come.

The horrible laughing noises now came back in full, piercing Mikal's ears painfully. However, he was so desparate to complete his task that he was able to ignore them.

What he saw when he looked up, though, was like a nightmare happening all over again, a déjà vu of past events. His heart dropped to the bottom of his stomach, and his hands started shaking as his mind went back to the frightening incident aboard the *Campekter*.

With that terrible thought in his mind, he watched as his helpless friends began a slow, deadly march towards the bewitched waters that swirled in delight.

52

...

Flight

Without hesitating, Mikal popped the berry into his mouth. He chewed quickly and swallowed. Like Samuel had said at Castle Orthox, it didn't taste like anything.

He watched a tiny sliver of sunlight slowly go behind the trees in the distance. *I hope this is close enough to night, because I'm not waiting any longer!*

Counting on his instincts, Mikal bent his knees and jumped into the air, flapping his arms wildly... and he crashed back to the ground.

"Ow." He said as he picked himself up, wiping some gloppy mud off of his arms. "I guess it just hasn't reached my stomach yet." His heartbeat raced as he watched his friends' slow death-march. "I don't have much time! That berry had better work soon!"

As if on cue, a tingling sensation began in his gut and soon spread to his limbs.

Without warning, his entire body lurched upwards and hovered, floating above the ground.

Not stopping to revel in this unique experience, Mikal imagined himself moving forward, and he was instantly soaring through the air towards his friends.

A stray tree branch whipped him in the face as he crossed the line between the swamp and the beach, but Mikal didn't care. He was flying!

The feeling was exhilarating. It was as if he was riding in a carriage on a smooth road, only he was four feet off the ground. He tried increasing his speed, and his heart leapt into his throat as the white rocks shot away from underneath him.

The wind from the lake smashed against his body, as if it was trying to push him back, but Mikal tightened his muscles and strained onward.

The dark figures of his friends drew closer and closer, until he was hovering right over them.

"Hey, guys!" He yelled, hoping they would hear him. Just as he guessed, they didn't answer. Their blank stares were fixed on the churning water of the lake.

Breathing hard from the exertion of battling against the wind, Mikal imagined himself dropping slowly downwards.

His body responded immediately, and he descended until his feet were less than a foot away from the white rocks that littered the ground. As he levitated above the surface of the lake, Mikal turned to the others, who were now walking stiffly towards him.

Mikal flew forward until he reached the first of the victims entranced by the evil laughing. This happened to be Kari.

"Oof." He struggled, trying to pick her up. Unfortunately, she was heavier than he had expected.

A bit awkwardly due to his lack of experience, Mikal circled her and tried to get her from behind. He put his hands in her armpits and willed himself to move upwards.

As soon as her feet left the ground, she gasped and looked around in fear, her whole body shivering violently. "Aah! W-what's going on? W-w-where am I?"

"S'okay, Kari. Rrg! I'm here."

"M-Mikal!" She exclaimed haltingly. "There was s-s-somebody talking t-to m-me, and-and she was telling me to w-walk into th-the lake!"

"Not much time to talk!" Mikal exclaimed, forcing his body to turn around and fly back towards the swamp.

When she felt the sudden rush of wind against her face, Kari finally realized their predicament. "Whoa! Why are we floating?!"

"Tell ya... later!" Mikal said between grunts.

In no time at all, they were back in the murky water. Mikal dropped Kari to the ground and started flying back to the others.

"Stay here!" He called to her from afar. "I'll be right back! And don't touch the white rocks!" Then he was gone.

It had been just under two minutes, but it had seemed like forever. Mikal had managed to carry all of them back to land except Samuel, and he knew that he didn't have much time left. They had been some distance from the lake when they started walking, but now they were closer than ever.

The last time he was at the lake, Rosh and Samuel had been fearfully close to walking in. Mikal knew in his gut that it was only a matter of moments before Samuel was taken by the ominously dark water.

A mist had settled over the lake. Now it was hard for him to see even a few feet in front of his face. Mikal couldn't see Samuel from where he was, but he knew the general direction in which to go.

Having adjusted to flying, Mikal soared towards the last victim. Because of the force of the wind blowing against him, his lips were chapped and his hands were numb.

The now demonic-sounding laughter was wafting through the air, striking fear into the hearts of those who had been rescued. Mikal held back a grimace as he tried his hardest to close his ears to the wretched sound.

Samuel's form suddenly appeared in the mist in front of him, growing larger as Mikal flew closer. He put on as much speed as he could to reach the last member of the team.

As Mikal started to lower himself, he saw something that caused his heart to switch places with his stomach.

"No!" He yelled, even though he knew Samuel couldn't hear him. "Stop!"

The bewitched boy took one more step that seemed dreadfully slow and set his foot in the swirling waters.

Myrth laughed.

Even though the evil lake had been laughing the whole time, this throaty chuckle was different. It was a laugh of victory.

She sensed a tingle on her outer rim, the feeling of a being's entry into her waters. She had been speaking to some young humans, using her entrancing powers to persuade them to come to her. This must be one of them.

She whirled her currents in a wide circle, threatening to sweep in whatever touched them. She willed riptides to appear all around her periphery, hoping that the unfortunate human would be sucked into her mass, so she could drown him in her depths and feast upon his saturated corpse.

Her eerie chuckle became louder when a splash sounded along her perimeter. She yanked her swirling currents harder, trying to pull the human in.

Myrth felt his presence, but it was stationary in her waters, as if he was resisting her pull. Not wanting to lose her prey, she drew the water in harder than ever.

Her laugh faltered as she realized that the human wasn't budging. She slowed her currents until they stopped completely, not even a ripple gracing her surface. Her wicked mind tried to comprehend what was stopping her from dragging the boy in, but Myrth couldn't wrap her thoughts around it.

She had been hungry for many years. Few travelers ever discovered her presence. When some did find her, Myrth would do all she could to draw them in and devour them as their bodies dissolved into the water.

To her surprise, the body she felt now started moving slowly towards the land.

Reaching a state of desperation, her instincts gave Myrth only one solution, and it required complete concentration of her abstract mind. She would be forced to focus solely on the one task. It was a large risk, considering the other humans in the area.

However, it was a risk she was willing to take.

"Do you think Mikal's okay?" Zane asked Ruth, Kari, and Rosh, who were staring into the thick mist.

"I don't know," Kari said, frightened. "It's been a long time."

Suddenly, they heard the crash of tremendous waves on the shore. A wild roaring of water sounded from the direction of the lake.

"Oh no! They're in danger!" Ruth said. "We need to help them!"

"But how?" Rosh asked. "We can't go on the rocks!"

Ruth turned to him, courage and desperation mixing in her eyes. "We have no choice. I don't know what's going on over there, but I *do* know that it's not good." She looked at them both.

"You don't have to come with me. You can stay here in the swamp and be safe. It's your choice."

With that, she turned around and stepped out onto the deadly, white rocks.

53

...

The Water

The waters that had once been swirling stopped and lay eerily motionless.

Mikal grunted and tried to drag Samuel away from the lake. It was taking all his willpower just to stay flying.

Samuel's weight strained against his arms. His muscles burned like fire, trembling from the effort. Now that the water wasn't pulling against him, he was able to move Samuel away more easily than before.

Come on, Mikal! He thought to himself. *You can do this! Pull him up!*

With a desperate heave, he managed to lift his dazed friend off the ground.

Samuel's eyes cleared. "Hey! Whoa! Where am I?!" He exclaimed, very surprised to be dangling from Mikal's arms above the ground.

"It's me!" Mikal said. "I ate a spellberry!"

"You mean you're... flying?!" He sounded incredulous.

Mikal hoped that Samuel wouldn't try to get free. "Yeah, but I can't hold you for long! We need to get back to the swamp! That's where the others are!" Samuel nodded slightly. "Just don't touch the ground!" Mikal warned. "If you do, then your mind is as good as a bowl of mush!"

Sweat beaded on his brow as Mikal hefted Samuel in his arms, trying to get a better grip. He felt the other boy's shirt begin to slip from his grasp, so he tried to wrap the stiff cloth around his fist.

It was no use. Samuel's body slipped out of his arms, and he fell screaming towards the ground.

"No!" Mikal yelled in frustration. He looked down to where Samuel had landed, mentally kicking himself for being so clumsy.

To his great surprise, Samuel stood up from where he had fallen and was now looking up at Mikal, gesturing and shouting something unintelligible.

Relief washed over Mikal when he realized that his friend was all right. He beckoned for Samuel to head towards the swamp, but the confused boy didn't seem to understand. He just kept shouting, trying to be heard over the noisy wind.

Then a thought struck Mikal. If Samuel's mind wasn't overtaken, then his wouldn't be either! With careful movements, Mikal maneuvered his way downward, trying to keep his balance at all costs.

In moments, his feet touched the ground. Mikal blinked and looked around. The evil force was apparently out of commission at the moment.

He turned to Samuel. "What were you trying to say?"

A disappointed light shone in his companion's eyes. "I was telling you to get out of here, because the lake is going crazy!" He pointed fearfully towards the once-calm water that was now boiling and frothing unnaturally.

"Yep. That's not a good sign. We should leave."

Right after he said that, a wave the size of his uncle's house erupted from the water and shot towards them.

"Yes," Samuel agreed, starting to run. "Let's go."

The two sprinted as fast as they could, the surging wave of water hot on their heels.

The mist was thick at this time of night. It was difficult for Samuel to tell where he was going. His breaths came in ragged gasps. His calf muscles burned from the exertion of running. His hands were numb with the frigidity of the night air.

Samuel didn't know how far it was back to the swamp, because he had been in a stupor when he first walked onto the white rocks. Mikal, however, was well versed in the path to safety, so Samuel trusted him to correct any mistakes.

He glanced back to check the wave that was chasing them.

It was pulling back towards the lake, a long sheet of glistening liquid sliding across the smooth stones.

"Hey... Mikal!" He said slowing his pace and breathing hard. "The water's... receding! I think it's... going away!"

Mikal's expression looked as if Samuel had died right in front of him. His face paled and his eyes became large with fright.

"What?" Samuel asked, confused by this reaction.

"If the water's... receding," Mikal panted. "That means... the wave is... going to come back... bigger!"

A feeling of dread settled in Samuel's stomach. He hadn't thought of that.

He turned his head forward to see if the swamp was anywhere near. He didn't think it was *too* far away from the lake.

Suddenly, a figure shot out of the mist and slammed right into Samuel.

"Oof!" He exclaimed as he fell over backwards, the breath knocked out of him. Mikal had also been knocked down and was gasping for breath.

"Samuel?! Mikal?!" Standing over them, surprised as ever, were Zane, Ruth, Kari, and Rosh.

"What are you guys... doing out here?" Samuel wheezed. "Go... back! The water is... coming!"

They seemed to get the hint, for their faces blanched.

Samuel rolled his eyes in exasperation. "Go!" He yelled to break them out of their trance.

As the others sprinted back to where they had come from, Samuel pulled himself off the ground, his chest aching from the impact with whom he knew must have been Zane.

After drawing in a deep breath, he gathered his strength and ran speedily in the direction the rest of the team had gone.

<><><><><><><><><><><><><><><><><><><>

A booming crash sounded in the distance behind Mikal. A roar thundered like a tropical typhoon. He heard the heaving breaths of the others next to him, and although it made his muscles burn, he picked up his pace.

With a rippling motion like a sheet being pulled away, the fog suddenly cleared in front of him, and he saw the swamp. It was so close and yet so far!

Mikal could hear the approaching wave behind him and felt the presence of an immense body of water, looming ominously overhead, ready to smash down on him at any moment.

He ran a little bit harder.

The murky treeline drew closer and closer. Mikal hoped with all of his being that the trees would offer refuge. He pumped his arms and lunged forward, putting on every extra ounce of speed he could muster.

With one final leap, Mikal threw himself into the swamp lunging forward, away from the roaring water behind him.

He picked himself up and turned around, hoping that the others had made it.

All of them but Samuel were standing beneath the trees, gasping for breath, their chests heaving spasmically.

Mikal raced back to the edge of the swamp and looked through the fog, his eyes darting back and forth.

Just as he had predicted, a roaring body of water thirty feet high surged across the wet rocks towards the swamp. He shifted his focus to the base of the wave, seeing Samuel.

The panting youth pounded his legs as fast as he could, flecks of foam from the wave behind him spattering his shirt.

"Come on, Samuel!" Mikal yelled. "Run!" As if the helpless boy didn't have enough motivation already.

Samuel reached for the trees.

Mikal put his hand out and grabbed his friend, pulling him under the trees with such force that they both fell into the mud of the swamp, away from the furious wave behind them.

Mikal squeezed his eyes shut and did the first thing that came to his mind.

"Adonai, help us!"

54

...

Exhausted

The thundering wave of water surged forward with unnatural speed, looming overhead like a raging beast preparing to devour them.

Ruth screamed and ducked down, covering her face with her hands. There was a horrific roaring as she braced herself for death.

Seconds passed. With her eyes squeezed shut, she waited. Nothing. Confused, Ruth looked up and gasped at what she saw: A wall of water rushing upwards into the air. The foaming façade was smooth and stationary, as if an unseen force was shielding them from its wrath.

Just as quickly as it began, the height of the wave diminished until it was nothing but a sleek layer of water running across the white rocks back towards the lake. It disappeared into the circular pit of water and was gone.

The stars shone bright in the sky, twinkling as if the harrowing experience had never occurred.

"What just happened?" Zane asked, confused.

Mikal slowly rose and stared awestruck at the calm lake. "I think... I think it was Adonai."

Ruth raised her eyebrows incredulously. "You mean *you* believe in Adonai?! When did this happen?!"

Mikal proceeded to tell them the story of his encounter with the Creator, not leaving out any details.

When he finished, the rest of the team shouted in triumph and embraced him, joyful that he finally believed. This confused Rosh. He'd never heard of Adonai, but he reluctantly joined them.

Not wanting to waste any more time, Samuel suggested that they move on down the road. Although it was night, none of them were tired. It was as if the experience had completely revitalized them.

Heartily agreeing with him, the ragged-looking group slogged through the mud towards the road.

Ruth recalled when they had done the same thing earlier that day, totally clueless about the travails ahead of them.

I wonder if anything else dangerous and interesting will happen, she thought, staring at the muddy ground. *Probably. I bet our hardest challenges are still to come.*

Morning had arrived, and the sun was just rising above the treetops, shedding its warm light on the six weary travelers that plodded along the worn path.

It had been about an hour since the swamp had given way to the dirt road, and Ruth's sore feet were happy to be walking on solid ground once again. Despite that bit of relief, her legs were aching from the ankles to the thighs, a dull, throbbing pain that shot through her body with every step she took. She did her best to ignore it, feeling that it would be a hindrance to have the others stop just because her legs were sore.

They had not come across any civilization in the night, but they were still hoping that a town would appear in the trees.

Ruth's eyes were sagging, and her mind felt as though it was shutting down. She figured that if they didn't find a village soon, she might pass out on the ground.

Another stab of aching pain shot through her leg. She groaned audibly.

Samuel walked up next to her. "Are you all right?" He asked. He seemed perfectly normal, but Ruth knew better. She could see the dark circles under his eyes and the way he held his head, as if he was afraid it would fall off.

Samuel noticed her heavy eyelids and drooping head, making a deduction. "I'd say you're not all right. We should take a break."

Ruth shook her head. "No, no. I can go on." She yawned widely.

"Let's take a break, guys." Samuel said, ignoring her.

Ruth thought of protesting but decided against it. *I may as well,* she thought. *I guess it would do us all some good to have a little rest.*

They turned and walked into the woods a little, keeping the path in sight.

Ruth sat down on the pine-needle-covered ground and stretched her legs out. It felt good to sit down... so good, in fact, that she didn't want to keep her eyes open any longer.

Figuring that the others wouldn't leave her sitting against the large pine tree when they decided to go again, she surrendered to the exhaustion that was overwhelming her and closed her eyes, succumbing to sleep's pull.

<><><><><><><><><><><><><><><><><><>

Kari's eyes popped open and she sat up quickly.

They had been walking through the woods all night, when Samuel had decided that it would be good to take a rest stop. The six of them had walked off the side of the road and sat down among the towering evergreen trees.

Rosh had volunteered to be on watch while the others slept, but it hadn't worked out that way.

Kari noticed the young adult leaning back against the rough bark of a Douglas fir, his chin resting on his sternum and his chest moving up and down rhythmically. A slight whiffling sound emanated from his direction.

She looked around and stretched her arms, yawning wide. It looked to be after noon, which meant they had slept for over five hours.

The spring sun was shining through the branches of the trees, casting spots of light on the dark forest floor.

Kari stood up and brushed the needles off her wool jerkin. She leaned back against a tree and gazed at the beauty of the forest. It was alive with the sounds of wildlife. A light breeze rustled through the branches. A brown squirrel leapt from tree to tree, vigorously searching for something. A brightly-colored jay landed on a branch across from her and twittered energetically.

Amidst the other noises, Kari heard a sound that she did not expect to hear. It was that of a wagon, its wooden wheels rattling over the hard ground, in chorus with the clopping of horse hooves.

She peeked out cautiously from where they were hidden and observed the newcomer. It seemed as if he was a normal traveler heading to his village, but it never hurt to be careful.

The man, dressed in a brown and gray cloak, was seated in the front seat of a wooden wagon that held multiple bales of hay. He had curled gray hair covering the back of his head; the top was as bald as could be. The horse was speckled brown and plodded along as if that was all it had done its entire life.

As Kari stood there watching him, she had an inspiration.

"Excuse me!" She said, strolling out from the woods as if she walked through there every day.

The man looked up and called "whoa" to his horse, which came to an abrupt halt. He peered down at her, his expression confused at her unexpected appearance.

"How may I help you, miss?" He asked.

"Do you know how far it is to the nearest town? My friends and I have never been here before and were wondering when we would come upon one."

He looked at her a bit suspiciously. Something about him struck Kari as familiar. The way he scrunched up his eyes when he was thinking reminded her of somebody, but she just couldn't put her finger on it.

"Your friends?" He asked, looking around. "I see no one else around here."

She figured that it wouldn't hurt to tell him. He would probably forget as soon as he left.

"They're back in the woods, sleeping. We've been walking for quite a while and were very tired."

He appeared to consider it for a moment and then acquiesced. "The next town, if I'm calculating correctly, is just about two miles up ahead. It'll take you no time at all to get there." He smiled at her. "I'd be willing to give you a ride, but I think you'll want to go with your friends."

"Yes, I would. Thank you for your help." He nodded politely and continued down the path, humming something to himself.

She remembered the time back in Aena, when they asked directions at a cabin they had found along the path. That cabin had been home to a very rude man, who apparently thought it was funny to lie to kids.

Kari was caught up in the memories as she watched the wagon disappear around a bend. She reflected on all that had happened since then.

We've grown so much, she thought. *Every one of us. All of those bad experiences have strengthened our friendships.*

As she was thinking, it hit her. Shaken, it took her a moment to process the revelation.

Kari stared down the road where the wagon had gone, a bad feeling rising in her chest.

She knew who the man was.

55

...

A Stalker

"Guys, guys, wake up!" Kari whispered harshly to the others.

Mikal opened his eyes groggily and sat up, squinting in the daylight. "How long have we been here?" He asked, the sleep evident in his voice.

She looked up at the sun through the tree branches and said, "That doesn't matter. I have something to tell you!"

Sensing that something was wrong, Mikal stood up and looked around, the others following his lead. "What? What's happened?" He asked urgently.

Kari looked quickly over her shoulder and then told them about the man who was traveling along the road.

Mikal rubbed his eyes and yawned. He wondered why a man on a wagon was so exciting to Kari. That didn't seem like anything to be worried about.

"This might seem like useless information to you, but I recognized the man after he left."

Their interest piqued, they leaned in unconsciously to better hear what she was about to say.

"Do you remember the day I was hit with the dart back in Aena?" They nodded. "Well, Ruth and Mikal took me to see a doctor, and..."

"You mean you saw Tarius?!" Mikal interjected, realizing what she was trying to say.

"Yes! I don't know what he was doing here, but it can't be a coincidence!"

"I agree," Rosh said. "We should move now and follow him. If he works for Yamal, then we're in deep trouble." He turned to Samuel, who pondered this thoughtfully.

"It's a hard decision," he said. "There are so many ways we could get trapped."

"How's that?" Rosh asked.

"If we stay here, he might come back with reinforcements. If we follow him, he might lead us into an ambush. If we turn back, which I definitely do *not* want to do, he might have more men coming behind him, and we would be attacked by them."

"I see your point. What do you say we do?"

Samuel rubbed his hands together and started talking rapid-fire. "I say we follow him, but not on the road. We move through the woods, keeping track of where the path is so we don't get lost. When we reach a village, we stay on the outskirts, never letting ourselves be seen together. Anybody working for him will be looking for a large group, and we'd be very conspicuous in a small town. When we leave, we'll head in a slightly different direction than the way we were headed, and maybe throw them off our trail."

Everybody stared at him.

"And that's why we let you do the thinking," Mikal said, breaking the silence. "Are we leaving now?"

Kari walked back to where she had been sleeping. "Yeah, I just need to grab my satchel and we'll be ready." She knelt down and dug through it, checking to see if everything was there.

She froze, her skin turning pale. She looked up at the others with a horrified expression on her face.

Knowing that something was terribly wrong, Mikal asked, "What? What's the problem?"

Kari looked utterly speechless, but she managed to stammer, "The... the key... it's gone!"

Elakhim crouched low behind a shrub, watching the six people.

His sharp, black eyes scanned the trees, taking in everything there was to see. He had a hawk-like nose that bent downwards, and bushy, gray eyebrows. His shoulder-length gray hair was bundled up in the hood of his mottled cloak. He didn't like the clothing, but it was a necessary part of his camouflage.

The kids were discussing what to do next. One of the girls, the taller one with black hair, had apparently recognized their accomplice on the road, but that was only a minor flaw in the plan.

Tarius was not important in the overall plot. He had been following them since Shala Province, but was only doing so to keep track of their whereabouts. He had posed as a traveling villager, just in case they happened upon him during their journey.

Elakhim's duty was to take out one of the enemy. According to his master, the girl with the black hair was his target. She was supposed to be the keeper of the key, but she hadn't done a very good job of that.

Another of his partners had tried to dispose of her with a poisoned dart back in Aena. Unfortunately, the other girl knew the cure for the poison, and no matter how impossible it seemed, they managed to find the remedy and use it.

The assassin smiled and clutched a small, wooden box closer to his chest. It had been extremely easy to steal. He had practically taken it right out from under their noses.

He was told to kill the girl while they were all awake and then escape quickly. Seeing their friend fall dead at their feet would strike fear into their hearts.

It seemed like they weren't being very careful at the moment, just enjoying a casual conversation.

Elakhim knew better. He knew that once they decided on a course of action, his target would grab her bag in preparation to leave. While digging through it, she would find that the key he had stolen was missing. They were already on edge. Something like discovering that the point of their mission had been stolen would bring chaos and disorder to the team.

He had to move fast, for he sensed that they were nearing the end of their conversation. Elakhim slowly lifted a small assassin's crossbow and took aim. It was already cocked and loaded. He had been prepared to shoot since they woke up a few minutes ago.

The girl walked over to the tree and stooped down. Elakhim centered his aim on the back of her head as she dug through the pack. He knew that now was the time to shoot, and he had best do it quickly.

He pulled the trigger.

"What?!" Ruth exclaimed.

Kari shook her head with stress and slammed it down on her pack.

Before anybody could say anything else, there was a click, and a black dart slammed into the wood of the tree, right where Kari's head had been.

Reacting immediately, Ruth whipped a knife out of her belt and stood at the ready. The others did the same, drawing their weapons and scanning the forest.

Ruth slowly swept her eyes over the ground where the bolt had come from. Nothing seemed out-of-the-ordinary.

But wait! There was something! In a large patch of ferns and bushes, a shape darker green than the leaves twitched slightly.

She responded by flipping the knife out of her hand and sending it spinning towards the ferns.

Almost immediately after she threw it, a man in a dark green cloak shot out of the shrubs and bolted away.

Ruth gave chase, sprinting after the man as fast as she could, while drawing another knife in the process.

56

...

Similarities

Elakhim raced through the forest, his legs pounding the ground as fast as they could. Sweat trickled down his face. His green hood had blown back in the wind, and his long, gray hair was flying freely. His chest heaved, but he kept running, ignoring the pain. *I have to escape, or I'll die.*

His mission had failed. The targeted girl had evaded his dart.

He hadn't thought about the possibility that she would somehow avoid it, and he definitely hadn't thought about any retaliation.

His sweaty hand gripped the wooden box under his cloak. He couldn't let go of it no matter what. He knew that the key it contained held immense power, though he didn't understand its purpose. All he knew was that if the enemy took it back, his master's plan would be ruined.

As if in direct contradiction to his thoughts, the box slipped out from underneath his cloak and fell to the ground with a thump.

Elakhim started to wheel around and dive for it, but before he could, something heavy hit him in the back. He fell over and lay sprawled out on the ground. His groping hand fingered the box numbly, trying to get a hold on it. It was no use.

Elakhim let out a long groan, the edges of his vision tinting red. He felt a dull pain in his upper back and wondered what it was. Reaching backwards, he brushed something hard. He struggled to grasp it and managed to yank it out.

A surge of pain pierced his entire body. He tried to yell, but his voice failed. He pulled his shaking hand back and gazed at what he was holding.

It was a knife. The blade was stained a deep red and blood was dripping from it.

His blood.

With that final revelation, Elakhim let loose a shuddering gasp and died.

<><><><><><><><><><><><><><><><><><>

Ruth knew that if the thief escaped, their quest would be a failure.

The taller man was outpacing her by this point. She panted for breath, trying to keep running. However, Ruth knew that she would never catch up to him.

Normally, it was proper procedure to take the enemy alive and question him. That wasn't going to work in this situation. Ruth had only one choice of how to deal with this assassin.

She stopped in her tracks, and before he could get too far away, she flung the knife at the man.

As it spun through the air, he dropped something out of his cloak and started to turn around.

At that moment, the knife slammed into his back, penetrating whatever weak armor he was wearing, if any.

Ruth grimaced as she saw the man fall down and struggle to pull the knife from his back. He stared at it, horrified. She was almost afraid he would get up again, but when Ruth saw him become still, she knew it was all over.

Everyone had followed her in pursuit of the thief except Mikal. He had stayed behind just in case any other intruders showed up.

Ruth knelt down next to the man's lifeless body and picked up the dark, wooden box. She handed it to Kari, who clutched it tightly with both hands, terrified of losing such an important item again.

Ruth wiped the crimson blade of her dagger on a patch of grass and sheathed it in the small, leather scabbard she had pulled it from.

"Here, help me turn him over." She beckoned for one of the others to assist her.

Zane bent down and heaved the man over with one fluid motion.

Ruth leaned in to look at the man's face.

He had a hawk-like nose and bushy gray eyebrows that hung loosely, overshadowing his black eyes that were open in a blank stare. His long, greasy hair was fanned about his head, some strands lying disorderly on his pallid face.

Kari and Ruth blanched.

"What? What is it?" Samuel asked the two girls. "Do you know him?"

"It's… it's Tarius!"

Mikal crouched down and surveyed his surroundings vigilantly.

He had volunteered to stay behind and watch for more of the enemy. They didn't know if there were any more assassins about, but it never hurt to be sure.

Mikal was crouching in a large shrub, his knees tucked underneath him and his head cocked at a strange angle.

He scanned the forest again, moving his head slowly enough to be almost unnoticeable.

A slight movement caught his eye in a cluster of trees to his left.

Mikal stiffened his body, trying not to move. He stared at the trees apprehensively, focusing on the location of the irregular activity.

As if on cue, a fuzzy, gray squirrel poked its head around a trunk and then scurried upwards, disappearing into the network of branches.

Mikal let his breath out slowly. It wasn't an intruder, just a squirrel.

As he relaxed, a man cloaked in green stepped out from behind the tree.

"Wha'?" Zane exclaimed. "This can't be Tarius. He was jest back thar!"

Kari shook her head, mystified. "That's what I thought! Maybe I was wrong, but either way, this is definitely him!"

"That's not possible!" Samuel said. "Are you sure this is Tarius?"

"Well, it looks like him," Ruth said, appraising his features. "But he didn't have long hair, and his nose was a little smaller."

"If it's not him, then who could it be?" They pondered.

Samuel's eyebrows were scrunched in thought, his deep stare focused on the leaflets of grass, on the tiny pebbles that littered the ground... and he had an idea.

The young leader looked up slowly. "Guys, what if this *is* Tarius?"

"Whad'ya mean by that?" Zane asked.

Ruth understood what he was saying. "You mean... he has a twin?"

"Yes!" He exclaimed, getting warmed up to the idea. "What if Tarius has a twin..."

"Had a twin," Kari corrected him.

"Yeah, I guess," he conceded. "What if Tarius *had* a twin, and they both conspired against us? Ogrion could use a couple of indistinguishable minions. They would be able to be in two places at once, to draw people into confusion."

"Also," Kari started, "twins are connected in ways unknown to humans. Sometimes they can almost read what the other is thinking! That would be a very helpful strategy in battle."

"I agree," Samuel stated. "Someone who was prey to those two could be utterly destroyed."

"It's a good thing we killed one of them, then," Rosh said.

The others were about to voice their agreement, when a deep shout rang through the forest.

57

...

Multiples

Mikal kept as still as possible.

The tall man looked from side to side nervously. He stepped forward from behind the tree and came into full view. Seeming much more comfortable now, he reached back and pulled the cowl off his head.

Mikal held in a gasp. The man looked just like Tarius!

As he peered at the stranger through the ferns, Mikal deduced that the man wasn't the treacherous doctor from Aena, but rather a very convincing look-alike.

Besides the scruffy beard that hung from his chin, the man would have been an almost perfect impersonation.

He stepped closer to the frightened boy and surveyed the forest. Then, without warning, he emitted a short, piercing whistle.

It was so sudden that Mikal almost flinched. Fortunately, he had been trained not to react to surprises such as that, and he kept his calm composure.

He grasped his hidden broadsword in his hand. The man was coming closer now, and it looked like he was going to walk right through the patch of shrubs where Mikal was concealed!

However, when he was so close Mikal could smell him, the man stopped and stood perfectly still, his hands on his hips.

Mikal prepared to lunge forward with his blade, but before he could, something grabbed him from behind.

A rough hand wrapped around his mouth and pulled him to the ground. He bit at the coarse fingers. His teeth sunk in and his attacker screamed in pain. Mikal felt warm blood in his mouth and spit it out.

Faster than he could see, the man that looked like Tarius jumped on him and grabbed his arms. Mikal kicked upwards, but it was no use. The man was pinning his legs down.

Remembering his sword, he swung it backwards at the person behind him, but the blade was easily knocked out of his hands.

All of a sudden, something solid smacked the side of his head and everything went dark.

"It's Mikal!" Zane yelled. "He's in trouble!"

They left the body lying on the ground, but took the green cloak with them. Their feet pounded the ground, and their hearts beat fast. Zane's mind was reeling with possibilities of what could be happening.

Spotting the area they had slept in up ahead, Samuel raised a hand in the air and signaled for them to slow down. With carefully placed footsteps, they crept closer to the campsite, dreading what they were about to see.

A small tree grew up from the ground in front of them, and several bushes and ferns were scattered around it. The group hid behind this foliage and watched the proceedings in the clearing beyond.

Two men clothed in green cloaks the same as the dead assassin's were holding someone up to a tree and tying his wrists together.

It was Mikal!

From the looks of it, he was unconscious, the men having ambushed him.

As they watched the lithe men bind their friend, a plan began forming in Zane's mind. He toyed with different ways to make it work, leaning his chin gently on his huge mace. Suddenly, it all came together.

"Guys," he whispered. "I have an idea."

Ilich wrapped the hard rope around his prisoner's wrists, making sure that his knots were tight.

He turned around and retrieved the boy's sword from the ground, gazing at it enviously.

"This, my brother, is a good sword," he said to his sibling, Qusab.

The other man turned and beheld the marvelous blade their target had been using. "Yes. I think that it will make a fine addition to our spoils," he announced in a deep, rumbling voice.

"Indeed."

Ilich and Qusab were brothers. In fact, they were twins. Their angular faces were identical in almost every way, from their bushy eyebrows to their sharp noses.

Ilich and his brother had been assigned to capture the members of this band and deliver them to Ogrion. Their other brother, Elakhim, had failed in his task to kill the girl.

He had also seen the knife-throwing one chase after Elakhim following his failure, so he knew that his brother's life was moot. A hot feeling of anger and vengeance filled his face. *I will destroy those wretches for what they have done!* He vowed silently.

He had already observed his third brother, Tarius, deceive the girl with the fact that a village was two miles from their camp, but unfortunately, the brats had seen through that ploy.

Now that he thought about it, though, their targets were likely to return soon, and he didn't want to be there when they found their friend tied up like he was now.

"Come on, Qusab," he said in a quieter voice. "We need to go. They'll be back any minute." His twin nodded in agreement, and they prepared to slink away into the darkness of the forest.

A deep voice spoke from behind him.

"Hey, where are you guys goin'?" They turned around and saw another man in a green cloak standing behind them.

"Is that... Elakhim?" Qusab asked, confusion framing his face.

"Yeah! I mean... yeah." The big man walked closer to them.

Suspicion started nibbling at Ilich. Elakhim's death had been almost certain. Now, there was a man in front of them claiming to be their brother. There was something fishy about this.

"How'd you get away?" Ilich's brother asked.

"Killed 'em all."

Now he knew something was really wrong. Elakhim didn't have an accent like that. His voice had been clear and sophisticated, and it wasn't that deep.

Ilich peered at the strange man. He was quite tall and powerful, but the cowl was pulled low over his face, so they couldn't see his features.

The slender assassin reached behind himself and drew a knife from his belt. He knew this wasn't Elakhim, but he didn't know who it was. *It must be one of those kids*, he thought. *I just don't remember them being this big!*

"You're not Elakhim," he stated.

"What?! How can you say that? I'm your partner!"

That just about confirmed it with Ilich. His brother had never called them partners. Elakhim always referred to them as brothers, never anything else. Before he could say so, however, the stranger spoke again.

"It's time," his deep voice rumbled.

"What? What do you mean, you imposter?!" Qusab cried, drawing his sword.

Ilich opened his mouth, but before he could say anything, he saw something out of the corner of his eye.

A sharp blade, gleaming in the afternoon light, shot through the air towards his body.

58

...

The Fifth

Ilich screamed in pain and fell to his knees on the ground.

The shining blade pierced his side, penetrating through the leather tunic he wore underneath his cloak.

Ilich saw Qusab battling the one who had claimed to be Elakhim. He could see now that it was merely a boy, albeit a very large boy, who was wielding a gigantic mace.

Ilich groaned and fell to the ground, pulling the dagger out of his side, the life draining from him as blood gushed from his open wound. Trying to stem the flow of liquid with his cloak, he bunched it into a ball and pressed it against himself. The makeshift bandage was immediately soaked.

With his other hand, he limply held the knife he had intended to use on the boy imposter. He tried to lift his hand and throw it, but he was too weak. The dagger flopped lazily back to the ground.

As he lay flat, groaning, he saw more movement out of the corner of his eye.

The rest of the young warriors they had been tracking emerged from behind a tree and some bushes, their weapons drawn and ready.

This should have made him desperate with fear, but he wasn't looking at them. Behind the angry mob, something else stalked silently.

He smiled as his vision dimmed. *They have no chance now, he thought. It's over for them.*

Ignoring the burning pain, Ilich watched a man in a green cloak step stealthily from behind the cover of the trees, a thin tube held in one hand.

Randan.

Zane swiped his mace at the shorter man in front of him. He seemed to be gaining the upper hand, but his foe was very skilled.

The man's accomplice was now unconscious on the ground, a bloody knife resting next to his hand. Ruth had taken him down with the same knife she had used on his brother.

By this time, Zane had guessed that there were a lot of people in Tarius's family. So far, he had counted four siblings. They must have been quadruplets, since they all looked about the same age. Zane pitied their mother.

The man he was fighting ducked a swipe from Kari and lunged forward. Zane just managed to parry the blade with the handle of his mace before the sword would have run him through.

Tiring from the fight, Zane decided to master his opponent with pure force. He lifted his mace for a powerful overhead swing. The other man raised his sword in a futile attempt to fend off the impending blow.

Before Zane could bring the mace smashing down, however, he felt a sharp sting in his shoulder. In his surprise, his grip fumbled in the swing, and he lost control of the mace. It flew out of his hand and hit his enemy's sword, barely hard enough to push him back a step.

Zane grasped behind him at his shoulder blade, trying to feel what was pricking him. As he did this, the world started spinning around him. He almost managed to keep his balance, but in the end, he fell to his knees, wondering what in the world was happening.

Then everything went dark.

Randan stood silently behind the trunk of a large tree. He fingered a small dart that was in his hand and slid it into the end of a long, wooden tube.

Being as discreet as possible, he poked his head around the tree and watched the battle that was going on between his brothers and the children. Unfortunately, Elakhim was dead now. He had witnessed his ruthless murder at the hands of these very competent warriors. He had also seen Ilich struck down by a flying knife from the same brat that had killed Elakhim.

Now he would have his revenge.

He put the tube up to his mouth and aimed it at the blonde girl. She was engaged in combat with Qusab, who was holding his own against all four of them, hacking and slashing every which way.

Randan had already taken down the main threat, the giant boy with the mace. Ilich and Qusab had dealt with one of the boys earlier. Their victim was lying unconscious against a tree, his hands and legs bound.

Focusing on the girl once again, he drew in a breath through his nose and then pushed the air out through his mouth. The force of his exhalation propelled the tiny dart out the other end of the tube.

His aim was true, and it hit the girl in her upper arm. He saw her step backwards and pull it out. She took one confused look at it and fell to the ground, unmoving.

In quick succession, Randan shot three more darts into the remaining attackers, watching them stumble about clumsily and then collapse.

Qusab was breathing heavily, staring at the fallen bodies of his enemies, bewildered. He looked up when Randan approached and spoke scornfully. "Did you have to go and kill them?"

Randan rolled his eyes. "I used a sleeping dart! They're not dead, but Ilich will be if we don't get him out of here soon!"

Swallowing his anger, Qusab agreed. "Yeah. We could put them all on that peasant's cart if Tarius were here. It would be much easier to get them to the ship that way."

Before Randan could answer, a familiar-looking, gray-cloaked man stepped into the small gathering.

"You called?" Tarius asked.

Not surprised at all that his brother had been there, Qusab said, "I was saying that we should load these people on your wagon and take them to the ship that way."

Tarius nodded his head thoughtfully and stroked his nonexistent beard. "Yes, we could do that."

Annoyed with the delay this conversation was causing, Randan abruptly stated, "So let's do it, then!"

After binding their ankles and wrists, loading them onto Tarius's wagon, and covering all the bodies with hay, Ilich's peril came to their attention.

Randan knelt down next to their brother and felt his pulse. He could discern a faint heartbeat in Ilich's limp hand.

"He's still alive. But with all this bleeding, he won't be for long." He looked up at Qusab and Tarius. "We need something for a bandage, a strip of cloth, maybe."

Tarius began searching in his wagon for cloth, but Qusab ripped a length off of his shirt and handed it to Randan.

The other man took it thankfully and rolled his eyes at the doctor's efforts. Tarius had always been known to be the laziest among them.

After he had finished binding Ilich's wound, they loaded the hurt man onto the hay, making sure to place him on top of the bodies of their prisoners, so they would be uncomfortable if they woke. Randan pulled the hood over his brother's face, covering the tattoo that was inscribed there.

He wondered why Ilich had chosen to have the mark put on his forehead. It was much simpler and easier to hide when it was on one's hand. He pulled back his sleeve and gazed at his mark.

Its deep black color reminded him of the ebony room he had pledged his loyalty in. He traced his finger around the eye-shaped symbol, a promise that his master was always watching.

"You about ready to go?" Qusab asked, startling Randan out of his thoughts.

The other man pushed his sleeve back down his arm and nodded.

"Then let's go!" The three brothers hopped onto the wagon, and Tarius grabbed the leather reins. He snapped them on the back of the brown horse, reciting the necessary command.

The horse began walking, plodding along at a slow rate, used to the burden of the rickety, wooden wagon.

As he traveled along the dirt road, thoughts about the journey ahead for the six captives wandered through Randan's mind. He laid his head back and closed his eyes, basking in the afternoon sun that shone through the cover of the trees.

Oh, yes, he thought. *They have quite the trip ahead of them. Quite the trip, indeed.*

59

...

At Sea

Samuel leaned his head against the wall of his cell, listening to the ocean waves splash against the side of the ship.

They had been at sea for several weeks now, after having been captured by the servants of Ogrion. When Samuel awoke after being knocked unconscious by the dart, he had found himself with the others in a dingy prison cell on the lowermost floor of a sailing vessel.

Every day, they received meager meals that consisted of stale bread and water. What was living in the water was a mystery.

From the tidbits of information he had gleaned hearing the conversations of passing crew members, they were on a pirate vessel, sailing across the Naska Sea towards Lanya. The four identical assassins had sold them to pirates.

At first, this had excited Samuel. They were being taken to the exact country they needed to be in! As time dragged on, however, his hope deflated. Samuel was forced to abandon any thoughts of completing his mission. They were deep in the enemy's territory, and there was nothing Samuel could do about it.

Fortunately, they hadn't been searched when thrown in the cell. The only things that were taken from them were their weapons. Kari still had the key half and kept it safely hidden somewhere in her clothes.

During the long nights, they had been discussing ways to escape. Kari suggested the way she and Ruth had fooled the guard in the swamp, but Samuel rejected that idea. It would be nearly impossible to fend off the pirates without weapons, and the large body of water that surrounded them would make it very difficult to escape.

Their dank prison cell was small for six people. There was almost enough room on the floor for Samuel to lie down, but he wouldn't dare do that. Besides the fact that his wrist was chained to the wall, the ground was covered with rotting straw and was crawling with insects of unknown origin. There was also a small privy in the center of the cramped space, which exuded a horrid smell.

After the first few days, Ruth's seasickness had eased off, but the guards outside hadn't bothered to clean up the floor. That was another reason to stay sitting on the crude, wooden benches that lined the walls.

The only door to the room was slightly shorter than Zane, with one, barred porthole in the top center. There was no handle on the inside, for that would be too easy for skilled thieves to pick. On the outside, it was locked with a keyhole and a rusty chain that connected the door to the frame. This gave less than a modicum of hope to any poor prisoners who happened to be kidnapped by these men.

Samuel's head hurt from dehydration and the constant rocking of the ship. His backside was sore from sitting down for weeks, and his stomach growled with displeasure at their unhealthy meals.

Feeling the strain of the journey, Samuel knew he needed to stay positive and keep everyone's hopes up. He was wondering what to talk about, when he heard a cry from the deck above.

"Land ho!"

A small line of land appeared on the horizon, a dark contrast on the blue sky before them.

Denor gazed upon the waves of the ocean, admiring their powerful beauty. He breathed in the salty sea air as it blew past, carrying the cry of a gull from somewhere overhead.

It was good to be at sea.

As he stared at the approaching mainland, he remembered the man that had hired him. Randan was his name. He had approached Denor, asking if he would carry some prisoners to a man in Lanya named Grale. The job earned him thirty gold shards. All that Randan had divulged to him was that the six captives were enemies of the rightful ruler of Aena and the world: Ogrion.

Denor didn't actually serve the rebellious warlord. He spent his time preying on cargo vessels that sailed unsuspecting through the Naska Sea. Denor had always admired the beliefs of King Ogrion. He figured that the King of old had been senile before his mysterious disappearance.

Those times were long ago, however, and he had the present to worry about.

"Garthor!" He shouted. His muscular first mate walked up to him, swaying with the movement of the ship.

"Yeh?"

"Prepare the men. By the time we get to shore, I want them ready to move on the double! We don't want to attract any suspicious eyes when we bring out the prisoners." Before Garthor could leave, though, Denor added one more thing. "Oh! And tell Kosta to check on our passengers. Have him see to it that they're ready to move."

"Aye, Cap'n!" The burly man walked away and began yelling orders to the crew.

Soon, Denor thought to himself. *Soon we will rid ourselves of those miserable children. I hope this Grale character has the money.*

"Everybody got it?" Samuel looked around at the faces of his friends in the dim light. There were no objections. "Good. Now, when they open that door, you know what to do."

Samuel had just finished informing his friends of a plan that he'd been mulling over.

With some flexibility and a little help from Adonai, Kari had managed to pick all the locks on their wrist cuffs with the key half she had hidden. Fortunately for them, it had fit perfectly into the holes, something that Samuel had originally doubted.

Heavy footsteps sounded on the stairway leading to their cell. Someone was coming to prepare them to leave the ship. What the incoming pirate didn't know was that they were already prepared.

Samuel took his place in the corner of the room next to the door. He contorted himself in an awkward position that the guard hopefully wouldn't notice.

A key clicked in the lock outside, and a chain rattled. The wooden door swung open on creaky hinges, letting in a man who was almost as tall and muscled as Zane.

Almost.

When the man was all the way in the room, Samuel breathed deeply. *Here goes nothing,* he thought, and swung down from his hiding place, leaping nimbly out the open door and shutting it behind him.

Kosta plodded down the wooden steps that led to the prison cells. He really didn't like doing guard duty for the prisoners, but the captain had ordered it. He couldn't deny the captain's orders.

Kosta sighed to himself as he fished the ring of keys out of his pocket and found the one that went to the cell. He unlatched the chain from the top of the door and then swung it open, letting the dim light in on the captives' faces.

When he entered, he noticed that one of them was older than the others. There was a certain solidity to his face that made him look more mature. He decided to watch that one.

Just as he stepped across the threshold of the cell, the door slammed shut behind him, and he was subjected to darkness. Having been in the sunlight for so long, he couldn't see anything.

He opened his mouth to yell for help, but before he could, something rock-hard slammed into his jaw and he groaned, falling backwards to the floor.

Kosta lifted his hands to fend off any more blows.

Another strike came, but it was not at his jaw this time. Instead, his assailant jabbed a fist into his stomach.

Kosta tried to scream, but he couldn't breath. Moaning one last time, his eyes closed, and he passed out.

60

...

Breaking Free

"You can open the door now, Samuel!" A muffled voice said from inside the dark prison cell.

Samuel released his grip on the door handle and let it swing inward.

The others stepped over the unconscious body of the pirate and exited their cell, stretching in relief. They squinted at the brightness of the outer room and reveled in the fresh air.

After taking in their surroundings, Ruth turned and addressed Samuel. "Do you know where to find our weapons?"

"Well," he began, looking around the room. "It doesn't seem like they're in here. The pirates must have locked them away somewhere. We'll have to make do without them."

Ruth shrugged. "At least we have Zane."

Samuel looked back and suppressed a grin as he observed the huge boy effortlessly move the incapacitated pirate further into the cell. He shut the door, locking it.

Samuel walked over to where the others had hidden, making sure that no more pirates were coming. They concealed themselves in an unobtrusive alcove that was near the stairway to the upper deck.

After waiting for a few minutes, Samuel felt the vessel moving slower and slower until it eventually stopped, bobbing slightly in the waves.

They had reached the docks by this point, which meant the final piece of their plan was about to begin.

He held his breath as heavy footsteps stomped overhead, and men yelled back and forth to each other, passing on orders and cursing. *I wonder why pirates curse so much,* he thought. *Maybe just because they can.*

As he sat there, his mind wandered, planning their next course of action after escaping the ship. The hope that had faded was returning. He didn't wonder if they would complete their mission now. He knew they would.

Loud feet thudded against the steps above the six uncomfortably positioned people.

Here we go.

"Where's Kosta?" He heard a rough voice shout. "Wasn't he s'posed to get the pris'ners?"

"Yeh," another gruff voice replied. "Sent 'im down 'ere a li'l bi' ago. Hasn' come back ye'."

"Wal, we might wanna check on 'im." The pirates' voices grew louder until they were right next to the hiding place.

"Looks like th' door's still locked," one of them said. "I won'er where Kosta wen' off to."

There was the clinking of keys, and then a noisy creak.

"Wha' the...?!" Samuel heard a pirate exclaim. He felt Mikal tensing his muscles next to him, but he held up his hand for them to wait.

The two pirates who were checking on Kosta called up for the others to come down and see.

Footsteps thundered above their heads. A horde of unruly pirates rushed down the stairs to see what was wrong, talking loudly and cursing. Samuel held up his hand again, waiting to give the signal.

As soon as all the pirates were clustered around the open doorway, he clenched his hand in a tight fist, the signal to go.

He and the others stormed out of their hiding place, clambering up the stairs as fast as they could.

A lone pirate stood in their way, staring at them in bewilderment. Zane pushed him aside, sending the man stumbling backwards. There were no other pirates on the staircase, but Samuel could hear shouting behind him. The ones in the lower deck had seen them escape.

A wicked knife flashed past them and embedded in the wall. Samuel pumped his legs as hard as he could, knowing that his only chance was to outrun the pirates.

Suddenly, there was something slick beneath Samuel's feet. He wheeled his arms around, trying to catch his balance, but it was no use.

Helpless, his feet slid out from under him, and he hit the ground hard.

Pirates' voices approached as he struggled to get to his feet.

The others had stopped at the top of the next flight of stairs and were beckoning to Samuel hurriedly.

"Come on!" Rosh shouted.

Samuel reached out his hand and grabbed a rail, pulling himself upright. With one fluid movement, he leapt off the slimy substance and hit the steps running.

The pirates' voices were directly behind him. Samuel felt a hand swipe his back, grasping at his clothes.

His panicked friends took off running again as he reached them.

They finally emerged onto the top deck of the ship. Sunlight glared down from above, blinding Samuel for a moment.

As his eyes adjusted, he could see the small town by which they had docked. It was nestled peacefully in the woods that surrounded the sandy shore. Red brick houses stood solemnly in the morning light, keeping watch over the busy people in the streets below.

Samuel looked at the wooden dock, and his heart dropped like a rock.

In their rush to check on the prisoners, the pirates had failed to put out the bridge that let them walk ashore!

Knowing that it was his only chance to survive, Samuel decided to jump. There was a ruckus behind him, and he knew that the pirates had made it onto the deck.

"There's no bridge!" He heard Kari yell from behind him.

"We'll have to jump!" He called back. Not waiting for the others' confirmation, Samuel reached the edge of the ship and pushed off, leaping with all his might towards the wooden dock below.

The dock approached ominously, but he bent his legs to absorb the impact, hitting it hard and rolling.

He popped back to his feet and turned, hoping that his friends had decided to jump instead of stay on the ship. Relief swept over him as he saw them hit the dock one by one.

"Come on, guys!" He shouted. "Let's get out of here!"

He started sprinting for the city, but before he could get too far, a cry of pain reached his ears. It was Ruth.

"Wait! Help! I'm hurt!"

Samuel whipped around, skidding on the slippery dock. He saw Ruth limping towards them, a grimace on her face.

Not knowing what else to do, he bolted back to her and yanked her off the ground, carrying her like a baby. He ran as hard as he could away from the ship, not caring about the strain in his arm muscles. He heard the sound of knives hitting the dock behind them and sticking into its soft wood.

Samuel watched the others turn towards the forest that bordered the town, all of them sprinting as fast as they could.

His arms burned like fire, but he couldn't give up now. Not after he had made it this far. Most of all, however, he couldn't let Ruth down. She was counting on him to save her, and he knew it.

Just when he thought he'd never make it, the cool shade of the forest washed over him, and he looked up, realizing that the others had all stopped running and were now sitting on the ground, breathing hard.

He gently set Ruth on the ground against a large tree.

"How's your ankle?" Samuel asked. He assumed it had been her ankle that was hurt from the way she had been limping.

She looked up at him, gratefulness shining in her eyes. "It's alright. Thank you for saving my life." Then she blushed and turned away.

Samuel straightened his back awkwardly and turned his head back to the pirate ship. His cheeks were turning bright red, and that was only partially because of the heat.

As he observed the docks, Samuel noticed that the pirates weren't giving chase. *They probably think we're long gone by now,* he thought.

"Hey, Samuel!" Rosh's voice called from behind him.

He turned back around. "Yeah? What?"

"I think you might want to see this." Rosh pointed up through an open spot in the branches.

Samuel caught his breath.

A massive tower of stone rose up in the distance, its snow-covered peaks glistening in the sun. Masses of verdant green forest blanketed its sides. The summit, which sat many miles above the ground, protruded outward, partially concealing a dark spot in its white sides: A cave.

"That," Samuel said, clearing his throat, "is Vanguard Mountain."

61

...

The Mountain

"That is one big mountain."

Mikal and Zane were standing on a hilltop, staring at the imposing Vanguard Mountain.

They had spent most of the day hiking through the massive forest. It had been a comfortable trek, with warm spots of sunlight shining through the shady boughs of the trees.

Ruth's ankle hadn't improved. Although they had splinted it, she had been limping most of the way, her injury paining her with every step. She was a strong girl, however, and had refused to be carried or helped by any of the others.

Except for when Samuel helped her on the dock, Mikal thought, smirking. *She didn't seem to mind that at all.*

They decided to make camp about a half mile from the mountain. Mikal and Zane had been instructed to scout out the path ahead, and Samuel and Rosh had been sent to gather wood for a fire. Mikal wasn't sure if it was a good idea to send up smoke like that, but the others convinced him that they were too far away from civilization for anyone to notice.

Ruth and Kari had volunteered to stay at the camp and start preparing some sort of afternoon meal with berries, leaves, and a small rabbit they had caught earlier. They figured that the boys would be happy to come back to a ready-made meal. All they had eaten in the past few weeks was stale bread, and they had all lost weight during that time.

Mikal peered up at the peak as the setting sun reflected off the bright snow. He strained his eyes to see if he could discern any movement in the dark cave at the top.

"Do you think they're up there?" Zane asked, talking about the mysterious dragons that were the guardians of the second half of the key.

Mikal was about to answer when he noticed movement.

"Look!" He exclaimed pointing up to the cave. "There's something up there!"

"Where?" Zane squinted.

"In the cave!" Mikal answered.

There was a slight flutter, and something green flicked out of the orifice and disappeared back into its depths.

Ruth reclined against a large stone in their campsite. She stretched her back, hearing it pop noisily. A dull ache still throbbed in her ankle. They had splinted it with a firm branch, wrapping it with a piece of her shirt and securing it with a long strip of cedar bark.

Leaning forward, Ruth ripped a large, green leaf into small fragments and tossed them into a kettle they had found lying neglected on the ground. She figured that their need to eat surpassed any desire to avoid diseases that *may* have contaminated the pot. She hoped that Adonai would protect them from anything too nasty.

"Hey, Ruth, can you pass me some of those berries?" Kari asked.

Ruth nodded and picked up the small bag of berries, passing it to the other girl.

They worked in silence for a moment, Ruth making the soup, and Kari preparing the rabbit.

It was a fair amount of work to prepare the animal before cooking it. Currently, Kari was squeezing berry juice onto the skinned corpse.

Back home, Ruth hadn't cooked much. Soup was actually one of her stronger meals. Her principle was, "Just throw everything in a pot and call it good." That seemed to work for most soups. Hopefully, the boys would like it when they returned.

Tired of the silence, Ruth nonchalantly inquired of Kari, "What's up with you and Mikal?"

The other girl stopped her work and faced Ruth with an annoyed look on her face.

"Seriously? That's the best conversation-starter you can think of?"

"I'm just asking. Just asking." Ruth snuck a look at Kari. The older girl's cheeks, although previously pale, now had a tinge of pink in them. Ruth firmed her lips, trying to keep a mischievous smile from breaking through. Her effort was wasted, however, for Kari looked up with an annoyed expression.

"Why are you trying not to smile?" Ruth didn't answer. She just kept working on the soup. Nonetheless, Kari deduced the reason.

"You don't need to make fun of me just because I like a boy, okay?" Ruth looked up at her, and Kari realized what she had said. "I mean… as… as a friend. Just a friend."

Ruth smirked doubtfully. "Sure. Just a friend."

Finally, Kari gave in. "Okay, okay! I… I like the guy, alright? He's a good person, and it's not often you come across an *actually* good person."

Ruth nodded understandingly. "I know what you mean."

Kari raised an eyebrow. "I'll bet you do! With Samuel carrying you like that back on the docks? I thought you were going to kiss him or something!"

"What?" She stared incredulously at Kari. "I wouldn't do that!" She paused and then continued reluctantly. "But he is a good guy, and as you said, those kinds of guys are hard to find."

To any bystanders, this would seem like a malicious argument, but to the two good friends, it was just a lively conversation.

"Well, it looks like we've both scored big on this one, then!"

"You make it sound as if they're items! They *are* actual people, you know!"

"Yes, yes, of course." They paused and continued preparing the food in silence for a few moments.

"What did you guys talk about when Mikal was spending so much time with you on the *Campekter*?" Ruth asked, pulling her hair back.

"Oh, we talked about what it was like back home and stuff like that."

"Are you sure that's all?" Ruth asked, wiggling her eyebrows.

"Yes, that's all."

Before Kari could make another retort, she heard yelling.

She stood up quickly, brushing her slimy hands off on the grass. Kari looked in the direction the shouts were coming from and saw the two brothers sprinting towards them as fast as they could, shouting something unintelligible.

"What?" Kari yelled back as they came running into the campsite.

Samuel stopped just short of the food they were preparing and pointed into the sky. "Dragon!"

Before he could explain more, there was a huge whooshing sound. The sunlight went dark for a moment, and there was an unmistakeable growl.

All four of them looked up in awe.

Rocketing upwards towards the cave in the peak of Vanguard Mountain was a powerful, green-scaled beast.

62

...

For The Love Of Money

The majestic reptile flew towards the mountain. It swished its tail back and forth, propelling its body faster and faster. Its magnificent wings beat against the oncoming wind, forcing it to soar up the side of the craggy mountain.

The dark hole in the peak loomed above. The great beast turned at a sharp angle and disappeared into the cave. It fluttered its enormous wings, landing on the rocky ground of the cavern. Its orange eyes flashed.

In response, two more resplendent dragons appeared from the shadows and ambled up to the first creature with dignity.

"Are they here?" The largest dragon asked in a deep, melodious voice that rumbled through the room like thunder.

"Yes, Varnul," the first replied in the slightly higher tone of a female. "They are making their camp in the grassy clearing below."

The dragon that hadn't spoke yet asked Varnul, "Should we retrieve them, or allow them to make their way to us?"

"A good question, Nuntuk," it growled in reply. "What do *you* propose we do?"

"I say we bring them into our cave. It is a hazardous path up the mountain, and their strength may waver. We should assist them."

Varnul, the alpha, turned to the female dragon. "What do you think, Miltah? Should we, or should we not?"

The smaller dragon looked down, deep in thought. "I think we should carry them. The journey up the mountain to our cave may be preferred to older humans, but these are mere children. They have not yet built up great strength."

"Then let it be so. Make ready to fly down. We must do this as quickly as possible, for evildoers lurk in the forest."

<><><><><><><><><><><><><><><><><><>

"Did you see that?!" Mikal exclaimed as he ran into the campsite.

"You mean the *dragon*?" Kari asked.

"Oh, no!" He replied mockingly. "I meant that colorful butterfly that's flitting around, not the gigantic, green, scaly beast that just flew over us!"

"Hey, no need to be sassy!"

Mikal sighed. "Sorry," he apologized. "It's just that I'm kind of freaked out right now."

"It's all right. And yes, I did see the dragon. It flew into that cave up there!" She pointed to the dark spot in the mountain.

"How're we gonna git up thar?" Zane asked, confused.

Samuel sat down on a rock and pondered their situation. "The only way we're going to get up there is by climbing, unless the dragons come down and pick us up, which I believe is highly doubtful." The others nodded, conceding his point. "I think we should rest down here until Ruth's healed and we've recovered our energy. Then a couple of us should try to find a path up, paving the way for the others."

"It's a good plan," Rosh said. "But how long will it take?"

Before Samuel could answer, there was a shout from the treeline behind them.

"Who's that?" Zane asked.

A bad feeling began eating away at Samuel as he observed the newcomers. He knew exactly who they were.

"Guys," he said in an apprehensive voice. "Get ready to run."

"Do you know who they are?" Ruth asked him.

"Yes. They're the pirates."

<><><><><><><><><><><><><><><><><><><>

Denor yelled in fury when he saw the escapees standing in the clearing. They had escaped the pirates with almost no resistance. Fortunately, there was a good tracker among the crew, and he had shown the pirates which way the kids had gone.

Those children may have thought he'd given up. But little did they know, pirates didn't give up money easily.

"Come on, Garthor!" He yelled to his first mate. "Let's attack!"

The muscular man nodded and brandished his Racouan scimitar. It had been a long time since he'd fought, and this was the perfect chance to refresh his skills.

Denor turned to the horde of pirates behind him and yelled, "Don't kill anyone! I want them alive!"

"Why can't we kill 'em?" One of his men shouted.

"If we kill them, then we don't get the money for their capture!"

The pirate nodded, acknowledging that his captain had a point.

"Let's not give them any more time to prepare!" Denor yelled. "Charge!" He led the way as the mob of burly pirates swarmed into the clearing.

<><><><><><><><><><><><><><><><><><>

"Help me up," Ruth said, struggling. "We have to get out of here!"

"Here, put your arm around my shoulder!" Samuel leaned down and helped Ruth up as quickly as he could.

Adonai help us, he thought, looking towards the shouting horde of men. He and Ruth began running from the approaching army. He was so desperate, he was nearly dragging her.

Suddenly, a rough hand grabbed Samuel's shirt and yanked him backwards. Ruth fell to the ground away from him, crying out in pain.

A calloused fist crashed into Samuel's face, making his head spin. He lay helplessly on the ground, watching the man out of the corner of his eye.

The burly pirate turned to Ruth and started towards her, cracking his knuckles threateningly. He laughed a deep, throaty chuckle. He had been told not to kill them, but giving them a good beating wouldn't do that.

In desperation, Samuel lunged forward and grabbed the man's leg, making him trip and stumble backwards.

The angry pirate caught his balance and glared at the pesky boy on the ground. He lifted up his fist once again, but before he could bring it down, a massive gust of wind pushed him backwards.

Samuel's eyes widened as he beheld the majesty before him.

The huge reptile opened its talons, plucked Ruth off the ground as if she were an insect, and carried her up into the sky.

63

...

The Cave

Ruth screamed as she dangled from the giant, black talons that were wrapped around her body. Although she wasn't being hurt, the surprise of being picked up by a dragon was quite overwhelming.

Managing to catch her breath, she looked down and saw the pirate army below. She glimpsed tiny figures being run down and beaten.

Suddenly, two more huge, green dragons swooped down and extracted people from the fight. The largest of the dragons held two of the boys, probably Samuel and Zane, and was scorching the ranks of the pirates with a white-hot tongue of flame.

Ruth gasped in wonder. She had heard the myths about dragons breathing fire, but it had never occurred to her that they might be true.

The landscape below became smaller and smaller as she realized they were flying right next to Vanguard Mountain, soaring up towards the cave.

The fear of flying had left Ruth now, and she felt only exhilaration. Her heart beat rapidly in her chest, but she wasn't afraid anymore. She knew that Adonai would protect her no matter where she was, even if she was dangling from the claws of a dragon.

The snow on the mountainside flew past her in a blur, blending its pure white with the brown of the rocky cliffs. Tall, imposing fir trees jutted proudly into the sky. Mountain goats leapt from stone to stone, comfortable in their natural habitat.

Then, in a single moment, the ground below disappeared, replaced by dark, moist stone underneath her.

Ruth's ears popped because of the pressure, and she was slightly lightheaded from the rise in altitude, but that was nothing compared to the excitement she felt from the flight.

The gigantic dragon set her gently on the floor, along with Kari, whom it had held in its other claw. Ruth hadn't noticed Kari being picked up. She had been too absorbed in her own experience.

She looked up at the dignified reptile and wondered if it could speak.

"Are... are you able to talk?" Ruth asked tentatively.

A low rumbling filled the cave, almost like a deep chuckle. "Yes, little one. I can speak." Its voice was as soft as silk, but also as powerful as fire.

Ruth turned around when more flapping sounds filled the cavern. Kari greeted Samuel and Zane, who had just been set down by the largest dragon.

"That was fun!" Zane said, pumping his arms above his head. "We should do that again!"

Obviously not agreeing with Zane, Samuel stumbled towards the two girls and leaned against the cavern wall, trying to steady himself. He had a purple bruise on one side of his face, but other than that, he looked no worse for wear.

"You all right, Samuel?" Ruth asked him. "You look a little pale."

"So… hate… heights!" He said between breaths.

She laughed, the pleasant sound echoing through the cavernous room.

Mikal and Rosh walked up to the group. Mikal had a thin cut on his arm, and Rosh was developing a black eye.

"Well, Samuel," his brother said. "I guess our mountain-climbing expedition's been cancelled."

They all laughed, but then, remembering the main reason they had come to the cave, they fell silent.

Samuel turned to the large dragon, which he assumed was the leader, and addressed it in the most eloquent words he could think of.

"Mighty dragon," he began, but the green-scaled reptile corrected him.

"Call me Varnul," the dragon rumbled.

"Okay, Varnul then. We have come here to retrieve a half of a key for our king, the ruler of Aena. He called it the key to Yamal, and said that you are the keepers of one of its halves, for it was split into two pieces long ago."

"Yes," it said slowly, staring down at him. "I know the key of which you speak. However, we must ask why your king seeks this great symbol of power."

Symbol of power? Samuel thought. *Is this what Y was referring to when he warned us? Is this why the king looked so uneasy when he was giving us our mission?* These thoughts raced through Samuel's head as he considered the possibilities.

"Our ruler, King Nunor, told us that he wanted the key to unlock a secret door in Yamal, to take captive any defiant people. Although, we learned at the Realm of Y that this key has a different purpose greater than opening this door."

The dragons looked at one another questioningly. Eventually, the one called Varnul spoke again.

"What Y told you is true, for the key holds power beyond what any of you could imagine. We are forbidden to tell you more, however, for the great Creator of our world has ordered that you learn it for yourselves."

"Will you not give us the half, then?" Samuel asked.

"We shall give it to you, but you must be wise with it. Your king's intentions are not what they may seem."

With that familiar statement, the huge dragon reached its powerful jaws behind itself and pried something shiny from one of its scales. Holding the object gently between its sharp teeth, it lowered its head.

Samuel slowly walked forward to retrieve it. He reached out and reverently took the golden key half, gazing at its features.

It looked the same as the other key half, just opposite. The carved lines in its stem were there, and the other half of the blue, diamond-shaped jewel was embedded in the gold.

"Kari," Samuel said. "Bring out the other half."

She blushed and turned around, retrieving the item from somewhere in her clothing that Samuel did not want to think about.

As she did this, the dragons watched them closely. Samuel thought this was kind of unnerving, but he knew they were servants of Adonai, thus he did not fear them.

"Here, Samuel." She handed him the dark, wooden box, opening its small lid.

He set the container on the ground and held the key halves, one in each hand. Samuel looked up at the dragons.

"What am I supposed to do? Just stick them together?"

Varnul nodded slowly, not saying a word.

Very carefully, Samuel pressed the two halves against each other.

A bright, golden light shone in the crack between them. The glow filled the room, shedding light on everybody's faces in a vast explosion of brilliance.

Then, just as suddenly as it had appeared, it was gone.

Samuel held up the faultless key, looking it over. The others gathered around him, peering in at the small object they had risked their lives for.

It glowed slightly with a shiny, golden hue. Carved markings ran across the stem, where the seam between the two halves had been.

Samuel gazed up at the dragons, a question in his eyes. Before he could ask it, however, they answered, seeming to know what he was thinking.

"The runes are written in Gerleuta, an ancient language that only the elders of the Axedarian race can read."

Samuel nodded, though he didn't know who the Axedarians were. *I guess I'll have to figure that out later.*

He looked back at the dragons and asked, "Can you take us back to our country through the air?"

Varnul slowly nodded once more. "Yes, but before we leave this place, all of you need rest. It has been a long time since you have had proper sleep." The dragon's scales rippled and a smooth gust of warm wind passed through the cave.

Samuel realized that he was, indeed, tired. In fact he was exhausted. Now that he thought about it, it was all he could do to not fall asleep on his feet.

Figuring that this was as good a spot as ever, he sat down on the ground, not caring about the cave water that soaked into his trousers.

"One more thing," Varnul added before Samuel's eyes could close. "Adonai has bid us to tell you this: The key you hold is one of three items of power."

"What?" Samuel asked, his tired brain confused.

"The key to Yamal. It is the first of the Triqan."

Turn the page for a sneak peek of

Adonai's Book

1

...

In The Dark

Prime Minister Lithel crept down the deserted hall, his eyes round with fear. A long, black cloak trailed behind him, making the slightest whispering sounds upon the cold, gray stones of the floor.

Reaching an intersection, he glanced from left to right, quietly sidling down the former. Drops of sweat beaded on his forehead, and his hands trembled with anticipation. A long, gleaming knife was clutched tightly in his fist, the flickering torchlight reflecting off of its sinister blade.

He finally approached his destination. An innocent, wooden door sat comfortably in the wall at the midpoint of the passage, a seemingly unimportant addition to the bland matrix of halls and doors inside the keep. A lone guard lay on the ground, fast asleep.

Lithel paused in front of the door, his conscience screaming a warning. *Why am I doing this?* He asked himself. *Why should I...* A different voice interrupted him.

"*Do it.*" It washed through his mind, blotting out the wiser voice and sealing his conscience in a cage of metaphysical steel.

Lithel's head bobbed down and then came back up. He stared at the door, a new look of determination written on his face. Glowing rings of red haze encircled his pupils, giving him a malicious aura.

With an unfeeling expression, Lithel withdrew a key from his pocket and inserted it into the lock. Turning smoothly, it emitted a short click. The Prime Minister gently swung the small door open and stepped inside.

Glossary of Characters

Adonai – (a'-dō-nī)
Ashan – (a'-shin)
Athanawty – (ā'-than-o'-tē)
Aubredax – (ä'-bru-daks)
Axedarian – (aks'-u-dār'-ē-en)
Barnus – (bär'-nus)
Bekuntakh Gunta – (bek'-ūn-tok gūn'-tu)
Bergal – (bur'-gul)
Bilt – (bilt')
Bofe – (bō'-fu)
Borgla – (bōr'-glu)
Bridoj – (bri'-dozh)
Brusall – (brū-säl')
Byran – (bī'-ran)
Chan – (shän')
Chemp – (chemp')
Creyan – (crā-in)
Ciath – (sī'-ath)
Courage – (cur'-ej)
Daniel – (dan'-yul)
Delba – (del'-bu)
Denor – (dā'-nōr)
Diamond – (dī'-mund)
Dol – (dōl')
Eger – (ē'-jur)
Elakhim – (ē'-lu-kim)
Ellan – (el'-un)
Essence – (es'-ens)
Eyla – (ā-lu)
Feentag – (fēn'-tok)
Flen – (flen')
Friada – (frē-ä'-du)
Garimec – (gār'-i-mek)
Garthor – (gär'-thōr)
Gerleuta – (jär-loy'-tu)
Gordo – (gōr'-dō)
Gorix – (gōr'-iks)
Grale – (grāl')
Gren – (gren')
Grogger – (grä'-gur)
Gund – (gūnt')

Hugo – (hyū'-gō)
Hylokar – (hī'-lō-kär)
Ilich – (ī'-lēch)
Jamis – (jä'-mis)
Jempetulum – (jem-pet'-yū-lum)
Jocas – (jō'-cus)
Johan – (yō'-hän)
Jos – (jäs')
Joy – (joy')
Jujong Abkh – (jū'-jong äbk')
Kari – (kä'-rē)
Kiyel – (kī'-yul)
Kosta – (käs'-tu)
Kymavay – (kī'-mu-vā)
Lenkim – (leng'-kim)
Lergenio – (lur-jē'-nē-ō)
Lithel – (lith'-ul)
Lora – (lō'-ru)
Lorndis – (lōrn'-dis)
Lurd – (lurd')
Maik – (mīk')
Malto – (mäl'-tō)
Marcus – (mär'-kus)
Margaret – (mär'-gur-it)
Maria – (mu-rē'-u)
Marken – (mär'-ken)
Marl – (märl')
Mayeth – (mī'-eth)
Mektah Ujeb – (mek'-tä ū'-jeb)
Mikal – (mīk'-ul)
Miltah – (mil'-tu)
Myrth – (murth')
Napzia – (nap'-zē-u)
Nasgatar – (naz'-gu-tär)
Nat – (nat')
Ngylin – (ngē'-lin)
Noal – (nōl')
Nostal – (nō-stäl')
Nunor – (nū'-nōr)
Nuntuk – (nun'-tuk)
Ogrion – (ō-grī'-un)

Olga – (ōl'-gu)
Patience – (pā'-shens)
Peace – (pēs')
Pheno – (fē'-nō)
Quiel – (kēl')
Qusab – (kū'-säb)
Raga – (rä'-gu)
Randan – (run-dän')
Rhubin – (rū'-bin)
Rihanna – (rē-hä'-nu)
Rosh – (räsh')
Ruth – (rūth')
Samson – (sam'-sun)
Samuel – (sam'-yūl)
Sandra – (sän'-dru)
Sayen – (sī'-en)
Schmidt – (shmit')
Shem – (shem')
Skyrcoh – (skr'-kō)
Solomon – (sol'-u-mun)
Sotiras – (sō-tī'-rus)
Sus – (sūs')
Sventor – (sven'-tōr)
Tamas – (to'-mus)
Tarius – (tār'-ē-us)
Ticha – (tē'-ku)
Tre – (trā')
Triqan – (trī'-kän)
Valentina – (val'-en-tē'-nu)
Varnul – (vär'-nul)
Vester – (ves'-tur)
Vin – (vin')
Vincent – (vin'-sint)
Wilhelm – (vil'-helm)
Xortahn – (zōr'-tän)
Yakob – (yä'-kub)
Yanonelias – (ya'-nō-nē'-lē-us)
Yimnural – (yim-nur'-ul)
Yurson – (yur'-sun)
Zalles – (zäl'-es)
Zane – (zān')

Glossary of Locations

Aena – (ā'-nu)
Belsh Desert – (belsh' de'-zurt)
Bielon – (bē'-län)
Campekter – (käm-pek'-tur)
Chambul – (sham-būl)
Chrume – (krūm')
Domilia – (dō-mil'-yu)
Evis Ocean – (ē'-vis ō'-shun)
Farnosh – (fär'-näsh)
Felid – (fē'-lid)
Filasky – (fil-ä'-skē)
Filitos – (fi-lē'-tōs)
Gejokt – (ge-jokt')
Grenga – (grāng'-gu)
Grudenheim – (grū'-den-hīm)
Kalh – (käl')
Kaltoid – (kal'-toyd)
Kar Toche – (kär' tū'-hyu)
Kogincheir – (kō'-gin-shīr)
Kremul – (krē'-mul)
Lorriet – (lō-rē-et')
Mal Grus – (mal' grūs')
Matopeia – (mu-tōp'-ē-u)
Mellen – (mel'-un)
Melyn Toche – (mā'-lin tū'-hyu)
Menator – (men'-u-tōr)
Myna – (mī'-nu)
Nolai – (nōl'-ī)
Oman-Yaml – (ō'-män-yam'-ul)
Orthox – (ōr'-thoks)
Plains of Adur – (plānz' uv' a'-dū-r)
Racous – (rä'-coos)
Ratkon – (rat'-kän)
Rydia – (ri'-dē-u)
Satayeha – (sa'-tä-yā'-hä)
Schnell – (shnel')
Shala – (shā'-lu)
Tesca – (tes'-cu)
Vanguard – (van'-gärd)
Velendaw – (vel'-en-dä)

Victon – (vik'-tän)
Virud – (vē'-rūd)
Wajaq – (wä'-zhäk)
Yalaj – (yu-läzh')
Yamal – (yu-mäl')

Acknowledgements

There are so many people who helped me in the process of writing this book. I just can't thank them enough for their encouragement and support.

I want to thank my Mom, Dad, Seanán, Gabriel, and Aubree, for being my first fans, and my Mom and Dad for being the most in-depth editors ever.

I would like to thank all the people who gave me their opinions of my writing: Al and Linda, Mike and Carole, Dr. Stoner, Jonah, Mikal, Eric, Hally and Dave, Gretchen, Eric, Dave, Sam, and Sandi.

Thank you, Sam, Mikal, Kari, Ruth, and Zane for the use of your names, and Ellen for posing for the cover picture.

I also have to thank my youth group, Boy Scout Troop, and drama class for supporting me in this process.

Thanks, all you readers and subscribers to my blog! You make my writing worthwhile.

And finally, thank you Jesus, for guiding me through this process and giving me my inspirations and ideas that have made this novel what it is.

- Tyler Appleby

Read the rest of The Triqan Trilogy!

Adonai's Book
2

After escaping the clutches of evil to retrieve the key to Yamal, Samuel and his friends are thrust back into the hectic life of Castle Orthox, only to encounter the aftereffects of a heinous crime. Following their arrival, the young team is chased out of the castle by an unlikely villain, who is bent on recovering a mysterious book in their possession.

Bane of the Hylokar

3

The culmination is at hand, and something is stirring. A being more powerful and evil than Samuel and his friends could have ever imagined is rising from its grave. Will this be the end of civilization in the land of Domilia, or can the chaos be stopped? There is one possibility... it is a blade... the most powerful blade in existence... the Bane.

About the Author

In early 2014, when he was fourteen years old, Tyler Appleby had an idea that slowly transformed into his first novel. In November 2015, he published *The Key to Yamal*, the first installment of The Triqan Trilogy. The next two novels, *Adonai's Book* and *Bane of the Hylokar*, were published soon after that, completing the series. In early 2017, Tyler achieved his dream... to be one of few teenage authors to publish a trilogy before the age of 18.

Tyler Appleby lives in Western Washington with his Mom, Dad, two brothers, and sister. In addition to being a published author, he loves Jesus, acting, and Boy Scouts.

Find out more about Tyler Appleby by visiting and subscribing to his website/blog:

thecorzanitecubicle.wordpress.com.

www.ingramcontent.com/pod-product-compliance
Lightning Source LLC
Chambersburg PA
CBHW071216250626
47163CB00001B/3

9780692585504